I studied the map, fo[...] huge chunk of it. "I'v[...] I'm here."

"You'll get a librar[...] Berkeley resident," the Ahram, Alex, said. "The library's okay, but you'll still have to carry out bound books—no terminal texts for non-students."

"Oh." I was so used to accessing texts through the computer that I'd forgotten about checking books out.

"Set up an account with the Bank of America near the Co-op. Electric money is waiting for you."

"Fake credit?" They'd make me an outlaw again, data-junking the Bank of America.

Alex said, "Don't be so touchy."

"It's his planet," the female Barcon said, bent over my right thumb, carefully rolling down the fake skin.

"I'm nervous. I broke parole when I left Virginia."

Alex looked at me as if he'd just realized I was not simply another rude human. "Okay, we're nervous too. You're the first human refugee ever to get home pass."

"I'm nervous about other humans here."

"You've got to learn how to deal with major humans," Alex said. "First contact's due in about ten years. Much better if you can help us deal with them."

"Are we really that awful?"

"No, no, not *that* awful." Alex smiled at me. "We'll stay in touch, I promise." He tapped my temple over the skull computer so I'd realize how.

They've set it up so I'll have *to meet people.* My face went hot. I didn't say anything more.

BEN BOVA'S DISCOVERIES

BEN BOVA PRESENTS

BEING ALIEN

REBECCA ORE

TOR

A TOM DOHERTY ASSOCIATES BOOK
NEW YORK

BEING ALIEN

Copyright © 1989 by Rebecca Ore

A TOR Book
Published by Tom Doherty Associates, Inc.
49 West 24 Street
New York, NY 10010

Cover art by Wayne Barlowe

ISBN: 0-812-54792-6   Can. ISBN: 0-812-54793-4

First edition: September 1989

Printed in the United States of America

0 9 8 7 6 5 4 3 2 1

= 1 =

"Easing Back to Earth"

The human woman, Yangchenla, lived with me on and off for three years while I learned what the Federation wanted me to know about dealing with other species of sapients. I was better, though, with the non-humans, even with difficult people like the Gwyngs, skinny, long-armed former bats with wrinkled fox faces—nervous, hypersocial—than I was with my own kind. I was afraid of my own kind, especially those descended from Tibetans, who'd been stranded on the Federation capital planet, Karst, five hundred years earlier. Asian rednecks. I was a Virginia redneck, so I'd been told when I was growing up, so it was a bad match.

After I kicked Yangchenla's drunk uncle Trung out of our quarters, she really left me. Or did I leave her? Perhaps she would have come back again, but after two weeks alone, I couldn't stand the space we'd shared: her Tibetan bed furs, her almost subliminal human female odor fading away from the clothes she'd left behind.

Granite Grit and Feldspar, two birds, let me move in with them and their son, Alchir-singra, who was still too young for a Federation working name. They were seven feet tall, wingless, feathered, with scales from elbow down to the hands, softer fingers than you'd expect, and different enough from me not to read my expressions closely. Another mobile-faced ape would have.

Yangchenla found me. I came back from a meeting with

cadets I was supervising and saw her waiting in front of Granite's door. "May I come in?" she asked, her flat face not really looking at me. She'd wrapped her body tight, band squashing down her breasts, two layers of clothes over that. "Or don't you associate with humans now?"

"I couldn't take any more, Yangchenla." I went to the refrigerator and pulled out a package of *villag*, strips like a cloudy bean aspic, more translucent and firmer than Terran bean curd. Feathers and scales littered the other alcoves of the T-shaped officers apartment, flecks of food, bill parings. *She probably wouldn't want to eat in this mess.* "Would you like some Yauntro *villag*?"

"No."

"I got tired of you leaving and coming back, the arguments, so I moved here." I sat down on a bird table, wiping aside slightly smelly feathers and flecks of rock-churned crop food.

"Hiding from me?"

I didn't answer that for a while, then said, "We weren't officially mated."

Yangchenla tightened her lips back. She brushed a bill paring off a hassock, then sat down on it firmly.

I said, "Children are messy, whatever the species."

She answered, "But most creatures do want them."

"Yangchenla, what kind of a life would this be for a human child?" I speared a strip of *villag* with a human fork. "Would you want him to be another second-class human hustling handicrafts?"

"I was born here." She cut short what she was going to say. I'd told her several times that she was grasping, her family overbearing, her drunk uncle a pest. They wanted me to get them privileges I hardly had for myself.

Granite Grit came home then with his son, Alchirsingra. When Granite Grit saw Yangchenla, he became flustered, face feathers slightly roused, haws flicking translucently across his brown eyes, scaley fingers gripping Alchir firmly by the wrist. He looked at me and asked, "Should I come back later?"

Alchir said, "Nervous creature. Afraid of us?"

"Not of you," Yangchenla said. "Of Tom."

"Mammal squish brain," Alchir replied before he picked up a bill-paring knife and trimmed his beak.

"He's bright for three, I think," Yangchenla said.

Granite Grit's face feathers puffed up even more, then he smoothed them down. "Alchir, come with me." He grabbed Alchir's pale yellow wrist.

Alchir stiffened, still staring at us mammals, until Granite Grit stroked his beak. He crouched and gaped at his father, begging for food, then ruffled his feathers, embarrassed. Alchir-singra's parents got orgasmic pleasure from regurgitating into his gaping maw and he was old enough to want no part of that. Granite, humming down low in his crop, preened Alchir's head feathers, then pulled him along through the door.

Yangchenla thought the Federation had favored me while neglecting her own people. But the Tibetans couldn't hack sophisticated interspecies culture when the Federation brought them to Karst 500 years ago. After one of them murdered an official, the Federation moved the whole Tibetan village to an undeveloped area on Karst Planet. Later, a few, like Yangchenla's people, gained skills enough to be allowed to live in Karst City.

But I wouldn't let her have another baby. She'd had a son earlier with a Tibetan and had been implanted with a birth-control device. If the son died, she could have another. Her ex-husband had the son, off in the wilder parts of Karst. I refused to let her have my child.

God, she'd exploded when she found out. Yangchenla said now, "Gwyng lover. Black Amber, your wrinkled-faced blood drinker sponsor bitch . . ." The full accusation stayed unspoken, this time.

Black Amber didn't approve of Yangchenla. Yangchenla didn't approve of Gwyngs either, the wrinkled faces who couldn't speak her languages. It took massive transforming to make even Karst Two, the Gwyng communication code, comprehensible to most species. And Yangchenla was a xenophobe.

"You're a xenophobe. She's my sponsor. And I told you I only helped keep the suitors in line at her matings."

"I am not a xenophobe. She lets her babies die."

"Yangchenla, I've got work to do. You've got a shop to run."

"You're a little boy, what serious work do you do?"

"I've got to keep a planet from bankrupting itself over advanced technology."

She stood up slowly, her arms wrapped around her body, fingers dug into her upper arms. "We have lived without you for centuries." Her body scents thickened in the room.

"You looked *me* up, Chenla."

She went, "hah," a sound she'd gotten from me, and left. I'd expected her to scream and throw things. Now, as she closed the door, I felt even more anxious, guilty.

I had a private office space in a building originally designed for crepuscular sorts, now re-rigged with bigger windows and stronger lights, the retrofit not quite as highly carved as the original exterior and interior trim. I was there, almost afraid Yangchenla would try to talk to me again, so lonely in some obscure way that I wished I could find a Tibetan like me, an isolate. Then Karriaagzh called me to his office.

Karriaagzh was over eight feet tall, all hollow bones and mammal-clothes-damaged feathers, utterly alien. He sat on his backward bent hocks, reaching down under his tunic to pull loose a feather sheath from a new feather. He wasn't Granite Grit's species, but he shared a non-mammal single-mindedness. He was an isolate, truly alone yet so able to cope that he ran the Federation's Contact Officiators Academy. I tended to be intimidated.

First Karriaagzh's nictitating membrane swept his yellow eyes clean, then he stared at me as if memorizing any changes—Karriaagzh, eighty now, would outlive me and mammal aging was said to fascinate him.

I said, "I was promised time on Earth once I finished the training."

"We hoped you'd be happy with Yangchenla instead."

"*Yeah.*"

"Your own people embarrass you?"

I didn't say anything. Karriaagzh's pupils contracted, eyes fixed, then he loosened his focus and said, "Tom, we'll send you to do research on Earth. There's a country there, *Japan*, which faced high tech challenge.'' The yellow eyes looked up at the hanging light piece in his high office ceiling: twenty feet up, retrofit scars in the paneling showed the ceiling had been lower. He looked back at his desk terminal and wrote an entry with his light pen. The terminal display flashed maps and figures at him, so fast I couldn't make them out.

''What can *human* experience have to do with Yauntra? They're much more group-oriented than *humans*,'' I said. Then as his display continued flashing, I babbled, ''Actually, I don't know if I should really go back to Earth.'' Going to visit Earth was my getting back on a horse that had stomped me. Bunch of primitive xenophobes in the Virginia hills who'd discarded me, left me for aliens to salvage.

Feathers around his beak twitched. ''We have an observation house in *Berkeley* . . . *California*, but *Berkeley* isn't rural *Virginia*, Tom, or Karst City.'' He gaped his beak at me slightly and rocked on his keel bone, the one that never anchored wings. ''You can do research on how Japan reorganized itself to deal with machine culture, reacquaint yourself with your own species. Someday there'll be official contact.''

''Maybe Black Amber would object to me going to Berkeley?''

''She *is* still your sponsor, isn't she?'' He spat air. ''She's with History Committeeman Wy'um again. If she were my kind, her sexual behaviors might be moral, but as she's not, they aren't.''

Back at my office, when I keyed up my mail, a message crawled down the screen: JOIN ME. I AM HERE. BLACK AMBER, SUB-RECTOR, ACADEMY AND INSTITUTES. The printer spat out a map. Amber was on a Gwyng island halfway around Karst.

The only way to get to that particular Gwyng island was by the Karst equivalent of air taxi, gate travel being blocked over most of Karst's surface, so I went to one of the outlying airports and hired another brachiator, one of the ones with tri-colored head hair, to fly me in a narrow powered glider that Black Amber would pay for.

I flew across Karst's empty spaces at night, dark below me, the sky lighter, glittering with star clusters and miniature suns. Most of the planet was just there to physically support Karst City; an artificial planet requires less maintenance than a space station. Dotted across the black were lights where various high Federation types like History Committee Members and Sub-Rectors had outlying residences. The farms were closer to the city. For five thousand years plus, the ecosystems, the carefully placed oceans and landmasses, managed themselves with minimal grooming by us intelligent beings. Each time I flew across Karst, I thought of what a massive thing it was, how small the life forms that built it.

The plane landed at an airstrip on what would have been the planet's Pacific Ocean, if I was oriented correctly. I don't really know—Earth is probably upside down as well as backward in relation to Karst.

Warm here, near the equator, but not as hot as July in Virginia. Behind the airstrip, I saw the black outlines of strap-leaf trees, like palms but botanically more complex. Shreka g'Han, a four-and-a-half-foot-tall fuzzy bear sapient, sat in Black Amber's bubble top electric car, the plastic cowling slightly sand-etched. Behind a fence, grazing creatures like Holstein-colored hippos stared up at us. Gwyng pouch hosts—they incubated the few baby Gwyngs who survived birth. One of them jerked around as though yanked by its tail, and a little Gwyng stared out of the beast's pouch.

"Red Clay, Tom, come." Shreka used both my academy and species names. "It's difficult to tend Gwyngs. I'm so glad to see you." He looked hot. The little fuzzy bear-stock types were weird. Perfect servants—except they served with a tinge of condescension.

I asked, "Open mating or are Amber and Wy'um still exclusive?"

He didn't answer, but hunched his shoulders. Black Amber and Wy'um were acting scandalously by Gwyng standards. They saw themselves as a Gwyng colony of two.

Not *always* exclusive, though. Gwyng politics forced Black Amber to invite others to her breedings. And one of Wy'um sisters adopted Black Amber's son—biochemically proved to be Wy'um's true son.

"They're teaching the child Gwyng languages," Shreka told me, his scalp hair ruffling even though the air was dead, "and even Wy'um doesn't respond much to Karst."

I could almost feel my skull computer whir, getting set to give me some sequential signals out of the Gwyng languages even if they weren't anything I could make sense of. *Garble, garble, Black Amber yourself.*

The car passed herds of pouch hosts and blood beasts—all dark grey and black bulk. Normally, even at night, more was visible—the stars being so bright—but tonight was overcast, just a glowing grey, like a half-moon glowing through the clouds, but all over.

I saw light shining though the woven planks of the house—a huge house for isolated Gwyngs—with a black patch in one corner, Wy'um's security office, a room-sized safe. Shreka ruffled his head hair again and said, "Don't let them tire you."

"I'm used to Gwyngs."

"They're being *very* Gwyng."

Black Amber would have to discuss my trip to Earth in Karst languages. My mind wasn't geared, even with computers, to radar-based languages that clocked time in light polarizations and embedded time and spatial relationship into all their meanings. Sometimes, I thought the Gwyngs just bullshat about Gwyng languages and their elaborate brains.

We parked by the veranda as two Gwyngs came out, dressed in Gwyng rigs, collars with strips of cloth going down the center of the nippleless chests to join up with a broad band of cloth around the genitals. The vestigial webs hung like loose black crepe from their armpits to halfway down their upper arms.

My computer babbled to my speech centers, failing to transform Gwyng into sequences I could hang meaning on, then my brain squealed when they went into ultrasonics.

Black Amber and Wy'um, dressed in Gwyng winter shifts with cut-outs for their webs, came out, twined together side to side. Their little child, almost the same age as Alchir-singra, held on to Wy'um's knee and stared at me with oily Gwyng eyes. The fur over the raised bone surrounding his eyes was paler than his baby sparse body hair, making him look vaguely like a photo negative of a racoon.

Gwyng irises and pupils looked no larger than my own eyes, but behind the bone surrounding the visible eye was a huge eyeball, with a retina as complex as most mammal's visual cortexes, so sensitive that Gwyngs could see infrared and polarized light, so quick they processed visual information five times faster that I did. Yet Gwyngs could be as doofus as any human.

"Black Amber, we need to talk," I said.

She stared at me, then said, in Karst Two, "Why code babble? Know (think I do) what you (lonely male) want?"

"Granite Grit's not all too happy that I'm living with him and Feldspar."

"Birds (only mild disgust, except for Karriaagzh—great meaning slippage/impaction in shift from Gwyng to Karst Two)." She stroked Wy'um. Another large Gwyng that I thought must be Wy'um's sister came out, larger than the males, but not so tall as Black Amber, who was taller than me when she stood, as she was standing now, defensively raised on the balls of her feet above me on the veranda steps. They talked a bit in Gwyng, then Black Amber said, "Come in (try our life)." She pursed her lips at me, her smile, like a human going *oo*.

All the Gwyngs oo'ed at me. She wanted to embarrass me, I realized, but I was used to Gwyng teases.

"Life and honors," I told her, having translated that out of an Earth science fiction book some Terran observer had smuggled out of the Berkeley Public Library.

"He (sleeper alone in his dreams) gets along with birds," she told the other Gwyngs in Karst Two so my computer would transform what she said into comprehensible phonemes, "and (almost) with us."

Sleeper alone in his dreams—Gwyngs thought being trapped unconscious alone in a bed was most peculiar. Black Amber's little son looked at her hands, nervously. She wiggled her long thumbs at him—no anger juice in the glands at the base of them.

Wy'um stirred away from her and their son tried to pull them back together. "The Federation is our home/life," Wy'um said. "We don't distort policy over sexual . . ." His voice trailed away; his facial wrinkles deepened.

"Tom, I consider as crippled but social Gwyng." Black Amber came down the veranda stairs and stroked me with the furred backs of her knuckles. "Come in. We plan to tease you about sleeping-alone-except-after-sex. Only wild pleasure tames humans to each other, then not for life."

The little Gwyng went to his aunt, hugged her knees and stared at me, then said something to Amber.

"No, you won't be able to understand him until your skull can take/get implanted with the computer," she told him. "No loss."

I bumped my body against her lightly as I passed her. She koo'ed slightly and took my elbow to steer me inside. The five others followed us. I sat down cross-legged on one floor mat while Wy'um and his sister twined together with Amber on another. The other two adult Gwyngs—males by the size of them—sat down on suspended swing chairs balanced at knee level with counterwieghts. One said something to the other, got out of the chair and crawled into a tube sofa. Ambers's child watched him, then crawled into a smaller tube that looked more obviously like a host pouch.

Don't watch them as though they were zoo specimens. I looked up instead at the pattern playing on the Gwyng flat screen on the wall, something they read as language. When everyone was settled, I said, "Black Amber, I think you'll sympathize when I tell you I want to be among my own people for a while."

She stopped and looked at me with eyes like greased black rock. "You went to Karriaagzh first."

"He was in Karst City. I'm sleepy," I told her. "Separating from Yangchenla."

"One hundred rotations of this planet ago," she said, but she got up and led me to a tiny room set aside for alien guests—pretty rare on this island, I took it.

Her son came to the door and leaned against it, stroking his stomach, web veins slightly distended although he hadn't spread out his arms. She spoke to him, then said, "He wants to touch you."

When I knelt, he came up, fingered my head hair with tiny long fingers that looked almost brittle, and spoke Gwyng to her.

"Yes/you're perceptive," she said in Karst Two. "He cut it short as our head hair."

"What can I call him?" I asked her.

"He won't understand you—Amber-son, if you have to name him something."

Amber-son leaned against me as she explained, in Karst Two, that I'd be calling him various weird sounds.

"He does understand Karst Two, then."

"A little," she said. "I spoke Karst to not exclude."

"Red Clay," Amber-son said, almost ultrasonically.

I cupped my hand and brought it down in the Federation signal for agreement. He squealed and koo'ed in a fit of Gwyng giggles, then curled up on my bed, not touching me, his head propped up on his left hand, web stretched and pressed against the mat covers.

"Is he going to stay here all night?" I asked Amber.

"Problem?" she asked, thumbs curling out slightly as the glands at their bases engorged with blood or anger juice precursors. I looked, then looked away quickly before she could notice.

"Well, will he be comfortable with an alien?"

"If you let him, it will relieve his fear."

I thought about her fear of Karriaagzh and said, "Then it is good not to be afraid of aliens, Black Amber?"

"Of mammals," she said smoothly before speaking Gwyng at him. She smiled at me as if she'd been waiting years to demand this of me. "Sleep with my true child and you can go to your planet afterward."

Black Amber had other pouch children, but Mica, stranded on Earth, killed there, was, had been, her only other true child. He'd scared me the first time he tried to sleep with me—odd, now I realized how he'd felt, alone among aliens. He must have complained about my coldness in journals Black Amber read after he died and the aliens found me. Well, I decided, Amber-son is small; it will be like sleeping with a big dog. I reached over to him and stroked his side.

Black Amber took my head in her long fingers and kissed me on the nose. Then she left, body rocking slightly over the bowed Gwyng legs.

Bats—they're excessively complicated flightless bats. Amber-son trembled slightly when I thought this, empathetic to the tension in my own body. *Poor baby.*

He whispered, "Red Clay, be good/kind (anxiety)."

I cupped my hand slightly, brought it down, then stretched my fingers toward him. He scooted over and curled up beside me before I could change into my Earth-style pajamas. *Oh, well, the tunic and pants are loose-fitting enough.* I eased my hand down for the covers—he sat up with a start, then must have remembered Amber explaining this strange alien custom and wiggled in beside me again. I took off my tunic top and he twisted his little fingers through my chest hair and sighed. "Need more (sleepers)," he whispered to me.

"Um," I said, suspicious.

"Can you-sleep-if-not-willing, not-Gwyng?"

"You know more Karst Two than Black Amber let on."

He still couldn't understand Karst One, though, and stared up at me, then touched my unwebbed armpit. *He's just a little kid,* I thought, rubbing his back. Fortunately, I was tired and fell asleep quickly, didn't insult him or Mama Black Amber with restlessness.

During the night, though, he woke me, whimpering in his sleep, hands locked around my wrist. I hummed, remembering how two Gwyngs once awakened me, and he opened his eyes and said, "Won't push me out?"

I shook my head, then signaled *no*. As I stroked him

along his side with the backs of my knuckles, the way Gwyngs like it, I wondered what a four-year-old Gwyng could have nightmares about. *Maybe me?*

But he cuddled closer, fingers still tight around my arm, and went back to sleep. I managed to fall back asleep and dreamed of when Mica was with me on Earth, of Black Amber's anguish over losing him, her hostility toward humans.

In the dream, after Mica died, gut-shot by my brother, I turned to Amber and said, "Even if Warren is nasty and crazy, he's my brother."

In the morning the adult Gwyngs of the house hummed us awake and Amber-son laughed, koo'ed.

"Did he have uncomfortable dreams?" Black Amber asked.

Amber-son looked over at me, breathing through his mouth. I shook my head, then said, "Is that why you made him sleep with me? Because he has bad dreams?"

"Know his non-sound symbol," Amber-son said in Karst Two. "Shakes head no. No. No-bad-dreams-no."

Black Amber told him, "Shook head because he didn't like/feared the question." She said to Wy'um's sister, "You've been teaching him Karst language (troubled)."

"He lives on this planet, not Gwyng Home," Ghring'um said.

"I thought he was having terror dreams over me," I said, anxious about my own dreams.

Amber wrapped her long arms around her thin body and hooked her hands behind her neck, thumbs bent, veins pulsing in the webs stretched over her chest. Then she stretched her hands toward her son, but didn't touch him, just held her long fingers near his face. They opened and closed like a hypnotist's. She asked, "Would you rather be back in the pouch?"

Amber-son watched her thumbs and, wiggling slightly, didn't say anything. Wy'um crouched slightly as though Amber had scolded him. Then they talked Gwyng, excluding me.

Finally, Black Amber spoke to Amber-son and then said to me, "Take him for a walk among the herds. We have some of your planet's food animals. Then find your food in the stale food room."

"Do you have a *cow*?"

"Horned milk oil animal from *Sherrsee*? Yes. And some egglayers," she said.

"What about a flat iron pan to fry eggs in?"

"Walk him *now*," she told me. When I began to move, she nibbled her thumb glands to suck out the anger juice.

Amber-son folded his own little arms around himself, then huffed out his breath slightly at her. They stared at each other—challenge eyes. He was a tough four-year-old.

I held out my hand to him. He sniffed and said, "You have funny web odor."

"Yeah, so I've been told." I realized this was one-way conversation and signaled *yes*.

"Outside?" he asked.

Yes.

"Good, Red Clay, I can show you . . . (no Karst word for her). I call her something you don't understand." He looked at me as if expecting a reply, then wiggled his shoulders. We went by the food storage room, that stale food room for foods already taken from the animals, where I poured myself a glass of skim milk, the Gwyngs having taken the cream.

"Better warm," Amber-son told me, sucking air slightly, the muscle between his chin and his throat bouncing.

My hand, fingers loosely curled, was going to get tired, bobbing yes all the time, but he knew the head shake for *no*. I jerked my chin toward the door and he ran out, clumsily like all Gwyngs—body rolling, arms as long as a spider monkey's spread for balance.

Other little Gwyngs rushed out of the stable, babbling in Gwyng and Karst Two—"Where have you been? Why did the big ones take you away? You smell funny?"

"They wanted me," he said, his eyes suddenly more

oily than ever. "I'm too important. This is Red Clay, my friend."

"Smells funny," one of the Gwyng babies said.

"Maybe if I talk to . . ." Another one-way conversation.

One of the brood beasts came out from the stable and lowed, then loped up to Amber-son and stopped. A little Gwyng hopped out of the pouch and hugged Amber-son sideways, then the brood beast nudged them both back toward her tail with her blunt black-and-white-mottled head.

I decided to leave him, go back to the house and tell Black Amber, Wy'um, and Ghring'um—all of them, mad thumbs or not—that Amber-son needed more time with the other baby Gwyngs.

Black Amber met me coming back from the stable, stopped, arms folded across her chest, fingers tugging at her body hair.

"Why did you take him away from the pouch host so soon?"

"Mica . . . We want him to be extraordinary for male Gwyng (like Mica/pain). Grow-need-grow-fast."

"He's not Mica, Black Amber."

She took me up against her hairy side. Her eyes looked down slightly into mine. "No, you are Mica/replacement. The bird will destroy my other pouch kin in dangerous missions (now happening)."

"What about going to Earth? I need to be better with my own kind."

She ran her finger down my nose bridge as though she'd never seen it before. "What about your people in the undeveloped area and in Karst City? Learn to be good/better with them."

"I want my own time, and *Americans*."

"Can't return to your cultural area."

"But if you people, even surgically rearranged, can hide in *Berkeley* without being noticed, then I should fit right in. When I was in prison, I met a guy who planned to go to *Berkeley* as soon as they set him free."

"You figure out much, awkward-with-own-kind."

"And, you had some people you wanted me to meet."

She fingered her side where she'd been shot on Earth. "Some (I am forced to admit) were kind. One woman will follow the sound of your voice. Go back, be intimidated (or possibly not), return to me (not to Karriaagzh)."

Berkeley was nothing, I was sure, compared to Karst City. But Berkeley wasn't rural Virginia. She saw my face go rigid and rounded her thin lips slightly.

I thought about Yangchenla as I flew from Ghring'um's island, Black Amber coming with me. Black Amber looked over at me and said, "I have so much to worry about."

"You've been a bad girl by Gwyng terms, haven't you?"

"Don't be stuffy/prig/moral dwarp. The Federation doesn't care as long as I do my job." She narrowed her eyes and twitched a foot as if Karriaagzh was before her, subconsciously kicking him off as though she were a small bat being attacked by a hunting bird. "And you saw the two other males."

"I ought to get my own place," I said, wondering if the two other males had had any chance with her, or were there just for show, to prove Black Amber's matings were open, honest by Gwyng terms.

"You needed company right after Yangchoochoo left." She never pronounced Yangchenla's name right, despite her ability to memorize what to a Gwyng were nonsense sounds. She pulled off her Gwyng rig and pulled on the Sub-Rector's uniform—full-length tunic and pants, twisting away from me so I didn't see her front, but still acting rather post-heat, humming and brushing up against me as we left the plane. I felt embarrassed, as usual. She knew. Being Gwyng, she liked to tease.

Before I left, Black Amber sent me a message on my computer terminal: THREE GOALS. TWO OBLIGATORY, ONE OPTIONAL. RESEARCH JAPAN, GO TO DINNER WITH TWO HUMANS, FIND A WIFE. KARRIAAGZH AND I AGREE.

I leaned away from the screen and worried. Everyone

told me that humans were weird. Even I wasn't allowed to spend more that sixteen hours on duty without taking sleep time. Federation rule for fragile species, near-xenophobes. Now I was going to have to face millions of my weird fellow creatures again. I was desperate to go back and scared, too. *Shit*, I thought in English, *no sooner than I adjust to here . . .*

= 2 =
Berkeley

Space gates eat angular momentum and the space-time we skip between departure and arrival. Outside at intersect was *nothing*, not even time, much less a stray hydrogen atom. Granite Grit, who studied astronavigation, explained that we intersected through vibrating multi-dimensional hypercubes, but Gwyng mystics claim we destroy and re-create the universe with every jump.

At a Karst orbital station, I wedged myself into a round transport pod and sealed the hatch from the inside with six four-inch wing bolts, tightening them good with both hands. The in-transit light, one of a pair of little diodes over the hatch, went on a minute or so later.

The pod lurched like some giant was playing tennis with it, whirled a few times, stopped for ten minutes, then dropped and rocked forward gently. Before I got really claustrophobic, the arrival light flashed. I undid the hatch and pushed it until the seal peeled off.

As the hatch swung free, a blond Ahram about thirty years old, his head real blocky without the usual skull-top crest, raised it to the catch position. He was lighter-skinned than the Ahrams I'd seen before—my shade—and seemed to be shaved down in the face. As I climbed out with my bag, he backed away as if he didn't know what to expect, getting a human delivered to him when Earth had billions of other humans around outside.

"You grow a beard?" I asked him in English.

"We're various, too. Call me Alex. Here's your passport and driver's license. If anyone asks about your accent, you've been in Asia." He spoke perfect English—the Federation had fixed his vocal organs just as I'd been surgically rearranged to speak good Karst.

I swung the hatch down on the pod and tightened the external dogs. The air turned blue around the pod a second before it skipped out of this space-time. I looked around the room—no windows, metal double garage door, gyp board walls—and saw two dehaired Barcons, looking like alien caricatures of Negro wrestlers. Dressed in jeans and UCal sweatshirts, they squatted by the wall, arms folded across their chests, a perfect match for size. Barcons made me nervous. They were generally Federation medics, remote in their treatment of our alien illnesses, but sometimes they used their medical knowledge to rebuild brains. They could kill for the Federation, but that was very rare.

But dehaired or in molt, they *could* pass for human—if you didn't notice the jaws with too many angles between chin and earlobe.

The air felt muggy, but cool, full of traffic gas. I was in the Bay Area near a freeway. One Barcon said, "We'd better fix his fingerprints now."

The other Barcon, wider at the hips, probably the female, said, "Be sure to tell him how to get his papers replaced if he gets mugged."

"We inserted all the right data into the computer," the Ahram, Alex, said, "so you're street-legal."

"*After* we change your fingerprints. Temporary, so don't abrade them. We'll re-do the tips in a month. Lucky your law doesn't take retina prints."

"What about my skull computer?" I'd just left Karst fifteen minutes earlier, being here so suddenly was weird, not that I hadn't traveled as fast before to really alien planets.

"If they find that," the male Barcon said, "you'd be made as experimental KGB and we haven't given you an address."

"Alex? Can I get in touch with you?"

"We'll be in touch with you," Alex said.

I didn't like that; it reminded me of major drug investors who sent out thugs in untraceable junker cars with muddy plates, the guys who forced my brother Warren to make drugs for them, back in Virginia before Karst rescued me from that life. "I'm loyal to Karst," I said.

Alex said, gesturing at one of the Barcons, "Jack here was mugged."

I got embarrassed for humans all over again. Of course, they couldn't trust *me*—I was from a long line of xenophobic/philic flip-flops who believed aliens would eat them or save them.

The Barcons wiggled their noses. Amused, the bastards. Alex said, "Tom, sit down. I'll try to get you oriented while the guys work on your fingers."

I sat on a metal stool while the Barcon sprayed both my hands with nerve deadener spray from a bogus Windex can. Alex sat cross-legged on the cement floor near my feet. "We'll put you on the San Pablo bus when we finish."

The only human city I'd ever been much in was Roanoke. "I could get lost."

Alex unfolded a map while the Barcons peeled off my finger skin. "Here. The main bus connections are at Shattuck and University. We've rented a place for you just off Shattuck on Milvia, so you can walk to the university and the co-ops. Black Amber rented an apartment in the same building."

"Near people she wants me to meet?"

The male Barcon grumbled Barcon language about *Gwyon-ngs* and *Black-re-Amber*.

"And you're going to leave me by myself so I'll get lonely enough to call on them." Black Amber gave me the woman's address just before I left Karst.

"Tom, you're acting suspicious, just like a human."

"Alex, he is right, though," the female Barcon said. "We will leave him alone to make contact."

I half wanted to spit in their eyes and go back to Karst. "So I have an apartment already. Do I have a bank account?"

"You've got to set one up. You've been in Asia, remember. You know Yangchenla's language."

"Shit, if anyone knows real modern Tibetan . . ."

"You learned an obscure dialect. Asia's very fragmented, even for a human territory."

I studied the map, found the university sprawled over a huge chunk of it. "I've got to do research on Japan while I'm here."

"You'll get a library card for about twenty dollars as a Berkeley resident," Alex said. "The library's okay, but you'll still have to carry out bound books, though—no terminal texts for non-students."

"Oh." I was so used to accessing texts through the computer that I'd forgotten about checking books out.

"Set up an account with the Bank of America near the Co-op. Electric money is waiting for you."

"Fake credit?" They'd make me an outlaw again, data junking the Bank of America.

Alex said, "Don't be so touchy."

"It's his planet," the female Barcon said, bent over my right thumb, carefully rolling down the fake skin.

"I'm nervous. I broke parole when I left Virginia."

Alex looked at me as if he'd just realized I was not simply another rude human. "Okay, we're nervous, too. You're the first human refugee ever to get a home pass."

"I'm nervous about other humans here."

"You've got to learn how to deal with major humans," Alex said. "First contact's due in about ten years. Much better if you can help us deal with them."

"Are we really that awful?"

"No, no, not *that* awful." Alex smiled at me. "We'll stay in touch, I promise." He tapped my temple over the skull computer so I'd realize how.

They've set it up so I'll have *to meet people*. My face went hot. I didn't say anything more while the Barcons stripped the rest of my fingers and rolled cultured fake print skin down the tips. They glued down the grafts with glop that was also an anesthetic.

"Don't grip anything too hard today," the male Barcon said. I picked up my bag strap with the palm of my hand—

a big duffel bag full of clothes that some alien, maybe
Alex, had bought me in Berkeley. Alex opened the garage
door and we went to the street.

Somehow, I suspected my brain would make Berkeley
look like Roanoke, around the railroad yard—good old
brain using its familiar templates. We waited at the bus
stop with weird half-breed sorts, Mexicans, Asians. One
black guy stared at the Barcons, at Alex, then at me,
shrugged as if bewildered. *Yeah, they don't look real negro, noses too thin, too many angles in the jaws.*

What I'd thought was a railroad line was the BART,
Bay Area Rapid Transport, which zipped by—overhead. I
hadn't noticed that the rails were elevated. It was like a
commuter tube train on Karst, but without the magnetic
levitation. The foggy air was too chilly for June. Was it
really June?

The San Pablo bus, wires sparking overhead, pulled up.
Alex said as I got on, "Get a transfer for the Shattuck
Avenue bus." If I'd dealt with really hostile aliens on
Yauntra, I told myself, I should be able to solo undercover
on my own planet.

Just before the doors closed, Alex got on the bus, too.
He sat down beside me and patted my leg. "Since you're
new to Berkeley," he said, "I should show you around a
bit."

I sighed, too hugely relieved. This trip was regressing
me back to my wimpy adolescent years. Alex said, "We'll
get you settled in and then hitch up to see the sunset from
Lawrence Laboratory."

What we passed continued to look like a flattened Roanoke. Denial is soothing, as I'd been told when I first
came to Karst. But why shouldn't Berkeley remind me of
Roanoke? Both of them are human cities.

"You're originally from the East," Alex said. "I heard
acid rain killed off the Frazier firs there."

"Not where I was."

"We'll change soon for a Shattuck Avenue bus."

When the bus stopped at a light, I saw a bizarre dingus
whip around the corner—a ten-foot-long fiberglass bullet
with bike wheels embedded in it, flying a flag on a pole

like a fishing rod. The hull looked almost like a Yauntry snow coach.

"What?" My muscles tingled as though I was ready to jump or had started and didn't notice.

"Vector—you see more of them since Iran took Iraq."

"Alex, what in the hell is a Vector?"

"Faired bicycle, recumbent. They made a few of them in the seventies, but they've only become popular on the street in the last seven years."

"I've only been out of the country five years." I closed my eyes and leaned back against the seat.

The bus rumbled on for a bit, then stopped. Alex pulled me to my feet and said, "Transfer."

We got out. Some of the people waiting for the buses wore clothes I was used to, jeans and sweatshirts, but others dressed oddly: black shiny pants that looked like exotic long underwear, men's jackets with asymmetrical openings like a woman'd have on a dress. Berkeley humans would give any alien an odd impression of my species.

The Shattuck Avenue bus pulled up and we hopped on board. A woman and man were arguing fiercely in a foreign language. Everyone on the bus slanted their eyeballs half at them, not quite staring. Alex grinned viciously at me as we sat down. *Look at the crazy humans*.

The woman was doing woman-stuff, thrusting her breasts out, seducing behind the arguing; the man was running a physical bluff of another sort: fists clenched, chin up, ready to drop her with man-violence. Exactly the way a woman and man argue; too typically human.

They went at it for ten minutes—I wondered what had made them so upset. Finally, another woman beside them said, "But, Yona, Demetrios, it's only ice cream."

All of us humans eavesdroppers giggled. Alex twitched his head as if shaking off a fly.

When he got off, he took my bag and said, "Human female and male survival strategies in the argument, yes?"

"Yeah, I guess." I'd had those symbolic sorts of arguments with Yangchenla. Too often.

"Down to Milvia and left," Alex told me. My building was two stories high, with balconies for upstairs apartments and tiny yards fenced with planks behind the ground floor units. In front of the building was something like a huge yucca but with thicker leaves. I scuffed away some mint by the road—the soil looked black. Maybe I could grow a garden, do something familiar even if I didn't stay long?

Alex waited while I went up iron stairs that boomed underfoot. The super was leaning against his door frame. I said, "I'm Tom . . . Gresham. Guy name Alex arranged an apartment for me." My real name would get me busted; Gresham, I told myself, not Easley.

He asked, without shifting, "Hard drugs, dogs, more than one woman a month?"

"No," I said.

"He tell you the rent was $700? Fourteen hundred, two months at $700 each."

He was robbing me, I thought. I almost went down for Alex, but instead signed over $1400 in traveler's checks. The super handed me the key and said, "Rent's due each month. Envelope will be in the door. You been in Berkeley before?"

"No, I . . . no."

"Call PG&E and tell them to hook you up. Don't know if you've got lights now or not." He went back in his apartment and came back with a greasy receipt book, wrote me off a receipt that could have been for anything and handed it to me.

I went back downstairs and asked Alex, "What is PG&E?"

"Pacific Gas and Electric." I unlocked the door and switched on a light. "Don't rush to get the bill in your name," Alex added, "as long as you've got power."

I looked up and saw glitter flecks in the ceiling paint, then looked around at the furniture—ruptured vinyl and chipped formica. "Alex, isn't $700 a month too much rent?"

"You've got two bedrooms."

"I could have rented a house for a year for $1400 in Floyd County. A good house."

"Yeah, yeah." Alex obviously had heard about Floyd.

He continued after a pause, "Tonight, we'll go see the sunset. Tomorrow, you can take care of business. Want to use the toilet?"

Pissing in my Terran toilet felt ceremonial. I'd expected to see a strip across the bowl—"Sanitized for your protection"—the place reminded me so much of a cheap motel.

Before we left, Alex checked to see that the windows were locked and that the patio door track was blocked with a steel rod. "Being here is like living in a xenophobia movie," he said, "almost too exciting."

On the way back up to Shattuck, I noticed that the side streets at right angles to it had houses on them, the parallel streets apartments. The woman Black Amber wanted me to meet lived in a house.

"Smoke?" Alex said. He pulled out a badge, stuck the pin though this shirt pocket. It was a Cannabis sativa grower/smoker's photo ID permit. "Berkeley's not like the rest of the country."

"Man, for you to be smoking is dangerous."

He pulled out a tiny joint, licked it, then said, "The sunset will be enough for you since you've never been in such a big city." He lit the joint and took two huge hits.

"Don't fucking bogart it because I'm being a prick. I'll smoke some."

"We'll wait." He pulled off the ID and put it and the joint away, then stuck out his thumb. "Marijuana doesn't relax you?"

"Shit, my brother got real messed up on drugs." I noticed I'd dropped out of the prestige dialect Tesseract trained me to.

"I'm sorry."

A car pulled up and Alex asked, "Going to the sunset?"

"Hadn't thought about it, buy why not."

I'd forgotten how smelly gas-burning cars were, but I hopped right in back. Alex and the driver, a guy with weirdly short hair and a drooping moustache, talked about anti-recombinant-DNA ordinances that some guy named Potrero was trying to pass.

Shit, Alex fits right in. But he sure wasn't like other Ahrams I knew.

As we went through a strip of park, a huge deer jumped in front of the car, crossed the road, and hopped over a hedge. *Bigger than a whitetail, a mule deer,* I decided.

"Blacktail," Alex said. "Seen one before, Tom?"

I shook my head.

"Maybe we'll have a little earthquake for you," the driver said. "Alex says you're just back from Asia, never been in California before."

"Nope."

"Southern boy once, though."

"Yeah." I looked up at the driver in the rearview mirror, but he wasn't concerned. Alex turned around and furrowed his brow at me, as if to say, *lighten up.* The skin corrugations went up in a steeper than human V, like the brow to crown bone crest that wasn't showing still influenced his face muscles.

Going to see the sunset was a Berkeley ritual—over fifty cars had parked along the overlook, people carrying beer cans or joints wandering from car to car. To the west were the sun and a wall of fog.

"Ocean's under the fog," Alex said. He pinned on his permit and started passing the joint around.

We sat on the hood of the guy's car. The sun seemed to touch the fog with pink light, then red. I was wondering if we'd stay until dark, took my second hit off the joint, and realized Alex grew two-toke whammo weed that skidded your brain like black ice under car tires.

The sun hung fire in the fog bank, then slipped down as the planet rolled away. The sky must be patterning like crazy, I thought, almost able to see what a Gwyng sees. "Damn, Alex," I said in Karst, too drugged to think, "you just met me and you've drugged me."

"Indian hill dialect," Alex explained to the driver. "Tom, remember to speak English."

Karst, damn. I froze in a paranoid flash as the lights came on in San Francisco's shadow—the whole horizon like a thousand searchlights.

"Hey, Alex," someone called.

"Carstairs, you here to see the sunset?" Alex said.

"Working." Carstairs, short, almost pudgy, with black-rimmed glasses, had a wicked little face, like a human version of a Gwyng. He pointed to the Lawrence Lab building.

"Here, man, be inspired." Alex offered Carstairs the joint. "This is Tom. Tom, this is Jerry Carstairs. Tom's been in Asia, sleeping with Asian women."

"Say something Asian," Carstairs asked. He inhaled deeply and looked at me; he didn't believe us a minute.

I told him, "Fuck off" in Yangchenla's Tibetan.

"Some hill dialect," the guy who drove us said.

"Really?" Carstairs inhaled a second toke, enough smoke to skid himself to Asia for a translation. Smoke trickling out of his teeth, he asked Alex, "Irish pub tonight?"

"I'll pass . . ." Alex looked at me and laughed.

"We ought to go," I said, meaning leave.

Alex said, "Not yet, Tom." Carstairs sat down on a post between the car and a brushy ravine, then winked at me.

"Mr. Carstairs, you work in the Lab?" I asked.

"What I really do is dimensional physics. You ever read a guy named Rucker?"

"No."

Carstairs looked at Alex, then at the sky and said, "Alex has. Dimensional physics fascinates him."

Does he know Alex is an alien? Or am I in drug paranoia?

Alex stood up, his scalp flushed where he would have had his crest. "Tom, we will go now, if you want."

"I do want," I said in my most formal English. I felt bewildered, as if a child among adults with secrets.

The driver said, "I'd like to stay a bit longer. I'm expecting someone."

"I'll drive you," Carstairs said.

"Can you?" I asked. "You're not too stoned?"

"Oh, I can do anything," Carstairs said, smile deeply curved into his cheeks.

"Brilliant man," Alex said. Carstairs went across the road to another parking lot for his car. He drove back, seeming suddenly sober, and opened the passenger side doors. We got in without speaking, me not quite sure what Carstairs knew.

"Could you take Tom by Milvia and Cedar?"

"Sure." Carstairs skewed to a stop just over the next crosswalk. When the yellow went on for the cross traffic, he jammed on the gas and popped out just before our light turned green to beat oncoming traffic in a left turn. I pushed his umbrella under the seat so it couldn't jab me when we crashed. I just knew we would.

We didn't crash. Why I don't know. Carstairs and Alex giggled as I got out of the car. Alex said, "I'll drop by tomorrow to talk more."

Blinking behind his glasses, Carstairs tapped his nails on the steering wheel and said, "And is Tom Gresham really your name? Gresham's Law always appealed to Alex here."

"Tom is real." I almost added, *And I'm human, too,* but I wasn't sure he knew Alex wasn't.

As they drove off together, Alex rubbed the air over his surgically flattened skull.

My Ahram colleague seemed demented. I wanted to go back to Karst, but didn't know how to contact the Barcons, so I fumbled at my door lock with the little round key, finally getting the bolt back. Difficulties of Berkeley—Federation doors opened to palm print and voice, or punched code.

The apartment was chilly, so I turned the gas heater to seventy-two. It whomped on, blue jets up and down a black pipe. No other heaters in the house, not even in my bedroom. People must freeze in the winters, I thought.

I pulled out my Terran pajamas and said to that mass of knitted cotton, "How do you like being home?"

In the morning, I woke up terrified, not sure whether dream or real police pounded at my door. I lay in bed, checking the noises: gas heater, rumbling pipes, a bed bouncing off the wall. That's what woke me, violent fucking upstairs.

I got dressed and stuck my head out the bedroom sliding glass door. Cold—I came back for a jacket and then went to get a traveler's check cashed at the Co-op.

The Co-op was like a Southern States for city people with a grocery on one side of Shattuck and a regular gardening and hardware store on the other. I felt most at home walking through the hardware store—washers, drills, and mattocks were like what I'd used in Virginia. "Hi," a bearded dwarf clerk about sixty years old said.

"What can you grow around here?" I asked.

"Where do you live?"

"On Milvia."

"Well, you *can* try greens and herbs, if you're willing to poison the snails." He stressed "willing" like I really shouldn't do that. "Soil's heavy, black adobe."

I'd never heard of black adobe, but I decided I'd get some gardening tools after I got situated. Across the road, I got orange juice, eggs, and biscuits, a notepad, and toilet paper, then realized I had no kitchen stuff and bought a frying pan. The checkout girl fingerprinted me on the back of the traveler's check. I tried not to wince—and prayed the graft glue held.

"Have a nice day," she said as she packed my stuff. "The ink fades in a minute if it's not fixed." She rolled the prints with a damp rubber roller.

Back to my apartment, I spread all my stuff out on the burn-scarred formica table and jotted down notes for what I had to do:

1. Set up bank account.
2. Get library card
3. Get computer
4. Get PG&E to put the bill in my name.
5. Get phone set up, phone book.

I rubbed my eyes, then stopped to fix eggs, sloppily poaching them since I'd forgotten to get butter or oil. No salt.

6. Buy salt, oil, pepper, flour, beans, cornmeal, frozen greens, fatback, bread.
7. Find out more about Carstairs.

I wasn't sure about that last. *Maybe I'd better not meddle?* If he suspected Alex wasn't human but had no proof, he'd be considered nuts if he babbled about dope-smoking aliens watching the sunset from Lawrence Laboratory.

8. See how lonely I had to be before I'd look up Black Amber's Berkeley contacts.

For a moment, I wanted to get caught, ease the tension of leading a false life. But my brain threw me a quick memory of two guys fucking in the prison bunk beside me—nobody doing a thing even though it was almost a rape. Warren's friends had watched out for me. And I had to kick hard once.

Most of the time, I blotted out my jail memories. Sitting in Berkeley with a new past, I shuddered—*no, I don't want to do prison again*—and checked my list over before I went out.

Yucko weather, fog a fine mist in the air. I'd never seen such summer weather on Karst or Yauntra. I found the bank, on Shattuck down from the Co-op buildings going toward the campus. The woman smiled hyperfriendly at me once she'd punched in my social security number. I thought I was about to get busted, but she said, "Tom, you've got $25,000 in electronic transfer funds waiting. Do you need a credit card?"

"I've never had one before."

"Well, I'll take your application."

I pulled out my passport to fill out where I was supposed to have lived during the last four years. But my alleged past hurt my credit rating with even a liberal bank. No VISA card, but I could get guaranteed balance checking, as long as I kept $5,000 minimum in savings.

So, phone deposit $250, PG&E $200. I could see that $25,000 in Berkeley wasn't altogether much.

Computer and radio. I decided I really needed a radio,

company-like. Maybe hook a voice reader/recorder into the radio, so I'd be warned if any radio program announced the arrest of aliens—*hey, maybe get a police scanner*.

Maybe Carstairs is another one of us?

I doubted that. And voice-readers—that was a bit paranoid.

About noon, I cut up Hearst toward the campus, walked through a redwood grove, and continued on, just looking at things—the old university buildings brick and the new ones pastel metal and glass. The students looked like any alien students with backpacks and pocket computers—maybe weirder face hair, agitated like Gwyngs. *A provincial university*, I thought in Karst. *Nah, it's bigger'n Tech*, a Virginia-educated lobe of my brain replied in low English.

Suddenly I only noticed women—guys faded into the bricks—and got a hard-on for all the human women, visible and invisible. My cock would explode if I walked farther.

I thought about Yangchenla's nastiest crack about me and Black Amber. *No, Yangchenla, I never slept with an alien*. The blood backed out of my cock. I asked a girl in a long blowing white dress, "Where do I get a library card?"

Her face did a subtle freeze shift—*oh, he's not a student*. She pointed to a huge, obvious building about a hundred yards away and walked off.

"Thanks anyhow." *Bitches, human women*.

The library crew fingerprinted me again, with a clear jelly that only made prints on treated paper, and took a mug shot for the ID card. Then, after their computer checked me for outstanding fines, they gave me a booklet that explained the various libraries all over campus on all the subjects that I could use. I asked about computer compatibility with the library's software.

"Go to Computer Mart," a woman said, "and tell them you want UCal compatibility. It'll be seventy-five dollars a month for modem linkup. Call in when you've got your system."

I looked at my fingertips to see if the graft lines were visible. Nope, the Barcons had done good work. Why hadn't the bank printed me, I wondered until I realized they'd had *my* money.

After I'd dealt with the library, I was really hungry and so crossed Sproul Plaza, headed toward Telegraph Avenue. First thing, I ran into a bicycle-truck selling tempeh sandwiches. *What the hell?* I asked, "Can I see some?"

The guy handed me a strip of tempeh. I sniffed it—smelled like paint—then looked down Telegraph and saw a Shabazz Soul Food sign. My brother Warren had told me about a Black Muslim place called the Shabazz Bakery. Shit, Black Muslim food had to be better than tempeh. "Thanks," I said to the tempeh dealer, handing him back his little strip of moldy beans.

They can't be racists here, I told myself. *It's California.* The door didn't look threatening—beveled glass in blue-painted wood. I looked inside, saw that I wouldn't be the only white boy, and smelled the cornbread.

Hope I'm not drooling. I sat down in a booth. A black woman in a long dress, head covered with a kerchief, came up and said, "Yow."

"I'd like pinto beans and cornbread. Glass of buttermilk if you have it."

"Cornbread with jalapeños, ginger, or plain."

"Plain cornbread."

"Home food?" She smiled at me.

"Yeah, originally. I've been away."

"Glad you aren't a Voudonist. We hate Voudonist here, especially druggy white Voudonist." She went off to get the food while I looked further at the menu. They had tempeh here, too, and I read the fine print on the beans—no pork, flavored with beef or spices, depending on the cook's mood.

Funny, I could eat anything compatible to my proteins if it was labeled alien. But on Earth, I wanted familiar food. Tempeh wasn't too different from Yauntro villag—that's what was so *bad* about it.

But I'd never seen all the variations of any planet, just city blocks and country acres here and there—and now I

was being provincial about the west side of my own con-
tinent. *Planets are huge, thrust into variations of space.*
The universe suddenly expanded exponentially around that
Terran soul food restaurant, and the edges of all the variations overlapped.

"You been thinking?" the waitress said to me as she
set down my buttermilk.

"I have," I said in my most formal English.

"Enjoy the food. The cook was in a good mood today,
white boy." She put the cornbread and beans down, then
poured me some water. "Beef in those beans."

I was just a tiny truculent creature moving through im-
mense space, invisible at any reasonable scale, bitching
about the food. *Scale can't be fixed; got to work on that
truculence,* I told myself in English, digging into the
beans. Not homestyle, but good.

Back at my apartment, someone knocked while I was
setting up the computer system the store clerk guaranteed
would be compatible with the UCal system, plugging the
phone jack into the modem. I jumped, wondering if the
fingerprints hadn't worked, then heard Alex say, plain-
tively, "Tom."

I unbolted and unchained the door. His face and bald
scalp across the top of his head were sweating and pale,
his eyelids puffy as though rows of mites had been chew-
ing on the eyelashes. Puffy eyelids seem to be a pan-
specific sign of debauchery or viral infection. He came in
and peered at the modem, breath hissing through his big
teeth. "Tom, you and I need to walk in Tilden Park."

"I've walked already."

"Now. Right now." He hulked over me in his red nylon
human jacket, caught in some bleak Ahram emotion. I
realized he wanted to talk where no humans could over-
hear us.

"Okay, Alex."

"Carstairs," he said, "works in a classified section of
Lawrence Laboratory. I didn't find out when I first met
him. He doesn't talk about that at all. Someone else let it

slip.'' He touched the wall and his ear. *The walls might have ears.*

Shit. Smoking dope with a weapons designer. We must already be under Federal surveillance.

Alex drove an odd car, license plate X-KALAY. When Alex opened his car door, it flexed. I closed it carefully. The whole car looked homemade, seats from an old VW, round dialed instruments, lawnmower-type gear shift, plastic and fiberglass body.

''What kind of car?''

''Berkeley eco-deco. Gets about seventy-five miles to the gallon, burns alcohol.''

''Okay.''

''Would you prefer pedaling a Vector?''

''Not up hills like the ones we went up last night.''

''I moved here after they passed restrictions on gasoline cars. More paperwork to get a gasoline permit than a marijuana user's permit, that's Berkeley.''

The little car didn't stink as did the gasoline burner we'd ridden in yesterday, but it threatened to balk in the hills. ''It's a real obvious car,'' I told him, meaning he could be followed easily.

''I didn't drive it to pick you up yesterday, did I?'' He sounded annoyed, like I'd challenged him in spy trade-craft. ''Even these pollute some.''

The oaks had shrunken leaves, small oaks—I was sure they were oaks, though, by the acorns. I didn't speak, just looked at the weird vegetation. Alex parked in a lot with signs pointing to various hiking trails, giving their distances in kilometers.

We began walking through sage plants, weird scrubs, things with twisted orange bark. Finally Alex plopped down on the ground and said, ''Sit down.''

''Are you going to smoke?''

''Never smoke in chaparral during the summer. Fire hazard.''

''Man, I don't want to get busted here. Carstairs suspects something.''

''He can't prove anything. Not a thing.''

''If he did a DNA-type on you, he'd *know* you're alien.''

"He hasn't."

"But he's a fucking weapons engineer."

"He never talks about that. Just the theoretical stuff, the dimensions stuff, worm holes." Alex sighed and nibbled at some sage. "Tom, I want to know when Earth makes gate contact. He'll know. I'm not a security threat, really. He doesn't even know where I live. You don't either. And he's exciting. Am I like other Ahrams?"

"No, most of you guys are calmer."

"Being around humans did it, almost like neural rewiring."

"If Earth made contact, would Karst hand you over to the Feds?"

Alex looked disgusted, muscles rippled around the big jaw. "I don't want to be surprised. Jail is horrible, isn't it?"

"I'm Academy; I don't like sneaking around. And you're teasing Carstairs, some way, and putting me in danger."

"You're a prissy little human." He got up.

I scrambled to my feet fast, suddenly aware of how isolated this trail was today; how big he was. "Do the Barcons know about Carstairs?"

"They're lucky; they don't need friends. Humans are enough like Ahrams to be . . ." He stopped talking and bit his lower lip.

"You made friends with a *weapons* designer? The Feds know he's got a big blond friend—you better believe it."

"Judging from the reports, I like humans better than you do."

"So I had terrible fights with the Tibetans."

We began walking down the trail toward his car. He asked, "And how is Black Amber?"

"Fine, she and Wy'um had a son."

"Behind every liberated Gwyng male is a truly ambitious pouch sister."

"That's cynical."

"But true. The males *are* useless. I had to deal with the crisis over Mica. After Black Amber was wounded, Rhyodolite coma'ed out, the stupid bastard. Cadmium, I guess he wasn't any more hysterical than usual.''

"Yeah. What do you know about the people Black Amber wants me to meet?''

"Nice girl. I'm glad I've been altered to speak perfect Midwestern English or she might have tried to analyze where I come from.''

"Are you from the Ahram home planet or are you Karst-born?''

"Karst-born.''

"Are all the Karst-born weird for their kind?''

"No weirder than you are for yours, Tom,'' Alex said.

We could see the car from the hill and began talking of other things, like manzanitas, black sage, oaks, and how most one-celled organisms had global ranges, lived in both fresh and salt water.

"So disappointing to get water from the Pacific and see the same damn diatoms that I'd seen in spring water,'' Alex said. "Even saw a Euplotes patella, looks almost like . . .''

I said, "Physical constraints on possibilities?''

"Or maybe all life is expressions of one mind?'' *Karriaagzh's line*. Alex said, "Relax, I was lonely today. Just lonely,'' as we got in the car.

When he let me out of the car at my place, I said, "Let me know next time you go drinking with Carstairs.''

"Okay, maybe.''

I didn't see Alex again for days. The next day, I worried all morning, studying the computer printouts on the UCal Japanese studies library holdings. Most of them were in Japanese—I wondered about getting a translation program, but didn't know if Earthlings had developed such things yet.

By ten A.M., when I hadn't been arrested due to being seen with an alien, I went to the Co-op and bought beans, pork backbones, and a loaf of bread. Then I called the computer store and asked if they had anything that could translate Japanese into English.

"Are we talking technical data? Are you willing to screen out invisible idiots?" the clerk asked.

"Technical data."

"Well, it's going to take a sixth generation machine if you're asking it to translate voice."

"I've got a KayPro XV. Bought it there day before yesterday. No voice, just text, printed texts."

"No can do."

I decided to read what I could in English before getting another computer to translate Japanese to English, get a general picture.

The next day, I stared at my glitter ceiling, then went out to buy a radio at the Co-op hardware store. While I was there, I got a few tools to make a garden: spading fork, mattock, shovel, and gloves to protect my fake prints. It wasn't that I'd be here long enough to eat anything; I just wanted something familiar to do.

I put the radio on a listener-sponsored station. In Floyd, we got three listener-sponsored stations, each one running the same PBS stuff. I'd listened enough to know who Bach was. But this radio station was playing fusion music— illegitimate daughter of heavy metal and calypso-oid music—and announcing programs that would debate second generation space defense programs.

I opened the door so I could hear the radio while I worked in the garden—then started clearing away some old boards in the little yard.

Newts under those logs? In a city? Newts and deer— Berkeley began to seem like they'd just last week laid the city over wilderness and the animals hadn't had time to leave. I threw the newts over the back fence and started grubbing out the ivy.

A huge snail the size of a tennis ball wiggled its eye stalks at me. *Shi-it.* I'd never seen snails that big. I threw it over the fence after the newts and tried to lift a forkful of dirt.

I bounced on that fork seven times before the black clay broke free. Another snail watched from where it was chomping down an oak. *Okay, we'll go back and ask the gardening freak what works with black clay.*

But instead of heading back to the Co-op, I walked down Milvia, just walked, checking out where I was now. A half-grown peacock ran across the road and behind one of the apartment buildings.

Something clicked. I stopped comparing the hills to the Blue Ridge as though they were both built the same way. Brown summer grass here, fine. The temperature rose to about ninety for a minute while I was walking, then dropped to forty-five when the sun . . . when the earth I stood on rolled behind the terminator, behind its own shadow.

Instead of expecting arrest as an alien spy, I began to worry about muggers, turned back home, walking on Shattuck which I figured would be safer. There, I spotted the store where Alex had bought my Earth-style clothes.

Still no sign of Alex the next day. I checked out a Lafcadio Hearn book at the insistence of an Asian library clerk and two books on Japanese industrial development.

"Industrial development in Japan was very sudden," she told me. "About the time of your Civil War. We had been insular before then."

"Was it better being insular?"

"Read this." She handed me some copied sheets.

She was Japanese; I wanted to talk to her more, but I saw her face twist away from me and the eyes dart back toward me—a human sexual interest behavior that I'd studied from books and life on Karst, so I thanked her and left. No more Oriental women.

You're a prissy little human, Alex said from my memory. Alex was playing with a weapons designer who did dimensional physics on the side. *Maybe he's sneaking gate design information to Carstairs?* Suddenly I didn't want to even be in my apartment. I went to the Co-op bookstore and bought a Bay Area guidebook, called up the BART schedule on the computer, then went to San Francisco.

Something odd about this train. I couldn't quite put my finger on what, dangling from a strap surrounded by a human mob, then realized I'd never been on a train filled with just one species. Humans all of us. I stared at bearded and shaved men's faces, then at women's lips, all painted various shades of red and pink, cheeks chemically flushed, too. *Wow, we are a weird species.*

Five people in yellow robes got on the train at the first San Francisco stop and began chanting, "Hari Krishna, Krishna Rama, Rama Rama."

Yangchenla's people, shit. The robes looked so much like the Karst Tibetans' robes that I couldn't watch, but instead stared at black hulks whizzing by the window until the train burst out into bright fog and multi-colored houses.

San Francisco looked like a magic Roanoke that had been kept up and painted colors (my brain did some wish landscaping, but Roanoke *was* built when San Francisco was being re-built). Suddenly the houses disappeared as the train went into a tunnel. On the other side of the tunnel were metal and ferroconcrete apartment buildings.

At Seal Rock, I saw the Pacific Ocean, big and chilly with real seals in it. One stared back at me from the rock—that creature to creature stare you only get from really intelligent animals or fellow sapients.

Would the stars tonight be the same as the stars I saw in Floyd, I wondered.

I didn't feel like checking and headed back to the BART station. The train back wasn't entirely mono-specific—I caught a glimpse of one Barcon getting on a car behind me. I was relieved to see them. *They must be tracking me through my skull computer.*

I walked home from the university station, catching one more glimpse of the Barcons. When I got home, the phone was ringing. I almost didn't answer it, but thought that it might be Alex.

"Tom, did Alex drop by today?" It was the male Barcon.

"No. I saw you guys behind me on the train."

"We didn't have time to say hello." He hung up.

I fixed a late lunch, but I couldn't feel the time in Berkeley. After lunch, I was bored, the boredom edged with tension. I couldn't do anything about Alex—I didn't feel like helping the Yauntries today. Fuck the research. I pulled out the address Black Amber had given me.

Amber had traced the address from the journal she'd kept when she knew English, when she hunted in human shape for Mica, saying as she'd traced, "Humans, untrustworthy, except for this woman and you, Red Clay."

But Karriaagzh said if only a few were different, then humans didn't have to be xeno-flips, I remembered as I found the street address on my Berkeley map.

The woman lived on Cedar, between Milvia and Martin Luther King, not far from my apartment, in a house. Who'd be home during the day? I'd leave a note. Black Amber's friend was the older sister, Marianne, the younger was Molly. The Schweigman sisters—but not from hill German folks like some of my kin. I wrote: *I'm a friend of John Amber's and would like to talk to you. Tom Gresham, 1607 Milvia, 555-6641.*

As I walked out of my apartment and crossed Cedar, my sweat mingled with the chilly fog. My fingers rolled the paper back and forth, back and forth. By the time I got to the Schweigman door, the note looked like a crumpled joint.

Voices inside the house paralyzed me. *Knock, knock. Who's there? Alien. Alien? I been alien for your love, Marianne.*

Hush, head, and let the hand up to knock. Finally obedient, my knuckles tapped the door, then I saw the doorbell and pushed the button.

A young, redheaded woman, about twenty-three, came to the door in a long skirt, bra-less under a Bach t-shirt. "Hi?" she said like it was a question, her toes twisting in the carpet as if they were cramped.

"Are you Marianne?" I didn't think so—Marianne was older than me, by about two years.

"No, I'm Molly. I'm busy."

I looked closer at the skirt and said, "Handspun? You're a weaver, John Amber told me "

"That one? Mum . . . m."

"John wanted me to give Marianne a message. I was going to leave a note if no one was home."

"Don't ever do that in Berkeley. You'd get us robbed. Where are you from, to do such a thing?"

"From the country," I said. "Virginia."

She looked at me like *what an idiot*. A black man, almost asleep, padded downstairs and snuggled up behind her, arms reaching around her waist. He asked, "Who's this?"

"Sam, he's looking for Marianne." She leaned back against the black guy. The black guy was her lover—I felt weird, then ashamed of my racist streak.

"We'll give her your address," Sam said in most proper and chilly English.

"Please do," I said. They stared through me hard enough to have spotted my computerized plastic skull bone. "I wanted to thank her. For helping John Amber."

"Yeah, John Amber," Sam said.

I didn't go home then. Virginia or Federal law might be waiting on the corner of Milvia and Cedar to recall me to jail.

At sunset, on the corner of Shattuck and University, I stuck out my thumb and hitched to the sunset. Carstairs wasn't there. After the night came, electric glitter under us, I rode back down with the guys who'd driven me up. They discussed sunsets in Mexico, Japan over Mt. Fuji. I almost told them about the sky around Karst.

Back at my apartment, the phone rang as I put the key in the round hole. *Maybe someone's watching?*

"Have you seen Alex?" The female Barcon sounded worried.

"Nope. I went by the Schweigman house."

"Wait on that."

"I left word. Marianne wasn't home."

"Put her off until we find Alex."

I told them, "He's been hanging out with a Lawrence Lab researcher named Jerry Carstairs. Drinking at an Irish pub. Have you seen Alex's car anywhere?"

"Parked at his apartment."

"Well, do you want me to check with Carstairs?"

"Do." The Barcon hung up. I got out the phone book and looked up the number for Lawrence Laboratory, called and asked, "Do you know when I can reach Jerry Carstairs?"

"Doesn't work here anymore."

"What about his home number?"

"Call personnel, ten to four, work hours. Sorry, okay."

"Okay." I didn't know what to think. Whatever, I'd have to wait until morning. I turned on the radio and tuned in the weird listener-supported station, but that was playing some squealing code.

I froze in cold sweat, then the announcer broke in, "We're going to black-box twenty-four hours a day next month, so subscribe now for a descrambler at present subscription prices."

Code but not for me. I collapsed giggling on the ratty couch, part of my brain rather coldly watching.

Nobody came by or called the next morning, so I began reading *The Japanese Discovery of Europe, 1720–1830*, by Donald Keene. The Federation, I thought, was fairer than the Dutch traders at Nagasaki.

At noon, I heard a knock on my door, light fist, not like a Barcon's. Slowly, I got off the bed, marked my place in the book with a grocery slip, then went to the door. "Who is it?" I asked, slipping the chain on. I looked through the open bedroom door and calculated how fast I'd have to run, how long the door would hold up if Feds were behind it. The backyard fence I could get over fine.

"Marianne. You came by yesterday?"

"Yeah." I opened the door as far as the chain allowed. Her hair was long, black, held away from her face by a silk scarf. She turned her head and stared at me through one brown eye, a tongue stuck out between full lips. She licked the chain, nibbled it as though she was mocking my paranoia. She was mocking me. I'd seen women like her buying organic groceries with food stamps in Floyd when I was twelve, sneaking around, watching hippies.

"You said you know John Amber. Is he okay?" She sounded female over "him." I unchained the door, wondering about what had gone on before the Gwyngs found me in Virginia.

"Yeah, he's okay. He's back in Asia now."

She stared at my mouth as though seeing the surgery that gave me all the Karst phonemes. "He didn't sound Asian. And where are you from?"

"I was born in rural Virginia, but I've been in Asia a few years."

"Speak some."

I told her "I'm sorry, but I don't know much," in Yangchenla's Tibetan.

Her eyes widened. "Holy shit."

I opened the door all the way and said, "Do you want some lunch?"

She came in and stared at me, then spoke two sounds, one a dental *t*, the other alveolar. "Can you tell the difference?"

"Oh, yeah." I pronounced them and realized that my alveolar ridge had re-shaped from human norm.

"Yeah?" She sat down. "Okay, I'll have lunch with you. I'm curious. Am I getting myself in danger?" She grimaced as though that hadn't come out quite the way she'd wanted it to.

"Nope," I said, concentrating on putting phonemes where they belonged in my mouth the old Virginia way.

"How did you meet John?"

"Through some friends of his who got stranded in Virginia. How did *you* meet John?"

"He and a black girl were living here, and my sister and her husband thought they'd help out another interracial couple. I'm not sure John and Rhoda were lovers, though. Big tension between them, like they were illegal aliens stranded together, used to being in a larger social group."

"Yes," I said. She guessed well, made me quite uneasy.

"I worked mainly in linguistics, but we got exposed to considerable social anthropology, too, in that."

"You teach?"

"No, I just fool around." She suddenly sounded sad—*drop this*, I thought.

"I'm doing some research on Japan now."

She went *um*, a noncommittal *um*. I put two frozen pies

in the microwave. "You don't eat tempeh, do you?" I had to ask.

"My parents were nuts about it."

"My parents are dead, too."

She stared at me, her finger rubbing between her lips, then said, "So we're both orphans," with a cryptic smile playing between the words. She sure didn't remind me of Floyd stock come from Germans.

"Were your parents Californians?" I asked as I pulled the pies out of the microwave and put one in front of her.

"They came here from New York in the sixties, following a rimpoche. Burnt radicals." She opened the pie crust with a fork and looked in dubiously.

Rimpoche—Yangchenla used the word sarcastically to mean *darling*, but the other Tibetans used it for priests, *precious one*. "I just can't escape Tibetans," I said.

"What you spoke? You learned that in Tibet? How did you get in?"

"Snuck. I don't believe in passports."

"Speak more."

"Come on, I've told you I was illegally in Tibet."

"Um, um, uh. I don't believe John Amber had traces of Tibetan patterns in his speech. And there's more to yours."

She'll crawl up your mouth after the strange sounds, Black Amber had told me. I said, "Minor stroke," wondering if I should trickle out some drool.

"Not if you can hear the difference between dental and alveolar *t*'s."

"I'd prefer that you not analyze my speech," I said, arching into high English but slopping into Karst phonemes. She stared at my mouth like a bird dog on point. *Oh, shit.* I bent over and shook her knee.

"Tom, tell me if I'm in trouble with my questions?"

"No." Her knee was knobby under my hand, the thigh above it muscular. I lifted my hand before my fingers could squeeze harder.

She tried to spear a chicken nugget out of her pot pie, and half giggled, half choked. "God, we're nervous people, aren't we? How long have you been in Berkeley, Tom?''

"Couple of days. I'm doing research on industrial development in Japan." I was a bit bewildered by her near giggle.

"Why?"

"To help some people get industrially developed without getting swamped by an alien culture."

"John Amber's people?"

"People in the general area." *Let's not have her and Carstairs putting their guesses together.*

We finished eating without saying anything more. Then as I crumpled up the pie pans, she said, "Hey, don't throw those away. Recycle."

"What?"

"Wash all aluminum cans and pie pans, take them down to the recycling center. If you don't need the money, tell them to donate it to the Job Corps. Sorry to snap. It's the way my parents brought me up."

I swayed slightly on the balls of my feet, pie tins still in my hands, and said, "When in Berkeley, be eco-deco."

"You say John is okay?"

"Yes."

"And the others."

"Fine."

"I'm glad they sent word." She looked around the apartment, then up at the glitter ceiling. "I could show you where recycling is."

"Sure."

"I've got a freight bike."

"Is it like a Vector?"

"Nope. Like an Asian freight bike."

I tucked my chin down, wondering if she was trying to trap me into admitting I'd never been in Asia. She took the pie pans out of my hand, washed them, and put them in a paper bag. "So, Tom, you have secrets. Relax, I won't make any more guesses."

"Thanks. Now take me to recycling."

"Wait a few days. We'll have a full load between your house and mine."

She left and I felt infinitely more lonely. No Alex, light-years from Granite—and Marianne'd gone, too. The book on Japan lay spine up, pages spread over grease patches on the table. *Shit, that Japanese librarian will kill me.*

For the rest of the week, I lived off things that came in aluminum, collecting a huge heap of cans for recycling.

I also bought lettuce plants. But snails by the hundreds, huge ones, led by a snail big as a softball, I swear it, ate the lettuce down to the ground.

The female Barcon called to ask if Alex had stopped by, hung up when I said, "No, not yet." I couldn't do anything except read about Japan or defend my lettuce. I went to the Co-op and asked the garden clerk, "What kills snails?"

"Corey's Snail Kill, but . . ."

Fuck ecology. It's Corey's Snail Kill time.

I bought my box of Corey's and was walking back to the apartment with it when Marianne pedaled by on a contraption that looked like a torturer's bike—little narrow seat, straps, clips, skinny tires, toothy metal gears spinning on the back hub. She wore skintight pants and a jersey zipped down to between her breasts, black plastic straps over her hair.

Ecological Berkeley women wouldn't approve of Corey's. And if Alex was gone, in Federal hands, I ought to be making plans for another life, not be pissing around saving lettuce from monster snails.

"Hi, Marianne. Is it ecologically unsound to poison snails when they eat my lettuce?"

"Fatten them on cornmeal and eat them instead. Tell me if I ought to send out more resumes or work on getting my time trial time down to a sub-26." She sounded tired.

"What are you talking about? Sub-26? You're a linguist, right? Get a job in that if you need money. Do your time trial if you don't." Time trial on a bike?

"Sub-26 minutes for a ten-mile bike time trial. The CIA has jobs, but they'd never trust me. I'm a third generation red diaper baby."

"Communist?"

"Weather Underground. Grandparents were stodgy Stalinists and my parents rebelled. So I had to become a serious scholar except for a bout of Zen mysticism."

"What happened?"

"I converted my parents to Buddhism. Weather Underground had a high burn rate."

"So you pedal around wondering what to do next?"

"Tom, training for racing doesn't let you think." She stroked the bike's lugwork with a hand in a punk glove. I thought punk had died decades ago, then I realized that the punks had stolen bikers' gloves. She saw me looking and pulled the gloves off—half fingers peeled inside out— to show me sunburn spots on her hand. "Matches the mesh."

Bike racing—that explained the knobby knee, the firm thigh under my fingers the first day she'd come over. "I've got lots of stuff to recycle, Marianne."

She pulled her glove back on and said, "Oh. Yes. You can ride a bike, can't you?"

"Sure."

"Probably Sam's will fit you."

"I could ride the freight bike."

"Nah. You'd . . . is your male ego fragile?"

"No, sort of," I admitted.

"Well, let the freighter slow me down. I'll spin a low gear, and we can ride together."

I shrugged, male ego plotting to outride her, and walked home to flatten my cans. Ten minutes later she knocked on my door, still in the funny bike clothes, with rocker-bottomed shoes that lifted her toes up off the ground. Behind her I saw the three-wheeled freight bike and the other bike.

She told me, "I took off the toe straps so you wouldn't go down if you forgot them."

"You ride to the dump in those clothes?"

"Normally, not. Recycling's in the flats."

As if that explains something. I was about to hop on the bike and ride, but she pulled out a hex key and fiddled with the seat and handlebars. When she'd adjusted it, I lifted the bike. It almost flew through the air, it was so light.

"I eyeballed it, so now let's see if you need to fine-tune the fit," she said, wiping the hex key and putting it up her pants leg. The nylon was tight enough to hold the key in place.

She beat me—downhill on a fucking freight tricycle. I got off and walked around the recycling yard to cool off while she talked to the halfbreeds that ran the place.

"Tom," she called to me.

"I'm not pissed."

"If you'd trained for as long as I've trained, I'm sure you could beat me, okay. I feel awful when guys act like I've castrated them when I beat them on a bike."

"O-kay."

"Take it easy. The freight bike falls faster, too, and we were going downhill."

"You could have let me beat you," I said, then wished my tongue had gotten bee-stung before I said that.

She put her bike-gloved knuckles on her hips, then said, "Tom!" like I'd exasperated her. Then she pushed her hair back and pulled on the helmet made of fat plastic straps. *Commie idolatrous bike racer.* "Train me. I'll get a bike."

"Do you know how expensive these are?"

"I've got money." I'd beat her eventually.

"Okay."

On the way back, I noticed the slums we'd raced through the first time.

"I lift weights," I told her when I handed her back the bike. "I should have gone faster."

"It's cadence," she said. "Women generally get better form quicker than guys, even if we aren't as strong. And we were going downhill. The freight bike falls faster."

"So you ride a bike all the time?"

"Yeah. I . . . well, since I didn't have anything better to do, I started when my last grant proposal was turned down." She took the handlebars of the bike I'd been riding in one hand, grasping them in the center where they joined the bike, and pulled it along beside her as she pedaled the freight bike toward her house. "But I'm too old to be a pro, so I'm just wasting my time," she shouted back.

When I unlocked my apartment door, I heard the phone ringing. It stopped before I could answer.

I put out the snail bait that night, *fuck Berkeley ecological women*. In the morning, the backyard was littered with snail bodies, most curled back into their shells, some dangling out like misshapen penises. I gathered the dead and dying, all slimy, into a paper bag which I dumped in the dumpster. *Marianne, come back and I'll never poison snails again.*

A dragging ass Lincoln pulled up by the dumpster just as I let the lid bang down—Carstairs driving, with Alex. They'd both grown beards, grubby weirdos in shades. "Alex, you dwarp!" I yelled at him. "People been calling asking if I'd seen you. And Carstairs, you don't work at the Laboratory anymore."

"We were out celebrating that," Carstairs said, pulling off the shades and putting on his black-rimmed regular glasses.

Alex fished a pack frame and pack, with a sleeping bag strapped to it, out of Carstairs's trunk. "Just like Kerouac—mountain climbing, Zen shouts. Jerry, come in."

"Who was this Kerouac?" I asked. Carstairs looked at me and blinked, then shook his head slightly. He seemed somewhat nervous. Maybe real nervous and hiding it.

He said to Alex, "I didn't want to get you in trouble."

Alex looked very alien then, squatting down by his pack. The scars where his crest had been cut off showed as fine raised white tissue running from his hairline over the bald crown of his head. He fingered through one of the outside pockets and got out his keys. *Alex, what have you been doing?* His beard hadn't grown in a human pattern, missed his lip as though he'd shaved off a moustache and left the rest stubble.

"Are you a danger to your friends," I said to Carstairs. "You drink a lot."

"I think not," he said, rather disdainfully. "Because Alex . . ." He shut up.

"Tom, Jerry's my friend. Really."

"We need to talk about this. We all have to talk."

"Jesus, Tom," Alex said. "Let's get inside."

"I'm really Alex's friend, Tom. Really."

"Please, Jerry," I said, more and more afraid Carstairs would babble about aliens to whiskey-treating bar pals who'd be FBI getting him drunk to find out the truth about his weird companions. Of course, it would sound so crazy that he'd get locked up, not Alex.

"Come on in," Alex said again.

"I have to think about things," Carstairs said. "Let's all go to the pub Wednesday night." He turned the ignition key, his head cocked to the side as if listening for tuning problems.

"Wednesday, then," Alex said. He looked around him and put his keys in his jeans pocket. Carstairs backed out into the street, waved as he pulled away.

"Where's your car?" I asked Alex.

"Parked. Can I come in?"

"Sure. The black guys have been worried about you."

"*Hnyeh*, I'll call them, but don't you tell them you saw me." I unlocked my door and we went in. Alex pulled what looked like a pen out of his pocket, pulled the pocket clip completely off, and began using the pen-disguised scanner on the walls, behind the sofa, and around the stove.

When he'd finished, he pulled out the ink barrel and scraped off the micro-electronics with a Swiss Army knife from his pack. As he put the pen back together again, he called on my phone and said, "Gee, guys, don't be paranoid. I went camping with a friend. I'm not a parolee, for pete's sake." He stared at me with suddenly alien eyes when he said that—brown with whites too small, tinged yellow. "Okay, I'm at Tom's apartment, but I won't be staying long."

I heard one of them grumbling in English about "second-rate academics who . . ."

Alex's fingers strangled the coiled phone wires. "I'm not a second-rate academic."

"Why don't you both discuss it later?" I said.

"Yeah, Tom worries about me, too," Alex said to the Barcon on the phone. "I'll drop by later tonight, okay." He hung up and stood looking at me for a while, then picked up his pack, pulled it on, strapped the waistband tight. "Tom, be cool."

"I . . . forget it." If I got him really pissed, he could leave me stranded in Berkeley, even call in to the police with an anonymous tip after my fake fingerprints grew out. "I got used to lots of strange companions when I was in Asia." I was proud of myself; I didn't put any weird stress on Asia.

"Well, I need companions," he said, voice suddenly gentler. But then he said, "Maybe *you* befriend aliens because you can't rank among your own?"

I was bewildered by that. He went all the way out the door, closed it behind him. *Marianne!* I'd sworn I wouldn't jump the bones of Black Amber's designated good female human, but sex with her now would connect me to humankind.

The phone rang. I answered it. Barcon. "Is Alex still there?"

"No, he just left," I said. "I don't expect to see him before Wednesday."

The Barcon, the male this time, hung up.

The next morning I called Marianne and asked her if she'd help me buy a bike like the one I'd ridden the other day. We transferred buses all over Alameda County to end up in a warehouse district knocking on a metal-cased door to a shop with windows painted black and grated over.

"Yo," a male voice called.

"Reeann and a friend," she called back.

The steel-sheathed door groaned open—a police lock bar rubbing in a slot behind it—and I saw a thin guy with prematurely grey hair straggling out of the rubber band holding most of it behind his neck.

"Tom, this is Roger Strigate."

"Hi, Roger."

"What you need?"

"Prices. Scare him away."

"Twelve hundred dollars stock frame, silver brazed. Fifteen to seventeen hundred dollars custom. If you can ride stock, I start at fifty cm."

"Try stock," Marianne said almost flirtatiously.

"You're a bit big for a bikie, not too long in the leg though for stock. Reeann's perfect size for a bikie, five feet eight."

"Give him the fully fitted price," Reeann said.

"Dr. Schweigman, does the man get a club discount?"

"Can he get mine?"

"Well, okay, so the whole bike is $2500 with Frageolo-Campangnolo, or $2300 with Toyota, or $2000 with used bits and pieces."

Whatever happened to the K-Mart special? I said, "I'll need those rocker bottom shoes, too, won't I?"

"Reeann, has he ridden bike before?" The guy picked at a solder burn on the back of his hand between the wrist and the index finger—scuffy-looking hands, muscled for hands the way Reeann's legs were muscled.

"He wants it," she said.

Roger chuckled. No bike could cost so much. "Are your frames worth it?" I asked.

The man's face almost crystallized, muscles rigid. Shadows from the overhead fluorescents made him look gaunt, like a movie priest. He muttered, "There's a store on Telegraph for people who want toy bikes."

"No," I said. If she wanted to scam me for an ex-lover, maybe she'd feel guilty later. I took out my checkbook and began writing the check. "Bike clothes, shoes, the works. We'll call a cab from here."

"Relax, Tom. You said you wanted the best."

Hell, it isn't real money, anyway. And I felt the need to spend some—like wasting money would reduce my tension. Roger put me on a contraption like an exercise bike with plumb bobs. While I pedaled, he shifted the metal angles of the thing, muttering to himself about "mashers" and jotting down figures.

Finally, he said, "You can take a stock fifty-eight centimeter frame if we're fitting you for racing. I'll use a 150 millimeter stem. You'll take a medium skin short. Medium jersey might not fit—you're long in the torso.''

"And a helmet and gloves," Reeann added.

"He really hasn't ridden *any* kind of bike, has he?"

"Not a ten speed," I said.

"It's too much bike for you," Roger said, battered fingernail tacking out the bill on a photoelectric hand calculator.

"No toe-clip overlap?" Reeann asked.

"Na, just about a thirty-eight inch wheel base. You want to buy extra tires, extra wheels now?"

"Give him itty-bitty clinchers and gum tubes."

Totally adrift in their jargon, I felt my face getting hot before I laughed at myself among such alien humans on my own planet. Skitter, skitter, my pen on paper wrote out a big check without hesitating. We couldn't take the bike with us. Roger had to put it together from components. I asked, "Marianne, want to come with me and some friends to an Irish pub on Wednesday?"

"Thistle and Shamrock? They've got free hors d'oeuvres Wednesday.''

"Friend's taking me—don't know which bar."

"I'll come by Thistle and Shamrock if I can. If you're there, you're there," she said, maybe making an attempt to evade me.

On Wednesday, Alex was at the door with his grower/user ID dangling down the front of a gray ribbed sweater, beard grown out even more, with a fake moustache slightly darker than his real face hair. "Ready?" he asked.

I looked at him carefully, but even though the yellow whites of his eyes showed swollen blood vessels, he seemed sharp, unexpectedly sharp. "Can you drive?" I asked him.

He shrugged and said, "You can do it. Car's not too far off norm if you can handle a stick shift. Did you tell our friends where we were going?"

"The black friends?" He nodded, so I said, "I just said I wouldn't see you until Wednesday."

"Shit," he said. After I got in the car and checked out

the controls, he dropped drops in his eyes which seemed
to make the blood vessels swell more—faking stoned, I
realized, fascinated.

"Shit, man, yourself. I did tell Marianne." I turned the
key in the ignition, to the right. No? To the left—the en-
gine sounded like a pillow-smothered motor boat.

"Don't want to see them. Chilly black bastards."

I wondered what a quarrel between Earth watchers
would do for me—alien assholes. "Tell me where to turn."

"It's out Telegraph."

"We going to pick up Carstairs?"

"He's meeting us there." Alex rolled another number
and smoked it as though it was a cigarette.

I didn't even ask for a hit. "That doesn't affect you
much?" *Did that sound enough like an ordinary question?*
He rolled his bloodshot eyes at me and laughed, almost
an ordinary dope-stoned giggle. I thought, *I hate people
from the Institute of Analytics and Tactics. A and T, T and
A, I hate spies.*

A cop on a blue-cowled motorcycle flashed me over.
Fuck it, I thought, almost jamming us against the dash as
I jerked through a gear change, swerved up against the
curb, and braked. I smiled up at my reflection in the cop's
helmet visor. *Boy, they expect trouble here—not mirror
shades, a wraparound helmet with brow to chin visor.*

He held some high-tech kin to a short cattle prod in one
hand and said, "Roll it."

Alex reached over me and rolled down the window,
smiling stupidly at the cop. My hands coiled around the
steering wheel, my asshole began to pucker. "Give him
your driver's license," Alex said. I turned red and pulled
it out of my pants pocket, s-l-o-w-l-y.

The cop pulled my license up to about eye level, sucked
up some of the car air with a small vacuum cleaner rig,
read a meter on it, and told me, "Any more smoke in the
car and I'd bust you for operating while contact high." He
flipped his fingers to the visor joint, then waved us back
into traffic.

I looked over and saw that Alex was sweating. He asked,
"What was jail like?"

"Hideous," I said, "but you'd be in a different jail. Federal prison, I believe, with tennis courts."

Alex looked at his eyes in the rearview mirror. "You think *I'm* teasing Carstairs. He's figured out something and he's teasing me." He got one of his pens and cradled it in his hands as though it was hot.

I looked down at it when we stopped at a traffic light, noticed the yellow cap was turning dark. *Is he bleeding?* Alex dropped the pen out the car window when we got going again and leaned back against the seat. He didn't say anything about the pen, so I worried as I drove, he directing me. *The traffic cop bugged us. The Barcons. The Feds. My parole officer. Shit.*

"If Carstairs is there, the black guys will be too nervous . . ." He didn't quite finish the sentence, sucked in his lower lip, and ran his tongue between lower gum and teeth.

I parked behind the bar. Alex touched my arm just as I was about to get out. We paused there, headlights washing over us as more cars came into the lot, his face half shadows and scars.

"Go," he said. Gravel creaked underfoot. I looked back. Alex's body rolled almost like a Gwyng's, his legs swinging wide before he planted them. "I know my business," he told me quietly. "You'll see how well in a moment. The blacks won't dare mess with me here." He meant the Barcons.

The front of the bar was dark glass with spotlit weird harps and tin whistles behind it. As we walked through the swinging doors, I noticed that most of the people were white, divided between college types and older, coarser. Two blacks, no, two Barcons waited for us at the end of the bar, hunched over drinks, with space around them, even though the crowd was hip to ass in the rest of the bar. The Barcons got up and began moving toward us.

"I won't pay you for a burn," Alex said loudly.

The Barcons stopped. "Nigger dealers," someone in the bar muttered, face lost in the crowd. I saw the smaller Barcon's jaw seem to break between the chin and ear, and both their noses pulled in. *Why doesn't someone see?*

"We must talk, outside." The Barcon male shook his hands as though flipping off sweat.

"I'm meeting a friend here."

A beefy guy stepped through the crowd, pool cue in one hand with a razor scar running across his knuckles. "We know Alex," he said. "Leave him alone."

"We have to discuss business with him," a Barcon voice said behind me. A second pair of Barcons stood near the doors. Another white guy in a blue nylon jacket stepped through the crowd, oil on his jacket, hand in his pants pocket—*brass knucks, heh, boy, or a gun?*

"Leave us alone," I said to everyone. The two other Barcons came up behind me. I didn't want to choose sides.

Then Carstairs swung the doors back and stopped, arms blocking the entrance. He stared with twisted delight at the whole scene, glasses askew on his nose. He saw me and shoved his glasses back, index finger against the greasy bridge, then giggled helplessly as the door on that side flapped against him.

The Barcons froze, the smallest female at the end of the bar quivering, jaw bones jerking. *Is everyone too drunk to see how alien they are?*

I expected the cops any minute—saw the headlines as though they were hanging in neon in the bar smoke: ALIEN SPIES CAPTURED IN BAR BRAWL.

Carstairs got out of the doorway and said, too loudly, "Tom, what *is* going on?"

"I don't know."

"No?" He pulled a barstool up and grabbed my hand. "If I . . ." He had a small trocar ready to plunge into me.

"He's taking tissue samples," I said.

The Barcons behind me grabbed the trocar, broke it against the bar. The crunch sound brought a white boy around to face us. The female Barcon at the end of the bar whimpered.

Then Marianne came in. "Tom?"

"Help me get all these people out. Alex needs to talk to the four black guys, but not here."

She loosened her shoulders as if cocking them, then did

the same for her hips, and said, "Very definitely not here." I couldn't believe it when she walked up to the guy with the cue stick and took it out of his hands. "Trust me," she said to him, jutting her hip out against the man's thigh, "they won't hurt Alex."

The female Barcon began making funny noises, *huwh, huwh,* deep in her throat. Her mate pushed his knuckles down on her spine.

"Who are *you*? the guy with his hand hidden in his pocket asked Marianne.

She ignored him. "We ought to try down the street. Better bar for our discussion."

"Why?" Alex said.

She said very loudly, "I met you with John Amber, didn't I? Was he pimping the black girl or were they lovers?"

Alex paled along his skull where the bone crest had been.

"I'll come," Carstairs said, still amused. "I like black bars, too."

"Holler if you need us," the man who had the cue stick said. He looked at Reeann as if thinking *how did this little bitch get my cue stick away*.

She put it back in his hands and walked toward me, hissed in my ear, "Racists," her hand on my shoulder.

"Carstairs wanted to take tissue samples," I said to Reeann as we walked to the cars, adrenaline still zinging at my fingertips, my gut cramped. "I should have let him."

She patted my cheek almost like a cat, violence padded behind the fingertips. Or sex? Then she said, "Was John Amber a DNA recombinant experiment?"

"Carstairs was a weapons designer. Alex is crazy." I told the others, "I'll ride with her."

"I took the bus," she said.

"In the car with us, then," the female Barcon who'd been scared in the bar said. "We want to thank you."

"I know it's tough on blacks in parts of Oakland."

The Barcon put her hands on either side of her nose, trying to hide the wiggle, nearly hysterical for a Barcon.

Reeann looked carefully at them as she got in the car, then looked at me, at Alex getting in his car with the other pair of Barcons, and tucked her chin down, her tongue making little wet sounds inside her mouth as though she wanted to be talking.

She knows now, just like Carstairs. She almost put her hand on my leg, but the hand rocked in the air.

"Miss, are you Tom's friend?" the male Barcon asked almost casually.

"We just met," she said, eyes focused on the door handles, then twitching up to the locks.

"Which bar?" I said.

"Go back down Telegraph. It's on the left."

"Noisy, but I know why you chose it," the male said, sounding non-human. Marianne looked away from the locks and door handles and stared at him, breath hissing in against her teeth as she raised her head.

"Why did Alex want to avoid you?" she asked.

"He has problems," the female said. "And we're his therapists, right, Tom. He fears something yet courts the disclosure of what he fears."

"Right," I said, pushing my shoulders back against the seat and arching my spine. The adrenaline had stiffened my muscles, and I wasn't sure what was coming next.

"Crazy?" Reeann asked, touching the door lock button.

"Tempts public ridicule and jail," the male Barcon said. "Tom, you must tell Alex about jail."

Reeann stiffened as though *now* she disapproved.

Wounded recombinant experiments okay, jailbirds no. I felt like I was reliving my first day out of prison, and realized what she thought mattered to me. "Marianne, it was over drugs, in Virginia." I hated my voice when I said that, a draggy whine, con voice deep in hustled cigarettes.

"Can I . . ." she began to say, then stopped. "I always wondered where John Amber and Rhoda came from, but I didn't want to get them in trouble. I have no real loyalty to things as they are."

The Barcons shifted in the front seat, looked at each other. "Tom does come from Virginia," the male said, looking back at us through the rearview mirror, utterly alien, inspecting a potential human breeding pair. He stopped talking when the female touched one of his odd jaw angles with her fingertips.

"Virginia was wasting him, his talent," the female said. "He . . ." She broke off to speak in Barcon to the male.

Reeann listened hard to them, then pulled away from me, body arched away from me, rigid. "So what happens now?"

The male wiggled his nose. "Maybe you can become friends with us?"

"I'm not going to be kidnapped."

"No, not kidnapped," the male said. "We need to talk to Alex, and with you."

We parked behind another bar, in Berkeley on Telegraph, not in Oakland. Carstairs, alone in his car, pulled in behind us, got out and watched, his eyes trembling in their sockets, as a Barcon got out, then Alex, both huge males, easily 220 pounds and over six and half feet, then the last Barcon, only slightly smaller, got out and stretched. At first, I thought Alex was in cuffs, but he was just rubbing his wrists, holding them together. Then Alex looked at Carstairs as though he hadn't meant to involve his human friend in this, whatever *this* would be.

The Barcons looked around the parking lot, then began discussing the situation in Barcon. "All right, you humans know," the male Barcon who hadn't ridden with Reeann and me said. "But it's worthless knowledge."

Carstairs looked at Alex as if Alex was his connection for maximum head candy. Alex shrugged slightly, then we went in, by black and white couples and singles, to an empty back room. We all sat down in a booth.

"You used drugs," the littlest female, the one who'd been scared in the bar, told Carstairs. "And you resigned your job. Why?"

Carstairs hunched over a beer in a frost-rimmed mug. "You are . . ." He didn't sound straight and he didn't finish.

"Alex," her mate said, "why?"

Alex sighed and reached for a pecan in a bowl set on our table, cracked it with his teeth, smiled at Carstairs as he tongued the meat separate from the shells, spit the shells out onto his fingertips. Finally, he answered, "I think the bird is right." *Meaning Karriaagzh.* "We should expand contacts, give these people gate systems."

"No," the littlest female said, "the wait magnifies your terror of jail, so you'd like them to know now. You may have to be rotated out before the contact."

"Why?" Carstairs asked.

"Because of you, in part," the chief male said.

"I resigned. I suspected . . ." .

"Alex told you?"

"No. I got a sweat sample. It wasn't conclusive."

Alex looked up at Carstairs and picked up another nut.

"Tell Alex about jail, Tom," the smallest female Barcon said. She looked just like a big black man slumped over a beer and stirring it with a swizzle stick. Alex flinched.

I said, "Federal prisons wouldn't be quite like the state prison camp I was in."

"But they give such time to spies," the female Barcon said to Alex. "Very cruel to disguised outsiders, no?"

Reeann said, "Let Tom and me leave. I'm not part of this."

"I'll take you all Goddammit down," Alex said.

Reeann began laughing. *Is she hysterical,* I wondered. Carstairs giggled for two seconds, then said, "You befriended me because of my weapons work, Alex?"

Alex said, "No." Veins in his eyes seemed to be enlarging. Then I saw a tear roll out of his eye, larger than a human tear. Maybe his skin had a different surface tension? "Someday, you'll find a way into space, and the Federation will turn me over to the FBI as a peace gesture. The more I'm with you, the less I want you to see me as an alien."

"Oh, Alex," Carstairs said.

Alex said, "Jerry, my wife was with me here for two years. She died, a trivial accident, on Karst. I'm alone

here except for humans. These are no company.'' He
swung an arm at the Barcons.

''He wouldn't re-mate,'' the other female Barcon, silent
up until now, said softly.

Carstairs looked nervous—*hey, what are the implications, Carstairs baby*. Then he asked, ''You aren't going
to hurt me?''

''No,'' the chief male said, ''as long as you don't betray
him ahead of time.''

Carstairs began to smile, then he frowned and asked,
''Time dilation?'' Meaning, did you get here by flying at
near light speeds?

''Time doesn't play a part in it,'' Alex said.

''I knew the accents were odd,'' Reeann said. ''You're
not recombinant DNA experiments. You're not humans.''

''I went camping with you, for two days,'' Carstairs
said softly to Alex.

''Prisons here could hold us all, I think,'' the chief male
Barcon said, leaning on his elbows, his hands shredding
napkins on the table.

Alex lurched up and said, ''I have to go to the bathroom.'' One of the Barcon males followed him.

I told Reeann, ''I'd go back to prison, if the State of
Virginia found out. I broke parole.''

She shook her head slightly, real fast, as though a bee'd
buzzed her. ''You, then, *are* human?''

''Yeah.'' I felt ashamed.

''And you've been in jail, for drugs, and aliens took
you away and did what with you?'' Her voice got edgy;
she heard her own hysteria rising and grimaced.

''They trained me to make contacts with other sapients,'' I said. ''I'm good at *that*.'' *But I fuck up with
my own species*. I remembered Yangchenla's harangues on
how I never questioned what was done to me.

She said, reaching for my hand. ''Is it difficult, being
back?''

''Yes, but the Federation wants me to be as good with
my own kind as I am with others.''

The Barcons were watching Reeann and me intently;
Carstairs seemed bored, writing something on his napkin.

When Alex and the second Barcon male came back, Carstairs shoved the napkin at Alex who said, "I don't know."

"Or can't tell me," Carstairs replied.

The Barcon chief picked up the napkin, looked at it, and said, "You're thinking along the right lines, but I suspect you have been all along, or Alex wouldn't have been so interested in you. Perhaps we can tell you when you're right. So better to keep showing us your theories, stay away from the FBI. Does that help?"

"How close? Could we make contact with you next year if I tried this?" Carstairs took the napkin back, scribbled on it, shoved it back at the Barcon.

"Not that way either, but . . ."

Carstairs carefully folded his napkin and put it in his wallet.

Alex stared at a waitress until she swung by the table. "Four pitchers of beer," he ordered. She brought them promptly and he swallowed two mugs full in about three breaths, deliberately trying for a drunk. Then he leaned back from the table and shuddered.

"They don't kill you for breaking cover?" Carstairs asked. His glasses were askew again; his face looked pasty, as though the skin was loaded with sweat about to bead through his pores.

"You think we lied about not hurting you. You wonder if they'll kill you for finding out?" I asked. The sweat slickened on Carstair's face.

"You can't prove a damn thing," the chief Barcon said. "You're a notorious drug user. You want an exclusive on the physics. Why should you betray us?"

"What about me?" Reeann asked. I felt her body shift, shoulders squared, as though she'd die fighting if the answer was wrong.

"Will you mate with Tom?" the smaller female asked.

For a second, there was no sound, no air. Then Reeann's eyes seemed to spin. "Mars wants women," she said before collapsing on spilt beer, choking on her laughter, legs thrashing under the table.

She settled down, breathing hard, tears in her eyes, then looked over at me.

"I said something wrong," the female said, jaw flexing.

Reeann fled to the ladies room. Carstairs looked at us and bit into his hand, teeth really in the flesh, sparkling eyes surrounded by the black-rimmed glasses. The waitress came by and mopped up the beer, face utterly impassive with curiosity.

"I guess I'll never be good with humans," I said.

"You're fuck-ups," Carstairs said. "Not machine-brained invaders of superior ruthlessness."

"It's a hardship post," the female told him.

= 3 =

Alien Landscape With Woman

Marianne—I dared not walk by her house after that night in the bar. The Barcon couples left the bar quarreling between pairs, solidarity in marriage as I've never seen in humans. One real black whispered to his lady, "Must be Africans."

Again, I hit the books, saw an old video of an almost kamakazi sales school, read all *Harvard Magazine* had to say on Japanese, discovered obscure articles about nuclear reactors in Zaire and on the Navajo reservation. All my friends were aliens—and on another planet. I didn't have friends here, human or otherwise, I kept thinking to myself as I booked down with Japanese data.

Then, three days later, Marianne came by, smelling of warm skin and gardenia perfume, in shorts as if the weather were warm, with a rugged hippie shoulderbag dangling below her elbow. I opened the door and was terrified that she'd burst out laughing again. She said instead, "Roger Strigate wants you to pick up your bike."

That was another life, Reeann, but I said, "Okay."

"Then we can go riding, out," she said in a small voice, "away from the city." She looked at the walls near the door as though searching for bugs.

"Yeah," I said.

"I want to know all about John Amber," she said. "He was odd."

"Odder than you think," I said as I got my shoes on.

In the drive, her car, another eco-mobile, sat on fat dune tires, all sunburnt fiberglass and chrome bike racks.

"I'm sorry I laughed," she said.

I didn't reply then, but as we got closer to the bike shop, I said, "I hate having my women arranged for me."

She didn't speak herself until I paid Strigate with $3000 for the bike, riding clothes, funny shoes with slotted plastic biscuits on the soles. Then she said, "Let's pretend none of this weird stuff is going on."

"Yeah, I'm researching Japan to help an African country develop without getting economically in hock to the West."

"An honorable profession," she said. "Better than being an out-of-work linguist who won't do government work."

"What I'm doing *is* government work."

"CIA, USA. My parents' bad guys." We loaded my bike on the rooftop bike rack beside hers, then put the other stuff behind the front seat. "The government that put you in jail for drugs."

"I wish I had turned my brother in. No, I don't . . . Reeann, he was tabbing Quaaludes, making speed, using. But he was crazy, too, and my brother."

We drove though modern suburbs planted on western movie set type hills, then out farther. "Tom, you don't have to be back soon, do you?"

"Hell, they're giving me an opportunity to slip back into human culture if I want to hide forever under a phony name."

"Do you want to go back?"

"Shit, yes. I don't want to get stuck here."

"Does Earth seem provincial to you now?"

"Yes and no."

She found a park by water she called a slew. "Spelled 'slough.' "

"*Sluff,*" I said.

"*Slow,*" she said as she began getting the bikes off the rack. "I thought we'd ride about twenty miles in flat country."

"Twenty miles!"

"Sure, you're in basically good shape. I've seen you running around the campus ParCourse."

"You've been watching me?"

"Yes," she said with a little, very unsouthern hiss.

I turned from her as I felt heat rise in my face and reached for my bike. She moved closer to me, hip to hip, and unhooked what I'd just learned to call a quick release, a cam-operated squeeze bolt loosened and tightened with a chrome-plated lever. The front wheels were in the car, with more quick releases skewered through their hubs.

Silently, she showed me how to put the wheel in the front fork and adjust the quick release to clamp the wheel firmly, then she said, "I thought about telling someone there were aliens in Berkeley, but too many people in Berkeley claim to have met aliens already. And I found out lots of fringe academics know Alex. A popular fellow."

"He's manipulative," I said.

"No kidding. What about the fake blacks?"

"They're hard to get to know."

We leaned the bikes against the car and pulled on our fingerless gloves, strapped the helmets tight. I swung one leg over the bike and stood straddling it while I watched her put one cleated shoe in her left pedal, wiggle it until the cleat slot went down over the rear pedal bar. She pulled up and tightened the strap. "Leave one strap loose, so you can yank that foot out. Make it a habit to leave the left or right loose—just one side all the time."

"Could you give me some books on this?" I felt weird taking instructions from a woman, especially one I was sexually attracted to.

"Tom," she said like both she was sorry and I was a jerk. She pushed stray hair under her helmet strap and looked at me with her gloved right hand knuckles against her left cheekbone, elegant inside her weird clothes. I did as she said and felt trapped on the bike, pulled the strap right and then lifted my foot. She pushed down on her raised pedal and swung her foot up into the other toe clip. I tried to imitate her but ended up with my foot on the wrong side of the pedal, the clip dangling underneath.

"Keep pedaling. When you build up momentum, flip it with your toe."

I pedaled like a crippled man, flailing at the pedal with my toe. Finally, I slid my foot in the clip, and began pedaling furiously. The bike went smoother the faster I went.

"Fun, isn't it?" Marianne said from beside me, her bike going without little jerks from side to side.

We began giggling. Like normal teenagers, I thought, having never had normal teen times. All the languages I knew zinged through my mind, making up epitaphs for her—*karrer zullila*, op wul, lost bossy bitch, *frantul*—I decided I wanted her as all of them. She took me away from my fear of being trapped as the parole breaker, alien sympathizer. We were just two kids on bikes, anonymously zinging by suburban yards now, too fast for our ages to show. Still giggling.

Then she said, breathing hard between phrases, "Alex . . . really terrified of jail? You sent here . . . to urge him to be more discreet?"

Well. Probably. "Nothing . . . is done . . . on Karst . . . for just . . . one species's . . . reasons." I noticed there was more air gulping between my phrases than hers. Suddenly I felt what had to be my liver, metabolizing lactic acid that burned back. "Slower."

She tightened her lips and sat up on her bike, coasting. I said, when my lungs settled down, "I hate talking about jail. My brother got me into drug making."

"Where's he?"

"I don't know."

"Shouldn't you find him?"

"I couldn't, but maybe someone else could."

"Is he dangerous?"

"Not to a woman." I guessed that was a safe answer.

"You were pushing the pace, Tom," she said. "Is this more comfortable?"

"Yeah." Yeah.

"What do you do for your . . . Federation, is it?"

"I arrange trade contracts, watch non-contacted sapients' television programs. I've learned two non-contacted languages as best we could extrapolate them. I study contacted sapients' behavior and history. If two species are quarreling, a lot of times a third species can figure out how to solve the problem.''

About a mile down the highway, we passed other bike riders going back toward the parking lot. They waved at her, she at them. Then, just as I'd decided she wasn't going to respond, she said, ''I wish I could do that. I'm a linguist, but primitive tribes are so glicky. Really, fleas, leeches . . . do I sound bigoted?''

''Leeches are . . . glicky.'' I'd never heard that word before.

''I'm never going to do shit on a bike.'' She bent down and loosened her toe straps. ''And I'm whining again. Don't kidnap me. I'd miss my sister.''

''She could go, too.''

Marianne's bike swerved. ''And Sam?''

''Yeah, they want a human social group.''

''And your brother. We're all wasted on Earth, no?''

''Yeah.'' I didn't tell her she'd be Support, not Officiator.

''Is there something horrible up there that you're not telling me about?''

''Other humans. From Tibet, about 500 years ago. They helped a ship during a contact war. I think there were two Federations then, but the computer's got nothing on that.''

''Uhm, well, Tibetans. I guess I can't escape them.''

''They do have fleas. And the women tape down their breasts and run little shops in the city, some of them. City Tibetans don't have fleas, just the Preserve ones.''

''Well, we won't be the only humans there, then?''

''Not hardly. About 200 of them, maybe fifty or sixty in the city.''

''Just one city?''

''The planet's artificial. It gets to you sometimes—every plant is imported. The geology is faked. The *vr'ech*—that's Karst for sapients or aliens—wanted the Federation held out in space off from inhabited planets.''

''*Vr'ech*, what's the singular?''

''*Ech*, but it's considered too alienating.''

"Why?"

"Like you're real and the other guy isn't. We aren't really supposed to speak of other sapients as *vr'ech*, but rather *uhyalla*, creatures, both sapient and non-sapient, us and them. Uh, the inclusive plural prefix."

"Unofficially, then, there's bigotry?"

"Some of the *uhyalla* are very *ech*. We have to know the differences, really, even when we try to smooth them over."

"Would you want to stay here?"

"I have obligations."

"Also, you skipped parole. But you could buy false papers so easily."

I didn't answer her. A line of skinny guys on bikes like ours came whizzing up, amazingly silent for things going over twenty-five miles an hour. Chattering among each other, they began to pass us. Marianne looked up and said, "Mike."

"Marianne, jump on back."

She said, "I'm just cruising."

"We won't make you take a pull. Just suck wheel."

"She doesn't want to," I said.

The guy laughed and stood up to stomp his pedals and catch up with the others. He pulled in so close I thought he'd run into the other bike rider's back wheel but hung in at three inches, drafting like a race car.

I said, "They wouldn't hunt me down if I left, but I couldn't do anything here as interesting as what I've been doing. And I'd miss the other species. It's like living in a zoo where the exhibits explain themselves, or listen to your theories about how they evolved socially."

"Super neat."

"You wanted to ride with them?"

"I don't know what I want. Yeah, I want to know what would my status be if the other humans have fleas?"

We rode on by oaks with normal-sized leaves growing by the water, up hills covered with manzanita, those orange branches twisted so much they looked like they had muscles, sage, then past houses sunk in the earth with huge black solar panels covering their rooves.

I said, "Here looks as alien as any place else."

She said, "I grew up here."

"They logged off the trees, so you've just got brush."

"No, rainfall's scanty."

"Marianne, if you come back with me, we can find a place on Karst where the rainfall is scanty. They made the planet to suit all sorts of creatures."

"I feel so odd."

We pulled over to a BP station, not a brand I'd seen sold in Southwestern Virginia, and got organic ginger beers, very peppery in almost round glass bottles. I walked around the pumps—unleaded gasoline, gasohol, alcohol, methane—my heels getting bruised, my toes tipped up by the plastic cleats. Marianne sat down on a wood bench under the station's windowboxes and stared out across the road at a citrus grove. She kept wiping sweaty hair out of her face, off her shoulders, throwing the long strands behind her, and sipping her ginger beer.

"Tom," she finally said, looking at me, "I need to get to know your friends better."

"I . . ." I couldn't explain that I didn't have their addresses. "I'll try to arrange it. Right now, I've got a problem I'm researching. Guys spending themselves bankrupt trying to get all the new computers."

"Need self-sufficiency? I'd love to do what you're doing."

I wasn't sure whether I liked that or not. "Maybe you could work with the Institute of Linguistics," I said, meaning not first contact work like the officers/officiators, us *uhchippran*, *vrchippran*, depending on whether the speaker is one of us or not. From *chiwu*, one of the oldest words in Karst One, meaning, reduce tension/create closeness. Even the Institute of Defense used the term for their personnel, like they reduced tension with weapons.

She took off her helmet and tucked all her hair back, then buckled the straps back on. "Let's go before we tighten up, Tom."

"How much farther?"

"About six miles."

You can't really spell or pronounce *uhchippran* or *vrchippran* with American letters or phonemes.

The sun got hot and beat all my languages together under the helmet straps. I rode behind Reeann as close as I dared, bile rising up my esophagus, swearing to myself that I would get in better shape.

When we finally got back to the car, Reeann pulled a varnished wicker picnic basket with leather straps and brass fasteners out of the back. I leaned my bike up against a tree and said, "Expensive-looking basket."

"It was a gift from one of my professors." She looked guilty as she unstrapped real china plates from the lid. "There's a blanket in the trunk."

I opened the trunk and put my fingers on wool softer than I knew it could be, grey and black woven in lozenges with red silk bindings around the borders. "Your sister make this?"

"Yeah, spun the wool and wove it when she was on unemployment after a weaving store fired her."

"They love handspun on Karst."

"Aliens in handspun." She laughed as she poured a cold soup into bowls.

"Weavers are covered by the city minimum wage. If you can afford to wear handwoven stuff, it means you're rich."

"I visualized a giant lobster wearing one of Molly's skirts."

"Nothing's odder than bipedal birds, about eight feet tall, no wings, but beak and feathers. But they wouldn't . . ." An image of Karriaagzh in a long skirt—I started to laugh, too, as I spread the blanket.

"Here's some vichyssoise," she said, handing me a bowl. "Have you had this before?"

"Not on Earth," I said, sipping a spoonful, afraid it was pureed bean mold. No, it tasted like liquified potato salad. "Cold potato soup?"

"Yo."

"Little furry guys drink something like this."

"Try this." She passed me, on a plate, a breaded

chicken leg, thigh and drumstick, with a wedge of cornbread. The cornbread was hot.

"Um, yes."

She smiled. "I knew you'd like that, at least."

"Oh, hell, I like the vichyssoise, too. I'll eat anything
that agrees with my proteins."

"Really?"

"Except tempeh." The vichyssoise did seem more ap-
pealing, now, for some reason, than chicken and cornbread. "Tempeh reminds me of work."

"Why?"

"Tempeh reminds me of *villag*, which is an alien bean
jelly. Yauntra . . . God, what a bummer." I remembered
my Yauntry contact, Edwir Hargun, sitting across the room
from me, eating villag. As he ate, he told me his people
wanted him and me punished if Federation technology
caused trade wars between the Yauntry corporations. Fuck
those laser-read computer data matrices more tempting to
Yauntra than trade beads to American Indians. "If I don't
help the people I'm assigned to work with, I'm a convenient . . . I guess 'scapegoat' is the word. I don't have a
planet species to protect me."

"Whoa, boy, you want me to leave Earth with you and
you could get your butt in trouble. Where would that leave
me?"

"I better help them. Or convince the Federation that
Earth's going to get gates for contact soon. We probably
should feed information to Carstairs."

She said, "God, not to Carstairs. He's FBI-bait."

"I don't know how the gate transitions work, anyway.
Alex doesn't either. I bet ninety percent of Academy and
Institutes people don't. It's like how does your car work."

"I know how my car works. I helped build it."

"Oh, Reeann, say like television, or computers. You've
got a couple of guys who know how they work, and then
the rest of us know how to use them. Aliens, out there,
they mostly just know how to use more things."

We finished eating in silence. I seemed doomed to run
into hypercompetent females when I wanted to be protective. Reeann took my empty bowl and the unfinished

chicken when I leaned back on the blanket. Overhead, leaves cut flickers from the sunlight, shifting in the wind.

"I'm not too tough, am I?" Reeann asked. I looked at her quickly and saw that she'd loosened her hair and was kneeling at the edge of the blanket. I raised myself on one elbow and stretched out my arm to her. She lay down on the blanket beside me, the nylon pants sweaty and cool between us. As she lay down, some of her long hair spread across my throat. "I'd like you to hold me."

I thought about the picnic basket, then looked at her eyes, rimmed around the bottom lids with tears not quite large enough to fall. "Is it something I said?"

"No, just everything. Maybe my period." She wiggled slightly and I rolled to my side and put my arm over her breasts.

No. We just fell asleep, and nobody stole our expensive bikes, either. I woke up hearing her pulse clinking near my ear and gently moved her wrist and wiped her hair back.

"Tension," she murmured.

"Yeah?"

She rolled onto her back. The wind blew through the nylon shorts and the padding in my crotch was clammy. She said, "Tension made us sleep." With her bottom lip pushed out and up, she blew stray hairs off her face.

I raised up on my elbow, checked the bikes, then looked down at her. "And why are you tense?"

Her lips were swollen slightly, as though she'd rolled them against scratchy wool when she was asleep. "Because." She smiled, moved her shoulders and her hips slightly. "Because we both may be crazy. That's the most reasonable explanation."

I sat up. "I'm not crazy. My brother may be, but I'm not. The Barcons tested me."

"I saw one of them bend in the jawbone. Humans can't do that. But . . ."

"Why don't other people see that?" My voice went shrill.

"Tom." She sat up beside me. "I'd like to talk to Alex and the others again. And I want to see you again." I stood up and she raised her hands to me. Up she rose as I took her hands and tugged, but we just held each other like children. This woman, I realized, wasn't like Yangchenla at all. We loaded her car, put the bikes on the roof, and drove home through the long hill shadows.

"Next time," she said as I unloaded my bike at the apartment, "bring a change of clothes. Short chamois gets pretty soggy. You could get boils down there. I wouldn't like that."

"You wouldn't?"

"No."

"You want to come in for a bit?"

"Tom, I've got to change or I'll get boils, down there. I . . ."

"I wouldn't want to see boils . . . there." I remembered the Barcons telling me that resident bacteria and other parasites often proliferate when the host is under stress.

She tucked her full lips between her teeth, trembling with giggles.

"I won't have any hard feelings if you go."

"But if I stay."

"We're both nervous, aren't we, Reeann?" I bent down and kissed her through the open car window. She just ran the very tip of her tongue in through my lips, then bit my bottom lip gently.

"I'll be back, Tom. But just because I know doesn't obligate me, does it? I'm not going to be kidnapped?"

"No, I wouldn't allow them to do that to you."

"Well, I think I will come inside then."

I brought her bike and my bike inside with us. We were more like teenagers than people who'd had lovers. She ran her tongue over my raised velar ridge and giggled when I leaned back and said, "Surgery. Yes, I'm human."

Her breasts were very different than Yangchenla's little tight ones. They tilted her dark nipples up—not the pale beige ones of the high school girl back in Floyd County, not Yangchenla's small dark ones that came so quickly to a point—big oval nipples. Big breasts, more flesh on her than I thought she'd have with all the bike riding. Slippery legs, shaved, sweaty.

I wondered vaguely what she'd wear out of the house—her bike clothes were so sweaty, clammy in my hands. She turned on the radio as we passed it on the way to the bedroom.

Then we heard furniture slamming into the wall overhead. "They said they were Swedish," I told Reeann before we began laughing helplessly. Finally, I said, "I can't get it up if I'm . . ." Helplessly squirming.

"That's all right. They'll be through soon, then it's our turn."

We both lay back and I watched her breasts roll as she laughed. Suddenly I couldn't laugh. I closed the drapes to the garden sliding glass door and crawled back on the bed as though my cock were glass and could break.

I wouldn't have noticed if the Swedes had broken through the ceiling and landed on top of us.

Then it was over. Reeann and I slept a bit, then she got out of bed naked and opened the drapes to stand there looking out into the little garden. The room was dark, so I didn't think anyone could see in. I sensed she didn't care.

After a while, she said, still looking out in a way that would have been distancing in a Yauntry, "I love men who get lost in me, who don't watch themselves. Promise me, though, that you are human."

"I am. The Barcons can prove it."

"I know human molecular biologists who could prove it, too, Tom. Would you mind if I had one test you?"

She has samples in her cunt, I thought, my cock worming backward. "Okay." I went to the bathroom and showered all the sweat and sex juice off.

"I'm sorry I asked when I did," Reeann said, "but I'm scared." She looked at her bike clothes wadded up on the floor, walked naked to the bathroom. I sat there, listening to music I'd never heard before and running water. She came back out wrapped in a towel, her hair wet. "Could I borrow a shirt and a pair of your pants?"

"Come back here and sleep," I said. "We'll have breakfast in the morning, talk." I got out of bed and turned off the radio, then found a shirt and handed it to her, saying, "You can wear this to bed if you need to."

She looked younger than me as she put it on and climbed back into bed with the towel between her legs. She sighed and stared at the ceiling, her arms wrapped around her waist. I pulled the covers over us. In the living room, the little gas heater whomped and ignited.

"Grits!" she said in the morning and I didn't know whether she was joking or really protesting. She dipped her fork in them tines down and spread them, then lifted the fork with about one grain on it and tasted.

"If I cook breakfast," I told her, "that's it: eggs, bacon, grits, toast, and coffee."

I should have told her to eat the grits with butter and salt. Or with hot sauce, like Warren did, borrowing from migrant Mexican apple pickers.

The phone rang then—Barcons. "Marianne wants to meet you and discuss things," I told the one who answered.

"Has Alex been around?"

"Not in the last three days."

The Barcon sighed. "Alex. He should remember we have his pride on ice." Meaning Alex's skull crest. "We'll be by to visit soon. At your place or Marianne's?"

"The people you wanted to meet," I told Marianne, "where? Your house or here."

"How soon?"

The Barcon must have heard her question. "Today, when we can get over."

"Here. I haven't prepared Molly and Sam for this yet."

"Here," I told the Barcon.

"We need to go out to Tilden Park for some exercise this afternoon," he replied.

I wondered if the FBI or CIA had heard what Reeann and I'd been saying this morning. But I could prove I was human. If all the fake paper checked out and my fingertips held up, I'd be okay, but nervous.

Real nervous. Damn Alex and his weapons-designing doper buddy. Marianne pulled on a pair of my pants, zipped them best she could, rolled the cuffs up and went home, rolling her bike beside her. I went out to the laundry and put in both our skin shorts and jerseys, plus the towel.

By the time she got back, dressed in baggy green pants and a cotton sweater, I'd done the dishes. When I let her in, she smiled very slightly and went over to my computer, looked at the printouts of the library holdings on Japan. "You think Japan had the answer?"

"Maybe. But high tech you crave always changes your society, looks like."

"You should also study the Hopi Indians. They didn't want to modernize, just survive as Hopi."

I thought about Yangchenla's people, some who wanted to be part of Karst's multi-species urban culture, others who wanted to follow their yaks. Less than 500 Tibetans, almost all originally from one village, and they couldn't agree. Three non-villagers—maybe Indians, maybe Chinese—had been visiting when the Federation ship crashed, but that didn't explain Yangchenla's craving for Federation position. She was purely village stock. I said, "Humans are weird."

"You're human."

"Yeah, and I'm weird, too. We should be careful about what we say. People might think we're crazy, not just playing a game, about this alien stuff." I pointed to my ear and to the walls.

"But your friends are coming."

"Yeah, we'll go take a walk with them."

About that time, I heard a knock, just one fist blow, on the door. Marianne stepped farther into the room, by one of the sliding glass doors, as I checked out the peephole. Barcons. I pulled the chain stob out of the slot and opened the door to two of them, dressed in jeans, plaid shirts, and Nikes, the smallest female, still over six feet tall, and her mate, not the first ones I'd met.

The female looked at Marianne and said, "I'd like to thank you for your help the other night, and to apologize for embarrassing you."

Marianne said, "I dislike bigots." I looked at her closer and saw that she was paler than usual.

"We'd like to take you on a picnic," the male said.

As we left the house, the male sidled up to me and whispered in Karst One, "Change the bed coverings. I can smell them from here."

I turned around and locked the door. They had an old two-door green Nash, funky-looking and rigged to burn gasoline. Marianne shivered slightly as she got in.

"Don't be afraid of us," the female Barcon said.

"Why not?" Marianne said, shifting her hands to her knees, squeezing them.

"Because it makes us nervous," the male said.

"What are your names?"

"Jackie and S'um," the female said. "I'm in the Jack job. He's the S'um, or Sam."

Shit, I thought, the first non-humans she meets knowing they're aliens would be Barcons. She looked over at me as if asking does it get any weirder than this?

S'um said, "We tend not to get too close to other species, sapient or not, but don't be afraid of this."

"I taught her *vr'ech* and *uhyalla*."

"We don't get close to *vr'yalla*. Our species has *vr'ech* parasites that destroy brain tissue and ride the emptied bodies," the Jack said, jaws trembling slightly. Marianne drew back as far as she could from the front seat.

S'um spoke to Jackie in Barq. Then he said to Marianne, "We will take good care of you, your reproductions. We're excellent physicians, can fix or cure most anything, learned from getting parasites."

We stopped at a light. When it changed, S'um hit the gas and the little Nash leaped.

"I thought I heard a big motor," Marianne said.

"Eight cylinders. Very surprising in such a small old car. We've restored it," Jackie said.

"Good mechanics, too, but we're not known for that," S'um said.

"It wastes a lot of gas," Marianne said.

"We only use it on special occasions. It beats the heat. Alex doesn't know about it either."

"Is Alex a problem for you?" Marianne asked.

"He is resident here, but unorthodox."

I remembered another Analytics *yalla* describing Karriaagzh by a Karst word that meant "unorthodox." We pulled into the Tilden parking lot. The two Barcons got out first, then pushed the seats forward so we could get out. S'um pulled out a backpack and put it on. Marianne looked down at her feet—she had thongs on.

Jackie said, "Well, we won't walk far. But you did want to ask questions, didn't you?"

"Yes."

"You want to be more than Support?" Jackie asked.

I realized the Barcons had bugged my apartment or listened to us through my skull computer's link to my auditory centers.

"What's Support?" Marianne asked.

"Support is not officer or investigator. Helpers. Married women who tend Karst businesses, raise children."

"Do I have *any* bargaining power in this?"

"Tom's first mate was unsuitable. He didn't operate at maximum efficiency because of worries," S'um said. The two Barcons discussed us in Barq—I heard fragments of my Academy name, "Red Clay," and "Marianne" bouncing around in their speech, phonemes English rather than their own.

"Your *first* mate?" Marianne said to me.

"Yeah, Yangchenla. Tibetan ancestors. We were too different from each other."

Marianne laughed.

"Marianne, stop it. We were very different."

"And you and I aren't?"

"We're both from the same country, same century."

S'um interrupted, "Marianne needs work in linguistics?"

"Yes," Marianne said, "Marianne needs work in linguistics. If Marianne is to bring a social group, then Marianne's sister needs weaving work and her husband needs music gigs."

"So perfect," S'um said. "No hidden agendas?"

Marianne asked, "Must I bear children?"

"You can if you wish, two, without discussion."

"No hidden agendas, then," Marianne said. She sighed the kind of sigh you twist with your tongue, changed its pitch. "But I haven't discussed this with Molly and Sam."

I thought this was too easy. If they could promise Marianne an Institute position, then why couldn't Yangchenla's brother have gone to the Academy? We sat down and the Barcons began pulling squat cans—bare metal, no labels—out of their pack. Su'm handed two with ziptop lids to Marianne and me. S'um said, "We always eat out of cans."

Marianne said, "Because they're sterile."

Jackie pulled out a can opener and a Bic lighter, flamed a third can's lid and the opener, then opened it. S'um put a fourth can in something that looked like a thermos, turned a knob. Marianne pulled back the top of the can and sniffed. She asked, "What is this?"

Jackie said, "Complete human diet."

I pulled back the lid of mine and saw chunks of meat and lumps of white—noodles, dumplings, potatoes?—mixed in a glossy brown gravy. "I need a spoon," I said.

Jackie gave me a spoon, handle forward, then gave Marianne one. "Would you like them warmed?"

"Yes, please," Marianne said. S'um took his can out of the heater and slid hers in. He wrapped it in a dish towel when he took it out. As she took her first bite, I handed him mine.

"It's Campbell's Chunky Beef!" Marianne said.

"Supplemented to be completely nutritious," Jackie told her. "We would like to meet Molly and Samuel Turner. Can we come to your house?"

Marianne said, "I suppose. Will you tell then you're *uhyalla*, aliens, whatever?"

"We shouldn't until we clear your agenda with Karst," Jackie said, picking up the cans with tongs and putting them and the can heater in the pack. She handed each of us a square of foil and said, "Wrap your spoons in these please."

We did and she put them in a larger foil pouch. Marianne said, "Do you need to be that sterile here?"

"We don't want to get into lethal habits."

"Okay." She looked back at me. "When you come over, bring Tom."

"You trust Tom. Wonderful," S'um said. We went walking back down toward the car, weird little quail with solitary feathers bobbing over their eyes flushing out from the brush as we passed.

We left the Barcons' car parked in my apartment's parking place and walked down to Marianne's. In bright light, the Barcons looked even more alien.

Reeann opened the door and said, "I forgot. Molly and Sam went to the city to discuss a wall-hanging commission. But they should be back soon."

"May we see the house, then?" S'um asked.

I was curious myself because all I'd seen had been the foyer with the staircase going up behind Molly and her husband when I dropped by before.

"Sure. It's an integral urban home from the early nineties. We compost our wastes and have a garden and fish pond outback."

"We do much the same," Jackie said. "The Clivus Multrum is a very efficient design."

"You use a Clivus Multrum?"

"We copied it on our planets," the male said. "We'll owe much for the design use when contact is made."

"The kitchen's in back," Marianne said, sliding two paper-covered panels into wall pockets. The back of the kitchen was an attached greenhouse, full of black barrels and red clay pots with tomato vines sprawling out of them, mint, parsley. I saw three bins by the sink—metal, paper, organics. By the stove, a small metal can labeled meat scraps.

"We recycle meat scraps through chickens," Marianne said.

The Barcons wiggled their noses and touched each other, showing more excitement than I'd ever seen from Barcons, chattering away in Barq. The male said, "Less outside system penetration this way?"

"Less waste. We've got a solar hot-water heater, passive solar with the black barrels and a blower system that stores heat in the basement in rocks.''

''Where does the water come from?'' the female asked.

''From the Berkeley main water line, but I recycle water through the plants and then catch condensation from the greenhouse panes.'' She walked into the greenhouse and pointed to a trough and tubes. ''We collect it and run it out to the garden.''

S'um looked at the sink, then went around back. From the sink drain, we heard his voice, ''Do you only use your own composted shi . . . manures on the garden?''

''Visitors can contribute.''

He said something in Barq and Jackie put the stopper back in the drain. After a while, he came out. ''Our parasites won't affect you,'' he said as he washed his hands. ''We compost most carefully,'' he said, ''and I'm sure you do, too, in a city.''

''Do you want to see the solar hot-water heater on the roof?'' Marianne asked.

''Can it run full boil?'' Jackie asked.

''I know of one design that can, if you have sunlight enough.''

''We'd like to see that design,'' S'um said.

''I never knew you all used composting toilets,'' I said to the Barcons.

''Mandatory to sterilize urine and shit,'' he said, ''before they leave the home space.''

''Would you like tea?'' Marianne said. ''We could make some from fresh mint, each gathering our own.''

''You are quick to be understanding,'' the female said. ''Our security habits make most *vr'ech* nervous.''

''I hope I'm *uhyalla* to you now.''

''You have a good ear,'' S'um said. The female said something to him in their language. He added, ''But then you are a native linguist.''

They shambled out through the greenhouse door to the garden after her. While they gathered mint, I went into the living room where I saw a harpsichord. I'd read about them on Karst, in books smuggled there from Berkeley.

I stood and looked at it, touched one of the keys gently,

an odd sound, though I'd thought I'd heard it before. Not live, on tape, over the radio.

The door opened, and Sam Turner came in. He looked at me and said, "The cracker who wanted to paste a note to the burglars on our door, 'Hey, they're not home at all.'"

"Do you play this?"

"Yeah, does it surprise you?" He came over, his hand like a blade in the air twisting to get me to move. I stepped aside and he sat down and began to play Bach, something I'd recognized from PBS radio stations. One brushy eyebrow arched up as his thin, long fingers flexed across the keyboard, keys black and white in reverse of a piano.

S'um came in. Beside Sam, the Barcon looked extremely alien—multi-jointed jaws, skin texture minutely pebbled, nose bulbous where even most blacks' noses are thin, right below the eyes. Sam looked up and asked, "What are you?"

S'um looked at me. Jackie and Marianne came in from the kitchen. "Where's Molly?" Marianne asked.

"She stopped by Fiberous Distractions. Who are these people? CIA, FBI?" He reached slowly under the harpsichord strings.

"We're hard to kill. And I thought there was a metal block on the sounding board," S'um said.

"Cracker, do you have anything to do with these people being here?" Sam began to play jittery Bach, spider music.

S'um spoke before I could. "We have a job offer. You can play music any way you want to with us."

"They're friends of John Amber's," Marianne said.

Sam raised an eyebrow again. Jackie flexed her jaw joints. Sam asked, "Illegal aliens?"

"Not humans," S'um said.

"You're not from outer space. We both know that's impossible. You're CIA."

"We travel through space folds. That's the simplest explanation."

"Yeah? You can't let us walk around Berkeley saying,

'We've been privately contacted by aliens and they've offered me a job playing harpsichord for them.' ''

''Yes, we can,'' Jackie, the female Barcon, said.

''Authorities will think you're insane, which is convenient for us if you're not willing to accompany Tom and Marianne back to the base planet.''

S'um took the gun out from under the harpsichord strings and said, ''Too small a caliber.''

Molly, two huge bundles of fibers in her arms, came in the door about this time and stared from Sam to the Barcon S'um. The differences seemed utterly vast now—scars where the sixth fingers on both of them were removed, funny muscles in the face. She turned to me and said, ''Why are you here?''

Jackie looked at Molly's skirt and said, ''We're looking for some volunteers in an exploration. You could earn the equivalent of $40,000 a year spinning and weaving.''

''For aliens?'' Sam said, almost choking. ''Aliens wear handspun?''

''It's a luxury item with them,'' I said.

Marianne heard the teakettle whistle and went back to turn it off. Molly shuddered and followed her back.

Sam said, ''What do you want us for?''

''To increase the human gene pool on our planet. Representatives were here about 500 years ago,'' S'um said, not mentioning the space wars.

''For a zoo?''

''No, ask Tom.''

''I've been trained in diplomacy, making contact with new species, coordinating trade exchange.''

''Yeah, and I've been trained in classical music.''

''They let me use what I've learned.''

For some reason that stung him. Sam began picking out jazz riffs on the harpsichord. His hands trembled.

''May I play with you?'' S'um asked.

''Better not break down my bench.''

S'um knelt down at the bass keys, huge, fuzz showing down his collar as he bent his head. His body proportions were different than human—his legs shorter, torso longer. He spread his big fingers and laid them carefully on the

keys, seeing if the tips would sprawl over more than one
key. They fit, but barely. He wiggled his nose at Sam. The
human, sweating now, arched his eyebrows again and began to play with his right hand, his left curled up against
his groin.

The Barcon played the same melody but in a lower
range, then reversed it.

Sam shifted his lip corners slightly and brought his left
hand up to the keyboard. He played and left the music
dangling. S'um reached up the keyboard and completed
the phrase, reduced the tension, musical and otherwise.
Then he played a skittery piece, missed one note. His jaw
wiggled and he corrected himself.

Sam played something tentative; S'um transposed bits
of it into something faster. They both began playing together.

Arguing, the women came out of the kitchen, Jackie
holding four teacups. Molly stared at the two males playing the harpsichord and said to me, "And are you alien,
too?"

"No, I'm from Virginia."

"You humans were wasting him," Jackie said, setting
the teacups down on a banged-up redwood burl coffee table. "This is okay for the cups?"

"Sure."

S'um quickly ran his dark index finger along Sam's
sweaty jaw and sniffed his fingertip. "You're still tense.
Would beer help?"

"You drink beer?" Sam got up and began to pace.
Molly looked at Marianne.

"Tom, go get beer," S'um stood up and fished out a
wallet. He handed me a twenty. "Olympia."

"God, they drink Oly," Molly said, her voice harsh and
wavery.

I left, feeling weird, like a teenager who watches parents discipline children, knowing too much, identifying
with neither. If I'd gotten involved with the counterculture
in Floyd, I could have learned to live in an integral urban
house, moved to Berkeley, lived a simple life among my
own species. Too late for that now. Past Milvia and onto

Shattuck—I went into the Co-op, the fluorescents cold overhead, the shadows harsh. As I fished four six-packs of Olympia out of the beer cooler, an image of Black Amber kicking a worshipful Molly off her knees rose to my mind. My kind, but I couldn't blame them for being nervous. The checkout clerk put the six-packs in a box so I could carry them easier.

I was nervous, too. I'd never seen a Barcon be so personable. As I walked back down Cedar, I saw Alex's car in my parking lot. He came out from the entranceway and waved for me to come over.

When we could hear each other, I said, ''We're all down at the Schweigman sisters'.''

''All?'' Alex asked, a pseudo pocket radio in his hand. He fiddled with the dial and answered himself, ''Yes, all.''

''Come on down,'' I said, ''it's getting weird.''

''A party might be premature,'' Alex said. ''Carstairs had his security clearance revoked.''

''What does that mean?''

''Let's go down and talk about it.'' Alex took the box from me and began striding off with it. I had to jog to keep up.

When we knocked on the door, Alex stood by the hinges, away from the peephole, then came in when the door opened.

''It's the bigot from the bar,'' Marianne said.

''I'm not a bigot,'' Alex said in English, then in Karst One, *''This meeting is not a good idea. Carstairs lost his security clearance.''*

The two Barcons looked at each other, then at Sam, Molly, and Marianne, who'd moved together toward the kitchen. Jackie said, ''We need your cooperation, please.''

Marianne asked, ''What about Carstairs?''

''He was a Lawrence Lab weapons designer,'' Alex said. He opened a beer and drained it. I noticed he had no Adam's apple in his throat.

''KGB-manipulated DNA creatures, then,'' Molly said.

''No,'' Alex said. ''Can't you believe we're aliens? And we don't need your piddling weapons. Jerry Carstairs is my friend. I . . .''

"You weren't trying to help him," S'um said, folding his arms across his chest which was too rounded for human.

Marianne's eyes darted to me, to Alex, then to the door. S'um went to the phone, called a number and put the receiver against his skull computer, then said, "Check."

The phone whined, then went dead and S'um hung it up. "Nothing on Carstairs that involves us. They probably revoked his clearance because he resigned from the weapons project."

"If Carstairs is your friend, bigot," Marianne said, "I'd like to meet him."

"My name is Alex."

"Okay, Alex."

The Barcons picked up two six-packs. Jackie asked, "Is there a bedroom upstairs?"

"Yeah, I'll show you," Molly said.

As they disappeared upstairs, Alex grinned and said, "They have to get away from us to get drunk."

Molly came back shortly, clumping down the stairs, and said, "They closed the door on me."

"Leave them alone for a while," I said. "Being around us is a strain."

"We need more beer," Alex announced, taking another can. "I can get it."

Sam said, "No, I'll go."

"Can I go, too?" Molly asked, getting up and standing close to her husband.

Alex said, "We'll still be here when you get back." He got up and played what I recognized as an Ahram music motif on the harpsichord, but the notes were slightly skewed, as though the harpsichord wasn't tuned for Ahram music.

Molly and Sam hugged each other. Alex turned his head slightly toward them, then looked away fast. He said, as they opened the door, "Take your time."

"I'll stay here with them," Marianne said.

Molly said, "Oh, Marianne, do you have to?"

"I'd appreciate it," Alex said. He sat down on a green velvet loveseat, sprawled out over the whole thing.

Molly looked at all of us as Sam went out, then she practically jumped through the doorway after him. The front door banged closed, keys whizzing in the locks.

Alex sighed. He told Reeann, "I'm not a bigot to human blacks."

She said, "I like those two . . ."

"Barcons," Alex said. "The male is their top wild sapient tamer, brilliant."

"Don't be nasty," I said.

"But he is and both institutes trained him. Don't worry, this house isn't bugged. Yet."

"Who trained you?"

"Analytics. I watch a lot of late-night television, waiting for you to stop playing alien space horror movies." He sighed. "And you think I'm a bigot."

Marianne squeezed her arms around herself and said, "I'm not a bigot. I'm not having hysterics, being in my house with aliens, outnumbered, huge . . ." She heard herself, laughed, then forced her arms to dangle.

Alex pointed to the beer at his feet and said, "Drink."

I twisted two cans away from the six-pack, popped them, and gave one to Marianne. We both sat down, me on the floor, Marianne on the harpsichord bench. I asked Alex, "Can you get drunk?"

Alex looked down at the whole six-pack and two cans remaining at his feet. "Yes. I'll stay at your apartment tonight."

"I've met other people who know you, Alex," Marianne said. "You're odd enough to be memorable. What do you find out from fringe academics?"

"Affinity. Plus I need humans. You're close to us, closer than Barcons, Gwyngs, the others who've been here. I grew up on Karst. Tom thinks that did something to me. It made me need others, not just Ahrams."

Marianne said, "Alex, do you know that the FBI does a termination-check when someone's security clearance is pulled?"

"Yes, they've talked to me already. I'm just a druggie." He pulled out his user/grower badge and showed it to her. "See."

"I don't know what your species is supposed to be like," she said, "but I think you're genuinely fucked up. The Barcons are aliens. You, there's something wrong."

"But humans are so good for me"—he smiled at her, finished his beer—"lift me out of my lethargy."

Marianne said, "I think you want to get caught, get it over with."

I wanted to get all of us off Earth, safely away to Karst, get Marianne what she wanted. "Marianne wants to be Institute of Linguistics," I told Alex.

"They'll have a bit of trouble arranging that," he said, already into his third can of beer.

She hissed, almost like a Gwyng.

Alex said, "Normally, you'd be Support, under Academy and Institutes." He yawned, exposing huge flat teeth, then asked me in Karst One, *"And what's Black Amber going to say to your woman's ambitions?"*

I said in English, "Black Amber likes Marianne."

"Black Amber was a hysterical ninny," Alex replied.

"I want to work in non-human linguistics," Marianne said. "Those are my terms."

Alex got up out of the loveseat, went up to her, and took both of her hands in one of his, squeezed gently once. As she began to cry, he ambled back to the loveseat. He asked, "Have you read Kayakawa?"

Tears in her eyes, she nodded.

"Fear is not just one thing. I don't want to terrorize you—easy to do with humans and Gwyngs—but do you think your sister and brother-in-law will come back without trying to convince the authorities that we're here?"

"They haven't had time to get back yet," I said. "Marianne, I'll do my best to see that you get an Institute position."

Marianne's tongue moved inside her mouth, her lips parted slightly, then she swallowed. The room became so silent, I heard her teeth shift against one another.

Then the Barcons began lurching down the stairs. Marianne raised both eyebrows and said, "You couldn't really promise me anything, could you? We're just going to be kidnapped." She went pale, face rigid with nostrils tight.

"What did Alex tell you?" Jackie said.

"That I'd be a Support person."

"We promise otherwise," S'um said. They both smelled weird, like skunk cabbage or broken stink tree.

Alex began to jabber at them in Barq. Marianne said to me, "Can't they agree?"

"It's not a monolithic federation," I told her. "But we don't kill one another."

"That's so reassuring," she said, dragging out the "so." But then she said, "Well, I guess actually that it is." She wrinkled her nose. "But tell them to go shower."

S'um stopped talking to Alex and pulled out a spray can, puffed himself and Jackie with it. The odor vanished.

"Pheromone disruptors," I said to Marianne.

Molly and Sam came back then, with beer and food. Sam said, "You were holding my harpsichord hostage."

"See any grey cars on Milvia?" Alex asked.

"No," Molly said, "no FBI."

"Your parents were Weather, weren't they?" Alex said. He looked almost boneless on the loveseat, drunk.

Sam said, "I'd like you all to leave. Now. Don't come back. We have nice quiet little lives here and don't need aliens and FBI to tweek us."

S'um said, "But Marianne and Tom . . ."

"What about Marianne and Tom?" Sam asked.

The Barcons and Alex began discussing *T'i'om* and *Re'i'an* in Barq. Jackie finally said in English, "It's not polite to tell you, but they're lovers."

I almost laughed. "I'm sorry, Marianne."

"It's all right, Tom."

"Sam," Jackie said, "it would not be fun to betray all of us to the FBI."

= 4 =

Leaving and Reasons to Leave

A grey car rolled into the driveway a day later, big gas-burner, and two guys in business suits got out, one with a briefcase. I saw them in the peephole and thought about running, but opened the door.

"Hello, Tom Gresham?" the older of the two men, the one without the briefcase, said.

"Yes," I said, praying to my fake fingerprints.

Before he said another word, he held up a glossy of Jerry Carstairs. I figured they'd start there. Something buzzed in my head and my muscles relaxed as if by remote control. Remote Barcon control.

"You know Jerry, Tom," the older man said. "We're field agents of the Federal Bureau of Investigation. I'm Special Agent Peter Friese." He showed me his badge.

"I'm Edward O'Neal," the other one said, flipping open his badge case. "I hope you'll be willing to tell us what you know about Carstairs without a subpoena."

"I don't really know much about him. I've been traveling in Asia a bit. Look, I've got a trust fund."

They stood in the door, looking at each other. "May we come in?" Friese said.

"Sure." I backed away from the door.

"What do you do with your computer?" O'Neal asked, almost conversationally.

"I'm trying to write about Japan. I get bored just living off a trust fund."

"You have an odd accent?"

"Asia. I also jammed a spoon up against the back of my upper teeth one time when I was tripping."

They smiled at that. "What does Jerry Carstairs like to talk about?"

"Weird stuff, like dimensions. Drugs, but I guess that's not so weird for Berkeley," I said, having seen them relax slightly when I lied to them about acid and spoons up the mouth. Cops always feel superior to sloppy druggies.

"Did you ever ask him about Lawrence Laboratory?"

I shook my head. O'Neal opened his briefcase and pulled out a photo of Alex. Shit. "Alex. People in Asia got him to meet me at the plane."

"Do you have his phone number?"

"No."

They stiffened. "Can we see your passport?" Friese said. I got up and went back to the bedroom, O'Neal following me, found the passport and showed it to them. Damn Institute better have forged a good one.

They pulled a small copier from the briefcase and ran my passport through it, every page with stamps. I figured they also had my fingerprints.

"We're concerned about Jerry," O'Neal said. "Perhaps he needs hospitalization?"

Yeah, I thought, for talking about these aliens he's met. "Why?"

"We don't understand why anyone who had a good job like his would suddenly quit," Friese said.

"And then apply for a grant to study dimensionality?" O'Neal said. "Was Alex putting pressure on him? Did you ever see signs of a quarrel?"

"They went on a camping trip together." I hoped the FBI knew this already.

O'Neal tittered. Friese looked at him, then back at me. "Are they lovers?"

"Not that I know."

"Ah, Alex. Lots of marginal types know Alex, Tom. Ex-post-docs, dropout weapons designers."

"I think Alex is crazy, not Carstairs. He tells people he's an alien sometimes."

The folks monitoring my skull computer weren't happy right then. But the FBI guys laughed and relaxed. "Tom, would you become friends with Alex for us. Tell us if you think he's asking Carstairs about his old work?"

"Sure," I said. Inside, a little mental me was jumping up and down. I'd lied to the FBI and got away with it.

Then O'Neal unplugged my phone, opened his briefcase, jacked a small computer into the line. "We're wiring your passport photo and prints in to Washington. Just a routine check."

"Sure," I said. The little mental me went into a crouch. The computer hummed like a hard-disk, then I heard an ink-jet hiss over paper. O'Neal ripped the sheet off, showed it to Friese. They nodded, but didn't show it to me.

O'Neal pulled out his modem jack and shut the briefcase, leaving my phone unplugged. "We're going now," Friese said. "We'll be in touch."

"You have a card so I can call if I find out anything?"

O'Neal pulled his cardcase out of his jacket pocket and handed one to me. "And we're in the phone book if you lose the card."

Sub-vocalize, a voice in my head said, the skull computer tapped into my brain's verbal centers.

I sub-vocalized, *They didn't ask about Barcons*.

No, nor about the Schweigman sisters.

Alex came by later that afternoon. "The FBI were asking about you," I said. "One left his card."

"Let me call them, Tom. Where's the card?"

"The FBI card?"

"Yeah." I reluctantly gave him the card. He dialed and asked for O'Neal. "Mr. O'Neal, this is Alex Hinderland. Look, do you want to talk to me? I'm a friend of Jerry's and I didn't like him working for the Feds, okay, so I asked him to quit or I'd stop sharing my cannabis with him. Shit, how do I know whether he has a permit or not. Yeah, I'm an alien, sometimes. When the astral projections are right, I share this body, just like in *Radio Free Albemuth*. Maybe I should . . . you wanna see my passport? You know my car, license X-KALAY, it's in memory of Philip K. Dick. The man knew. Stop me and we'll talk. But talk to *me*, okay, when you have questions. Don't bug my friends.''

I almost expected hundreds of grey government cars to come squealing into the parking lot then. Then squads of Barcons gating to Earth, to this apartment.

Alex listened to the man for a bit then. Finally, Alex said, "I'd rather tell when Tom can't hear.'' Alex hung up and laughed. Then he took out some trade tools and programmed the FBI bugs to pick up synthetic conversation about drugs and sex. "The program,'' he told me as he worked, ''will let them hear Marianne synthetic talk if she comes over, real-time radio or TV when you turn them on, computer noise.''

"Yeah,'' I said, "and if they find out what you've done, I'm fucked.''

"It's done with little microgates. They'll collapse if the apparatus is moved. If we have an earthquake even.''

"Terrific. Are you being sloppy so you can get pulled from this place?'' He seemed obsessed with getting trapped on Earth in jail, and yet loved how our human energies, behaviors, languages, jazzed him up.

Marianne didn't come over the next day, but two days after the FBI visited, she came over in brilliant green bike shorts and a matching green and white jersey. "Get your bike. We need to set up your training routine,'' she said.

"Have the FBI been by to see you?'' I asked.

"Oh, just foolishness over some weapons engineer who developed a conscience,'' she said.

I changed into bike shorts and the jersey while she loaded my bike on the roof rack. She seemed so cool. Outlaw cool—maybe her family wasn't so different from mine? I didn't say more since at least Alex and maybe the Barcons had technology enough to bug my apartment.

What with all the combined speeds and variations, I doubted a gate could be focused on us while we were erratically pedaling. Of course, they could bug the bike frame.

I got my waterbottles out of the freezer and wrapped them in a towel—a trick Strigate the frame maker mentioned when I picked up the bike and equipment. Marianne was waiting out in the living room, rocking on her cleats, heels in the air, then toes.

We loaded the bikes on top of the car and she said, "You need to start training regularly."

"I need to get away from that apartment regularly."

"You still reading about Japan?"

"I need to read about Japan, but I don't think it's really relevant." In two senses—I was beginning to think that we'd have to solve non-human problems in non-human terms, not copy from humans. "I need to be better with Americans."

"Socialize more?"

"With you."

"And with others, Tom?"

"Yeah. I've become a recluse. I can survive but it lacks something." Like Black Amber's approval.

"I could take you to some parties."

"Fine, Reeann."

"Reeann, I like that. My kid nickname was Pot." She wrinkled her nose up and bared her teeth.

"Marianne, Mary Jane?"

"Marijuana's not the same, but most Berkeley kids don't read Tennyson and Shakespeare."

"I have friends who made me read Shakespeare."

"Marianna in the moted grange, besieged on all sides."

"Parents shouldn't name kids things like that."

"Better than Action Faction, Sun Power, Moonberry."

"Yeah. Take me to some of your parties."

We drove straight back into the hills, not as far as the delta this day. When we got away from the car, I began explaining my life to Marianne, including Warren's contribution to my delinquency. She said, "I'll help you find your brother. If these people are advanced, maybe they could cure him."

"I feel like he's my responsibility, but he'd embarrass me on Karst, worse than the Tibetans."

"Don't you need to find him and deal with it?" She stared at my down tube as we began climbing. "Shift down."

I shifted, then again in back to the largest rear cog. The bike became heavier and heavier. "Yeah." I couldn't say more and she didn't speak again until we went over the hill.

"You were poor?"

"Yeah, we were poor orphans. Why do you think Warren got involved in drug making? It was the best money he could get, better than Amway, real estate, farming."

"Being born poor isn't your fault."

"If I make a lot of first contacts and work with linguistics crews and trade treaty crews, I could do well in the Federation."

"Bright country boy and the aliens saved you. My parents met a radical priest once. He was born poor in Virginia, too. The Catholics saved him."

"So, will you marry me and come back to Karst?"

"Promise me that I'll be trained in the Institute of Linguistics. And leave Molly and Sam here."

"They want to bring you all out now."

"Then we bring your brother out, too. My agenda."

The Federation would probably like that—get out all the humans who knew, except Carstairs, who was too fascinated to blab. And if he did, who'd believe him.

"Alex," Reeann said as if thinking along parallel lines, "is a slop."

"Slob?"

"Slop, and a slob, too, I bet. Are his kind like him?"

"No." I thought about Tesseract. "Most of the other ones I've met are dark-haired, bald over the skull crest. The Barcons rearranged Alex's skull bones so he could pass for human."

"They scrambled his brains, too, I bet," Marianne said. We had to drop back into single file because of traffic, then another hill took my breath away. I wanted to pull my feet out of the toe clips and walk up, but as long as Reeann could pedal, I would, too.

"Maybe growing up on Karst does that to you? I'm not

sure I'd want to have children there," I said, then added, "I can't write Warren directly."

"I could write him. Why was John . . . Black Amber looking for her son around Berkeley?"

"Warren sent an alien locator device to a guy in Berkeley that he didn't like. Had a guy in Roanoke do the actual mailing."

"So John Amber found them and got shot."

"They thought it was stolen military equipment."

"Well, it was, wasn't it?"

"Tell Warren you know I'm okay. Make it that you met me on a bus and I begged you to start writing him."

"And I felt guilty about not doing it sooner. Haven't seen you since . . ." She thought a bit. "You were riding through the country with bike camping gear, a very quiet guy, but I never thought anyone could be hiding out from the law on a bicycle."

That struck me as so hilarious I choked on my laughter.

"As soon as we know where he is, we snatch him." She sounded gleeful.

Another hill, and another hill on top of that—all these hills began pulling my quads. "Gear down and spin," she kept telling me.

Marianne sent her letter out to find Warren. Then we all went on with our lives as though we had nothing to hide from the FBI. Both the Schweigman sisters and the Barcons thought that was the best way to deal with them. The Barcons came by the Schweigmans once a week and told an FBI agent who cruised by one afternoon that they were fans of Sam Turner's.

I didn't ask the Barcons about Alex. If I'd been his case officer, I'd have pulled him off planet.

"You've been ordered to socialize more?" Marianne said one day when she came over. She was dressed up, in heels and a slinky purple dress with bare cut-out ovals in back. I didn't know if Alex's weird distortion devices still gave the FBI some innocuous warped version of what we said or what.

A task? Precisely. I felt . . . there's no one word for it in English, socially convalescent, breaking a transitory maladaptation and feeling awkward about it. *Farisch*. "Yeah," I told her. I got the canned clams out of the cupboard and the garlic out of the refrigerator. *Farisch* is an optimistic word, though. "After dinner . . ."

"Put the stuff back. We're going to a dinner party."

"I just learned how to make this."

"Tom, come on. Do you have good clothes?"

"Check the closet." She went into the bedroom and came out with my corduroy suit.

"This will do." She looked at the suit more carefully. "Someone taught you how to shop."

"Alex, I think, bought them for me."

"You should get one good wool suit, though. Italian with a vest. I love guys in vested suits."

"It's in there somewhere," I said.

She went back to my closet and brought out the wool suit. "Okay. Now do you have black socks?"

"Black socks?"

"You need black socks with this."

"Jesus, I have brown socks, I have red socks, I have white socks. I don't know if I've got precisely black socks or not."

She rummaged through my chest of drawers and came out with black socks dangling from her fingers. "Here, these go with that."

"Do I need a special color jock?"

"No, Tom." Almost embarrassed, I changed in front of her. She came up to adjust things from time to time, then tied my tie. "You look great."

"Aren't these clothes old-fashioned for Berkeley?"

"Dr. Baseman loves retro."

All dressed up, we got in her eco-deco mobile very carefully, brushing the front seats with our hands before we sat down. We laughed like kids about that.

Then up into the hills to a Berkeley I hadn't seen: brick houses, stucco houses, huge shade trees, children riding bikes and adults jogging with Afghan hounds and Malteses in the late July sun. We parked and walked to a house with a steeply sloped roofline dipping down on the left side of the doorway and rosemary bushes in front on the brick-walled bank. It wasn't a huge house, I noticed as we went up the walk to the door, but it was elegant—black iron frames in the bay windows, stained glass in the door. Marianne bounced the brass knocker off the strike plate twice.

I heard footsteps, then a blond woman opened the door. "Hello, Cynthia. Tom, this is Dr. Cynthia Baseman."

"Hello." I realized I'd been expecting a man.

"Tom, Ree, come in," she said. She had an accent, not quite German. "We're toasting *nori* now. Oliver caught an early salmon up north and flew it down on ice."

Marianne asked, "Where's Oliver?"

"Oh, he's still fishing." Dr. Baseman looked at me, and said, "Are you a student here?"

"No, ma'am," I said, remembering a bit of Somerset Maugham, "I'm a remittance man."

"How refreshing to hear someone actually admit it. Most of your fellow trust fundies these days try to pass as aleatory music revivalists. Where did you get that accent?"

"I fell on a spoon and it scarred my mouth."

She frowned at me, looked at Marianne. "Ree, I've heard there's going to be a tenure-track opening in linguistics at the University of South Carolina."

"I don't want to leave Berkeley."

"Ree, you should *visit* the campus at least. Tom, Ree says you're interested in Japan. Meiji? Modern?"

"How they handled technology without giving up their essentially Japanese culture."

"You'd love talking to Mr. Sato, then." She wrapped her right arm around Reeann's waist and grappled my elbow with her left hand.

She led us through the house into a walled garden half the size of a basketball court. On one side, water gurgled down rocks into a small pool with three giant gold carp, *koi*, in it. In the other rear corner was a gas hibachi about three feet long, a foot wide, where the guests were toasting what looked like crumpled sheets of green cellophane. Beside the hibachi, a Japanese guy bent over a butcher's block, cutting raw slices out of a bloody salmon. When people finished toasting their *nori*, they went over to the salmon, wrapped the seaweed around raw fish, and popped the nuggets into their mouths.

A Japanese woman came out behind me with a silver cocktail shaker, saying, "Cynthia, I made them with just a touch of vermouth. And stirred, not shaken."

Then Alex came stepping through the crowd around the hibachi, with a black teenaged boy following him. He nodded to Reeann and me.

"Do you know Alex?" our hostess said. "That's Wallie with him. He's trying to get Wallie a scholarship to Berkeley. Met him playing basketball in Oakland."

Reeann asked, "How long have your known him?"

"Not long. He read my articles on zoosemiotics in *Brain and Behavior*, and came by my office to talk to me about innate brain patterns and meaning matrices. A fascinating man. Wondered if one could actually have a holistic sense of language if the sound system involved was modified radar scanning."

Alex brushed by me and said, "Circulate, circulate." The young black guy looked really nervous in his jeans and running shoes among all the be-suited-and-tied academics. I wondered if Alex was really trying to get him into Berkeley. He clung to Alex the way I would have if I could have during my first days back on Earth, before I found out what an asshole Alex was.

"You want to go to Berkeley?" I asked him.

He stopped, looked at Alex disappearing into the house, and nodded. "Out of Oakland, anyway. Even to suit-life."

"It's different," I said.

"I tol' him I know Tagalog, Spanish, English, Samoan. But all street, you know. Street." He sounded desperate.

"They'll teach you proper," I said, remembering something I'd heard black kids in Floyd saying about the Yankee schoolteachers.

"Oakland isn't backassward, just . . ."

"Is it like here?" I waved a hand toward the hibachi and raw fish.

He loosened his shoulders. "No, it isn't like here."

Reeann just stood by listening. Then she said, "Have you had some salmon?"

Wallie said, "Not outside a taste in krill cakes."

She made us neat little balls, rice around the raw fish, then *nori* around that. "Taste."

"Like raw meat," I said.

Wallie ate his without comment, then watched to see how to make the balls. He began moving around the hibachi, making balls, gobbling them, going away, then coming back as if by shifting places he'd be less conspicuous.

I thought raw salmon was only okay, but I wasn't starving.

Reeann whispered in my ear, "Alex trying to prove he isn't a bigot about some people, just about S'um's kind?"

Alex came back from the house just then and stared at Reeann as if he'd overheard her. For the rest of the party, he stayed about ten feet away from us, not getting conversationally close, not getting too far away. I sub-vocalized, *I've now had dinner with more than two Berkeley people.*

His voice whispered in my mind, "Yes, I am listening."

I wondered then if the FBI could pick up the transmission. Reeann said, "Cynthia wants you to meet Mr. Sato. He's finished cutting the fish."

We went over to the Japanese couple. Cynthia introduced him and he bowed slightly. Remembering my reading, I bowed just a little farther down. His wife passed Marianne two full crystal martini glasses smelling of gin and ripe olives. Marianne gave me one.

"Gin goes excellently with sushi," Mr. Sato said. "Cynthia tells me you want to know how we Japanese coped with Western intrusion."

"Yes." I saw Cynthia turn to other guests.

"We had a terrible time. Westerners thought we'd ruined ourselves becoming wealthy and raising six-foot-high boys." He laughed and reached behind him. His wife put a cocktail in his hands. "One has no choice, really. It is more productive to become more productive, right?" He laughed and clapped me on my shoulder, then drained his martini and flushed.

Mrs. Sato tittered. Reeann looked from the man to the wife, and tightened her lips. "I like what Japanese did with the Memphis furniture style," I said timidly. "You make things over in your spirit."

"Aw, we can't help it. Now all things are looking functional, right. Japan was too poor to waste materials on anything rococo. So now, the whole world is Japanese styled. Hoopie shit." He reached back for another martini, but Mrs. Sato shook her head and said something in Japanese that he didn't like hearing.

"If you were an African, what would you do with Western technology?" I asked.

"Learn how to make lasers, fusion generators. Drive the children through school. *Banzai* learning. Like the black child your blond Kraut friend is dragging around— make them learn high tech. Any old crafts people you want to save, make them National Treasures and support them with tax money so nobody has to buy the junk."

"Aren't you being cynical?" Reeann asked. "There are low tech solutions, like the Urban Integral Homes . . ."

"I know those stupid Integral houses. You spend all your time fiddling with the four collection bins, the three compost piles, the bioenergetics of bunny and chick. You might as well live in the country and be poor. You have a job and run a house full-solar, recycling your shit? Or do you simply fritter your time on the fucking house?"

Reeann turned red. I tensed, ready to grab her if blood suddenly shunted from her face. Sparse-haired sapients with hemoglobinned blood, they get red or darker, it's a warning. When they pale, they're close to jumping. She slowly lost her color but didn't go pale. Gently, I laid my hand on her arm. She said, "I want to leave, Tom."

"Would it be rude?"

"Let's tell Cynthia we really enjoyed it, but I've got to get resumes out."

"Sato?"

"I've worked very hard, Tom, but he's right. I do have nothing to show for it. Your offer . . ." She pulled her face into a beaming smile as we approached Cynthia. "Loved it, Cynthia, but we've got to go. I'll get some resumes out tonight."

"I can call the departments and tell them to pay special attention to . . ."

"Thanks, Cynthia, but . . ."

"Consider the Carolina job, Ree. They're much more progressive than you'd think. Really."

"I think I'm going to do freelance fieldwork."

"Ree, you finished the degree two years ago. The book we pulled out of your dissertation was lovely, but you need . . ."

"Cynthia, Tom and I may be leaving Berkeley soon. I'll give you a forwarding address."

"Ree, you've done some excellent work." Dr. Baseman thought Marianne was being a fool.

I said, "I enjoyed it, Dr. Baseman."

"Is she going wandering around the globe with you?" Dr. Baseman asked me. I didn't realize how bony and tough her fingers were until she poked her hand into mine and squeezed. Not a handshake, a warning.

Alex stared at me across the garden, his large shoulder slightly hunched, watching as we left.

As she drove down to our neighborhood, Reeann said, "Come over tonight, okay?" She sounded whipped and little.

"Okay."

"I love the academics and yet . . ." She sighed. "It's crazy to consider leaving with you. I got a letter from your brother."

"So where is he?"

"Richmond, Virginia, in a halfway house."

"Richmond." Odd to think he hadn't left Virginia. "We could fly out to see him."

"You have the money?"

"Yeah, I had a $25,000 bank draft waiting when I opened my account."

She sort of vibrated her eyes at me, being heavily involved in traffic problems at the Shuttack and Cedar intersection. Then she gunned us through the intersection and down Cedar into her garage. We sat in the car. "Tom, I don't know."

"Do you want me to go home?"

"No, talk to me."

"Everything will be all right."

"It's crazy. Does your life really work for you?"

"I have to work at it. I tend to think of people like Alex as sort of like cats. They mean well, but they've got different motivations. Some maybe don't mean well, but those, too, have different motivations. Yeah."

"But, we can learn signals."

"Yes, semiotics. Now I know why one of my mentors made me study that."

Reeann shivered. "But, Tom, how do I know you don't have some different motivations?"

"Mine are within human norm," I said. "Test my DNA."

"Be careful." She said that playfully, but her face frowned. "People make funny assumptions."

I ran my tongue between her lips and pried at the stiff cheek muscles. Gently, she pushed me back and we got out of the car. "Semiotics," she said and smiled.

"Don't take me for granted," she told me as she pulled back the feather quilt lying over her double futon. "I want to go with you halfway because I am scared. Being scared is exciting."

"That's why Alex teases Carstairs."

"Carstairs really thinks Alex knows something. I'm sure that none of you could put a gate mechanism together, or you wouldn't be allowed here."

In the morning she said, "Do you want me to make the plane reservations for Virginia?"

"You in a hurry?"

"Yeah, I'm getting excited. Let's do it."

"There's nothing to be scared about for you."

"I met your black friends yesterday, before we went to the party. They approved of my doing linguistics work."

"Oh." She wasn't going to be Support then. "I'm glad for you."

"They tested me." With her hands, she shaped the brain function test helmet over her head. I remembered the colored lights, shifting forms. "I was excellent."

I'd just been high average for a cadet, but maybe the Barcons were just talking, so I said, "I'm glad."

"You'd really rather have me three paces to the rear, like Mr. Sato."

"No, I'm really glad. Make the reservations."

She slithered through the bedclothes and hugged me. "We can both handle it."

We landed in Richmond in the rain. Reeann handled the car rental, paid cash while I watched water trickling down the lower lobby's plate glass windows.

"I'll drive," I said.

"Are you used to city driving?"

"I'll drive." We went from the airport toward the city, sliding by the brooding James River on elevated steel and concrete. Reeann called out the exit just in time. I went down the ramp between a steel hauler with plastic wrapped girders on his flat trailer and a U-Haul that wandered into right-hand lanes as if blind on that side. Probably was, an amateur driver. We ended up on a little street filled with late nineteenth-century town houses, too plain to have attracted remodelers. Reeann watched the street—mostly black women sitting at upstairs windows, their arms crossed on pillows, yelling at their children who played on the sidewalk.

"It looks like Oakland," Reeann finally said.

We came into a fringe area—this was where the halfway house was, not in the total slum because social workers would freak, but not in a good neighborhood either. We saw signs in Vietnamese, Cambodian, and Spanish. Three black Rastafarians in grey peg-leg pants suits walked out of the Vietnamese take-out with little white cartons, their long dreadlocks bobbing as if to music we couldn't hear.

We passed the halfway house—two bay-fronted buildings each about three stories tall. "Not too bad," Reeann said. "I'll go in."

"I'll get some take-out whatever."

"Just ask for something with chili garlic sauce."

I said, "I didn't realize Virginia could be this weird." Reeann laughed as she locked the car. We stood beside it a second, then walked down toward the halfway house. She went in and I kept walking, thinking that I had to look different at twenty-four than I did at sixteen when I was arrested. I opened the door to the take-out place and realized I was overdressed for the neighborhood, wearing the cord pants and a white shirt. Wet, too.

"I'll have three orders of anything with chili garlic sauce," I said.

The man cook and the counter girl smiled at me and babbled to each other in their language as the cook scooped various cut-up vegetables and chicken out of white plastic containers lying on their sides behind the wok. He splashed in oily sauce, then stirred everything up, while the woman put ladles of rice in the bottoms of each carton.

"Want it be super hot?" The cook's accent was black, as though he'd learned English on these streets.

"Do one hot, the other two mild."

I walked back toward the halfway house and saw Marianne and Warren, yes, Warren. His face was rough, wrinkled but gaunt, like the bone was wearing through the flesh. He looked drugged, his brushy eyebrows straggly and greyed, more bald, even his still black hairs were duller.

"Tom?" he said. "You're still alive?"

"Yeah. Yeah, I've been to something like college."

"They told me you disappeared. Tom, Tom."

I wasn't sure what he meant, repeating my name like he was shaking his head over me. "Here, do you eat this?" I handed him a carton.

"I'm sick of it," he said. "Damn garlic chili sauce or rotten fish gunk on everything at that shop."

"Did Marianne explain things?"

"No." He looked at her as I handed her the container with the most sauce.

"That guy who helped us; the one who couldn't talk English. His friends took me away."

Warren seemed slow, 'luded. Finally, he said, "But they treated you okay? Better than what I got?"

Marianne said, "They can help you."

"Better than Prolixin shots. I'm a crazy man. I need a structured environment."

"Warren." I felt more numb than I could ever imagine, each finger lead bars, nerves zinging up and down my arms and legs. Flesh jumped in my shoulders, my face.

"Come with us," Marianne said. "We've got a car."

"Drove from California?" Warren asked.

"No, flew. We rented the car at the airport," I said.

"In chips," Warren said dully. He took the carton of take-out food and began picking at it with a plastic fork as we walked through the drizzle, hair plastered to our heads. "Little brother's in a real deal."

"Warren, I came back as soon as I could." Marianne looked at me funny when I said that.

Two black women—no, two midget Barcons or made-over sapients of another kind—were leaning against our car when we got to it. "We'll explain," they said.

Warren goggled at them as one got in the back seat, then said, "Come on in, Warren." The other waited until he got in, then took the gutter side window seat.

"Where are we going?" I asked.

"We want to talk to Warren," they said. "Privately."

"I don't want to," Warren said. I looked back and saw that he was sweating almost as much as he'd been when the drug investors bullied him into tabbing drugs for them.

"What are you?" Marianne asked. "Where do we go?"

"We're members of the Federation. Drive, we'll direct you. Barcons, we thought, would be too intimidating, but we're somewhat medically skilled ourselves."

"And Karriaagzh sympathizers," the other one said, speaking for the first time. "Marianne, you'll appreciate that. Karriaagzh wants to make contact with Earth."

"Don't you have any central leadership?" Marianne said.

"There's no one correct solution when dealing with composite entities," the first one said.

"You influence the good, discourage the bad," the other said. "Turn left at the next light."

Marianne and I went to Maymont Park while the two Federation fake-humans talked to Warren. The rain had quit but it was still grey.

Marianne asked, "When should we go back to them?"

"They'll find me. I've got a computer in my skull."

"Oh. Will they do that to me?"

"I don't know about the Institutes, and don't tell me I don't ask enough questions because that's what my first human woman said."

"I don't know what this is going to be like." She sat down on a bench and looked at the James flowing down below us. Her head twitched once, faster than shaking it no. "Am I just a misfit?"

"No, my God, you have a Ph.D., a house."

"All my friends have Ph.Ds. Hiding out in Academia."

I almost asked her why she didn't do something with it, but realized how bad that was going to come across. I felt very protective of her. And, in a sneaking way, I was glad she had some weaknesses.

"Tell me, how many other humans on Karst?" she asked.

"About 200."

"Can we come back for visits? They let you come back."

"Yeah, to find someone like you."

"Would you have just left Warren here?"

"I don't know. He haunts me, but he's more like the Tibetans than a modern person, I think. Except he was real high tech with drugs."

"Here, Rehab is training him to be a lathe operator."

I remembered the grounds crews with their automatic garden machines. "He can find work on Karst."

"Did he do a lot of drugs or was he crazy before that?" She almost crouched as she asked the question, looking very European, Jewish. I suspected how serious the question was for a woman.

"No, not before drugs, but he was restless. And he started doing drugs when he was in grade school. Some."

"Well," she said, straightening up a bit, "if we have children, it's a real outcross."

"Are you afraid?" I asked her. "People are pretty decent there, even if there are political squabbles."

"And the Barcons told me that people do get killed in first contacts," she said. "Don't try to reassure me too much."

"Does the idea of aliens fascinate you?"

"Yes, it does."

That's all that really matters, making a mutual zoological city with others, different ones, all those complex lives touching, diverging. "You'll do great, Ree."

" 'Zoosemiotics,' " she said, quoting her professor's topic.

"Karriaagzh says that just because we can't all understand each other bare-minded there's no reason to quit working together. He said that all life aspires to capital M Mind."

"I've heard other arguments on Earth," she said.

The two fake-women brought Warren down to me. The largest one said, "Marianne, the brothers need to talk."

She got off the bench and went walking off with them. When I looked away from her, I saw Warren watching me.

"Nice," he said. "You gonna steal her from Earth, too?"

"Warren?"

"Joking. Drugs screw the tone." He leaned his hips against the back of the park bench, one leg bent, foot on the seat, the other stretched out. "Do I have any choice?"

"We can help you better than Virginia Rehab."

"Everyone in the whole fucking universe thinks I need help. My brain . . ."

"They can regrow brain tissue."

His eyes widened slightly, but I saw the pupils pull to points. "But would it still be me?"

I didn't know how to answer that. He said, "What I did, then, was for money for you."

"That wasn't all of it, Warren."

"Yeah, maybe not. We should have taken your little bloodsucking buddy and just dumped him down a mine shaft."

"If he'd been alive when his kin found me . . . Warren, they wanted to brainwipe me until they found his will."

"Decent of them not to, considering that *you* didn't kill him." Warren drew his leg up and crouched on the bench and stared at me, the wrinkles shifting on his face.

"They know he pulled the shotgun on you when you stopped us from escaping. Warren, he didn't know shotguns could kill."

"You should have explained, maybe. While we were all communicating so well. Did you ever understand his kin?"

"By computers. But some of the other sapients you can understand bare-brained."

"What I really want to know is do I really have a choice? Can I stay here?"

I didn't answer right away. I wanted him with me, if Black Amber wouldn't attack him, if he'd still be Warren, or become again the Warren I'd known when I was just a kid. "I don't want to leave you here."

"I don't feel like I've got a choice," he said. "Got a smoke?"

"No." He looked down at the ground, eyes going side to side and I felt sick, afraid he'd grab up a butt. "Warren, I can't leave you here. I want you to share what I've got the way you shared what you had when I was younger."

"You're still my *younger* brother, boy."

"Yes, Warren, but my luck's up now."

Warren stood up and cuffed my ear. "You a man now, ain't cha? Get me off this damn Prolixin, it bloats my brain."

The fake-human women came back with Marianne then and the biggest one asked, "Is he okay about it?"

"I'm okay," Warren said. "What do you look like when you're not in human drag? Screaming tentacles?"

"I guess he's willing," I said.

"Go back to the halfway house for now. We'll take you out later. Kick and scream if you want to."

"Shit," Warren said. "Either you bitches have a cigarette?" The smaller one brought out a pack of Kents from her purse.

We drove back together, Warren on the window this time, and waited until Marianne signed Warren back into the halfway house. Then the smaller fake-human said, "Marianne and Tom, you go now. Visit Williamsburg, have a good time, then be back in Berkeley next week."

"Drive us up a few blocks before letting us out," the larger one said. "You've got a tail."

We drove on to Williamsburg that night and checked into the cheapest motel we could find, then explored the next day. Marianne hadn't been this far south before, or this far back in American time. "Quechuan past, yes, Anglo, no."

"You don't think of it as your past."

She gestured at her handbag, her handwoven top. "No, my people didn't land before 1890. We didn't even fight to end slavery here."

I saw a couple of guys in leather aprons working with a spinning wheel and dye pots and led her there. "Your sister does this."

"Bet this is probably more alien than what you see on modern planets a hundred light-years from here."

We went in a house that from the outside looked like a replica Williamsburg house in the good part of any small town. Inside, the ceilings were lower, everything was slightly uneven. I felt vertigo, like I was in a fake fake, and said, "It's not real."

"No, it's a reconstruction."

"Isn't it odd to be so concerned about the past."

"Maybe," Marianne said. "Most human cultures have myths."

"You'll get along fine where we're going," I said, mindful of the possible tail.

Marianne looked at her tourist map and said, "There's a graveyard, here."

We walked there and Marianne looked at the graves, counting the children who'd died before five, the mothers who'd died before thirty-five. She fingered each date as though blind, as though memorizing an essential fact about humanity. I began to worry about her, as though she was already pregnant with my child. Barcons would deliver her baby as though she were an exotic animal—but they were technically superb medics. She stared back over the eroded tombstones at me as if we'd suddenly become mere humans together in a huge inhuman universe.

She began walking toward me by the old graves, her loose hair swaying over her breasts. I thought of all of us, quick and dead, struggling to stay alive in our times. For her sake, I'd try to love my kind.

"You know what I was thinking when we were in the graveyard?" she said on the plane after takeoff.

"No. I know what I was thinking, though."

"We're utterly important and nobody knows it. We're representing our planet, our species."

"I was thinking that we're both human in a basically inhuman universe."

"Not cruel, though, is it?"

"Sometimes I think humans are assholes. Takes brains to be cruel. Takes more brains not to."

"We're not cruel people. Not even your brother."

I'd never thought of myself as a representative human.

Down below us the Mississippi glinted in the sun. Marianne leaned over my shoulder to see it. "I bet no planet is as beautiful."

"You'll see."

"Tom, I'm leaving all my connections behind, good ones, bad ones. Now all I'm going to be is a raw human."

"You'll make new connections, Reeann."

"But I *want* to see what it's like to be a raw human."

We landed and transferred from bus to bus to bus back to Cedar Street. In Marianne's mail was a note from Alex, telling us he'd be over on August 1. That was two days away.

Reeann, Molly, and Sam went out to Tillman Park to talk about the move, while I went back to my apartment to print my research notes on Japan. As I watched the printer whisk across the sheets, I wondered about minimum social units for different species. For humans, maybe six to eight—we were going to be claustrophobic as a social group unless we brought someone for Warren. Too late for that.

After all was printed, I had a stack of folded sheets four feet high. I put the sheets back in the two empty boxes and taped them up.

The phone rang. "Your reservations for the JAL flight 405 to Tokyo on the shuttle are confirmed for August second," a woman's voice told me. "Will you pick up the tickets for your party or do you want to give me a card number?"

"I'll pick them up."

"If your visit will be less than two weeks, a consular officer will stamp passports at the airport. If more, then you'll need to contact the consular office. You know the currency restrictions?"

"I'll check," I said.

"We thank you for making your reservations with JAL," she said and hung up.

A cover, I hoped. I was ready to get back to Karst.

On August 1, Marianne called. "Alex is here with a moving van."

As I walked down Cedar I saw a grey car parked next to a restored Volkswagen. Don't duck, I told myself. They didn't seem to notice me. Alex and Sam were moving the harpsichord into the moving van. I went up and looked in. Already they'd gotten Molly's spinning wheel and looms in, plus six trunks and three suitcases.

Alex said, quietly, "Austin's Mini-warehouse, Block six, unit thirteen, in Walnut Creek. Meet us there."

I looked at Sam. His eyes were glazed; he'd been tranquilized. He mumbled, "Don't hurt my piano, my flute, my harpsichord, my sitar, my . . ."

"Alex? What's wrong with Sam?" Molly asked.

"He was nervous," Alex said. Molly herself was sweating. "Molly, if you need sedation, it makes the transition easier for humans."

Molly said, "I guess we never had any choice, did we?"

Alex didn't answer, just went into the house with Sam. I left to rent a car.

In Richmond, two black women snatched my brother from the front stoop of the halfway house. Later, I saw the article from the Richmond *Times Dispatch*. Even though he'd been carried off screaming, he couldn't be found. The police dragged the James and sent a SWAT team up to our old Floyd County house, but Warren wasn't on Earth by then.

Karst had sent a transport pod to the mini-warehouse that fit nicely—we sent Sam and Molly across first so Sam could unload the harpsichord. The second load was equipment: the harpsichord, Molly's loom. Third load: Warren, unconscious on a stretcher, and I, with my bicycle and all my Earth clothes. Marianne came through last.

"Alex said he's going to see to it that we can get back to Berkeley from time to time," she said as she stepped out of the transport pod. "Are we on Karst yet?"

We were inside one of the outer transport stations, in Karst's Oort Region. I looked down at my brother on the stretcher. "Not quite yet. Take a look outside."

Her sister and brother-in-law stared out already at the massive cargo containers and the tiny space-suited aliens moving over them, the global clusters off the ecliptic—metal glints in the far distance.

Marianne walked to the window and hugged Molly and Sam, didn't let them go as she looked out, too. They didn't notice as an olive-feathered bird and two Barcons entered the station room.

The Barcons took Warren off on his stretcher. Marianne turned around as they talked in Barq. Her pupils were dilated, then she focused on the bird who crouched slightly and looked away from her, his tan hands flexing slightly. "It has no wings. Can you say you got used to this?" She swung her arm stiffly at the viewport, then at the bird.

I said, "I could arrange for us to take a chemical rocket into Karst if you think you'd like to get there more slowly."

"I don't know if I want to or not."

"It might be hard on the musical instruments," the bird said in perfect English. "I'll bring tea. My Federation name in your language is Travertine."

= 5 =

Fresh Imported People

Marianne and the other two hunched on the bottom of the transport pod as it lurched through the final transition to Karst. They trembled and stank like captured animals and I didn't know how to comfort them. As someone outside began unscrewing the hatch, Marianne kept her eyes fixed on me.

Black Amber opened our transport hatch. Her long fingers held onto the door as though she wasn't sure she should let us out. "You can stay/remain together for eight rotations," Black Amber said. "Tell her/your human woman I was John Amber."

I reached out and stroked Black Amber's fuzzy hands with the backs of my knuckles. "Marianne," I said, "it's John Amber, what she really looks like."

Molly half sobbed and half giggled, then stuck her fingers in her mouth. Sam asked, "What is that hanging under its arms?"

"Vestigial wings," I said. Black Amber drew her lips back and pumped her hands once. I saw her through their eyes—the wrinkled face, broad forehead with the eyes set in saucer-sized bone protrusions, the tiny chin at the bottom of the muzzle, nostrils deep slits like a goat's.

In the back of the huge receiving loft, a second transport popped through in a haze of blue light. The hatch opened and Travertine said in English, *"The looms and music instruments rode through perfectly."*

Sam swung his head around at the sound and helped Molly up. Together, his arm around her shoulders, they went to check their work tools, running their hands over the loom frame and the harpsichord legs.

Marianne asked, "Female?" Meaning Black Amber.

"Yes," I said. "Black Amber has a neat little son." Black Amber oo'ed, then gently reached her hand out, fingers bent at the first joint, and brushed her knuckles across Marianne's upper arm.

Molly and Sam kept their hands on their equipment even as small fuzzy guys loaded it into a trailer. "It looks just like a truck trailer," Molly said, tears oozing down by her nose, eyelashes stuck together in clumps. Sam walked with the movers, one hand pressing the harpsichord keyboard cover as if to prevent aliens from opening it.

"Yeah, the shape's ergonometric for lots of *uhyalla*," I told her.

"This building is square," she said, making "square" sound like an insult. I translated for Black Amber.

"Tell them that the plants are green," Black Amber said in Karst Two. I blushed, remembering how awed I'd been when I got off and saw blue skies, green plants, and flower colored flowers, and actual dust on the plastic runway.

Reeann stood, her head turning in quick jerks. Then she asked Black Amber, "Can we go somewhere and be alone with Tom?"

"She doesn't understand English anymore," I said before I translated.

Black Amber replied, "No, I'll go with you, rough out xenophobe edges. Need to reduce fear/hostility with humans before facing the killer."

"Warren, where is Warren?" I asked.

"I prefer not to face him." Black Amber folded her arms and hooked her thumbs behind her neck. The elbows snugged in against her sides at about waist level. I noticed then that she was swollen slightly around the pouch.

"It may die," Black Amber said, noticing where I looked. "Beyond breeding permit. Barcons sterilized my herds. Have to find host on Gwyng Home/difficult gossip about Wy'um here.''

"Maybe it won't pouch," I said before I realized the swelling was higher than usual, larger.

"But it *has* pouched (agony to me)," she said.

Gwyngs traded babies to build ties between groups, but if nobody would take this one and her own host herds were sterile . . . I wondered then how many true children Black Amber had placed with other Gwyngs and moved to embrace her side to side.

Marianne watched, then asked, "What's the matter?"

"She may have to have an abortion." That saved the explanation for later. "We're only allowed to reproduce ourselves here, otherwise Karst would become too crowded."

Marianne said. "Tell her I'm sorry."

"Marianne's sorry."

"Appreciated/acknowledged," Black Amber said, "but she wants you to step back from me, thinks sexual."

When I did as Black Amber suggested, I noticed that Marianne's spine unstiffened and curved into a shallow S. Black Amber oo'ed, then muffled a koo against her high shoulder.

The moving crew backed in a truck cab, with two long bench seats that swiveled to fit various body types, and hitched it to the trailer. "Tom, your social group has a floor in a building between the Academy and the Linguistics Institute," Travertine said. He picked at a cracked scale at the base of his right thumb. Then, as he lowered the driver's seat to the floor, he added in English, "You can all ride in the cab. Except for Warren, who will go to the hospital with the Barcons."

Black Amber flexed her feet in her soft skin slippers. "I'll ride beside Travertine," I told her. She bared her teeth at me slightly, then the lump between her chin and throat bounced. I looked at Molly and Sam. If they freaked, they could get us from the back seat. "Are you all okay, Marianne?"

"I want to ride with my 'sichord," Sam said, voice slurred still from the drugs.

"No, no, come in with us," Travertine said in English. He ruffled facial feathers as if frowning with the skin under them.

Molly helped Sam into the back seat of the cab. I saw Travertine check a knob on the dash and figured that we had some sedation control. My, but this was getting embarrassing. "Shit, folks, climb in. We're going to have a whole building floor to ourselves."

"And I will teach them Karst One, all except Marianne," Travertine said, his nails clicking against the steering wheel. "Marianne will have the language operations."

Marianne's eyes locked with mine in the mirror strip across the top of the windshield. "It's all right, honey," I said.

"She'll be with your new Rector's Man/Person when we get back."

"Has anything happened to Tesseract?"

Black Amber said, "We've decided that you need close contact/cultural understanding with/of another species. Jereks."

I didn't much like Jereks after one of them bit me in the thigh during a quarrel on Yauntry, but if that was the way the Federation wanted it, then I was going down a chilly burrow to deal with giant ferrets with shiny T's of naked black skin across their eyes and down their noses. Bipedal and tailless weasels.

As the truck drove out of the receiving building and locked into the traffic control grid, I watched my fellow humans through the truck mirrors. We rolled through Karst City's outer neighborhoods.

Molly gasped and said, "They use wood here."

"Yes," said Travertine. "It can be recycled, modified with resins."

"It's all fucking squares."

"Some houses are round," the bird said, "in other neighborhoods."

"And most of the skins are dark," Sam said. He smiled for the first time.

"Pale skin," Travertine said, "is an adaptation to extreme cold. There are white and gold Jereks, white-haired Yauntries with fair skins, birds with paler feathers than mine." He raised his shoulder feathers slightly as if putting them on view. "Do I speak English well?"

"Yes," Marianne said. "How did you learn?"

"From the same Ahram who taught Red Clay Tom prestige English."

Black Amber ignored us, hunched up against the far door with her webs strained tightly across her chest, arms at her sides, thumbs behind the neck.

Marianne said to the bird, "But with your beak? You have a slight . . . accent." She frowned as though that wasn't quite the right word. "But . . ."

"Surgery," the bird said, releasing the truck from the traffic control grid and turning a corner before locking us into the system again. We passed stucco and foamed aluminum houses, with little statue-filled parks spaced about five blocks apart.

The buildings got higher near the Institute of Linguistics, a walled campus with six skyscrapers and several dozen smaller buildings, then we passed shopping streets headed off at right angles to the street we were traveling on. "We'll give you bracelets to make sure you can get directions home," Travertine said.

"Shit, we wouldn't dare go anywhere," Sam said.

Travertine released us from grid control and waited until traffic was clear to make a left turn. We drove down a ramp in front of a twelve-story building about half the block long, fifty to sixty feet, and twice as deep. If we had a whole floor of that, I thought, we've got more space than a typical human house.

We all loaded Sam's baby grand piano and the harpsichord into the huge elevator. As we rode up together, Black Amber said, "You have Gwyng neighbors." Sam held onto both instruments—maybe he thought they'd bruise when the elevator stopped. I reminded myself that he was still drugged.

The elevator door slid down to reveal a loft space about sixty feet by forty feet. In the front facing the street were two picture windows, thicker than usual—I suspected they'd play computer graphics. Long slit windows on the side walls let in lots of light. Sam and the bird shoved the harpsichord out, then we all got Sam's piano in place. I walked through a passageway behind the elevator onto a wraparound balcony overlooking a courtyard. I opened the first door off the balcony and saw a room with a bay window overlooking the building's side yard. The windows in the neighboring building, like dark mirrors, reflected our building's stacks of mirror-like bay windows.

Slightly dizzy from counting how many reflections in the windows mirrored each other clearly, I turned away. This room was about fifteen feet by twenty, not counting the bay. Closets? I walked in both interior doors—one was a closet, the other a duplicate of my toilet facility in my Academy dorm, but with a tub added.

I heard a noise and saw Marianne, pale, eyes huge, standing in the doorway. "Come in and see this."

She came in and said, "There must be four bedrooms or whatever." Then she looked through the toilet door and said, "I need to use this."

I started to close the door behind her and she said, "Don't. I have to keep looking at you."

"Marianne, don't embarrass me."

"You weren't scared at all?"

Oh, that. "Oh, yeah, yeah. But they didn't hurt me."

She urinated, then fumbled for paper. "I guess that should be reassuring. Explain this language operation?"

"They re-activate your language centers, like when you were a child, so you can learn Karst One quicker. Like in two or three months instead of years."

"A brain operation. Shit, Tom, you didn't tell me about that. I can learn any language without that."

"Then they put a computer in your skull that transforms Black Amber's speech into sequential patterns. Without that, you'd never understand holistic language people."

"If this operation messes up my Quechuan, I'll kill you." She pulled her underpants up and then pulled up her jeans and zipped them.

We went out together and looked through the next door

into another room like the one we'd been in. In the back of the apartment, behind the courtyard, was a kitchen equipped just like Marianne's had been, down to the recycling bins with stenciled labels. She kicked at the paper one and swore, crying and giggling, "Damn literalist fools."

"Have you ever considered that we might have recycling?" I didn't know, but if she kept on like that she was going to hurt her foot.

"I guess they're trying to make us feel at home." She began turning on stove burners. Each lit with a little whomp of gas and burned smoothly from high to very low. Along the sides of the gas holes, a fine wire glowed red. Marianne said, "The wire?"

"I don't know what it does."

"Bet it keeps the gas hot when the flame is low."

"Or make sure that it all burns," I said, trying to remember how other stoves on Karst worked.

Marianne cut the gas completely off and checked in the refrigerator. I saw glass bottles of milk. She asked, "Real milk?"

"Gwyngs raise Jersey cows."

"They raise *Jersey* cows?"

"Yeah, Jerseys give high butterfat in their milk and Gwyngs metabolize lipids differently than we do."

"Jersey cow lipids? Well," Marianne said. She ran hot and cold water in the sink and said, "I guess it would be too much to expect that to be solar-heated."

"We've got fusion generators here," I said.

"Nice enough kitchen," she said, looking out the windows over the sink. I was relieved to see American chairs around the table. Marianne said, "Let's see the rest of the house."

On the other side of the courtyard air shaft were two more sixteen by twenty bedrooms, each with a bathroom. Beside the elevator was a fifth bathroom, this one multispecies with a sliding basin on a rail, a sandbox, a slit against the wall, and a shower with controls for heated dust or chilled water. Travertine the bird saw us peer into it and said, "That's for visitors and me."

"But it's got a little regular basin," Marianne said, fiddling with the water lever and temperature dial. Steaming water ran into the basin. She rolled the dial to the left and got cold. "This work like your dial thermometers?"

I tried to remember if I'd ever seen a dial thermometer on Karst. Nope. I shrugged.

"It's the opposite of Earth," she said. Her body seemed to jerk itself into alignment. "I want to see the sky tonight."

Molly and Sam were asleep on the sofa we'd brought from Berkeley to here, wedged together, gripping each other.

"Let them alone," Black Amber said. "You've got eight days together, Red Clay, then you'll come with me while Barcons put language in Marianne's skull."

"Where are we going?" I asked.

"Gwyng Home," she said, pinching her shift and pulling the cloth out over the pouch hole.

In the morning, Sam woke up restless, the tranquilizer metabolized out. He played jumbles of music on his piano or the harpsichord or paced the perimeters of the loft, stopping to look out each window, his feet bare, the pale sole skin showing around the edges.

Travertine ruffled his feathers and said, "If you think you wouldn't freak, Sam, I'll take you to hear music."

Sam stopped pacing.

"Let's all go," Marianne said. "We won't have much time together."

"That's right," Travertine said, "Tom will go with Black Amber and you *all* will have the basic langauge operation. We . . ."

"Thought we'd freak?" Molly said.

"Well, we thought it would be easier if you stayed together in your social group. And better socially if you have the proper accent. We have enough tangle-tongued humans wandering around."

I sighed. Marianne asked, "That rough?" she said.

"Alone, it wasn't all that nice," I said.

"Tonight," Travertine said, "we'll go out on the town. Is my idiom correct?"

"Sure," Sam said. He went digging through a bag we hadn't moved into a bedroom yet and found his shoes, a pair of Weejuns, and slid them on sockless. Then he pulled out a glasses case, tried on a pair of mirror shades that made him suddenly sinister.

"The light isn't bright at night," Travertine said. "That's when the music is usually played, even on Karst."

Sam pulled them off and snapped the earpieces together so hard that Travertine's beak reflexively recoiled and snapped, too. I asked in Karst, "Travertine, what did he do?"

"Your dark-skinned human is snappish." Travertine's head drew back on his long neck that was usually hidden in his feathers. "Perhaps we are overcrowding you *humans*, two males in the apartment?"

"What did he say about humans?" Marianne asked.

"That you were getting bored in the loft," Travertine said. "Your bicycles are here. Tom could take you out."

Sam sat down at the harpsichord and began playing runs of high baroque music. Travertine moved the piano bench out of the way and pulled a sofa cushion over to sit on, knees bent backward. His nails, almost like ours, clicked over the keys without pressing down enough to strike a note, patterning after Sam's fingering.

"Do that again," Travertine said.

Sam slowed down and played a phrase.

Travertine's fingers stumbled through it. Sam laughed and relaxed. "You're not so good, it's a relief." The bird's face feathers puffed up. He had tried.

"Ree, we'll be okay if you and Tom go out," Molly said.

"Nobody's going to freak out if they see us in bike shorts?" Marianne said.

"Wait, put your wristband on," Travertine said. He added in Karst, "Tom, pull a map."

I pulled a map up on the computer, printed it, and asked, "Can we ride bikes anywhere? They go about half as fast as Karriaagzh runs, and they need a hard surface."

"Try the electric cart paths, then." He pointed to the map I'd called up. "Here's the closest one. We're here."

We began giggling in the elevator ride down to the street, holding our $2000 bikes, dressed in skin shorts, rocking on our cleats. "Going out to explore an alien planet," Marianne managed to get out between giggles.

"We better be able to stop giggling," I said.

We stopped when the elevator doors slid open and two tall shiny blacks, not human, not Barcons, got on. They asked, "What home?" in Karst One.

"A non-contacted planet at present." I fished around behind me for my wallet.

"Are the plastic rockers on the bottoms functional?" the female asked.

I lifted my foot so they could see the pedal slot. They murmured to each other in their home language and said, "Thanks," more or less in Karst One.

Marianne's abdomen began jerking at irregular periods. At ground level, as the other couple walked out of the elevator, she asked, "Did they ask about the cleats?"

"Yes." She laughed until she choked. I didn't know why she thought that was hysterical. We continued down to the basement. We wheeled our bikes out through the basement doors and up the ramp, down two blocks, and then we began to pedal on the electric cart path.

"How big is the city?" Reeann asked.

"About fourteen million sapients."

"What do they do?"

"Everything from make interplanetary trade deals to farming and cleaning houses."

The path we were on ran behind the buildings through gardens, then down or up over the streets and train tubes. Faintly reddish green trees with mat grey trunks and drooping skinny leaves bordered the path for a mile or so—each tree hit by extra electric lights. Three shiny black kids darted after a flat doughnut-shaped airfoil like a Frisbie.

"They aren't even surprised?" Reeann asked.

"No, you expect to see different-looking sapients here,"

I said, realizing the shiny skins and reddish trees came from a hotter sun than ours.

I turned away from the Institute the way we'd come in the night before and headed for the third river. This was to the northwest of where I'd lived when I was first in Karst City, learning Karst from a family of bear-stock creatures. Now the buildings were transparent glass, small rooms that one could see into or stacks of open spaces framed by chromed poles, inhabited by the olive birds.

"Does everyone live in a species neighborhood?" Reeann asked. "And they don't need privacy?"

"No, they've got feathers. Some species live together. Most Gwyngs do, but Black Amber says we've got Gwyng neighbors in our building."

On farther, the neighborhood was mixed, several styles of buildings. Marianne said, "It's like Berkeley here."

The buildings were foamed metal and foamed plastics, deep-space products where you whip the metal or plastic up and cast it in a null-grav environment. Some of them had bays, though. Other than that, I couldn't see even the vaguest resemblance. "How like Berkeley?"

"Multi-ethnic."

A Barcon officer stopped us and checked our IDs on his wrist computer. He told me, "Be careful she doesn't panic and run away."

"I don't think she will."

"She doesn't know the language yet."

"She won't do anything stupid. She's from an Institute of Linguistics on my planet."

"What are you saying?" Reeann asked.

"He just wanted to see our passes."

"Passes?"

"Humans, well, the Tibetans are a bit crude, so the Federation only lets selected ones of them live in Karst City. They, and I, carry IDs at all times."

She said, "There'd better be a good reason for restricting human access to the city."

"They're primitives."

"Shit, are we talking pass law here, like in South Africa?"

"Reeann, we're talking over one hundred different species of sapients, sometimes a bit anxious about each other, okay. I'll take you to see some xenophobia movies sometime."

"Xenophobia movies?"

"Like Earth horror movies, only we don't need special effects."

"I wish you hadn't told me about this right now."

"Sorry, I tend not to think too much about my early days here. I had to trust them, and I'm not dead."

"Terrific. Let's ride just to the river you were telling me about and go back . . . home. Home?"

We rode to the river and down a bit along a paved cart path. "It looks just like a river," she said.

Another bicyclist came by, maybe a Yauntry riding it. "And that looks just like a bicycle," I said to her.

She watched the rider pedal down the path. "I'm not hallucinating. He's got cam cranks."

"Parallel evolution," I said, meaning both the humanoid appearance and the machine.

"I will need a new language for this, I'm sure."

When we got back to the apartment, all the others were watching movies on a VCR. "What's it like out there?" Sam asked Marianne.

"Sort of okay. We got stopped by a furry giant thing who asked to see our passes, though." She walked back to a bedroom, stripping off her jersey as she went.

We ate dinner together in our apartment, Travertine gulping whole dead rabbit-sized mammals, fur and all, the Berkeley humans rolling forks around in a pasta dish heavy with Gwyng-made Jersey butter. I felt like I needed meat, so I skinned and broiled half of one of Travertine's mammals.

After dinner, Travertine regurgitated his grinding stones into his scaly fist and went into the visitor's bathroom by the elevator.

"Can he eat any other way?" Sam said.

"Ask him," I said.

Marianne moved her pasta around on her plate a bit more and said, "I bet it's rude to criticize someone's eating habits here."

"But is it going to store its dead animals in our refrigerator?" Molly asked.

"I was cruel to one of his kind once," I said, "so don't nag him."

Travertine came back, his stones wrapped up in a white cloth. He pulled out a drawer and put them in, then said, "If you'd prefer, I could cut my meat up."

"No, eat the best way for you. I suspect it's hard on you being alone with us," I said.

"I must understand humans, then Rhyodolite's Gwyngs, then the Yauntries." My fellow humans didn't understand the context, but I did. He was the same species as Xenon. And Xenon panicked under Yauntry guns—no friends around him at all, just aliens, a Gwyng and a human, both cold and remote to him. The Yauntries killed Xenon, thinking he was about to attack them. Misunderstandings all around.

"I felt tremendously guilty later," I told Travertine, "and Rhyodolite has tried hard, for a Gwyng, to become used to birds. Rhyodolite felt guilty, too, when he got to know Granite Grit." Travertine's tending us was another multi-agenda Federation deal.

"Granite Grit is not my kind. If I haven't made you too uncomfortable," Travertine said, "then might we go out to the music?"

"Sure," Sam said. He whistled Doo, Dee, Da, Du, the notes from *Close Encounters of the Third Kind*.

Travertine swept his eyes clean with his vertical inner eyelids, less transparent than Granite's or Karriaagzh's nictitating membranes, and said, "Music may connect more than semiotic systems do."

We took a red bus filled with bald cadets in black tunics and pants. "I was like that four years ago," I told my fellow humans.

"Will they do that to me?" Marianne asked.

"Not in the Institute of Linguistics," Travertine answered. Our bird guide nodded slightly at me when the cadets got out at the xenophobia movie house. Out on the street, the species differences were blurred by harsh overhead lights.

"Looks like a street," Sam finally said. "Alive."

We got off the bus and went up an outside flight of stairs by a white wall covered with thousands of alien graffitos in maybe one hundred different scripts. Sam traced a big red Gwyng glyph with his index finger and looked at Molly, who handed him a pen. He scrawled, "Sam bring music."

Inside the club, two Ahrams on a dais played blue-glazed clay flutes while, down in a pit, a gold-furred Jerek danced in a tooled leather loincloth, front and back panels hanging down to the floor. The naked T of skin across her eyes and down her nose was pink, not the usual black. As she swayed on her short legs, the black leather panels blurred in the shadows at her feet. Among the other aliens, I saw two of Granite Grit's bird kind watching, sitting down like nestlings, their heads bobbing to the music.

Sam said, "My God, she's got little titties down near the hip band." Then he asked, breathing it out, "Can I see what they're playing."

Travertine got up and talked to someone standing behind a curtain made of short wood slats. He came back with a small drum. Sam tapped it. The sound was like an apple dropping in a rain barrel. He rested his palms on the rim and looked at the Ahrams. One of them cupped a hand and brought it down. Before I could tell Sam that meant yes, he drummed, the Ahrams played under his drumbeats, and the Jerek's feet moved with Sam's right hand, while his left hand fingers tapped out rain tones.

Molly said, "The dancer's hands go with the flutes." And I looked and it was so. Sam's drumming sped up, slowed, caught the Jerek's pulse. The beat was inhuman. She began wailing high tones that might have been a language, gold fur swaying, darkening with sweat that rolled down from her hip band and chin.

Marianne leaned against me, body tense and swaying across the music, syncopated. I put my arm around her shoulder, then noticed Molly. She was crouched forward, her hands gripping her knees, head cocked slightly, lips slightly parted so I could see that her teeth were on edge.

I bent toward her and whispered, "Do you like it?"

"Do they fuck across species lines?"

"Yes, but mostly males whose females breed in season."

She leaned back and closed her mouth.

"Beers, people?" Travertine asked. "Made from Tibetan barley, in fact." He set down squat blue cans with pop-tops not entirely in the Terran mode.

Finally, Karriaagzh and Black Amber decided to give all the humans the Karst One language operation. I went with them to the same hospital where I'd had my own language operation. In one of the patient rooms, I kissed Marianne good-bye and hugged Molly. Warren was sedated, in an adjoining room with Sam.

"We'll keep him on Prolixin for the present," a Barcon told me. "His brain is warped in the ventricles."

"What can you do?" I asked.

"Re-build and insert pre-programmed sections, if you insist on keeping a consistent identity."

"I do insist," I said and went home alone to my new apartment. Black Amber arrived a moment after I did. She was dressed in Gwyng rig, neck collar with a narrow cloth attached that draped down her chest and over the pouch slit and genitals. Over her shoulder she carried a zippered sling purse. I let her in and went to stand by the window, eyes half focused down at the street, all the *uhyalla*, *vr'ech*, whatever, just ovals and ellipses of heads and shoulders. She asked, "Need help with packing again/so soon? Ready for Gwyng Home."

"I can manage." I packed my most human clothes. She threw my blue officer's uniform on top of that.

In the elevator, she leaned against me, wrinkles brushing my cheek. "Karriaagzh paid for all the language operations. Is your kin threat to me?"

"The Barcons can take care of him."

She parted her lips and put her mouth up against my

ear, then nashed her teeth together to sharpen them. "Don't let him hurt a least one of us (threat)."

We got out in the basement where she'd left her plastic-hulled electric car and drove through the bright night. Karst nights are never darker than dusk—I'd have to get used to that again. She turned into a driveway leading to a gate station by the third river, a giant masonry building all windowless white. She drove the car through the building's double doors and up a ramp into the gate transport. A bear and Gwyng crew fastened the car down, then Black Amber pushed a button and the hatch closed. "We end and begin," she said as the gate transition light went on.

A minute of slight wobbles, two and a half minutes of stillness, and the arrival light flashed. Gwyng Home.

"Priority, so fast," she said, leaning on the hatch door switch. When the seal broke and the hatch swung up, we drove into a building that looked dusty, unused. Six or seven Gwyngs watched, nostrils twitching slightly. Black Amber stopped and one with a tiny plastic ring clipped through the bottom of his left nostril slot came up, talking in a Gwyng language. My computer squealed and babbled, trying to transform his speech by Karst Two rules.

"Show him your identity slip," Black Amber told me. I gave it to him. He stuck it inside a small cube with an eyepiece and examined it. When he took my Federation ID out, a plate of wavy plastic came out of a slot in the cube. "Take the plastic and show it the next time anyone with a nose ring stops you."

I took it and slipped it in my wallet. The Gwyng touched my armpits and babbled again. Black Amber oo'ed slightly.

She was going to take a nymph out of her pouch and then go into heat. I wasn't sure who'd be the one to help with that. "I packed human-style deodorant," I told her.

"I have heat suppressants this time. Cadmium is here/ on Gwyng Home/not near. We will stay in this urban area tonight, join with him (both traveling to meet at third location)." Cadmium was the fourth live alien I'd met, back in Virginia, a serious little cuss.

We got back in the car and drove by stacks of plastic

round apartments, other buildings with smokestacks like factories, heaps of plastic scraps, then other trash mounds of paper and cardboard. Black Amber's was the only private car on the unpaved shell road that ran along beside a rail line. The trees here looked stunted compared to strap-leaf trees on the Karst Gwyng islands, and the air had a metallic tang to it. The landscape didn't look slick the way Karst City, outside the slums, was. "We synthesize food for most of our people, oils, proteins. Herds are for the wealthy."

"What about pouch hosts?"

"Enough wealthy to breed too many Gwyngs," Black Amber said. The computer transformed that with odd flatness.

"What do you get from the Federation?"

"We eat alien hydrocarbons."

I saw two ruins—granite building walls that looked fused. Nuclear war here? "Is this the poorest part?"

She didn't answer, but rolled her huge eyes so far under the bone protrusions protecting them that I saw only a murky yellow brown, her sclera.

"You use plastic for everything?" I asked, touching the hotel room's woven plastic walls. They were stiff, like celluloid. "Then the Gwyng houses on Karst are primitive?"

"Not primitive, extravagant," she said. "This hotel is (almost) poverty, recycled into food after we use it."

The plastic in the living-room ceiling glowed—no switches—and the single bedroom was dark, just one mat. I looked at her and she said, "You, I, and bought sleepers will share that."

"Bought sleepers?"

"No kin here," she said. "Hotel provides fake-home warmth." I saw one tube sofa like an emptied silkworm cocoon, the Gwyng news screen playing moire patterns that they read as language, and an enameled box the size of a refrigerator. Black Amber found an intercom and spoke Gwyng in it, then told me in Karst Two, "I asked for real food."

"You haven't been greeted by anyone."

"My rank is with the Federation, not Gwyngs," she said, pacing on the plastic floor mats, fake tatamis, body lurching side to side over her short bowed legs. She stopped in front of the tube sofa and wiggled into it, crossed her arms and leaned her small chin on them, huge eyes fixed on me, bone protecting them, furred skin over that. Layers and layers—mentally shielded, too. I'd never known she had no rank among the Gwyngs. Or was this something new? Maybe gossip about Wy'um had gotten back to Gwyng Home.

"You don't have *any* status here?"

"Different status," she said, shutting her eyes.

The next morning, I woke up tangled in Gwyng limbs and gently unwound myself from them. Black Amber was up, leaning against a wall with a towel covering her pouch slit and crotch. One of the hired Gwyngs started, nostril slits flared, when he opened his eyes and saw me. He wriggled out from the sleepers, waking the others. "Did you (both) sleep well?" the largest female among them asked in Karst Two as the five of them stood up and stretched.

"We appreciated your warmth," Black Amber said.

"The non-Gwyng was not so sleepy?"

Before I could answer, Black Amber said, "He doesn't usually sleep/like to sleep in heaps. I'm teaching him to be polite."

I said, "I did sleep," but then realized that only Black Amber could understand me.

They all filed out, two naked females and three males with covered crotches. "Is nudity common?"

"Body coverings come from the Old Ones' ruin areas mostly," she answered.

"Were those Old Ones' ruins I saw yesterday?"

"Gwyngs evolved after the Old Ones died/killed selves."

Black Amber spent most of the morning talking Gwyng on the phone, sometimes lying in the tube sofa, sometimes sprawled on the floor. About every ninety minutes, she asked me to heat bottles of her blood drink or melt butter. She sucked up liquids through her oval glass straw—big as two thumbs held side by side—pushed down deep in her throat. I watched her breathe in and out while she sucked. Then she handed me the straw and glass to wash and got back on the phone. No other Gwyngs seemed really eager to adopt a Black Amber child.

Finally, somebody must have said yes. She put the phone down and stretched, webs rippling. She told me, "I (and you) will go North. Our North has many parallels with Linguist's city, *Barkaley*." She got up off the floor and dressed in Gwyng rig, her Sub-Rector's uniform in her shoulder sling.

We drove by tank yards and square gate station buildings. "Gwyngs hire out to prospect gas giants. Gas giant work (hint of danger, but Gwyngs can't/afford to/be intimidated)." I saw three runways, plastic like all the Federation runways I'd seen, but a Gwyng crew was digging up one of the runways in sections.

I asked, "For recycling?"

"Sun and landing pressure breaks down the molecules. Makes yeast/bacterial work easier."

"But you prefer food from animals?"

"All Gwyngs do," she said. I saw hangars, no airport terminal, but realized that Gwyngs arranged ticket purchases by computer and didn't carry much baggage. We went in one of the hangars where a female-sized Gwyng in a stained white shift looked at Black Amber's ID.

Black Amber said to me, "Bump bodies sideways but not too hard. They are kin for the flight/a formality." I touched the three Gwyng crew members very lightly, afraid they'd cringe. One stiffened and squeezed his nostrils shut.

We got on a small jet wide enough for tube sofas and a small aisle. Three cushioned tubes were on the right side, with legroom between them, the aisle on the left, then three tubes on the left and the aisle on the right, forcing the passengers into a serpentine path, and so, by threes, except for the last three tubes in the tail of the plane.

"Get in the tube during takeoff, then sit on it during the

flight until I tell you to get back in," Black Amber told me before she chattered in Gwyng to her con-specifics.

I sweated in the tube—no air-conditioning on Gwyng jets. But I guess the tubes were safer than seat belts in case of a crash.

The jet landed twice—passengers got off and others got on. One baby Gwyng burst into those oily Gwyng tears when he saw me.

Then we landed in chilly fog and went into a private room inside the hangar. Black Amber stripped off her Gwyng clothes and put on her Sub-Rector's uniform. Among other Gwyngs, she looked disguised in long pants and tunic.

"And you wear yours," she told me.

I dressed in the Academy uniform for the first time since I'd left Karst to go to Berkeley. The tunic dangled below my knees like a large hobble. "Do I need the sash?"

"No." She brushed her head fur against the grain, then dabbed a jell on it before brushing it back. Then she used a lighter bristled brush on her face fur, neck, and backs of hands. "Brush your head hair, and the visible hand hair."

I used her brushes, then slid my wallet in my tunic side pocket. Black Amber moistened her fingers against her tongue and smoothed down my eyebrows.

Then we went out; her contacts were waiting—seven Gwyngs in shifts with armholes cut deep for webs, three large Gwyngs, three medium-sized, one of them Cadmium, Black Amber's pouch child. They stood on the sides of their feet, toes curled inward. A big one, a female, said in Karst Two, "You brought a stranger, Black Amber zh'Wringa Vel."

"Only half stranger, zh'Wy'um Eshing. Red Clay is serviceable."

"Your herds have been sterilized?" They switched to a Gwyng language. Cadmium just looked at me, not speaking, his blond-streaked head hair slightly erected. Then zh'Wy'um Eshing, kin of Wy'um's, I guessed, said to me, "Come with us, Red Clay."

We got in a stretch limo that looked like a stolen 1930s Mercedes, but it had no driving wheel, accelerator, just a computer pressure pad. Eshing wrote a pattern on the pad, then said to me, ''We'll get something you can eat.''

''Fried blood cakes would suit him fine, with honey,'' Black Amber said. They talked Gwyng again. Eshing looked at me as though she suspected I understood, but all my computer did was squeal when they talked. Black Amber took a small curved plate out of her sling and laid it over my computer, saying in Karst Two, ''Now it won't record.''

Oh. I leaned back and watched the fog. Then we passed over a cattle guard, no, a blood and pouch beast guard, and drove through pastures, by sudden juniper-shaped trees, to the zh'Wy'um house—stone this time, built on a cliff edge, with the usual wraparound Gwyng porch. The stone was pierced with many long oval windows, no glass in them. We went into a gloomy, great room, cold with splashes of light coming through the stone windows.

''Do you chill easily?'' Eshing said to me.

''Give him some blankets and put plastic over his windows,'' Black Amber said.

''He sleeps alone (mild shock, not wanting to be rude)?'' Eshing asked.

''Alone and he's tired. Show him to his room, now,'' Black Amber said.

''Could I walk around a bit?'' I asked.

''I'll go with him,'' Cadmium said, ''I have the skull computer.''

Black Amber's nostrils slowly squeezed down into narrow slits, then she said, ''Yes (reluctantly).''

We went out of the great room onto the side porch overlooking the ocean, which I could hear below banging into the rocks. ''Late at night, the fog rolls back,'' Cadmium told me. ''In the morning you can see refractions—no, you can't. The sky will be fogless, more clear.''

''Blue sky when clear?''

''As on any planet with the right air. Black Amber's new pouch child—is it Wy'um (possessive).'' He stumbled over that construction; I barely made out the name. He added, ''The History Committee Person.''

''The matings have been open.''

His long finger caught my wrist, one finger on the pulse. "I don't know if you lie or not. Black Amber, is she angry with the bird?"

"I haven't seen her in a couple of months."

"We need to work better together, Black Amber thinks (I'm not sure). Hard with others, brains different. How are you perceiving this?"

"Correctly, I think."

He koo'ed. "Uneasy-don't-be-rude. Come." He began descending stairs cut into the rock. I followed him, afraid he'd lose me in the fog. We went down the cliff and onto a small crescent beach, mostly cobbles. Several large black animals wiggled back into the water.

I wasn't sure what I saw. "Hands?"

"Yes."

"What are they?"

"Maybe the next sapient. The Gwyng name wouldn't register in the computer."

A small diurnal bat flew overhead, peeping, then going into ultrasonics as it flew into the fog. My computer picked up the lower fringes of that. I asked Cadmium, "Do we have to stay outside?"

"Black Amber has business to tend to."

"She always wants the Federation to do more with the present sapient members."

Cadmium said, "Contact dislocates years after initiation. Even 400 years after. Do you want to swim?"

The air temperature was about fifty degrees; I didn't know if the water was warmer or colder. "I'm a subtropical brachiator."

"I'm not." He rolled his shoulders and took off his shift, then began wading out. One of the large seal-like creatures spy-hopped out of the water two feet from him and bugled through an inflatable nose.

He hit it on the shoulder and it dove and brought up strange lentil-sized things, gigantic shelled unicellular animals, parallel to something extinct on Earth. Cadmium passed several to me and bit into one of those lentil creatures himself.

Edible. Like sucking eggs.

* * *

When we went back up the cliff, the other Gwyngs except for Black Amber were on the veranda. They all were watching a barn off about a quarter mile. The doors opened and Black Amber, her Sub-Rector's pants draped over her arm, ambled out. As she got closer, I saw that her wrinkles were slack and her lips pursed in an oo.

Black Amber said, "Pouched. Female (satisfaction)."

Eshing said in Karst Two, "When she is twelve, we'll send her to Karst to become Rector if you can't manage." Black Amber looked stunned, lips parted, not oo'ing now. Eshing continued, "The bird threatens to outlive you."

"Karriaagzh refuses to age or resign," Black Amber said. She came up the veranda stairs and I saw she was damp, sweating. Drying her head with her pants, she asked, "Do you mind if I take suppressants?"

"No alien crudities here," Eshing said. "We'll provide your assistance."

"Cadmium and Red Clay can assist."

Eshing said, "We are not on Karst now, protégé. And this mating will be (I insist) open. Witnessed by us."

Black Amber threw her arms apart. Veins throbbed in her armpit webs. Eshing pinched a web and spoke in Gwyng, but I knew that she'd keep Black Amber from chilling down into an avoidance coma. Her web between Eshing's fingers, Black Amber shuddered, then she said, "Tom, Cadmium, leave."

"Can I go back to Karst?" I didn't want to be alone on this alien planet, but I didn't really want to witness another one of Black Amber's matings—her in blind heat, the males shoving each other, a pre-pubescent or three trying to keep the Gwyngs from damaging the female.

Eshing went eyeball to eyeball, belly to belly, against Black Amber, and talked Gwyng to her, then said, in Karst Two, "We want Red Clay to tell Karst we are still Gwyng here. You will stay close but will not be a visual witness."

Cadmium looked at me and shrugged like, *I'm sorry, I had no input,* a gesture he'd learned from me. Only Black Amber, among the other Gwyngs, could understand a human shrug.

* * *

Cadmium pitched a tent for us near the barn, but we still heard the noises. "We both spoilt by Karst," Cadmium said. He moved stiffly, aroused by the pheromones. "Eshing says Gwyng systems work best for all Gwyngs."

"Black Amber really loves Wy'um."

"That, in us, is perverse/selfishness." He spread his arms as if he, too, wanted to evade this stress with a self-induced chill-coma. "She won't impregnate fast (old)."

"Old?"

"Forty, forty-five planet cycles. Old."

"How many planet cycles do you live, using Karst cycles?"

"Sixty is beyond intelligent life. The body may wiggle."

"Oh. Oh."

She didn't settle for two weeks.

Cadmium and I went to the post-heat party. Black Amber was an ungracious hostess until Eshing took her outside. We pretended not to notice the screams.

On the flight down to the space-gate city, Black Amber stayed in her tube sofa, eyes tightly closed, beads of oil leaking out from between her eyelids. Other Gwyngs would glance by the tube, but their eyes never stopped, never really looked at her.

She opened her eyes when we landed and moaned as she pulled herself out of the tube. We walked to her car. She was stiff, bruised. "Should I drive?" I asked.

"Yes," she said and we went back to the plastic-walled hotel. Gwyngs were dismantling sections of it, quietly, with lasers, loading the pieces on trucks.

Black Amber ordered new clothes and a sleeping group before she went into the sleeping room. I heard water running and a hair drier. When she came out, she sat down on the floor beside me, her head hair still damp, and asked, "Do you know more about me now than you want?"

"I thought once first contact was over, then . . ."

"First contact is the beginning of 'then.' We have artificial food. More can live (more badly)."

"What do we do now?" I asked.

"We go back to Karst/bird terrors/bird idiocy."

Black Amber didn't say much more as Cadmium and I rode with her to the Gwyng planet gate facility. The Gwyngs who bolted her car down in the transport pod didn't speak to us either, although her transition still got priority, fast handling through the gates. A bear crew, no Gwyngs among them, unbolted the car when we arrived at Karst. Black Amber sighed and drove out on Karst, I asked, "Can I see Marianne now?"

"Not yet. Wait until she isn't embarrassed by her Karst-language ability." We didn't go into town. Amber drove on instead up the coast to her beach house through her herds of pouch beasts with older Gwyng children playing beside them.

"The children aren't yours."

"Nymphs are currency (Barcons don't understand)." She drove up to her woven plank house on stilts. A small blue electric car the size of a golf cart but completely enclosed was parked under the house.

We went in. Rhyodolite, her oldest pouch kin, sat in her great room, looking tragic, wrinkles sagging, oily eyes, nostril slits faintly rippling. I remembered, though, that he could be a tease. Cadmium's blond-streaked body fur rippled. Rhyodolite, tiny, still scarred from his third and last shape-shift mission two years ago, asked, "Gwyng-Home Gwyngs disapprove of you? My first contacts disapproved of me/of Federation. Hurt feeling with xenophobia. Lost trade shares/vast fear for no profit."

She opened her arms and bent forward slightly, they rushed awkwardly to her and cuddled against her sides, all three Gwyngs swaying together.

"But I agree with Gwyng Home (in policy issues)," Black Amber said. "They don't understand/xenocentric."

"But now Red Clay has new woman for us to tease," Rhyodolite said, his lips pursed so tight they dragged all his wrinkles forward. "Red Clay, relieve pain of scornful aliens. Here, bad xenophobe species name in Karst for slow minds." He handed me a piece of paper: SHARWAN, FIRST CONTACT FAILURE, NON-CONTRACTING SPECIES. POSSIBLE DANGER. SEE THE INSTITUTE OF CONTROL FILE 5897-A.

= 6 =

Some Kind Of Alien Wedding

The phone buzzed the next morning while the creatures at Black Amber's house were all sleeping tangled up together. At least, the Gwyngs were sleeping. Rhyodolite answered in Karst Two, then handed it to me. "The master bird, ready to send thousands to their deaths in hysterical first contacts, calls you."

"Come on, Rhyodolite, he'll hear you." I took the phone and adjusted it to fit human ears, then switched off the hold function. "Red Clay here."

Black Amber's eyes slowly opened. Karriaagzh said, "I sent a car for you, Tom."

"Thank you, sir," I said. He made a throat-clearing noise, deep noise with those hollow bones vibrating behind it and hung up.

Black Amber slid away from Cadmium and found her plastic plate that fitted over skull computers. She stuck a fine wire into it, said, "Put back standard functions," and laid it behind my ear.

I dressed in my officer/officiator's uniform, wishing I'd washed it after we left the strange Gwyng house on the cliffs. But I hadn't, so it'd stink of Gwyng arguments. Karriaagzh had no sense of smell, but his Barcons would know.

The car, driven by a Barcon, not a bear as was more usual, came up to Black Amber's ten minutes after Karriaagzh hung up. I slid on my black shoes. Cadmium bent down to close the straps. "Don't make Karriaagzh wait," Black Amber said. "He wants immediate contact with the entire universe."

Rhyodolite said, "Tell him the Shangwarn refused/not my fault (possible?/doubt/nervous of being blamed)."

Sharwan, he meant. Rhyodolite had no ear for what to him were nonsense sounds.

The Barcon opened the rear door from the driver's seat and said, "Your people are doing well. Now at Rector's People Chalk 137 and Agate 120. Jereks, very solid couple."

I said, "I haven't met them." Jereks—the weasels who worked so much for the spy Institute of Analytics and Tactics. Aliens with eyelids shiny and black as their eyes so you could hardly tell when they blinked. Carbon-jet, the Jerek spy who bit me in the leg when he was arrested by the people we'd just admitted to the Federation—he didn't have the nerve to bite anyone more directly responsible. "Can't they go to a Rector's People I know better, a species . . . ?" I couldn't tell him I didn't like Jereks. I had to like most sapient species—why couldn't I have one species that I didn't like, didn't have to get along with? Why not a little xenophobia after sympathizing with so strange a creature as Black Amber?

"No, you need to be tamed to Jereks."

"What about Gwyng Rector's People?"

"You have a Gwyng sponsor." Rigid, inflexible, remote—typical Barcon, not S'um, who'd calmed Sam Turner by playing harpsichord duets with him.

"What does Karriaagzh want to talk to me about?"

"About Yauntra, about Gwyng Home."

I leaned back against the seat cushions and stared at the rolling coastal hills, the glints of ocean beyond them. We crossed the northernmost river that fed into Karst Bay and were suddenly in the city near the water landing docks. The Barcon drove though the slums as if they didn't matter. I thought I saw Yangchenla's oldest uncle, selling buttered and salted tea from a pushcart.

Then we turned inland and I saw the Academy walls

and towers, and felt an odd rush of relief, at a somatic level.

"You do stink of Gwyng," the Barcon said as he let me out in front of the Rector's office.

I walked inside and took an elevator to Karriaagzh's floor. Almost no one was in the building—I remembered that it was spring mating season here—behind Earth's seasons. I went through the huge Karriaagzh-sized doors into the outer office.

"Come in," Karriaagzh called. I did; he sat behind his boomerang-shaped desk. On the desk, beside his terminal, a teapot suddenly steamed, went to full boil, then simmered down. As I looked at it, he said, "From Yauntra." He dropped in some loose herbal tea, turned the pot off, and brought out a University of California Berkeley cup for me and his spouted bird cup. "From Alex."

"Thank him for me," I said.

"He likes humans very much."

"He got us in trouble with the FBI."

Karriaagzh stared at me. One hand scribbled on his keypad. Then he looked at his computer screen. "Federal Bureau of Investigation," he said in English before translating that to Karst equivalent terms. "Ah, Alex. He has interesting ideas. If only people could gradually become accustomed to the idea of the intelligent other."

"I don't think humans can half believe intelligent other sapients share the universe with them. Should Alex go up to the FBI and say, 'Maybe I'm an extraterrestrial'? "

"Let's not talk about this right now," he said. Karriaagzh slid his transparent inner eyelids vertically over his yellow eyes, dimming them. I watched the muscles around his eyes bunch, relax, bunch up again, until he saw me watching and raised his crest. He wrote on his pad again and the terminal display changed. "The Barcons said you have traces of thumb gland odor on your body. Gwyng were angry around you."

"Not enough to wipe the juice on me."

"But enough to leak slightly." Feathers around his beak twitched and his inner eyelids relaxed. "Black Amber— can she be separated from Gwyng Home policy?"

"She can't do enough for them." Karriaagzh's beak gaped slightly and I regretted saying that much. "Gwyng Home seems like a poor planet."

"Overpopulated," Karriaagzh said. "They would starve if not for gas giant industries, which the Federation made possible."

"She thinks we need to work more with present Federation members, not send out additional observation teams. Gwyng Home thinks she's been morally corrupted by alien contact, but they don't disagree with her politics."

"Observation teams don't speed up on-planet technological development." Karriaagzh shielded his eyes again with the transparent lids. "We didn't have an observation station at one system and the species spread into another planetary system. Rhyodolite was on the team that tried to contact them. Not effective. Not convincing."

"He said there were problems."

"If we'd contacted the Sharwan just before they developed gate technology, they might have been friendlier." He slid his nictitating membranes back. "We need to expand contacts, now, before the Sharwan form their own Federation."

I went to Marianne at the Jerek Rector's People's place, in the north by the polar sea. Big polar sea, so the place wasn't freezing all the time, just in the winter. It was early summer now and just froze on occasional nights.

But Chalk and Agate's house looked just like Tesseract's—sprawling, lots of porches and wings—only they'd backed the main wing up against a mountain. My little plane landed on a runway near the swimming pool placed on the same side of the house as Tesseract's.

I climbed out of the plane and looked into two Jerek faces. Their noses were up, so I wasn't getting threat-face, but they were otherwise unreadable. Chalk was the male—he had slightly lighter fur than Agate.

I asked them, "How are they?"

Chalk said, "Marianne is well beyond the rudiments."

"Warren?"

Chalk looked at Agate, then answered again, "He heard about other humans. We're arranging a meeting. If he joins them, he'll still have a city pass."

"With the Tibetans?"

"Yes, the Barcons checked his sperm and found it unaffected by his brain malformations, so he has a duplication breeding permit. Is this too upsetting?"

"I want Warren to be happy." I didn't want to break his balls by switching from younger brother to boss, either.

All my twentieth century human colleagues came out now as if signaled. They wore grey tunics down below the knees except for Marianne who wore white with a green stripe across the shoulders at clavicle level—pre-Linguistics. Then Warren shuffled out, in jeans and a plaid wool shirt, his feet in felt slippers.

"The clothes are boring," Molly said.

"They're a disguise," I told her. "Do you have other learners here?" I asked Chalk.

"We don't do this generally," Agate said, lowering her nose slightly. No, they were Rector's People, not near-poor language-trainers.

"But you've all learned Karst One?"

Warren said, "Thought I'd really gone crazy. Language worse than a bad drug."

"I enjoyed it," I said. Marianne and Molly looked at each other.

"They cut off my music," Sam said, "English and my music. But it came back. Weird language, this one."

"So many meanings," Marianne said, looking at me as though I was strange to her now.

"Meanings driving me . . . ." Warren began.

"Don't say it, Warren," Sam said. "Remember the Barcons."

Warren shuddered and I wondered what happened in the hospital. "We're refugees . . . stinks," he said.

"Can we move back to the apartment?" I asked.

"When Sam learns his subjunctives better," Chalk said. "Come in. The house is Rector's People, like Tesseract's, but we have Jerek quarters below."

We were housed in the restriction wing. Sam raised one eyebrow—that frustrating gesture I couldn't master—as we passed armored doors now pulled back in their pockets. I said, "Do you have other people here now?"

"Travertine and our daughter, Uteece, Academy name Lisanmarl. We have another child, a son, but he's studying now, multi-Institute."

Sam said, "Lisanmarl's teaching me sarai drums."

I felt odd, as though the four new humans had aged while I hadn't, and vaguely threatened. They were getting along with Jereks. Had they explained all the social connotations of *Virginia high school dropout ex-con* to Chalk and Agate, I wondered to myself.

Marianne hugged me, disconcerting me by the very attempt to reassure me. I kissed her and rubbed my cheek against hers, then saw Warren staring at us, his eyelids swollen, bottom lip curled down. He saw me looking and his scalp flushed. *Oh, Warren, so sorry there's no woman for you after all that hospital jail.* Probably he should go to the Tibetans, I thought. If he ate take-out Cambodian in Richmond, maybe he'd like buttered tea.

The Jereks put me in a room with Marianne, but gave us two beds and something like a velvet-padded Henry Moore sculpture: holes, tunnels, curves, and protuberances. Warren followed us to the door.

When I touched the velvet-padded thing, Warren said, "For sexual stunts." I flushed. Marianne pretended not to hear. He said, "I'll leave you now."

When he closed the door on us, Marianne said, "I'm thinking about an old beat era poem, 'Marriage.' We're being mated like cattle."

"No," I said, "like geese," looking for a place to hang my clothes, wishing I'd bought more jeans while I had the chance.

"*Damn, Tom,*" she began in English, "the term 'officially mated' has bioterminological roots." She saw me fumbling with my clothes and said, "Here, they put a closet in for us. Molly and Sam share the other half." She pulled a wall section back into a door pocket.

I remembered that Yangchenla practically spit at me

when the Barcons tried to put us in a room with too sexual a bed. "I could sleep in Warren's room."

"No, there are two beds. And it's not like we're virgins." She smiled.

"But it's different now. Knowing Karst One is like having a new mind, isn't it?"

" 'Esperanto' that really works," she said.

"I'm tired." I fell back across the bed with my shoes on and she knelt by the bed and slipped them off, then began massaging the soles of my feet. "This one's for kidneys," she said, mashing down on the ball of my foot.

I looked down at my toes. "For kidneys?"

"Reflexology. Berkeley weirdness. And this is for the bladder."

"Speaking of which."

"Bathroom's down the hall," she said. "It's huge and very weird.

"Dust showers, cloacal slits, huge tubs, tiny hand bowls, urinals, squat toilets, sitting toilets."

"You've seen it?"

"There are reliever-cleaners like that all over Karst."

"Poor old jaded Tom." She lifted my left foot and tickled around the base of my big toe.

"What's that for?"

"For fun. Let's get in the big tub together."

"I am exhausted."

She took both my feet and shook me. "You're tense."

"Okay, let's get in the tub, but I don't want to try anything on the velvet sexual jungle gym." I got up and went to get my robe from the closet.

As we left our room, I saw Warren leaning against his room's door frame, smoking a cigarette, scowling. He watched us pass down the hall without saying anything. Marianne and I didn't speak to him either.

When we got into the bathroom, we locked the tub cubicle behind us. Marianne asked, "You're worried about Warren?" She dialed hot water and opened the tap.

"About lots of things. About how contact with different sapients changes us, more than culture shock, brain pathways shock."

"But we can all understand Karst One." She stripped, her legs paler now than when she rode bide every day, her breasts and hips fuller. So pretty it hurts—that's what Warren used to say.

I took off my clothes and laid them down over the robe. "Not all understand Karst One. The Gwyngs and some others can't. And the Karst languages were formulated to make contact seem easier."

"Sapir was wrong, then." She sank into the water up to her chin. I stepped in and our legs tangled.

"Sapir?" The name seemed vaguely familiar.

"Man who thought language formed perceptions. Karst languages are an example of the soft Sapir-Whorf Hypothesis."

"But not every species *can* learn a Karst language. The ones who can't aren't considered fully sapient. Maybe that's not right."

"Warren's having trouble, but I think he's fighting the language." She pulled her legs back.

"He's learning a language that said he was stupid before."

"Tom, the language expands things. Contact with other sapients—that makes life fuller, doesn't it?"

"They're all what we wanted animals to be when we were kids. Tesseract, my first Rector's Man, said the Federation was like a giant zoo without keepers."

She said, "We're all one another's keepers."

"Yeah, it can be really brutal."

"Your life was so innocent before?"

"No, that's why I make a good refugee. But yours was."

"Officiator Red Clay, I was a 'Berkeley brat.' "

"But you get involved with other sapients, then find out they die at fifty or live to 200, or get set up and killed to make someone else look bad. Some go crazy."

"Tom, I met Alex. I wasn't an idealist." She climbed out of the water and wrapped herself in a bast fiber sheet. "Get a towel, come back to the room; I'll give you a massage."

Warren had shut his door. Sam and Molly were giggling

behind theirs. I remembered that this wing of a Rector's People house was bugged.

Back in our room, Reeann spread a mat on the floor and said, "Lie down on it and relax."

"Naked?"

"Yes, naked. I've seen your cock before. Massage, really, just a massage."

I started to say I was a massage virgin, but I remembered the Barcons rubbing down my legs, Rhyodolite and Karriaagzh, on different occasions, massaging my shoulders and back. "I've never been massaged by a human before."

"California deep body massage. Tell me if I'm better than an *ech*." She poured oil on her hands and then dug her thumbs in on either side of my spine, almost fiercely, leaning her weight into me.

"I want a ceremony," she almost chanted. "Wedding ceremony. Human wedding ceremony."

Ceremony, yes, but it wasn't what I'd have called a wedding back in Virginia. Cadmium and Rhyodolite took me away to their Gwyng officers' quarters while the others prepared for the wedding at the Jerek Rector's People's.

Rhyodolite didn't say much to me during my stay, just oo'ed when he looked at me. Once he said, "Perverse, placental, fake pair-bonding (and human snob)."

Cadmium brought me back to the Jerek house for the wedding. As I came walking from the airfield to the house, I saw Sam and the girl Jerek Lisanmarl on the porch. Both knelt, drums between their knees, and shook big wooden tubes Sam rigged up and called African rainmakers that sounded like they ought to go with a lava lamp and LSD. They sat on either side of the door, she in Jerek leathers with her little breasts beginning to show on her lower abdomen, Sam in freshly tie-dyed tunic and pants. As I came up, they began to play alien fertility music. Does it matter whether it was human or non-human? The music was alien to me. The rainmakers made sounds like sand brushing tight wires while they tapped the drumskins with their fingertips, squeezing the drums between their knees to change the tones. Lisanmarl whistled from time to time, brushing her nose, then playing more.

Another plane landed. Karriaagzh got out awkwardly, then stalked up in his gold-threaded Rector's uniform, only his head feathers showing. Sam stopped playing and just looked up and down at the yellow eyes, the scaled forearms, the odd booted feet.

"Is Black Amber here yet?" he asked Sam.

Sam said, "No," and began playing again.

"Good, I want to talk to Marianne Schweigman."

"She's in back, dressing," Lisanmarl said, crinkling her facial skin.

Karriaagzh went in. I was about to follow him, but Sam said, "Bad luck to see the bride before the wedding."

"What does he want to see her about?"

Sam played and shrugged. Warren came out with a bottle of raw, unaged alcohol, and said, "Here, grooms need this." He drank first himself and handed me the bottle.

"Sure it's not rubbing alcohol."

"No, I distilled it from the beer."

"Warren?" I drank a slug and felt it etch out my esophagus and sit in my stomach like a small fireball. My eyes watered. "Warren."

"Good, huh," Warren said, taking the bottle back.

"I don't want to be drunk." The Karst word for that commented medically on the brain physiology involved.

"One swallow." He took another pull on it.

"Warren, stop."

"Shit, Tom, it's a wedding," he said in English. A Barcon that I didn't know was at the Jerek house popped its head out the door and glared at Warren.

We heard another plane coming in. It looked bigger than the others. Cadmium said, "I hope Rhyodolite didn't . . . (embarrassment if he did—I wish to disassociate)."

The plane landed and I heard Tibetan. Seven Tibetans got out. As they approached, I recognized Yangchenla's voice. Who would have invited them? Rhyodolite. Hips moving more than seemed biomechanically necessary, Yangchenla strolled across the yard in a new bottle green dress like the one she'd worn when we first were lovers, with six of her Tibetan kin in multi-colored Karst City clothes following her. She stopped about twenty feet from me, then came some closer. A wind fanned the dress back against her legs.

"Why did you come?"

"I heard. Will you throw me out?"

"Yangchenla, I don't want to disturb the occasion."

"I wanted to see what happened to humans over the past 500 years." Then she saw Sam drumming and frowned. "He's not a Barcon?"

"No, he's human like us, just even darker skinned."

"Perhaps he'll give me a child." She smiled at me.

"He's mated officially."

"I don't know what that has to do with children."

"Who told you about my wedding?"

"A Gwyng, through signs." She wiggled her hands. "We Free Traders can communicate even if we don't have computers for skull bones."

Damn Rhyodolite, he probably thought it was funny.

Warren, sweating drunk now, came out and overheard more of this than I'd wanted. "I'd give you a child," he said in Karst One, offering her the liquor.

She sniffed at it and said, "Where did you get this?"

"I made it."

In Tibetan, she said something about this skill being useful, and her kin laughed. One of the younger uncles came up to Warren and asked, "You only let women drink with you?"

"*Hell*, no." Warren offered him the bottle. "You from *Earth*?"

"From Karst City." Despite some murmuring from one of Yangchenla's grandmothers, the young uncle drank after he answered. He squeezed his eyes shut tight and pursed his lips.

"The original stock is Tibetan," I said.

"Next war," Warren said, breaking his sentence with a small swig and handing the bottle back to the uncle, "is going to be over Tibet."

Chenla's grandmother said, "Trung, stop it."

"My brother had me stolen from *Richmond*. Brought

me here with a bunch of freaks.'' Warren had acquired an amazing amount of Karst slang, probably from the Jerek adolescent, and sounded like himself even in Karst One.

The Barcon finally came out and took the bottle away from Warren. My brother looked as if he'd tried hitting a Barcon earlier and still wanted to try again regardless, but then he shrugged and said, ''He's going to refill it.''

Trung laughed and embraced Warren while Chenla's grandmother clapped in irritation. Yangchenla asked, ''Does the bride need help?''

''Karriaagzh is talking to her.''

The other Tibetans went inside when Agate called to them, all except for Chenla, who said, ''Everyone seems so interested in the new humans.'' She smiled for half a second, then walked up to Sam and stood by him, listening to the Jerek/Human music.

Another plane landed then—Black Amber and Rhyodolite, who came running up in that lurching from stumble to stumble Gwyng way with his lips pursed. Oo, oo, oo, what a joke to tell Yangchenla about my wedding. Cadmium looked embarrassed. Yangchenla locked eyes with Rhyodolite and went inside the Jereks' house.

Rhyodolite brushed his side against my arms and said, ''Yangchooshao didn't bite new woman?''

''I didn't appreciate your telling her.''

''Me? I didn't make a sound.''

''I understand.''

''Humans need to socialize together, like post-heat party. You all have mated.''

Yangchenla came out of the house with a dish of spiced nuchi and black Terran beans, a full protein for us Terran types even if nuchi evolved under completely different conditions. Picasso-grain, like too large buckwheat kernels with gaudy colors on them.

I went inside. The Tibetans didn't get too close, but made their eyes even beadier and the grooves in their faces deeper. Warren and Trung were squatting in the corner, making liquor talk.

Black Amber looked at me from a doorway of a guest

wing. Chalk and Agate cupped their hands and brought them down, then the Gwyngs and the Jereks grabbed me and wrestled me outside, down the stairs, koo'ing and whistling, and dumped me in the now heated pool. Chalk and Agate stripped off their uniforms and came in with me—pulling my clothes off and washing me with bristle-brushes while Rhyodolite and Cadmium splashed at us. Black Amber backed well away. Chalk chanted in Jerek as he and Agate helped me out and dried me.

Then, while I was still naked and beginning to freeze, the Gwyngs ran off back into the house. Travertine and three other olive birds came out waving brass pans full of smoking incense. They weaved around me once, hocks lifted high, feathers roused, beaks parted, tongues dangling, then went back into the house.

Chalk whistled softly, then said, "Now that you're washed and smoked, dress and come in."

Black Amber and the other Gwyngs stood touching sides to each other, arms intertwined, looking at the door leading deeper into the house. I heard Karriaagzh's voice, then Marianne's saying, "Are we ready yet?"

Sam and Lisanmarl began playing "Here Comes the Bride" on human flutes.

Karriaagzh came out carrying a carved wood sound-reflecting shell. He stood it against the wall. When he turned around, it flared behind his head. Marianne, in a white silk dress that flounced around her calves, followed behind him. Black Amber clenched her feet, then stared at Karriaagzh until he covered his eyes with his nictitating membranes. The muscle lumped between her jawbones bounced as she looked away.

"We are here today," Karriaagzh began, his harsh voice ringing off the sounding board, "to celebrate not just a human mating pair, but the start of a relationship built of mind as well as sexuality."

Black Amber, Cadmium, and Rhyodolite immediately turned to look at me as though I had told Karriaagzh to say this. Mind, he dragged his favorite paradigm for the universe into my wedding.

Karriaagzh flared his crest a tiny bit and said, "Tom, step forward and join hands with Marianne."

I did. Mine were sweating; hers were cool.

"Do you, Tom Easley, agree to cherish your companion for as long as there is love in your relationship?"

I said, "I do," stunned that my vows weren't for life.

"And do you, Marianne Schweigman, agree to cherish Tom for as long as you love him?"

"I do."

"And do you both swear to maintain this relationship as long as necessary to benefit your mutual offspring?"

"We do."

"I pronounce you an officially bonded pair."

I kissed Marianne and whispered, partly in English "When Earth is part of the Federation, we can have a *real church wedding*."

"This is a real wedding," she replied, all in English. "What's the point of 'til death do us part when half the marriages break up?" Then she nipped my earlobe almost to bleeding.

Everyone pelted us with rice, dried up bits of umbilical cords, and shed milk teeth.

"Throw them in the pool," Rhyodolite shrieked, waving a stuffed brood beast tail over his head.

Two hours later, after we cleaned up, I glanced at a security screen and saw Warren walking to the Tibetans' plane. "Warren, wait, don't." I ran out onto the porch.

One of the Barcons came out after me and said, "We'll continue to help him."

Warren turned, looking old and hideously hungover, bloated, the sharp cheek and jawbone angles blurred, but not padded with healthy flesh. "Tom, give it up."

"We'll track him down and inject him with Prolixin every two weeks," the Barcon said.

Trung took Warren's shoulder and said to me, "He needs us more than he needs *vr'ech*." Yangchenla just watched, dressed now in a knee-length Karst City tunic top, but with her legs bare, as though she'd learned more about human dressing from Molly and Marianne. She smiled, faintly, her eyes slitted even more than with the epicanthic fold.

"He'll drink himself to death," I said to the Barcon.

"We could do a personality rebuild, but you want identity continuity. That identity?"

Brainwipe—the body lives, the person dies. "Warren, be careful." I ached. "*Jesus*, Warren, I'm sorry."

"I'll still be in the city. They gave me a permit. Tom, I want to be around people. My kind. I . . ."

The Barcon whispered in my ear, "He had some trouble when we did the language operations—we had to isolate him for four days. Let him go."

"Warren, you know you're always welcome at my house."

Yangchenla said, "Come on, Warren, let's go."

Chalk came to the door and said, "Tom, come in with me. Karriaagzh and Black Amber quarrel for Marianne."

I went rigid, wedging myself in the doorway, until Warren disappeared into the plane, then I let Chalk pull me back into the house. We went into the second wing where I heard Karriaagzh say, "But she herself put Tom in danger."

"What?" I asked. Marianne lay curled up on a cushion, her head propped up on her hand, elbow on the cushion, staring out between Black Amber and Karriaagzh.

"Translate (correctly) for me, Red Clay," Black Amber said. Her feet were writhing, her arms flicked out once to help her balance. "Tell your female that your people are xenophobes, that we're now facing another xenophobic group."

I translated for Marianne. She said to me, "Does she understand what I say?"

"Her skull computer transforms our sequential signal to something hologramistic, only done in sound, like sonar."

"Black Amber, Karriaagzh, when you quarrel, you make me very nervous," Marianne said. "Black Amber, you're afraid of Karriaagzh."

Black Amber hissed. Karriaagzh raised his face feathers, but not his crest. "The fear can be managed, Black Amber," he told her in Karst Two.

Black Amber crouched and turned toward him, eyes gone blank, non-sapient. Marianne said, "Black Amber, no. Karriaagzh, you both ought to separate now."

Karriaagzh pulled his feathers tight, the membrane slid out slightly over his eyes, looking like a thick tear in each corner.

"I'm still getting used to *vr'ech*. Karriaagzh, don't be as bad as she is," Marianne said.

"*Uhyalla*," Karriaagzh said, muscles bunching around the eyes to pull the membrane back. His feathers jerked stiffly.

Black Amber looked down at her hands, fingers curled, sinews rigid, and said, "Red Clay, Red Clay, so difficult." She spread her arms and pulsed blood through the webs, then slowly began to topple over. I ran up and caught her, the webs hot and sweaty against my arms, her head dangling.

Karriaagzh hopped over, a gait I'd never seen him use before—terrible gait in these circumstances—lowered his body and took Black Amber's left web between his beak mandibles, crouching. He tightened slowly, his eyes closed, stiff quills erected over his rigid brows.

Black Amber opened her eyes and shrieked. He dropped her web and bounded backward, arms thrown out for balance. I tried to hold her as she began thrashing, but ended up falling with her to the floor.

"You stupid whore," Karriaagzh said to her. "With Wy'um."

Black Amber said, "The last *was* open. Contact with your crippled brains contaminates, perverts." She rolled to her back and touched her left web with fingers that jerked back. She wouldn't look at Karriaagzh.

Marianne said, "I can't stand this. Get out, both of you."

"They're both high Federation officials," I said.

"If I can't get them to go away now when they're upsetting me on my wedding day, this Federation is a farce."

Karriaagzh said, softly, "She would have damaged her embryo with a coma now."

"They'll all die from now on," Black Amber said. She closed her eyes and hugged herself, webs stretched over her chest, head thrashing. "Translate that. She's female."

"I'm leaving," Karriaagzh said. "Tell Black Amber I am willing to desensitize her." Karriaagzh walked out of the room, wiping his beak.

"Shit," Marianne said. "Shit. Black Amber, you had better get desensitized if you've got such a problem with him."

Black Amber's body quivered, then she tried to get up, floundering. "Cold," she said. I turned around and saw Chalk and Agate watching.

"We'll bring hot water and a vasoconstrictor skin rub," Agate said. "So she can't trade off her nymphs anymore?"

"It's more than web-creeping predator with him. He pursued me with his policies," Black Amber said.

"You like snakes, spiders?" I asked Marianne.

"I get startled weirdly when I see a snake suddenly."

"Yes," Black Amber said, "Karriaagzh is my snake."

"For her, Karriaagzh represents a primordial threat, the way snakes threaten monkeys. We react to fingernails on blackboards—primitive monkey alarms . . ." I felt dizzy myself and went over to a cushion by Marianne. Chalk came up and gently stroked me across the eyebrows with his thumbs. In English, I said, *"I feel caught between Black Amber and Karriaagzh."*

"Terrific," Marianne replied. Chalk touched her hand gently. She just blinked, moved her hand up on her lap.

I continued in English, *"Just because they've got more technology, you expected them to be morally superior?"*

Agate came back with the hot water and skin rub, heating Black Amber's body core with a warm drink, closing the peripheral veins to send the blood back to the major organs.

Marianne watched Agate, then asked me, *"The hippies were right then? Technology fucks you up?"*

Chalk said, "If you continue to speak in that language, I will call Travertine to translate."

I didn't think a bird in here would be a good idea, so I spoke in Karst. "Some species have been technological longer that we've been. But technology just makes life easier, not perfect."

"Brings us in contact with much complexity," Agate said, sitting by Black Amber, rubbing the Gwyng's nippleless chest. "Most of us find a few species to work with, leave the other ninety alone. None of us understands all of one another."

Black Amber sat up. She said, "Nothing can make me desensitive with that one."

"You need to walk around," Chalk said. "You could begin desensitizing with Travertine."

"Not today," Black Amber said as Agate and Chalk, both much smaller and lighter than she, helped her to her feet.

"Oh, Tom, what did she say?" Marianne asked when Black Amber and the Jereks had left the room.

"She wouldn't work with Karriaagzh on desensitizing her aversion to birds."

"I've already figured out that Black Amber doesn't work with Karriaagzh period. Tom, Karriaagzh said he could teach me Karst Two. After my skull computer is installed."

But Black Amber wanted my humans with her.

The next morning, while Marianne still slept, I walked into an open elevator with speakers softly playing Brahms. If I shouldn't be here, the machine won't work, I decided as I pressed the down button.

But the door slid up, the compartment sank, then the door slid down again. I stepped out into a tunnel lit with glow tubes, some twisted and dropped on the rough stone underfoot, others hung in wire baskets. A spring ran down between black stones, faint light glittering on its ripples. Down the hall, I heard water dropping, echoing against stone, then something hollow and metallic hit stone, a tube chime down in the darkness that pivoted forward when water trickling into it filled it beyond the balance point. Empty, it pivoted back, hit the stone, and caught more water.

"Agate, Chalk?" I began to see doorways off either side of the tunnel and stone Jerek figures in a niche at the end of it.

"Tom, you came down," Chalk said from the first room.

Agate added, "He's curious. That's a human trait, isn't it, Tom?"

"Agate? Did you want to be alone?"

"Come satisfy your curiosity. You're cold," Chalk said. He was right. The water in the hall was nearly ice-cold. I slipped off one of the stepping stones.

The three of them, the parents and the young daughter were playing silver flute-like instruments blown like bottles, not held transversely like human flutes. They put the flutes back under their noses, mouthpieces pressed against the shark-like lower jaws and played. Lisanmarl lowered her flute and said, "I wish I was a Gwyng or a Barcon."

Before I could ask why, Agate said, "Don't." I didn't know whether she meant that I shouldn't ask or that the young Jerek shouldn't elaborate.

"Maybe . . ." Lisanmarl began. She picked up her flute and blew out discordant notes.

"I'll leave," I said.

"Make them leave me alone," Lisanmarl said. "I don't want to be spayed now."

"I don't understand," I said, beginning to move back.

"Lisanmarl is sterile," Chalk said. "Don't tempt her. Watch your brother around her, and Sam."

"I'm sorry I came down here if . . ."

"She's maturing fast. You needed to be told. Steriles are always in low-grade estrus. Please don't take advantage of her. We know you're not happy with Jereks, but please."

"Human women stay in low-grade estrus, too," Lisanmarl said, "so he won't want me." Her black facial skin began to gleam in the cold light.

Chalk said, "We invited you down with human music

and pheromones. Maybe you think Jereks can be too oblique. Here's your pheromone disrupter."

Lisanmarl played human music at them. I felt very awkward and slightly angry. "I'm sorry," I said again. "Should I lock the elevator when I leave?"

Chalk and Agate looked up with blank Jerek faces, naked skin over their noses wrinkled. "We don't like blocked exits."

"Blocked exits," Lisanmarl said, "remind my parents of avalanches, but I was born on Karst."

"Being born on Karst explains it," Marianne said when I told her about my walking down a pheromone line to the Jerek tunnel. "Lisanmarl knows other species do things differently."

"But what does she want? Sam?"

"She's come on to him already. He said he didn't want a furry girl with tits below her navel, but could Molly and I tell him how to get out of it gracefully? Tell her we permanently pair-bonded like Barcons, we said. Molly's not sure he didn't sleep with her."

"Lisanmarl believes that?"

"Precisely what's going on? Permanent heat?"

"Same human women, they said, always in low-grade estrus."

Marianne laughed, then asked, "Why spay her?"

"I don't know."

One of the house Barcons told Marianne that Lisanmarl could die of pernicious anemia in ten to fifteen years if she wasn't spayed. Estrogen in heat quantities washes out the hemoglobin's iron. Some Jerek steriles wait until the first effects show. Chalk and Agate didn't want to let their daughter take a chance, or live the sterile life.

Chalk came up to me a day later and said, "We thought you ought to know why we're tense now. We may resign as Rector's People because of this."

"Don't," I told them. "I had no idea you were upset. I thought you were like the first Jerek I met."

"That's because you think all Jereks are tense."

"No, it's because I was preoccupied with my brother."

Chalk laid his hand on my forearm and said, "A problem's shape depends on species, but we all have troubles enough." He raised himself on the balls of his feet and rubbed his chin against my clavical.

"Will I stay here while Marianne has the skull computer installed?"

"No, you have an assignment. Black Amber sent word. Take your bicycle—they installed a device for it in the space station gym."

= 7 =

Crocs and Pretty People

Being an officer/officiator in the Federation, I would have duties. And so, having just registered us as a mated pair, the Federation separated Marianne and me. During the last four years, I'd spent a total of seven months on Watch Species 467 Station monitoring radio and video signals from the Watch Species 467 planet, learning one of their languages. Now space-time around that planet writhed— they'd done gate experiments—so ten of us who'd learned at least one of their languages came to wait to see if Watch Species 467 would develop space gate technology during this watch.

In the langauge I'd learned, Wreng was one of Watch Species 467; I'Wreng meant two; Wrengin, the many; Wrengee, the people. They looked more reptilian than any creature I'd seen before. The structure of their solar system, few comets, coolish sun, should have produced birds. But, while their sun was a bit distant, the planet atmosphere was a bit high in carbon dioxide. So, sparse feathers, scales on the hands. No beaks, either. They'd never been runners. We'd seen their porn movies, so we had a good idea of what they looked like—feathered heads and leathery bodies, dotted with saucer-sized erectible scales some of them pierced and hung gold rings on.

A shiny black couple, Argon IX and Argon X who I'd worked with before, opened my transport and asked in English, "Did you bring your new wife?"

I missed Marianne and I hadn't been gone from Karst more than an hour. "No, she's having the second operation. Who's here that I know besides you guys?"

They looked at each other uneasily when I said Marianne wasn't with me, but I thought maybe it was because someone I didn't like was there. "I promise to behave, whoever it is."

"Barcons from before, and the ape-stock, Wool, from the Institute of Science, plus a bird-stock. We don't ask species."

And Wool wouldn't tell you what he was. Yes, it's divisive to ask species, and I'd been bad about doing that. We were supposed to class people only as to temperate zone terrestrial evolvers, cold zone terrestrial evolvers, tropical zone evolvers: bats, bears and birds, and apes. There was a non-obligatory bound morpheme referring to travel modality that let us distinguish apes, bats, and bears from birds. Everything except birds had changed travel modes, bats from flying to walking, us from brachiating to walking, bears from four-footed gaits to bipedalism. Bird-stock was always bipedal. "So, who are they?"

Granite Grit came out. "Tom, Red Clay, so we're separated from our females for a month. The space warpage here has been in the wrong direction. The gates self-catch, so don't fall into gravity wells or our nets."

Argon X, the female, said, "Wool doesn't think the Wrengee are gating out. Someone else is trying to gate into this space-time."

Wool said, "Red Clay again?" He wore only pants, a thin creature that would have looked almost human except his skin was thick, mottled browns and greys, face almost immobile, and the eyes solid brown, no white showing, with a crepuscular creature's slip pupils. He was yawning, too mid-day for him to be up, stretching a body that showed more ribs than I had, scratching the hair that covered his head, neck, and shoulders. "Maybe this watch won't be so boring."

"I want it to be boring. I've got a wife now."

"And didn't bring her with him," Argon IX said.

"Some of us can live without our mates," Wool said.

I asked, to change the subject, "How are we dividing the watches?"

"You're limited to sixteen hours up, as usual, although I think it's foolish," Granite said. He settled down on his hocks. "Take some of the dark part of the rotation."

Wool said, "Karriaagzh sent a message pod. If the creatures making the gates aren't Wrengee, check to see if they are Sharwan. If they're Sharwan, we call in the Institute of Control and contact the Wrengee immediately."

The station, like all observation stations, was huge, studded with holowalls and digital sound systems, multispecies bathrooms, room to avoid the others if one's companions got on one's nerves. Fake lights, tunable as to frequencies and intensity, gave the place a strange sense of spaciousness. Research on humans indicated that I'd be happiest with windows on at least two walls, so three bright fake windows played Virginia scenery, with artificial sunlight timed to match the station's cycles.

Granite and the Barcons shared this space with me during the day. The Argons and Wool, with different light needs, tended to communicate by holophone, although they liked my light at some times of our rotation.

In his cubical, Wool monitored the twitches in space time, then wandered out at odd hours. He had two sleep periods a rotation and woke up desperate to talk.

The Federation wants you to be as happy as possible in the observation stations, get plenty of rest, don't get too bored, because at any minute, you may have to come face to face with folks who had no idea the universe had any other templates for sapient beings than theirs. Or people whose worst nightmares were distorted versions of themselves. Or people who were just plain hysterical.

Marianne sent me a letter:

Dearest Tom, Loved Red Clay, wha'Fran Rock Flour Red,
    As you know, I'm at Black Amber's house on the

beach just north of Karst City, missing you. Molly and Sam are with me, but not Warren, who seems to have taken up with a Tibetan tribal woman.

Black Amber—strange to think of her as John now, she's so alien. Once I began to read the computer auditory input as language, she began haranguing me. While she loves you and me, the whole business of looking for new planets is dangerous, the watch stations provocative. Tom, I can imagine the fury the Air Force would have if their first space probe was captured by aliens who then told them humans would have to join a union or avoid whole categories of space.

Do you know Rhyodolite, her pouch kin (adopted child, I take it)? What can he do, sexually? Sam goes around muttering about alien sexual exploiters, but Molly still thinks *he* slept with the Jerek kitten.

We are back at the house for a few days while Black Amber has her baby and goes through heat. One of the Barcons explained it to me. I met Wy'um, who stayed around even after Cadmium, the blond Gwyng who seems sort of "puritanical," ordered Wy'um off.

Black Amber's son by Wy'um is neat, a brash little daredevil. I feel a biological pressure to breed— like there aren't enough humans here. I'm a bit frightened by the urge, though.

Come back soon, I miss you. It's bad to be the only single human female on the planet. I've been studying more Karst Two with Ewits, who aren't quite as weird as Gwyngs, but, Tom, they are all aliens here.

The Institute of Linguistics gives its candidates names almost everyone can pronounce, so I'm Ree now here, too, but I'll always be Reeann for you. People without high-bridged noses tend to muff nasals. I asked why then did Karst One have nasals, and a Barcon who does language operations says they enlarge the nasal cavities and install a valve if needed, then neurologically tie all that into the speech centers. What, I asked, about people who don't have tongues. We'd install them, he said, but we haven't run into those people yet.

Love,
Marianna, Ree

I wondered who had read her letter and felt a bit annoyed that she said humans would be angry if we had to deal with other species on Federation terms. And the biological pressure to fill the sapient niches with humans?

Space was empty without humans. Pressure, maybe the same pressure, built up in my cock. I locked myself in my toilet to jerk off, but realized as I groaned and spurted that someone was probably watching me. Dizzy, I sat down on the toilet seat and put my head down between my knees until my blood re-circulated.

I went back to my room and lay down on the bed. Obligingly, clouds rolled through the sky in my fake windows, dimming the sun. I wondered if they'd ever be programmed to fake rain. Granite Grit called me on the intercom, saying, "Did you get a letter from Reeann?"

"They call her Ree just like her Berkeley friends."

"You can continue to call her Reeann. Need company?"

"You need company, too?"

"Yes."

"Come in then. Are all the rooms bugged?"

"If they are, Wool watches."

"*Shit.*"

"Excremental times again? I'll be there soon."

I sat up slightly, but the clouds thickened. Big fat raindrops plunked down on the illusionary tin roof over my head. When Granite Grit came in, I was a bit startled that he wasn't wet, then I laughed.

"Very realistic," he said. "Does it soothe you?"

"What do they give you?"

"Snow. Muffles all the sounds." He cocked his head so that one earhole pointed at the ceiling.

"They spent a fortune on special effects here."

* * *

I was asleep, dreaming of a Reeann who sometimes seemed to be Yangchenla, dream breasts swelling and shrinking, eyes developing epicanthic folds, when the intercom broke through my sleep, "Officers, we have company. Officers, we have company." Tangled in my sheets, I woke and tried to get my cock to subside, the dream excitement and the contact excitement making that doubly difficult. Finally, I managed to dress and went into the command room.

"They aren't Wrengee," Wool said. We had a transit pod, a big one, trapped between a double artificial gravity net, rigged like the Yauntry one that had trapped Rhyodolite, me, and the bird Xenon. A crew from the trapped transport crawled out in space suits and began cutting the cables around their vehicle.

"Robot camera?" I asked.

"Send," Wool said.

I maneuvered it up to a space-suited figure. Before the space-suited figures swarmed over the robot camera and dismantled it, we saw blond mammal faces behind helmet glass. That visual and their radio signals proved they were Sharwan.

"What are those little shrimps doing here?" Wool said.

I thought they were beautiful, golden furred with human faces, only more delicate, their angular cheekbones almost geometric, big blue eyes.

"Who contacts the Wrengee?" Granite asked.

I said, "What do we tell them? They've been watched by Federation people for years, but now they're being invaded by another species that we don't control?"

"Granite, you contact them. You've got the most scales," Wool said, handing Granite a microphone.

Granite Grit sent out a radio message in what he hoped was good Wrengu, "We are from another solar system and would like to make contact. If this is agreeable to your government or governments, please contact us on this frequency. We will send a visual signal scanning 600 lines in the units of times between the beeps." *Beep, beep.*

Granite wouldn't look too weird, except he had a beak,

too many feathers. All of us were going to be alien to the Wrengee. The Crocs, I'd been calling them to myself.

"We've got to send Karst a message, too," Wool said. "By pod." He keyboarded data into a crystal and loaded it into a small message pod, set the gate for an Institute of Control destination, tried to send.

The message pod wouldn't leave. "Someone's jamming us," Wool said. He brought out additional boxes and rigged them into the line. The box pulsed out.

"We're getting incoming signals," Granite Grit said.

One of the beautiful Sharwan guys stared out of the set again, then the signal stopped.

"We got the Institute of Control message away," Wool said, shoving himself back from his terminal. "Now, in about twelve hours, we should hear from the Wrengee, if the Sharwan assholes let us."

"But why should we trust you?" the Wrengee signaling us asked. "You only chose to reveal yourselves when . . ." He shuddered, then continued, ". . . when the other space creatures broke into our signaling pattern. I understand this signal has to travel six hours, return six hours. Don't let your reply come faster."

Granite patted his hands on the floor where he sat, body tense on his thighs. His hocks moved out from his buttocks, lowering his body slightly. Still with his feathers clamped tightly to his head and body, he said, "Well, at least they understood me."

Wool said, "Tell them if they don't come to terms with the Sharwan, we'll give them the gate technology."

Granite muttered in bird, then transmitted to the Wrengee, "If the Wrengee do not deal with the single species group that broke into their communications, this multi-species group gives them matter transfer. To move matter from one space point to another almost instantly. We do this if you need proof."

The video screen pattern shivered. A Sharwan face baring teeth in a grin or grimace formed from the visual static. In terrible Karst One, the Sharwan said, "Federation, too much control."

They'd learned some Karst One from Rhyodolite's linguistics team before they fled. They'd been listening to us now.

Great, we had some serious waiting to do. Granite tuned in one of the Wrengee television stations. After the first scene, I realized it was a rerun. Wool and the Argons began hiccuping. Granite switched the channel.

"Another rerun," Wool said. "They're trying to figure out what to tell their people."

I said, "I imagine we look like monsters to them."

Granite fixed an eye on me and bobbed his head once. "Speak for yourself, Red Clay."

We were all too tense. I said, "Okay, okay," but realized I snapped it out.

"Granite, were you joking?" Argon IX asked.

"If you don't think I was joking . . ." Granite rose up, almost to tiptoe, then slumped, hocks braced against each other. "We've got eleven hours and forty-nine minutes to wait."

We had a big gym room in each of the thousand some odd observation stations around the galaxy, including the one at Earth and this one. I went in—we had a problem here and I had a wife, there, on Karst—and in the gym, I put my bike on the windstand and rode, closed my eyes and pretended Marianne was with me, that I wasn't alone here dangling out in a vacuum waiting for intelligent neo-dinosaurs to decide whether they trusted us or not while savage pretty people propagandized against us.

The Wrengee gave me a slightly creepy feeling. I hoped I'd be okay when I met them in the scaled flesh. Snakes and spiders—well, they weren't much like snakes, really.

Eleven hours and five minutes to wait—I couldn't ride the bike anymore. I'd dripped sweat all over it. Roger had told me his paint was very durable but don't push it, don't leave sweat on it. I cleaned the bike, then greased the chain, not spraying it because the propellant couldn't be diluted in a planetary-sized atmosphere, would muck up this enclosed one. My brain kept coming up with odd little items like that. Ten hours and fifty minutes to wait. I blanked my watch face—let it keep time without reminding me.

Wool called me over the intercom, "We've got reinforcements. Institute of Control."

"From Karst?"

"They have their own stations. Don't ask coordinates."

The gate had brought us twelve sapients, all masked with visors down to their noses, lower faces naked grey and brown and pied skins, different species, but without facial hair or stripped of it. As I came in, the squad leader took off his visor—species something like a Jerek, but bigger—and said, "We brought a Control station half this volume full of robot devices."

Wool said, "We don't know what the Sharwan want."

"We are only here to control," the squad leader said. His men took off their visors—a wide range of people—and went wandering around the station.

We waited. I went into the food storage area and fixed pork and beans, comforted to have home food at a time like this. "Maybe," I said to Wool when he came in, "we should give the Wrengee the gate formulas and technology whether they want it or not?"

"Maybe," he said. He found a bag of nuts with thin pistachio-like shells and began splitting the shells with his teeth, flicking the hulls onto a tray with his tongue.

When Wool and I went back out, the Control squad leader was watching a Sharwan face up on the screen. I didn't know whether it was an actual on-time Sharwan transmission or a stored image. The squad leader pulled out a portable computer and began writing on its screen, looking up from time to time at the Sharwan.

"Can they block Class A gates?" the squad leader asked.

Wool said, "Yes."

"We'll trap one or two of those little blond boys, show them that we're nice brainy *uhyalla*, too."

"What are you called?" I asked the squad leader.

"Just call me Squad Leader."

Nine hours and an eternity to wait.

* * *

"We haven't had anything to do since the Yauntra blockade," one of the Control squad people was saying, waving a beer in his six-fingered hand, nostrils sort of loosely writhing around the edges. "Nothing except drills." He was playing a game with square cards and eight-sided dice with the others, sitting around a table. "But we'll wait to see what your guys sunward have to say."

I remembered when I was a kid, I snuck speed away from Warren, doing it to study for a test and then having to wait, wider than wide awake, for morning and then the school bus. Just like now, each minute buzzed into hours.

"How'd your people take it?" Squad Leader asked me.

"We haven't been contacted yet."

"Refugee, huh."

"Give us an apparatus and operator, coordinates to your whatever you're signally from. You're close." The Wreng sounded aggrieved. He lowered his eyelids halfway down, exposing a tattoo or natural design, then his hand snaked out to cut off the transmission.

Everyone turned to look at me. "I don't have any non-aligned people with me," Squad Leader said.

I almost said I was neuro-programmed to avoid snakes, but didn't. Wool and Squad Leader took my elbows like I'd bolt and led me into the gate room. The Barcons had already laid out the cables and the Control guys were dragging up a shiny white transport pod.

"You know how to set coordinates?"

"Yes, Rhyodolite taught me."

"We're sending you into the Wrengee transmitting station. The closure bolts will be under your control." Wool tucked a stack of bound printouts in the capsule, then a couple of the white and black boxes.

I crawled in beside the boxes and printouts. "Don't let the Sharwan get me instead."

Squad Leader said, "If they do, we'll bust their little blond asses."

I dogged down the wing nuts and watched the transit diode. It flickered, then the arrival diode went on. Just where was I? Cautiously, I undogged the hatch and swung it up. Sighing with relief, I watched the Wrengee twitch their scales and head feathers, scale rings on some of them tinkling.

Please, God, Mind, Universe of Biodiscourse, give them teeth. One of them spoke, "You can take me to the broadcast spot?" No teeth in front, just a curved blade of tissue going around the front of the mouth, flaps of tissue dangling from the roof of the mouth modifying that noise, a thick tongue that only pushed food.

"Yes," I said, telling myself they were as nervous about me as I was of them. Maybe mammals ate their eggs? No, they were viviparous. This was my first First Contact in a vertical position, not as a captive. "We want you to join us in a Federation that protects the rights of all intelligent animals."

"You're crippled in the mouth," the one who'd spoken to me said.

"No, born this way. Sorry. Can you understand me?"

"Something about a Federation and all intelligent animals. You're alone in that?"

"Alone in the transport? Yes." I felt like crouching and bowing, chattering like I used to do when I chased snakes off the road, saving them, but nervously. Then I wondered if I was offending them with my fear.

"Why were you spying on our planet?"

"Waiting to see if you were ready to deal with us, able to . . ." I didn't know their word for "conceptualize," so I continued, "think about intelligent species beyond your planet." I was about to add that the Federation required gate technology as the entry into system, but remembered just in time that we'd promised to give them that. Wouldn't give it to humans—no, we were too xenophobic—but the Federation would give it to these guys.

"Slow down. Speak clearly," the one I'd been talking to said.

"I apologize." I felt like I was going to faint.

"Speak bluntly."

Why? I said, "Want to meet some of the others?"

"Can I take a weapon?"

I hadn't cleared that with the guys back in the station, but what with armed Control people there, I wished he wouldn't. But anything to make the new sapient feel at ease. "Sure."

He flicked his tattooed eyelids at me—a gesture I couldn't read, but it seemed negative. I asked, "Should I stay here?"

"Your Federation put you out front to absorb the shock. You're our hostage either way, aren't you?"

They had an amazingly blunt way of talking, pretty sharp-witted, too. I said, "Yes. May I call you a name?"

"I'm Ersh. Who are you?"

"I'm called Red Clay. Having names that translate into almost all languages is a *Federation* custom."

"Wet and sticky," he said. I tried not to shudder or sweat when he climbed in the transport with me. He saw the printouts in the transport and asked, "What are these?"

"Space transforming guide book and boxes to make the transitions."

"We'll take those now." He handed them out and watched me close the dogs and turn on the gate generator. This trip, I controlled it from the inside. The transport jerked. When I rolled against him, his skin was softer than I'd expected, dry.

He said, "Scared. Afraid I'll find a lie?"

"Ersh, you're not nervous about my appearance?"

"Aliens *should* look alien."

I began to worry about Granite Grit. He said, "You're incapable of reading my body language, aren't you?"

"Yes, now." The arrival diode went green and I began to undo the hatch again, my hands sweating.

We had company—Sharwan. One, not holding the station crew hostage, or fighting the Control unit, just standing away from the Federation types, its own transport like a coffin behind it.

Its. Our guys had sex, at least in my private language; potentially dangerous strangers were *its*. I just noticed this as Ersh-the-Wreng and I climbed out of the pod. "What is the Sharwan doing here?"

"Hasn't said," Squad Leader said. He looked down at a grey box he was holding in his hand. "Your guy is armed with a metal projectile weapon."

"Yes, I said it was okay."

The Sharwan stayed close to its transport. "Federation over boundary," it finally said, rippling its blond fur. "This ours. Work for us."

Work, the Karst One term, implied work smoothly together and didn't take a subordinating preposition, but the Sharwan used the word it learned for its own purposes. The golden alien jumped back in his coffin transport and gated away.

"What did he say?" Ersh asked.

"Do you want to be their underlings?"

"No, not yours either."

"All are equal in the Federation," Granite Grit said.

"You're deformed," Ersh told Granite. "Feathers, beak. We exterminated your kind on this planet before we were fully evolved."

Squad Leader slammed his hand against a bulkhead and we all jumped, including Ersh, and turned to him. He spoke in chopped Wrengu, "Wrengee, protection us from Sharwan, no, yes. Get answer radio signal turnaround time plus tenth." In a little over thirteen hours, my mind translated.

Ersh stared at him and sat down, joints going the way my joints did, but with an extra hinge in the hip region. He trembled, then his eyes rolled up. We thought he'd fainted, but no, his eyes rolled back down out of his head, glistening now. "I can't make the decision for the whole planet. The whole planet can't make a decision that fast. What does this mean? What did that one who traveled in the oblong mean?"

Squad Leader said to me, "Tell him that we have to act fast, because we're assuming the Sharwan are already setting up their own blockade of your planet."

Ersh lowered his eyelid marks at me after I translated that and shook his scale rings. Then he radioed his own people. We duplicated the message and sent it to Isa in a mini pod.

Dear Marianne,

   I'm sorry I can't come back now, but we have had a first contact. The situation is complicated by the Sharwan who've threatened to bomb Isa, that's the Wrengee planet, if the Wrengee and others of their species join the Federation. We're rigging defenses for Isa. But the Wrengee and other Isa governments aren't committing themselves to the Federation without a trial of the defenses. If we can keep them from being bombed, then they'll join us. If not, not. Since we wouldn't threaten to bomb them to get them to join the Federation, that would be that.

   If the situation wasn't so tense, I'd wish you were here. I miss you.

Love,
Tom

I never realized I could be so lonely for a particular human face. After I sent the letter, I turned the hologram walls black, curled up on my bed, and just ached for her.

Ersh came in, looked at me, and said, "You hurt?"

Without speaking to him, I got up off the bed and went to my toilet, washed my face, then came out. He was still standing there, a flesh flap protruding slightly over his bottom lip. I said, "Sorry if I was rude, but I was just connected to a woman recently." That wasn't going to make sense in Wrengu, but he figured it out, old lizard.

"You wouldn't bring your breeding partner to a place so dangerous, would you?"

"Actually, she's still learning."

"Actually, this is very dangerous."

"Yes, I guess it is."

"If we let the Sharwan rule us, then no bombs will be dropped. If you can't stop one bomb, your help will damage us."

"The Federation is supposed to protect you from species like the Sharwan."

"I'm glad to press you while you're vulnerable. You've given me information no one could give us, 'supposed to protect.' "

He had mental gears I didn't. "Give you information?"

"Joining the Federation is dangerous."

"Giving in to the Sharwan is dangerous."

"The Isa governments are talking to the Sharwan. They won't drop bombs if we join them. Will you then attack us?" He left then. I lay back on the bed in shock, then got angry. We'd done all the work of a first contact, now they telling us if the Sharwan got one bomb through, Isa governments wouldn't have anything to do with *us*. Then I wondered if I'd done anything wrong, if Rhyodolite had insulted the Sharwan.

But, if I had vestigial webs, they'd twitch when I saw Ersh.

One bomb—I wondered if the Sharwan who'd gated into the Federation station had bugged us. One little flash of light—wasn't a bomb from space, either, Squad Leader said. Ersh's scale rings rang like wind chimes in March as he watched the flash and heard his people call him back.

The Sharwan cut in with a video—grinning, grinning, those high cheekbones like folded hawks' wings.

"Call us back if they exploit," Squad Leader told Ersh. Ersh rolled his eyes back, then flicked out his thick tongue. He said nothing, pulled his tongue back and climbed into a transport we were giving him.

After Ersh left, Wool stared at the television screen and said, "I pity them."

Squad Leader sent down capsules to Federation spies surgically altered to look like Wrengee and already in their cover positions. I saw Granite Grit watching intensely and realized the spies on Isa were his kind of bird. Isa wasn't abandoned yet.

The Institute of Control people began mock-scrapping with each other as they loaded their transport pod and gated to their secret coordinates.

Those of us on the observation team wrapped the whole station in gate cables and moved it back to the fringes of the Karst System. Wool asked, "Does anyone want to go back the slow way?" His grey mottled skin looked ashy.

Granite said, "I don't want to do anything next, not right now."

"A Sharwan group fled Rhyodolite's linguistics team," I said. "Maybe someone then did something wrong . . ." And then again, maybe my fears insulted Ersh.

We took a week to get home, cruising through the Karst System, not talking much to each other, just looking at the ice planet, that supposedly lucky thing to see, and at the gas giants, then the shuttle came spiraling down out of Karst orbit like a wounded bird.

Marianne was waiting at the terminal with Black Amber. I climbed down the shuttle ladder with my bag and said, "Isa turned us down."

Marianne said, "They were fools."

Black Amber said, "You (both) can go home (Karst City) now. Marianne is now in training. Bright female, almost like a Gwyng."

We embraced then, Marianne and I. "Warren okay? How are Sam and Molly?"

"I've got to talk to you."

"The brother," Black Amber said, "Defended himself (dangerous to pick on/city Gwyngs only tease/hissing). He's crude/primitive. Embarrassment to you, I think." She didn't offer to drive us home, just turned and left in her car.

"I know which bus," Marianne said. "She's upset over something."

"Nymph pouched, I bet, and nobody would take it."

"Tom, she's only forty-two, but that's like sixty for a Gwyng. She was sent here to become Rector. Now that won't happen."

I thought about the Gwyng planet, shattered into islands and small continents by super active plate tectonics— Gwyng healed fast, died fast. An image of a senile Gwyng falling out of a host beast pouch onto beach sand, mewing, nostril slit snuffing for other Gwyngs who avoided the aged, the insane—Black Amber twenty, twenty-five years from now? *"Marianne, I just want to be with you for a long while,''* I said in English. We got on the bus and traveled through the various districts like a cultural kalidoscope—glass houses, wicker houses, square and round houses, all filled with aliens who looked more or less alike, were wildly different inside their skulls. I changed my mind from minute to minute—alike, wildly different, alike.

"Was it awful?"

"I wanted them to join us, and not just for the first contact shares, too. The Isa planet people—they touched my xenophobia. I wanted to overcome it."

"Black Amber said the contact was outrageous—forced by Karriaagzh."

"No, it was forced by the Sharwan. Pretty little *vr'ech*, gold fur and blue eyes, beautiful, at least to me."

Granite Grit came up and embraced me, awkwardly, not his species' social gesture. "We tried. Now I go home and we breed again."

"Sounds like a good idea," Marianne said. "Lose something, gain something. Tom, have you considered that we ought to do that, too?"

I couldn't bear to argue with her right then.

= 8 =

Discovering the Humans

After all that, once we did land on Karst, the watch crew was ordered immediately to a terminal debriefing room. Grand Senior Officer Zircon XI, a grey-and-black-furred creature with slightly matted silky head hair, was waiting for us, his triple eyelids, like a bird's, sweeping out of sync over his black eyes, no pair of eyelids blinking synchronized with others. Like Wool, he never mentioned his species.

Granite Grit, crouched down on his hocks, body pressed to the floor, asked the Grand Senior Officer, "Do we get turned down often?" I knew Granite wondered if the failure was his fault. I felt, perhaps, it was mine.

Wool looked at GSO Zircon and grunted, then half lay on a long bench, one leg twitching, eyes half closed. He, not GSO Zircon, answered, "Rarely. Percentage-wise, more with non-mammals."

Granite's head feathers flared slightly. He stiffened, then slumped again.

GSO Zircon said, "We'll watch both of them. If we can get the Sharwan to talk again . . . we haven't had a problem like the Sharwan in years."

We continued talking, replaying the contact steps, trying to reassure each other that none of us did anything wrong.

The Grand Senior Officer Zircon finally said, "We're repeating ourselves here. Go home to your own."

I walked back into our apartment and something was right about the air. The harpsichord stopped. Sam and Reeann looked at me. I felt strangely out of place.

"Nice to be among humans again," I said. "Where's Molly?"

"Off with the Tibetans learning hand-sign since she didn't go through the second operation," Reeann said, somewhat stiffly. "She wants to communicate with Gwyngs."

"Warren?"

"He's out in the Preserve," Sam said. "Gwyngs have a grudge against him."

"Yeah, I . . . I'm tired. The contact didn't work out."

Marianne looked at Sam, then back at me, eyes going up and down, before speaking. "I understand refugees don't have much position here. So you take the most risks."

I almost wanted to invite some of the Tibetans over— almost. "We need more humans here, but not the Tibetans," I managed to say. I hadn't realized how terribly tired I was—*please cuddle me, Marianne*—and sweaty still.

"Karriaagzh and I have been talking about that," Marianne said.

I said, "Karriaagzh wants to contact at least everyone who has halfway conceptualized the possibility of decent intelligent life on other planets." The idea seems impossible now—dump everyone into a technological stew: plastic beggars, the lithium rich who'd sell centuries worth of energy for information on shifting molecules, and xenophobia movies to play to the doubts in all of us. I couldn't deal with that today. Every time I closed my eyes, I saw Ersh watching a bomb explode on his planet.

Marianne said, "Tom, let me fix you some tea." She went into the kitchen in the back while Sam and I stared at each other.

"Warren and Yangchenla?" I finally asked.

"No, not Warren and Yangchenla," he said, looking away from me. Warren and Molly, I thought, but he must have guessed what I was thinking and added, "Not Warren and Molly either. Your brother's quite the character. He's distilling liquor for anti-Buddhist Tibetans.''

"Shit no."

"You had me kidnapped. I had no idea what I was getting involved with. I didn't believe it was real."

"Are you working? Getting music work?"

"I play for the aliens. You ever see a xenophobia movie, holo?"

"Yeah, Karriaagzh is in an old one," I said.

Sam swayed back slightly and lowered his chin. "I've been approached to do one of those. And I play music, but the people here have every species' way of being tricky. Creature like me can get good and cheated here. Yangchenla says I have been."

"Yangchenla?"

Karst One has a slang term that means both meanly endowed in comfort/sex organs and stingy with one's lovers. Sam used it—the closest English is "prick"—when he said, "You were a prick with her."

"Sam, I couldn't adjust."

"Tom, you little refugee, you can adjust to *vr'ech*, *uhyalla*, but with other humans, you're just a *Virginia hick*."

"She wanted me to do things for her that I really couldn't do. You understand that we're not really high status beings here, don't you? Even with Academy and Institute affiliations." Maybe he was in love with her? Stupid to argue with a man in love.

"You hated her family. That's what really bothered her. You wanted to isolate her from the other humans. Just you and her, and you weren't there much."

Warren and I were like that, isolated back in Virginia. "Those humans were more alien than some of the other sapients," I said. "I wanted to be among people better than me."

"Now you've got Marianne—she's definitely your superior."

Marianne came back in and said, "Sam, stop."

Sam went to his room, came out with a keyboard under his arm, and went to the elevator, pushed the button for it, staring at the door, shoulders squared, knees slightly bent.

As the door slid down, he kicked at it, saying in English, *"Fucking alien elevator door."*

Marianne handed me the teacup and said, "And this is alien, too, for human nerves."

"Let's not go out for a while," I said to her, taking the cup and going to sit on a leather wing chair that she'd gotten while I was away. The hide was softer than the leather mod chairs Warren had bought with drug money— a non-Terran leather. I sat sipping the tea and stroking the arms of the chair. There were more changes: carpet on the floor, curtains on the windows, glass flower vases full of irises—where did she get irises? "You've fixed the place up?"

"Yes. Alex sent me the irises."

"How are you in touch with Alex? I thought you didn't like him?"

"Through Karriaagzh, who says that if we're discreet, we can visit Earth again, not Berkeley. London, maybe, or Toronto. Or Tokyo?"

"You been before?"

"To London and Tokyo. And Bolivia and Peru."

"God, I never went anywhere."

She curled up on the carpet by my chair and said, "No, just to Karst, Yauntra, Gwyng Home, this new planet."

"Reeann, all I get to see is little bits of a planet, for a few weeks. Except Yauntra, then we were locked up on a farm for a few months. And I was locked up in a couple of other places on Yauntra, by myself."

"We can travel. Academy and Institute people can go free to any planet that allows visitors. Lots of them do— there's a regular tourist industry. You're getting money from *uhyalla* visiting Yauntra already."

"Fir-in-Snow takes them out on tremendously expensive hunts. Karriaagzh brought back movies. It doesn't balance the trade."

"Tom, do you want to travel?"

"I don't want to see any *vr'ech* right now."

"Not even Karriaagzh, Black Amber, or Granite Grit."

Their images rose in my mind, but slightly transformed toward human norms, I realized after a second. "Not *right* now," I answered.

She took it to be a sexually charged answer. It worked out that way—get real alienated, then go push yourself into another human, it's wonderful, sort of.

The next day, I woke up, left Marianne sleeping, and padded into the kitchen naked to fix coffee, straight earthly coffee with lots of caffeine in it. Feeling weird, I looked down at my body, pale skin that oozed under tension, hairs up and down my belly and chest, but sparse, shoulders flat, like a Gwyng's, not rounded like a Jerek. Armpits marked with hair, bacteria cooking up what I'd always thought was a human odor out of raw armpit sweat. My face felt greasy—my hair seemed to creep on my scalp. Arrgh, a human, a wretched xenophobic human.

The water began boiling and I fixed up the Melita drip coffee the way Marianne showed me, wondering where we'd get more paper cones, if Karst would set up a Melita filter industry for us. No, we'd ask Alex to pick some up at the Berkeley Co-op and gate them several hundred light-years.

I fixed two cups and took them back to the bedroom. "Marianne, how'd you like to stay in here all day?" I asked, handing one to her.

She rolled around and wiggled up. I looked at her skin, darker than mine, studded with microscopic sweat glands, coated in even finer hairs. And breasts. What bioprogram made breasts so attractive, I wondered as I sat down beside her, staring from them to her armpits, tufts of hair like mine. Berkeley radical women didn't shave their armpits or legs, but bike racers shaved their legs, so she gave me the satisfaction of getting really close to her legs, getting to see all the curves.

But, looking at us as animals, we were ugly—sweaty cursorial runners re-rigged from brachiators. I didn't want to see anything weirder today than us.

"Tom," she said, "I've got language lessons."

"I just got back. Can't you wait a day?"

"Tom, you're sweating."

"I don't want to go outside today. I want you with me, a human with me." I saw my coffee began to ripple in the cup and realized I was shaking.

"Are you okay?"

"I . . ." Maybe we should call a Barcon, I almost said, but didn't want to feel like a medical specimen.

Marianne put her coffee down and went to the computer terminal, calling the Barcons, I just knew it. God, I was too experienced to go through xeno-shock again. "I'll go out. Jesus, I've been here for years."

"Tom, Chalk said that we should just stay in today, then go ride the bikes tomorrow. First contact rejection hurts, they said." She watched me while she drank her coffee. I finished mine, went to the bathroom and took a long shower. When I got out, she'd gotten dressed in a long silk robe her sister made for her, handwoven, worth at least five months work credit here on Karst. I put on an old pair of jeans, left my chest and feet bare.

"What we need now," she said, "is a big Sunday newspaper and melons."

I looked at the sky through the windows—sun not as yellow as my human sun. And Karst was smaller than Earth, so we were lighter. The lesser gravity generally felt like a vague up. But now I felt heavy. The gravity in the observation station might have been less.

"The light here is more blue," Marianne said. "I wondered how I'd look."

"You look great, a bit greyed, if I really concentrate." Maybe I was imagining that. Most minds correct for spectral differences.

"Sam said the air is different. He had to re-tune the harpsichord and piano to get them to sound the same as they did on Earth."

"Marianne, we *are* on an alien planet."

"And nobody's hurt us."

"Nobody's hurt you." I was about to say *yet*, but caught myself.

"You need to share some celebrations, Tom, like Black Amber's post-mating party."

"It's hypocritical. She's being forced to have open matings. She doesn't want to be a Gwyng; she wants to be a Barcon and mate for life with Wy'um."

"Tom, that was just an example. You want to be something other than human? We're human, Tom, and we've got to show them humans aren't xenophobes."

"And here I am, mildly xenofreaked."

"Tom, ease up on yourself. All the creatures who know you like you."

For a flash, I wanted a mother, then I stood up and went back to the kitchen and stared at the food in the refrigerator: Gwyng-raised Jersey milk with half a pound of cream floating on top of every quart, sliced meat, *villag* and bean curd, pods filled with triangular seeds, horizontally striped fish like trout crossed with aquarium zebra fish. My food was alien. Hearing her come up behind me, I said, "Know where we can get an ice cream churn?"

"We can fake it," she said. "I'll get eggs downstairs. A Gwyng sells food on the ground floor."

"I'll stay here." I planned to stay inside until I was too embarrassed to stay inside. Do other *uh'yalla* have attacks like this after years of living on Karst, I wondered, or am I just a xenophobe? Or am I just afraid of getting killed, by human or *ech*, not being allowed to fight back. I'd explain the Federation until some *vr'ech* didn't like what they heard. They'd kill me and another explainer would take my place, millions, billions of us. *Here we are and we won't go away.*

The Sharwan had said, *So what if we shoot and you won't defend anyone.*

I went prowling around. Molly's looms were in her room; Marianne's room was full of books; Sam's room looked ridiculously neat, a fitted green corduroy bedspread over a twin-sized mattress, shelves full of music, his piano and harpsichord both with keyboard lids down, a big plant in the bay window, a glass case of strange musical instruments against the left-hand wall. I recognized a dulcimer, then a fiddle. The others were strange to me, but somehow I recognized them to be human instruments.

When I heard the elevator in the shaft, I came back around to the common room.

"Twing's going to be closing for a few days," Marianne said, "but if we need anything, one of her pouch kin will be with her on the second floor and could open for us."

"That's her name?"

"That's what she recognizes as being close to a configuration of it. She seemed restless."

"She's going into heat, I bet," I said. Great, the building would be infested with pheromone-dazed Gwyngs, koo'ing and screaming on the elevator.

Marianne frowned at me for being an embarrassing xenoflip and said, "She had a freezer blender for sale. It should do the trick."

It did. We rigged the computer to print us behavioral illustration narratives as if they were news items, headlines and dot-matrix photos on big sheets of paper, and lay around on our bellies eating ice cream and reading about Barcon brain worm operations, bird-mating battles, and nervous system response to tonal patterns—music—in sequential and patterning-system brained creatures.

Marianne got the giggles when she read about an ape-type species represented by two refugee cultural groups that claimed to have both permanent and temporary pair-bonding. I felt even more depressed—our mating habits, our xenophobia, our other behaviors, and our literature, all common gossip. And the Federation couldn't stop one bomb against Isa.

The next morning I didn't want to go out yet, but as I drank my coffee, I heard the elevator coming up the shaft. Marianne got up and unlocked the door to our flat. The cab stopped, the door slid down, and there stood Karriaagzh, his head slightly cocked, body and legs slouched, a non-uniform tunic covering his body feathers. "Tom, I heard you were a little tired of us non-humans?"

I didn't say anything.

Karriaagzh came in, looked at Marianne, then stepped, hocks flexing very high, around the main room. Then he sat down beside my chair, head lower than my shoulder. "What bothers you the most?"

"Losing Isa, being half glad of it. Waiting years and making only two first contacts, one of them a failure, the other nearly lethal."

"We're going to expand station operations. Black Amber protested, but we must protect other species against the Sharwan."

I drained my coffee cup, then said, "So we'll be busier?"

"Yes. Marianne will go on station watches with you." Marianne nodded; I realized they'd arranged this earlier. Karriaagzh touched my wrist, rubbed the protruding wrist bone with his thumb. "We'll listen to music for a moment."

I realized Sam and Molly hadn't come back in the night before. "Where did Sam and Molly go?"

As Karriaagzh padded over to the player and looked through our human and alien digital discs, Marianne said, "Sam's playing for Tibetans who can't come into Karst City."

"Sam told me about this group," Karriaagzh said as he put on a Grateful Dead album. The Dead played about "Vitamin C and cocaine" as Karriaagzh twisted his head to catch the sounds with one ear, then the other. The Grateful Dead always reminded me of Warren, but I kept quiet.

I got three days more leave. Marianne and I went wandering about in Karst City—fourteen million aliens of 103 different species spread out over what Reeann figured was equal in land area to from Sausalito halfway to Sacramento then down to San Jose. Big city, dense in patches.

We took a maglev train in a clear vacuum tube to the Upper Preserve Gate, then took a bus through in-city agricultural lands: odd farms with mechanical tractors, multistory greenhouses, sewage sludge processing plants, Gwyng herds that included Earth cows among the bigger alien beasts, plastic reprocessing factories.

"The species run together. Some I can't tell whether

they're weird Barcons or fat people of our shiny black neighbor's kind," Marianne said.

"Federation over species. Rude to draw distinctions that might be *alienating*." The last word was in English.

"Like Alex?" After she said that, Marianne got up and asked the bus driver, a pug-faced creature, if we could tour one of the plastic reprocessing factories.

Without looking back, the bus driver told her, "I know one where the manager shows Academy and Institute curiosity seekers around for a bit of credit. Get out when I say, but you'll have a two-hour wait between buses."

The reprocessing factory was in a huge concrete and plastic building in a field of bone thistles all white stems and green spines. A boardwalk went up over them to the front entrance. Behind the building ran a maglev track, not enclosed. The building seemed ominous—dingy white in a field of bone thistles.

We walked over the bone thistles to the front door and went in. Three Gwyngs sat in front of a bank of switches, diodes, and analog gauges. I said, "We're curious about touring the facility."

A male said, "Boring/need break, so come for fifteen basic hour units."

"Can't afford that," Marianne said. "I'm still an apprentice."

The Gwyngs chatted in Karst Two, "questionably poor apprentice greed herself," as if we weren't there, then the male told Marianne, "Doubt/boredom (my greed) (sorry about greed). For ten units?"

"Say five for both of us," I said.

The Gwyng stared at his panels, then rolled his shoulders. "Acceptance/bored too much." He nodded slightly at the two females—bored with them, too, I bet.

We followed him up on a catwalk above machines grinding plastic into chips as fine as sawdust, then walked over conveyers that carried the plastic dust to vats. The hot air rising from the vats stank of yeast and rotten plastic. Fine screen skimmers dipped and twisted through the culture surface, then rose and whirled the yeast globs onto a moving trough. The trough, lined with leaky membranes, carried away the yeast in huge clots. The noise rose with the hot smelly air.

"Who eats that?" Marianne shouted at our guide.

"Creatures who fail their examinations," the Gwyng said, "or Gwyng host animals."

Marianne looked down, gripping both catwalk rails. "Yeast cake," she said. "Plastic recycling."

"Very high in proteins, hydrocarbon chains re-arranged by the bacteria and yeasts," the Gwyng said. "Automatic factory except for breakdowns (rare and dangerous/machines rule)."

"Very interesting," I said. "Gwyngs go out to mine hydrocarbons in space?"

"Make structural plastics, then eat plastics when bored with buildings and toys," the Gwyng said.

Marianne said, in English, *"The store downstairs doesn't even sell yeast cake. We're pretty far from the bottom of the social heap, Tom, refugees or not."*

"Processed further for Gwyng artificial food," the Gwyng added, "but not here. Barcon checkers necessary."

I said, "But Gwyngs make their own artificial food on Gwyng Home."

"Gwyng Home is a myth."

"But I've been to Gwyng Home with Black Amber."

"For Karst-born, Gwyng Home is not attainable."

I asked, "You don't know Gwyng languages?"

He didn't answer, just took us back to the office. We walked over the bone thistles to the bus stop and began to wait, in silence. Then Marianne said, "The Federation certainly isn't perfect."

"Something has to eat yeasts grown on plastic."

"What was he saying about Gwyng Home being a myth?"

"Rhyodolite and Cadmium told me that if a Gwyng doesn't learn Gwyng, not Karst Two, but a Gwyng language, at a fairly early age, then the mind doesn't develop properly. For a Gwyng."

"Gwyng languages aren't like Karst Two?"

"Karst Two is like a code for them, not as much information as the trained Gwyng mind can perceive."

"And so those Gwyngs are developmentally deprived and get to run a yeast factory."

"Yeah. That's why Black Amber makes her children learn Gwyng languages." We waited. Across the road was a seven-story greenhouse like a giant helix, with each long rectangular story at a slightly different angle from the others. I wondered what they grew in those, watched water spray inside one story. Small figures, too small at this distance to determine the species, walked through the fifth level pushing carts, harvesting the crop which grew in waist-high trays.

"At least," Marianne said, watching the same greenhouse, "there's no stoop labor there."

The Gwyng downstairs went into heat. Having a store, she knew lots of other Gwyngs; being a merchant, not inviting regular customers to her heat would have been rude.

At night, in bed, Marianne and I would hold each other but not having sex, listening, sniffing, as though we on the fifth floor could smell the second. Sam and Molly kept very odd hours, seemed to sleep in separate rooms.

All of us non-Gwyngs in the building, if we were in the elevator together, would stop speaking when we passed the second-floor landing, turning away from even our own mates. The elevator vibrated ultrasonics, oozed sex molecules.

Black Amber called the third night of the heat. "Cadmium and Rhyodolite (pheromones forced/driven) . . . if you can, help."

"Who called?" Marianne asked. She was reading some Institute study guide off the terminal.

"Black Amber. It's not important."

"She and Karriaagzh . . ." Marianne didn't finish, just trailed off and began to scroll through the material on her terminal, muttering, "I've worked with these semiotic concepts before. Signifier/signified drift, so that's why the linguists who devised Karst Two didn't work out a code, but rather an arbitrary signal shifting system. Karst Two

changes like a natural language. If the computers translated Karst Two directly into Karst One, then we wouldn't
be able to adapt to the shifts in Karst Two."

"And vice versa, somehow," I said.

"I don't quite understand how the shift works. I suspect the significant pairs . . . not pairs, I bet, in Karst
Two . . ." She stopped talking and pulled a couple of
pages of hard copy, then began scribbling on them, one
hank of her hair looped over a breast, the rest going down
her shoulders.

We went to bed shortly after Black Amber called. Marianne lay in bed, almost rigid, then asked, "Do the males
hurt the female Gwyngs?"

"Everyone gets scratches and bruises. Reeann, you're
tense. Want some warm milk or a backrub?"

"Sorry." She snuggled up against me and we drifted
off to sleep.

In the morning, I wiggled around under the covers, only
half awake. Marianne had left a warm spot in the bed, just
got up minutes before. Whichever of us got up first started
coffee, so I figured she was in the kitchen and pulled myself out of bed, used the toilet, then began dressing.

I just had my pants on when she called from the living
room, "Tom, quick." Barefooted and shirtless, I ran up
to the front of the apartment.

Two Gwyngs lay together facedown in a sleeping bag
on the floor. Cadmium, by the blond streaks, so the other
one had to be Rhyodolite.

"Black Amber told me to take care of them," I said.

"Didn't you lock up?"

Rhyodolite squirmed around in the bag. His face was
bruised, the wrinkles looser than usual, as though he hadn't
eaten in days. Probably hadn't. "Weaver's pouch kin," he
murmured, reaching up to Marianne with one hand. "Be
nice to a little Gwyng." The nail on his thumb was torn.

Cadmium punched Rhyo under the bag cover. "Red
Clay, heat is over (exhausting/exhausted of energy). The
one downstairs likes me (but many males, Rhyodolite too
small)."

Rhyodolite looked over at Cadmium and clapped his

nostrils open and shut a few times. Cadmium freed an arm and stroked Rhyodolite's face. Rhyodolite asked, "Can we stay here a few days, through the party?"

I looked at Reeann. She said in English, *"Yangchenla told me about Gwyng teases. Only if they leave us alone, is it okay."*

"No fair talking primitive jargon to discuss," Rhyodolite said.

"She says you can stay if you don't tease us when we're in bed," I said, not looking at Marianne.

"Spoilsport, fun rupturer," Rhyodolite began, but Cadmium Gwyng-talked to him and he settled down.

Then Cadmium pulled himself out of the sleeping bag. He went knuckles and knees down on the floor for a second, naked, then he unsteadily stood up, one hand cupped over his groin. He looked dried up. "Can one of you get our clothes and food?"

I said, coming up to steady him, "We've got milk and cream in the kitchen."

"I'll get it," Marianne said. She stared down at Rhyodolite—challenge eyes—and he looked away first.

"Why is she so touchy? What happened when she was learning Gwyng at Black Amber's?" I asked them.

"Rhyodolite and the Weaver," Cadmium said. "I'd like to sit in that chair." He pointed.

"Rhyodolite and Molly? Molly's the Weaver, right?"

"*Nice* placental female," Rhyodolite said. He closed his eyes and turned his head, submissively.

Oh, shit.

Molly herself came out, sleepy-eyed in a long cotton nightgown, and said, "Rhyodolite, what happened to you?"

"Where's Sam?" I asked her.

"Out, playing."

"I was bullied," Rhyodolite said, "ruthlessly/kept from sexual pleasures. Even Cadmium set me back."

Cadmium snorted. I'd never heard a Gwyng make that sound before, but they've got the flexible nostrils for it. I handed them towels just as Marianne was bringing out hot butter. Cadmium stood up, wrapped the towel around his waist, tucked the end in, and sat down. Rhyodolite stayed in the sleeping bag, his nostrils twitching.

"Molly," Reeann asked, "where is Sam?"

"Out. I don't know," Molly said. She knelt down beside Rhyodolite in the bag, held the cup for him. He wiggled his fingers at her; she wiggled hers back at him. Gwyng-sign, for people who can't get the second language operation. Reeann handed the second cup of hot butter to Cadmium who said, "We also need/would like formula. Storekeeper has it. Sorry to inconvenience you."

"I'll get it," Reeann said. "I'd rather not watch that." She kicked out a foot toward Molly and Rhyodolite and punched the elevator call button. Rhyodolite leaned on Molly's breasts, sipping painfully at the melted butter, stroking her jaw with his long furry knuckles.

Cadmium got up and paced, three steps away from Marianne and three steps back to the chair. He said again, "If the Weaver wants, she can stop him. He's little (and my pouch kin)."

Marianne went "errhh." The elevator door slid down; she got in and left. Molly looked up—not understanding what Cadmium said.

"No loyalty between sisters?" Rhyodolite asked me.

Cadmium said, "Don't be nasty."

Molly looked at me and pulled away from Rhyodolite, her face flushed slightly. I had missed over a month of their lives together. Poor Sam, I thought, married to a woman who goes for the most exotic available male. Cadmium said, "Would like shower. Pheromone disrupter would be better but don't have."

"Should we give him a shower, too?"

Cadmium looked down at Rhyodolite. His lips pursed slightly, then he said, "Your famous cold one?"

Rhyodolite brushed his knuckle fur against Molly's lips. She took his hand and pushed it away, but held it, eyes averted from mine.

Cadmium said, "Why don't we talk while I shower?" He walked over to the stranger's bath, put his head in and said, "This stinks of bird. I know the Linguist Aspirant doesn't want me in back, but . . ."

While Cadmium showered, he yelled over pulses of water, "He won't/can't hurt her. His sexual organ is shorter than human."

"It's more emotional with us."

"I don't know if Rhyodolite explained glass pheromone vials and their sexual significance to the Weaver before the Musician mated the Free Trader."

Sam and Yangchenla. "The Musician and the Weaver were pair-bonded."

Cadmium stuck his soapy head out and looked at me, wrinkles draining foam off his face, nostrils closed. He wiped off his muzzle and said, "Sure."

I said, "The Weaver's a female sex organ." Cunt, in English, but Karst One doesn't insult by sex organs.

"Come on/seriously, Red Clay, she's hands and brain, too. And other significant parts, like an asshole." Humans have them; Gwyngs don't.

"I've only slept with my own species."

"Never came close?" He pulsed the water so loudly I couldn't have answered immediately.

If, if, if . . . yeah, any species that sleeps with rubber Yokamama dolls and plastic vibrators can have a good time with any warm orifices or protuberances, intelligently manipulated. I'd been scared off the times I'd missed. "Close isn't doing it."

"Your crazy brother also prefers (the bigot) his own."

"A Tibetan girl?"

"Yes, but the Barcons won't give him a breeding permit. Sam and Yangchenla received one. When will you apply?" He sounded sexually preoccupied still.

"I haven't talked to Marianne."

"I understand noise for the Linguist in context."

"I think she'd be more interested in linguistics than a baby, anyhow," I said, feeling rather doleful about it. Should we have a child here, raise it among aliens?

We heard the elevator rising in the shaft. Cadmium said, "Back to the front row now, so the Linguist Aspirant won't be angry. Grouchy like most Red Clay species females." He took a second towel from the rack and dried off somewhat, considering how his body hair held water, then wrapped it around his waist. He explained, "First towel was smelly. Exhausted from that smell. Smell soap now."

"Rhyodolite definitely needs a shower," I said. We met Marianne at the elevator. She didn't say anything, just handed Cadmium a bottle of blood.

Molly and Rhyodolite weren't in the living room now. They giggled and koo'ed from her room. "He really needs rest," Cadmium said, slumping down on the floor with his bottle, "and food."

"You tell him," Reeann said.

Cadmium sipped at the bottle, looked at it, and muttered, "Stabilized, not whipped." Then he looked at Marianne and said, "Your sister is corrupting him."

Cadmium was loyal to his kin. And whatever Marianne did, I ought to be loyal to her. But the little runt Gwyng was my first friend here, perverse as he was. I said, "I'll take his food in." Marianne handed me the bottle.

They'd left the door open. Rhyodolite was in Molly's bed, covers up to his little pointed chin. She murmured to him in Karst One—he could understand her—then met me in the middle of the room.

"*Tom, you're a Bible Belt hick,*" she told me in English. "*Sex isn't just reproduction. It relieves tensions, makes us all one body.*"

"*How does Sam feel?*" I asked.

"*He needed a business manager. I couldn't help him.*" She took the bottle from me and went back to help Rhyodolite sit up, held him while he sipped it.

"*Yangchenla always was more interested in business.*"

"*And they're both primitive types to you, aren't they, you racist, yes,*" Molly said fiercely, still in English. "*You threw her out.*"

"*She left me.*"

"*I don't know why Ree puts up with you. You hicked up her name, Reeann. Sounds like someone on 'Hee Haw.'*"

Rhyodolite reached for her lips with his fingers and said, "Red Clay, she's angry?"

"Yes, at me."

He signed to her. She fleered back her lips and slid her incisors over each other, then looked out the window.

Rhyodolite took the bottle from her, drained it, and said to me, "I told her you were my friend."

I felt guilty. Maybe we all should embrace aliens with our genitals, be one flesh. I said, "Molly, he needs rest."

"Were we fucking when you came in?" she replied. I left, closing the door on them.

"Marianne," I asked when I came back into the living room, "do you mind me calling you Reeann?"

"No. I feel like a Reeann here."

"I didn't mean it to be a hick name."

"An innocent name."

Cadmium gulped, tongue muscle between his jawbones bouncing way up, and went toward the stranger's bathroom. Reeann asked, "Are you sick?"

He said, "No," and closed the door.

"He thinks we want to be alone," I said.

"Let's go back to your room," she said, "so he doesn't have to stay in there." We did. "Do you want to apply for a breeding permit now?" she asked.

"This is a crazy place to raise a human child."

"Sam and Yangchenla want one. We have priority on the child Warren's not having." She then said in English, *"God, Tom,"* sat down on my bed and wept. Her tears unsettled me, what bothered her most—Molly with Rhyodolite, Warren, me, having to get a permit for a baby? I sat down beside her and stroked her long hair. An eternity later—no, about five minutes—she went to the bathroom, ran cold water on her eyes, then came out and sat down in front of my terminal.

"You can't key in on mine," I said. "And the files on Earth aren't accessible."

"Ask Chalk and Agate if we can come visit." She got up and walked the floor while I sent them a message. The sun caught her face; she blinked and said, "It is morning, isn't it? I've got to go to a seminar."

"Are you okay?"

"Yes. You've got work of your own to do. Are Chalk and Agate going to reply now or what?"

"I sent it to his office." The computer beeped and I pushed the button for my mail. "Chalk says he has a few others the next slack days, but we could come if it's just to get away. Is it?''

"Yes," she said, "yes, just to get away." She scratched her back and stared out the window.

I typed that in. Chalk typed back, COME, GOOD.

Rhyodolite or Molly left a broken glass vial in the kitchen sink. Cadmium came in just after I did and said, "Please get rid of it before . . ." He fled to the hall.

I got rid of it, furious with the runty Gwyng and his human bitch, then sprayed the kitchen with Gwyng heat pheromone disrupter. Cadmium came back and sprayed the pheromone disrupter on his hand, sniffed deeply. I asked him, "Why did you come here?"

"I've been busy working on new contact procedures for Karriaagzh (don't tell Black Amber). Wanted to talk to you (get sex if possible, subsidiary reason)." He sniffed the room again and sat down in one of our kitchen chairs, turned it to face the atrium. "I'm tamed with Rector bird now."

"How's Rhyodolite?"

Cadmium's shoulder hair bristled a bit, then he said, "Sorry. Rhyodolite. The Linguist should be careful around him. He's loyal to Black Amber (more than I)." He folded his arms around himself, hooking his thumbs together behind his neck. The curved, long armbones fitted in against his sides, the webs stretched across his chest.

As I scrambled some eggs for my supper, I tried to remember when I'd seen him like that—not as often as the other Gwyngs. We didn't speak—finally, I heard the elevator stop at our floor. I went to the front room.

A knock. Neither Molly or Reeann would knock to come in. Sam had practically moved out.

I said, "Who is it?"

Sam answered, "Sam and Yangchenla. Who's home?"

"I'm the only human. Cadmium's with me."

I heard them talking but couldn't make out what they were saying, other than Yangchenla's "wrinkle faces." I said, "He's in the kitchen. Come on in."

They opened the elevator door and swayed toward each

other a microsecond as if uncertain as to whether they
really should come in or not. Both wore grey tunics and
their dark faces looked like formal tribal masks, rigid,
unreadable. "Cadmium and I are upset about Molly and
Rhyodolite," I said.

"We didn't come to discuss that," Chenla said, "We
need to work on being humans together." Had her lips
been that full when we were living together? I felt possessive and stupidly jealous.

"Humans other than you and Marianne live under pass
law here, like South Africa," Sam said. They both kept
standing in the elevator, not coming out. "We don't like
it."

"Humans are xenophobic."

"That's bullshit. Look at Molly. Look at you. Some of
Yangchenla's people are as sophisticated as any other Free
Traders," Sam said.

I heard the door to my room close and knew Cadmium
had gone in there, to let us go to the kitchen if we wanted.
Chenla's face darkened. Sam looked at her and reached
over to squeeze her hand.

"Sam, are you managing well? I feel responsible for
bringing you here."

"Don't worry. Chenla's teaching me."

Chenla added, "Tom, stop being a little alien asskisser
and be a real *human being*." She said that "human being"
in English, Sam's English.

Sam squeezed her hand again, this time hard, like he
might have called me an alien asskisser when they were in
bed, but he didn't want her repeating it. I shouldn't be
jealous; I kicked her out. I had Marianne. "I'll discuss it
with Marianne," I told them. "She isn't home yet."

"I don't want to run into Molly," Sam said. "I didn't
marry her because she was white. If I was . . ." He shut
up and his eyes rolled down. He looked suddenly more
vulnerable, then he looked up at me, the whites of his
eyes yellowish and almost bloodshot, not the cool urban
black guy. "You're the human in power here, so . . ." He
wanted to insult me, but knew it wasn't politically a good
idea.

"Does Cadmium . . ." Yangchenla began to ask. They came out of the elevator together, practically in step.

"No," I said. "He's an honorable Gwyng male."

Her lips twitched back as she looked around the living room. In Tibetan, she said, *"Nicer than what you gave me."*

I said in Karst One, "Marianne is also with Academy and Institutes. And the apartment was also for Sam and Molly, and Warren."

She looked at Sam as she sat down in one of my leather chairs and ran her fingers through the carpet. Then she turned to me and said, "It's not real animal fiber."

"So we don't have high rank."

Sam slumped down on a sofa and huffed, his legs straight out in front of him. Then he asked, "Do they say that humans always fight among themselves?"

"They say we aren't honest about our mating patterns."

"Tom, you told us Karst has a high minimum wage? But that doesn't work for musicians. We gig." There was a Karst equivalent for "gig." "If I didn't have Yangchenla, I'd be poorer than I was in Berkeley. Really Oakland flats poor. It's been no improvement for me with pass laws, being a refugee." He shifted on the couch, straightened up and started talking in black English, *"You happy hear that, white boy?"*

"No," I said. "Yangchenla, tell him it's worse for people in the Primitive Reserve, the Waste."

She said, "So what it's worse there? *Vr'ech* brought us here. You helped . . ."

I interrupted. "Say *uhyalla.* I have friends who aren't my species." *Uhyalla, as in human uhyalla, fellow sapients.*

Chenla finished, ". . . *vr'ech* kidnap Sam and Molly." *Not-us, those fellow sapients.*

Yeah, I guess I did. We sat with our eyeballs roaming in our skulls, not able to look at each other. Marianne came in then, looked around at us and said, "Glad to see you, Sam."

"Did Tom tell you about Yangchenla?" Sam asked her.

Reeann suddenly looked very wary. She went to the table and put down the printout she was carrying. "You were Tom's former mate?"

"I'm now Sam's mate for a child." She showed Reeann the scar where the birth-control implant had been. "We are sophisticated humans here, and maligned by the other sapient *uhyalla*. Perhaps the terms 'refugee' and 'primitive' don't affect you as they do us?"

"I don't like it, either," Marianne said. "Karriaagzh said to work with the History Committee. Closest way for us is through Black Amber."

Yangchenla frowned, "The top-rank wrinkled face."

"Cadmium is in my room," I told Marianne. "He's not utterly Black Amber's tool."

"We're going to Chalk and Agate's next break days," Marianne said. "Maybe you both should come. They're good people to discuss these sorts of things with."

"They have a Jerek sterile daughter," Yangchenla said. "*You* discuss it, then come back and meet more of us."

Marianne murmured, in English, *"Community Action. I love it."*

Sam laughed, then said to me, "A thousand light-years from Earth and she's still a red diaper baby."

"We need to get Molly . . ." Marianne began.

"Leave Molly to Rhyodolite," Sam said.

Reeann's head jerked back and she blinked, then said to Yangchenla, "How did you get a breeding permit?"

"DNA readings on both of us, pelvic exam, exam for him. From the Barcons. But your rank permits you to bear a child without anyone else's permit."

"Oh," Marianne said, almost breathing it. She wanted a baby, now. I could imagine her ovaries dying to shed live eggs—female, despite maybe being smarter than me.

"Do you have an implant?" Yangchenla asked her.

"No, they let me stock up on birth-control pills."

Yangchenla's eyes went as round as Oriental eyes could go. "You voluntarily avoid babies?"

Reeann said, "Yes, I take a pill every day."

Yangchenla began in Tibetan, *"What kind of stupid . . ."* then remembered I understood Tibetan. She leaned back and stared at Marianne as if Marianne had pulled off her human face to reveal Gwyng wrinkles.

Reeann said, as if apologizing, "I want to have a baby eventually. What's day care like?"

"Day care" didn't quite work translated into Karst One equivalences. Yangchenla continued to stare at her. I explained, "How are the children cared for when the parents are working?"

"Get a bear to tend you all. They love sapient pets," Yangchenla said, "but they eat pure meats and must be petted themselves."

Marianne said, "I don't believe in having servants."

"Bears," Yangchenla said, "take care of you. Out in the waste, some humans have human servants. One town human family is taken care of by two bears. The emotional difference is considerable." She spoke formal Karst One, but Yangchenla's human vocal apparatus made her sound weird, a pedantic primitive.

"Introduce me to that family," Reeann said. "If the relationship isn't exploitive, I might enjoy it."

"You'll have to see," Yangchenla said. "We must be going, but I'm glad to have seen you, Marianne."

"And you, too, Yangchenla." Reeann stood when they did. When they got in the elevator, Reeann turned to me and said, "Would it bother you if I got to know her better?"

"Does it bother you that she's sleeping with your sister's husband?"

"Molly wasn't faithful on Earth. I bet Chenla is faithful."

I felt shrunken as though the women had poured alum over me. "As far as I know. But I feel more comfortable with you, Reeann. Please."

"It bothers you?"

"If you ever are going to be pregnant, then I guess you want to be close to other human women in the same situation. The kids should be friends. But you and I . . ."

"Tom, if I'd been just another Berkeley Ph.D. and not radical, I'd have probably snubbed you."

"I'm not proud of my feelings about the Tibetans."

Cadmium came out and said, "Can this wrinkled face make you (both) some tea?"

Reeann said, "Sure, Cadmium."

"I am not Rhyodolite. You are not Molly. Good that we both understand." Then he turned and headed toward the kitchen.

After he'd gone, I said, "He doesn't tease as much as the other male Gwyngs."

The teakettles on Karst boil fast. Cadmium came back with three cups full, one for him, and sat cross-legged on the carpet, sipping through his tongue curled into a tube, not saying anything until he finished his tea. Then he said, "I have to leave now. I won't bed (not sexually or even just unconscious with them) with Rhyodolite and the Weaver. I know you wouldn't/don't want to embarrass us by asking/I'm lonely (need comfortable sleeping companions)."

He climbed to his feet, using his long arms for leverage and balance, then felt his wrinkles. "Dry," he muttered. I remembered seeing him oil his skin—just him, not the other Gwyngs.

"Cadmium, thanks for bringing us tea," Reeann said. "I don't know what that means for you."

He went over and brushed his knuckles against her upper arm. "A kindness, same as with you. We share an embarrassment." Reeann looked at me, then touched her elbow gently to his. He said, "Take care of Red Clay. Red Clay, be as Barcons with her."

Be mated for life.

He got his sleeping bag and left.

What work was I doing during this time? I was learning how to supervise cadets, among other things. My memory divided my human family life from my Yauntry negotiations and worries about cadets I supervised as the Institute of Control began training everyone in basic defense. We sapients continued studying one another and our histories, made behavioralist gossip, actually.

To take a break from both memory tracks, Marianne and I flew to the north toward our Rector's People. As the plane took off, Marianne said, "I'm going to pay more attention to the terrain this time. I was in shock before."

"They've tried to please everyone."

"But there's no permafrost," Marianne said, a non sequitur, I thought, until I remembered Agate's pets who ate food imported from Jerek Home. The creatures, who had bloated noses and ragged coats, sweated all the time. Too hot, even in Karst's north, for them.

North of Karst City—first plains and hills, then higher mountains which flattened out, covered by deep green forests, hundred of miles of them, threaded by creeks and rivers. Mountains surrounded the Polar Ocean, which was bigger than Earth's Arctic, not so landlocked. From what I'd studied about climatology, I knew both the bare black mountain rocks and the ocean itself warmed the far north here, but the sky stayed clouded all winter inside the polar mountain ring.

Marianne blinked when we hit the fog bank. "It's like the Aleutians," she said.

I visualized a map and said, "Yeah, water all round."

Our pilot began taking the plane down. A chain of little green lights glowed by the airstrip, snow in piles beside it. Other lights guided us to the Jereks' house. As we walked beside the row of small green bulbs leading to the house, I heard a high-pitched whistle. Lisanmarl came strolling on her short legs through the fog, naked except for a short leather loincloth, the tips of her fur wet from condensed fog, her black nose swaying from side to side. "They didn't do it," she said. I knew what it was Chalk and Agate didn't do—she hadn't been neutered.

Marianne smiled me a smile that said, *if I catch your hands straying below this creature's waist, I'll cordon off my pussy with barbed wire.*

"Hi, Lisanmarl," I said. "Marianne and I are here to talk to your parents. Marianne wants to talk me into getting a breeding permit."

Lisanmarl dropped her nose and hissed as if I'd smacked her. "I didn't ask to be a sterile." Marianne's lips jerked and she looked as abashed as I felt. Lisanmarl whistled softly and rubbed her hands down a leg of each of us, fast, and skittered away down the chain of green lights.

Chalk and Agate sat on the veranda in Jerek leathers,

the front and back flaps longer than Lisanmarl's, down to the ground. I shivered to see them, but they seemed very comfortable, drinking iced drinks with fog condensing on the tips of their fur.

Marianne said, "Your fur must insulate you very well."

"The design catches water when the temperature is around freezing," Agate said. "Did Lisanmarl pester you?"

"No," I said.

Lisanmarl hissed slightly as she went inside.

"You must admit," Reeann said, "that most human fathers would just have their daughters spayed if that would cure them of a permanent esterous that could be lethal."

Yeah, the Jereks allowed their steriles a lot of civil liberties. Lisanmarl could even sell herself as a sexual entertainer. Chalk and Agate were unhappy, but Lisanmarl hadn't had her malfunctioning ovaries stripped out.

While Marianne unpacked, I went to the bathroom and the kitchen to see what they brought in for us to eat: milk, greens, beans, white square curds—either cheese or bean—and what looked like two fryers—frozen birds the size of chicken fryers, at least. When I came back to our room, Marianne said, "Chalk said we should come down to the tunnel in whatever clothes it takes us to be comfortable."

I said, "It's chilly down there." We put on pants and tunic-length sweaters and carried our parkas. Down the elevator to their space.

The tunnel was as I'd remembered: dimly lit, cold water running between stones on the floor, water filling a tube and tipping it over, the plink, plink of dripping stones over pools. And the smell—wet fur, wet stone, mildew. Marianne blew out her breath—it barely fogged, the air was so humid. She said, not quite questioning, "You were led down here by pheromones and Brahms?"

We heard weird chimes then behind the first door on the right. "Come in," Chalk said, then the chimes began again, slightly discordant to a human ear. Marianne went in first and gasped. Chalk and Agate sat in front of rows of stones threaded on monofilament—jadeite, jasper, triple rows of stone chimes ran the width of the room against the left-hand wall. Candles on gold stands six feet, seven feet, high flickered in the air currents we'd stirred as we entered the room. There was another odd light in the room—then I saw chunks of luminescent wood—fox fire—strapped to the ceiling. When the bioluminescence died, they could take out the old wood and put in new.

"This wasn't here when I came down before?"

"No, we change our tunnels often," Agate said. "We will suggest something, and we want you to sit and listen to our chimes before you reply."

Chalk said, "You should work with Yangchenla, Sam, and the other humans. Improve your cultural level here."

Agate added, "Just because Yangchenla and Sam had a good idea first is no reason for you to be stupid."

"And don't talk until we've finished playing," Chalk added just before he struck a chime stone. They turned their backs to us and moved up and down the rows of chimes.

The music sounded almost like Yangchenla's music. I shuddered, wanting to grasp these notes, change them and make the music be what I'd expected. Instead, the slight discordances made me uneasy. I looked at Marianne. She exaggerated a wince.

The sounds weren't quite like nails on slate. I thought about being human with the Tibetans, with Warren. Shit, Warren and Sam adjusted better to the Tibetans than I did—were they more primitive than me? I felt a bit racist to think that—of course, Sam wasn't as primitive as I'd been when I first came to Karst.

I remembered one time when Yangchenla, naked, accused me of hating other humans, of wanting to be a Gwyng, an Ahram. Her kin were as capable as I, she told me; we were all hopelessly human. She then pulled on the Coke-bottle green American girl dress Tesseract had given her years earlier to wear for me when I first slept with her. After she'd jerked the dress down, she screamed—the air seemed crumpled by it—and ripped the dress down the bodice, stepped out of its ruins and put on Tibetan clothes.

"Why," I'd asked her.

"Because you want what isn't here," she had said.

Now I had Reeann and we both hung out with non-human sapients in Karst City and in space. Maybe Molly was right, give the aliens a good genital embrace?

Warren—Warren fit right in with the Tibetans. The Federation sapients mangled one another, cultural contamination, rebuilt language centers and organs—and sometimes went further than that. The Barcons could destroy and rebuild whole personalities, and I'd brought Warren to that possibility.

The stones quivered to silence.

"Do you hear them as being in tune?" Marianne asked.

"No, these are bitter stones," Chalk told her. "They unsettle."

"Do we seem like Tibetans to you?" I asked.

"We won't judge a whole species in a lump," Chalk said, his nose dropping as if I'd annoyed him.

"Yangchenla ripped up a dress I liked."

"You wanted to completely deny her family." Agate sat down, kneeling, her short legs splayed out to either side. She fanned out the leather loincloth in front of her.

"My family's dead," Reeann said.

Agate looked at Chalk and answered, "Not your sister. And Tom has a brother. Your parents are dead and that's sad. At least, it would be to us. But you could have children."

"I want a child, but we're not as pair-bonded as you," Marianne said.

"We have no choice. We nurse a child together; we bond. There seems such pain in breaks when the species has a choice."

Chalk added, "I hope you are both committed to taking care of the child. But Marianne can reproduce herself even if you don't want a child, Tom."

Since I saw by her face that Marianne wasn't going to say anything, I said, "We heard something about bears." Why were we talking about children?

Chalk picked up the stick he'd used to strike the chimes and bit it. Agate made a noise between a hiss and a whistle.

"If bears are a bad idea, tell us," Marianne said.

"They would take care of your child," Chalk said. "But you distort their mating patterns by providing yourselves as child surrogates." Agate interrupted in Jerek and they discussed us in a language we couldn't follow.

"Oh, get a bear," Agate said. "But human con-specifics would take better care of a human child than a bear would."

"No human child could grow up normally here," I said.

"It's very awkward for Tom," Marianne said.

"Having Tom try to be a non-human is also awkward. You're a human. He's a human. The others are human, too," Chalk said. "If their wombs aren't nourishing their embryos well enough to get good baby brains, or if they don't know the right experiences to grow the brains properly, then the Federation should help them more. You and Tom are fully intelligent."

" 'If their wombs aren't nourishing their embryos . . .' " Marianne repeated as if she'd just gotten a clue to the universe.

"Don't you know that the female must be well grown and then fed and exercised properly while the fetus is developing to make good brain development. Then as the child grows, learning helps the brain become more complex."

"We kept arguing heredity and environment when we discussed that," Marianne said.

Chalk said, "Absolutely everything is important. That's why we have fetus-bearing classes and child growth classes when we know the species's developmental biology."

"Oh," Marianne said like perhaps we were dumb.

"We're a bit harsh on this because of Lisanmarl. Barcons are researching that developmental problem."

"Will Barcons deliver me?"

"You're intelligent enough for a child-birth group. You'll learn to aid one another's births. I'll have another child to replace the breeding potential we lost with Lisanmarl," Agate said. "We can do it together. And with Yangchenla."

"I don't want to have a child now," I said. "When

we're ready, how, precisely, do we get a breeding permit?''

"This is for Ree's child, as an Institute linguist." Chalk reached into a cabinet and brought out a piece of fiber-surfaced material like plasticized paper, no, parchment. He slipped a needle out of a case and came over to me. When he showed me the form, his face shifted up and down as though he wanted to watch my expression but didn't want to give me a challenging stare. Printed on the form was "Officer/aspirant mated couple Red Clay/Ree Karst cycle 5,062, the nineteenth light period. A breeding permit for Ree with sera samples attached. Witnessed by Rector's People Agate and Chalk." A second circle was for the female's pregnancy test.

Chalk went over to Reeann, took her index finger, and pricked it. I said, "Reeann's baby. Reeann's baby? She's my wife. I . . . ''

Reeann looked up at me as her blood fell on the second circle. "Tom, better to nurse while I'm still in training. Being out on teams is risky, no?"

Agate said, "Would you want this to be a semen sample baby? And, Tom, the Barcons want your help in subduing Warren.''

"Oh, damn you all." I felt trapped by humans and aliens. The whole universe forced me to be a brother, a father.

Chalk said, "They're trying to bring him for brain mapping. He's being uncooperative."

"Did I deserve this?" Warren asked me. He was in a cage, hunkered up on the bunk with his arms around his knees, a cigarette in one hand. I was inside with him.

"I'm sorry, Warren. They say they can help."

"They've been netting me every month to inject that damn Prolixin." He dragged on the cigarette, pinching it between his fingers and squinting through the smoke. "Okay, they did ease down the dose."

"Why didn't you just come in when they wanted you to?"

He crushed out the lit tobacco and stuck the butt in his

shirt pocket—an American-styled shirt in Karst fabric. His Tibetan girl must have made it for him. "It's insulting. I was almost free when you guys dragged me off."

A Barcon came into the hall between the holding cells and watched us. Warren scowled at him. I said, "Warren, I couldn't have left you there, that way. You were . . . you're my brother."

"And you're a pouch-hole licker."

"Warren, don't be hostile."

The Barcon finally spoke. "Brain mapping goes easier with a cooperative specimen."

Barcon, specimen is the wrong word to use, I thought. Warren bit down on his lips, lips completely curled inside his mouth.

The Barcon plucked at his shoulder fur, then continued, "Warren, we're leaving your personality intact because you are a sapient. Your Karst language shows full structure, even though you try to distort it toward the primitive dialect variation."

"*Nifty,*" Warren said in English.

"Warren, please cooperate. They're going to help you."

"Whether I like it or not."

"Your drug use shifted brain chemistry and some structure," The Barcon said. "We will try to restore function."

"I did drugs because . . ."

The Barcon interrupted, "The environment changed for you and the other humans here. It can continue to change."

"We're not in Virginia anymore, Warren."

"Get me out of this cage."

"Promise no punching," the Barcon said.

"Yes, unless you . . . *shit*, yes." Warren still used English expletives. The Barcon came up to the cage door and keyed the combination on a number pad. Warren didn't look at the Barcon as he slouched out. I followed Warren, seeing how his shoulders slumped, how grey and bald he was getting, his neck coarse-skinned behind. What was he going to do here if they *could* fix him up? We walked into the brain-mapping room where three more Barcons surrounded a chair with a needled helmet like the one I'd been tested with before I came to Karst.

"The needles are so little they don't hurt," I told Warren. He looked at me like *you dwork* and at the Barcons as if speculating on their muscle insertions, the body leverage they had over him. Finally, he sat in the chair, gripping the armrests hard enough to push the blood from his fingers. His left eyelid twitched.

The Barcon who'd walked down from the cages with us cranked the helmet down, pushed a button, cranked the helmet down farther, then said, "Mapping the brain is a bit more complex than minimally testing it."

I held Warren's shoulders as they injected him with something that gave him slow breathing rigid flexibility. Whatever it was, it didn't stop his sweating. "Can he hear me?" I asked the Barcons, my hand dropping on his wrist.

"Feel the pulse," one of the three other Barcons said.

I did; it was racing. "Warren, it's all right."

The four Barcons began strapping Warren in the chair, immobilizing his head inside the helmet. "While a little needle motion isn't too harmful," the largest Barcon explained, "you want his brain map to be accurate, don't you?"

I nodded, not quite sure. A Barcon mopped out Warren's mouth with a wet swab, then fastened the helmet's chin strap. They left Warren and began to stand around a holotank and multi-keyed computer, muttering to each other in Barq, their backs to us.

Warren blinked slowly, with automated blinks. I kept saying, "Warren, I want you to be completely okay," rubbing his fingers.

Then one Barcon came back to lower a shield over Warren's eyes. Urine began seeping through Warren's pants. The Barcon said, "Warren, we're beginning repairs, like the language operations, setting up brain growth."

When the Barcons finally lifted the eye shield, Warren's blinks were as regularly timed as ever, but Warren's pulse ran fast, then slow, odd feeling him through the skin without him being able to tell me how he felt.

They injected a counter-drug to the one that had left

him paralyzed. His eye blinks became erratic. A Barcon unfastened the chin strap. Warren gasped, flexed his tongue, and said, *"Bastards."*

"Everything must stay in place. We need you to talk."

Warren's face seemed to age, wrinkles deeper, eyes filmed, not quite frowning, not quite. I said to the Barcons, "You're making it a confrontation."

"We're helping him," the Barcon who'd brought us into the room said. "We've done brain reconstructions for our own people after parasite-removal."

"I'm cold," Warren said. One of them loosened the straps holding down his thighs, then wrapped him with a paper-felt blanket. Warren rolled his eyes at the Barcon and said, "What do you need me to say? 'Poor stupid human craves interstellar master'?"

"Close your eyes," the Barcon who'd put the blanket on him said.

Warren squenched his eyelids tight.

One of the other Barcons at the computer spoke in Barq. The Barcon beside Warren said, "Tell us what you see."

"It's a small bird," Warren said.

"Are the beats regular?"

"Wing flaps regular. And it's going up to the right. Is that important?"

"Regularly, or in jerks."

"Jerked down."

"Here?"

"Bird flew backward and jerked."

"Discontinuity mapped," the Barcon at the computer said. "We'll rebuild the axons and dendrites in that area."

"Nifty," Warren said, "but what am I missing?"

"Fine discrimination," the Barcon said, "in threat evaluation. That's why you lost control of your bladder sphincter when we shielded your vision."

Warren turned brick red. I wished I wasn't here. They asked, "Are you ready to continue mapping?"

"Sure," Warren said like he was going to kill them when they loosened the straps. They continued with grids that distorted across injured parts of Warren's brain, washes of colors that shifted where neurotransmitters were inadequate or in excess.

Finally, they seemed to be playing with him, and I, wondering about my own paranoia, asked when they'd be finished with him.

They stopped and talked Barq, then said, "If he won't hit us when we loosen the straps, we won't play him out."

"Warren?" Pale and sweaty, his face looked as much younger from the sweat as it had looked older from tense muscles earlier. He nodded to me. I said, "Let him up."

"I've got to take a bath," he said.

I went out to a waiting room, then one of the Barcons brought me back to him. They'd put him in a regular Karst hospital bed, paper-felt sheets up to his chin. Beard stubs coarsened his skin. I'd refused to be depilated, but on his face, beard stubbles looked threatening.

"I can't remake my life just because *vr'ech* re-build my brain," Warren said, his head turned to the side, eyes blinking. His Karst was perfect now, as though the human accent earlier had been contrived. "I have a past."

"We can change your memories of that," one of the Barcons said, "and you have a slightly longer future now."

Warren rolled over to completely face the wall, the sheet slipping off his hairy shoulder. For a second, I was as intimidated of him as I'd been as a child, wondering if a completely repaired Warren would be my superior. An ugly surge of jealousy—I should feel happy for Warren.

He mumbled to the wall, "If you change my memories, you kill me. See you *bastards*."

The Barcon curled his nose to the side as if he knew what the English word "bastards" meant. I started out. Warren rolled over and sat up in the bed, saying in English, almost joking, *"Tom, am I gonna have to have breakfast alone?"*

"I've got to get back to Marianne."

"Tom. Well, be that way."

I felt quivery. The Barcon said, "He can stay overnight. Do you want him in this room?"

"Hell, no, he'd just talk all night trying to justify his space-bat friends. Let me see him in the morning."

As we walked out and down the hall, I asked the Barcon, "What kind of job can he get here?"

"Laser weld checker, stone cutter-layer machine driver. Not my problem, though."

Warren and I met behind the hospital for breakfast out on a patio. Huge birds with thick legs and brutal claws scratched, no, gouged out tubers from the earth around. Warren came to the door and watched them before coming closer. One of them sniffed the air and began walking toward us, a forty-pound bird trying to sneak up on our breakfast.

The Barcon with Warren shooed the bird back among the plants it and its fellows were thinning.

"You eat those things?" Warren asked.

"Some. They break garden soil for us," the Barcon answered. "Vegetarians, most of the time."

Warren sat down and looked at me so hard I wanted to say something, couldn't quite think of what would suit. "Are you doing okay?" I finally asked.

Warren pulled off the dish covers: eggs, toast, grits, butter. He said, "Looks just like home. Fake eggs, I bet."

"No," I said. "They eat eggs here."

Warren nodded at the earth-turning birds, "Those. Bet they're bigger than a turkey's egg. That's okay for a man kidnapped by his own brother to a planet light-years from the halfway house that was going to let him out in six months."

"Warren, I was trying to help you."

"You can't even get along with the other humans here."

"I'm trying."

Warren didn't answer. He put eggs, toast, and grits on his plate, tasted them, then put butter on everything and stared at his food, waiting for the butter to melt. Finally, he said, "They have any jobs I can do here? I'm not going to live off you. Sam wasn't going to leech off you either."

"They said something about weld checker . . ."

Warren laughed. "Damn whole universe wants me in some shit assembly-line job."

"Warren, Marianne wants to get together with Yangchenla and Sam, and the Tibetans in the city. We need to help the other humans, Yangchenla says.''

"You were a prick to the other humans, I heard."

"You're such a great example of human."

"My brain was drug-distorted, so I've got an excuse for hating . . . Tom, they treat us like animals."

"Not me."

"Me, the people in the wasteland. Round us up, brand us, stick us with needles."

"Humans are xenophobic."

"Oh, hell, Tom," he said in English. *"Maybe old humans get set in their ways if their brains aren't . . ."* He shut up and ate his eggs.

"You'll still be you," I said to him.

He gave me one of his wartime stares, light-years deep.

I said, my voice not quite matching the certainty of the statement, "You're my big brother. You'll be fine."

"Tom . . ." He almost said more, but didn't. One of the big birds raised up on claw tips to rake away my grits with a beak like a vulture's, no bigger. I noticed then that it had little paws tucked up under the feathers, not short wings. Unevolved Karriaagzhes. Warren whacked at it with a dish cover. Eyes wobbling independently of each other, the bird jumped backward before Warren connected.

"Maybe this is all an hallucination, but if it isn't, I'm in deep shit," Warren said. "Your Gwyng friends are going to pick on me forever."

"Black Amber didn't do any damage to me."

Warren laughed and scraped the rest of the food out for the big birds before the Barcons could complain.

"It won't just be your baby," I told her. "I don't think . . . ".

"You're scared," Marianne said.

"Yes, I am scared. My brother, what we face in first contacts. I don't want to leave an orphan here."

She sighed, eyes averted, hands rubbing her stomach, low where the ovaries waited. "Life is a risk, but . . . Tom, now's the best time. I'm still studying."

"Wait. A human baby here."

"Yes," Marianne said, "but only a little wait. Don't you feel empty spaces aching to be filled with humans?"

Funny thing was yes, I did, and both those empty spaces and my desire to fill them scared me. What if the whole sapient universe wanted to fill those spaces, too?

Marianne paced our apartment floor as she and I waited for the rest of the humans, no, just some representative humans, to come to our meeting. She'd set out buttered tea modern Tibetan style and a barley dish I suspected some Tibetan Buddhist wife passed around Berkeley. Warren was in the back of the apartment, sulking.

"Do we have to serve food?" I asked, prodding in among the barley grains with a Karst knife-spoon.

"Tom, it's pan-human hospitality, serving food. We eat only with those we trust."

"Or pretend to trust," I said, smoothing down the grains I'd ruffled.

We heard the elevator rise and unlocked the door. Yangchenla and Sam got out. She had on high-heeled shoes and a peach-colored sheath dress slit up the front to show her legs. Sam wore an electric green suit in glossy fabric I'd never seen before. Both of them wore big glasses, so dark I didn't understand how they saw through them.

Sam smiled at me and took his off. The shading was one-way. "We're showing them Terran style," he said, sliding his glasses back on. Yangchenla looked as if she was born wearing twentieth-century American clothes. The shades made her face seem less flat.

"My uncle Trung, my parents, three other shopkeepers, and Rimpoche Dorge Karmapa will also come," Chenla told Marianne. "I even told Molly, if she is interested in human problems these days."

Marianne looked more amused than hurt. She said, "Molly is still genetically human, isn't she?"

Sam turned darker, his nostrils spread, then he laughed, almost like Warren, that laugh, a man against a whole culture. He said, "Just as long as the bat doesn't come." Yangchenla leaned against him and reached her hand down to stroke his leg. I felt instantly jealous, not that I wanted to give up Marianne.

Just then the elevator went down. Yangchenla walked to the table to inspect the tea and barley while the rest of us waited silently for the others to come up.

Yangchenla's parents—funny how dignified they seemed here—in city tunics, he with his sparse grey beard trimmed. With them was a man in Tibetan clothes, padded shirt and pants and his hair tied up with thick cords—an old leathery man with slit eyes, skin so loose over them that the glitter was almost obscured. He'd pinned his city entrance pass to his shirt: Dorge Karmapa.

Just as they got off, the elevator went back down. "The others said they'd meet us here," Chenla's mother said. "That must be them."

"Are there not-us here?" her father asked.

"No," I said.

"We'll have to get them to cooperate sooner or later," Marianne said. "I hope you aren't bigoted."

Karmapa sighed. He had a funny rolling sort of walk, almost like a Gwyng's, and he went over to the table and began prodding among the barley grains as I'd done earlier. "Tsampa, I suppose, cooked alien style."

"From what your country became after your people left it," Marianne said.

"You're funny-looking people to be our kind, both paler and darker. The *vr'ech* don't consider you primitives?"

"No, Red Clay and I are being trained. We thought that all the humans should be offered Karst City educations."

Instead of answering, he pulled out some instrument I'd never seen before, blown like an oboe, with a reed, and played music more complex than any I'd heard among the Tibetans. Sam relaxed, then listened intensely, one ear tilted slightly toward Karmapa. But I could tell that Sam didn't recognize the music as particularly human either. Karmapa pulled the reed out of his mouth and said, "We are people who've been affected by time passed among strangers. We have not been static."

"No," Marianne said, softly. I did tend to think the Tibetans were sixteenth-century time travelers, then wondered what that village was like if it helped aliens stranded in the last contact war. Maybe not so primitive?

The elevator came up with the other Tibetans, including Yangchenla's younger brother, the one who wanted to be a cadet. Two were women, the third adult was a man. The man wore Tibetan clothes as did one of the women; the other woman wore Jerek leathers over her pants as a belt, higher up on the waist than a Jerek would have had the body strap, with front and back panels in tooled leather that went down to her calves. Her face was less broad than Yangchenla's, the cheekbones more angular and the nose more pointed. The elevator doors closed behind them and we heard the elevator sinking in the shaft.

Yangchenla's uncle Trung and her brother went up to each other and whispered, then looked at me. Both seemed annoyed.

Karmapa meanwhile had looked around the front room and down both corridors. He asked, "Is this for humans."

"For us," I said, remembering that Yangchenla's kin tried to move in with me when I had a smaller place. "For me and my wife, my brother, her sister and her husband." Sam pressed his tongue against his parted teeth. Woops. Ugh. Yangchenla had wanted her brother and her parents to live with us. Karmapa smiled at me.

"It comes with being Academy and Institute," Marianne said. "We'd like all humans to be able to take training in those places, to be educated and tested for that training."

"Dung hole," Trung said in Tibetan to Yangchenla's younger brother, "he sure has one if the wrinkled-faces don't." Did they remember that I knew Tibetan?

Warren came out then, his feet bare, shirt unbuttoned, listening while Karmapa said, "I represent the hill people to the city people and have worked with the other sapients in Support and Free Trade. We need to get to know one another better, Red Clay Tom."

Warren laughed. *"My little brother, he's saying you ain't boss of the humans,"* he said in English.

"My brother, Warren Easley," I said.

"Older," Karmapa said.

Warren said, *"But not even Support, yet."*

Karmapa said, "Warren has been with us, so we know there was madness in your family. Thank you for sparing Yangchenla the mothering of a difficult baby."

Marianne flushed. I said to her in English, *"This was your idea, bringing in these people."*

She replied in the same language, *"Well, actually it is an insult to an older man to find a younger guy has rank over him for reasons he never agreed to. You aren't a hereditary noble, you know."*

Warren laughed again. Karmapa kept his face still, then said, "We know much more than you realize, some of us. We . . ."

Yangchenla clapped her hands once. Marianne turned pale, her lips moving as though she was almost speaking. Karmapa smiled and bowed to the walls. "To the others listening," he said, "we mean you no harm; we want to improve our own situations."

"How?" Marianne asked, her eyes on Karmapa. He was in charge. "Have you petitioned them?"

"You might," I said, "begin with Karriaagzh if you haven't done so already."

"The bird's position is unsteady," Karmapa said. "Might we not approach the History Committee? You could introduce me to one."

Warren kept smiling at me, leaning up against a wall with one bare foot braced against it, his right hand on his chin. He said in English, *"Tell him to get dressed in city clothes if he wants to make a good impression."*

I couldn't tell Karmapa any such thing. Marianne said, "Rimpoche Dorge Karmapa, do you have any sense of whether humans are as law-abiding as Federation species?"

He smiled and said, "Unfortunately, my dear, we have put a name on the Memorial Wall within living memory."

One cross-species murder, recently. Not necessarily so recently, just within living memory, maybe his memory? He was old. Warren was the one who asked, "What were they trying to do?"

"Barcons were doing their duty."

Sterilization, birth control, injections of Prolixin, brain-wipe—Barcon duties. I asked, "So what happened and how long ago was it and what happened to the killer?"

"Twenty-seven cycles back. It is not important," Karmapa replied while looking at the floor, eyes averted even from my shoes.

Yangchenla said, "But others, Federation spies, have killed across species line for stupider reasons. They were going to expel all humans from the city. Rimpoche Dorge and his father won us the right to stay."

Trung said, "They sent the man back to our former place. In the middle of a riot."

"What were the Barcons doing?"

"Trying to control his births," Karmapa said. "But they have always done that."

"All Federation species can only have so many young on Karst," I said. "They limit everyone. This isn't just something they do to us."

"Some get unlimited breeding permits," Yangchenla said.

"Black Amber herself doesn't have one. She has to take her nymphs off-planet to get them pouched now."

Yangchenla's lower lip jutted out and she drew her head back. Everyone else shifted in their chairs or finally sat down except Yangchenla, Sam, and Karmapa. Warren eased himself down the wall and sat cross-legged, back against it, and picked at a callus on his big toe. Karmapa shifted his pelvis slightly, spread his legs, weight evenly over them, and folded his arms on his chest. "I don't say the Federation is unfair to us in that. They are unfair in other things."

"We don't have a sponsoring planet," I said.

"Yet you and your new woman are getting the training, without growing up on Karst."

"Maybe that's a plus for them," Warren suggested. "Not growing up here, getting warped by being low status."

Then we heard the elevator doors open. Black Amber, all alone in her Sub-Rector's uniform, stepped off the elevator, lips pursed. "Red Clay, (im)power(ment) gift. You can appoint two *hums*, your people, to either Academy or an Institute each year. The bird and your Rector's People, old and new, agree.''

She signed at Karmapa and pulled her lips back with her index fingers, turned and showed her teeth to Yangchenla, then touched Marianne's hand.

Warren looked at the Tibetans explaining the hand signs to each other, their faces suddenly more ethnic, less simply human than they'd been before Black Amber stepped off the elevator. He said, ''She must have pissed down their backs.''

''She just gave me the power to appoint humans to the Academy or an Institute,'' I told him.

''Sure did piss on 'um, little brother, unless they've got leverage on you,'' Warren said in English.

''Warren,'' Marianne began to say.

But Black Amber interrupted her, ''Marianne, go easy/ don't judge. I preserve Tom as alpha male human.''

My belly muscles went rigid as if I was going to fight. ''Black Amber, you could have helped earlier?''

''No agitation earlier.'' She shrugged one of her fake human shrugs, pulled up her lip corners to give me an imitation human smile, and backed into the elevator, but held the doors open. ''If it makes you feel better, I did not to help h'mins in general (killer xeno-flip-flops), but for you. And for the Linguist.''

Marianne said in English, *''I'm so thrilled.''*

Karmapa stared at Marianne, then smiled.

Black Amber koo'ed softly and the elevator doors closed in front of her, sliding up in a greasy hiss.

Yangchenla's brother squared his shoulders and looked at me like a young bird dog. I said to him, ''Let me tell you what they're going to put you through.''

''He knows,'' Yangchenla says. ''Operations, body dehaired, non-con-specific roommates.''

I said, ''And he'll still be a refugee.''

Marianne said, ''But that won't last long.''

Sam, who hadn't said much since he came in, said, ''Yangchenla's pregnant.''

I looked at Marianne. She stared a second at Chenla as

if my old lover had challenged her, then went up and embraced her.

Karmapa said, "We need more of us here."

"So everyone's been telling me," I said. "Marianne and I have a breeding permit, but . . ." But what? Knock her up. Give in to the ache of those empty spaces. Become a parent forever.

= 9 =

Babies

Actually trying to knock up Marianne seemed both great and horrid.

The Barcons washed the birth-control hormones out of Reeann's system, conditioned her ovaducts with a treatment they'd perfected on Tibetan women, checked my sperm, and turned us loose. "Don't think about it," one said. "Just continue your typical sex behaviors."

So we'd sat in bed one day watching rain streak down the outside windows. All the other humans were gone, our door to the courtyard hall stood open, and we shivered with the prospect of becoming parents.

"It would just be one child at first," Marianne said. "We don't twin in my family."

"Nor in mine," I said.

She looked at me as if to say something, like, silly, I supply the eggs, but just stretched out on the bed and hummed.

When I came, sweating and shuddering, she reached up with hot hands, ran her fingers through my hair and held my head. "It's the right time," she said.

"Marianne, you were an independent woman all your life, and now you're going to become a mother."

"It's all right, Tom. You're going to be a father."

Yeah. And that rainy day must have been the time, because within a week, Marianne came back from the Barcons with her test results.

* * *

Pregnancy had privileges—Chalk and Agate told us to take off three days vacation on top of the week break days. We went on a long bike ride on the electric cart trails. Both of us were as skittish as teenagers, me thinking how alien our baby would be, growing up here. Marianne claimed to be nervous about dislodging the fetus, but she still rode bike at twenty miles per hour.

"Nothing's changed," she said, eyeing a straight section free of other traffic.

"Nothing has changed yet," I said, hands clammy, skin shorts actually chilly as the wind beat the sweat out of them.

She began pedaling faster and faster, soon too fast for her to talk. I could keep up with her now—maybe I was in better shape, or maybe she was de-conditioned. I still had enough wind to tell her, "Don't overdo it."

Wind whipped tears out of her eyes or was she really crying? We reached the next curve and slowed down. "Marianne, you're not sorry, are you?"

"What, that I've given up bike racing?" She looked over at me and her bike wobbled. "Or your attitude about humans?"

"I'm sorry," I said, "Sorry I asked."

We rode on at a more reasonable pace, faster though than the quadrapeds a couple of Ahrams rode on the trail. The animals started, puffing through their nostrils at us.

"Are you staying at Tenleaving?" the female Ahram asked.

"Yes," I said.

"Beautiful place," she replied, "for ex-brachiators."

We began the uphill climb, pedal cadence dropping, downshifting. "I should have thought about touring gears," Marianne said, her face red, sweat trickling down into her eyebrows.

Tenleaving was set in cliffs and trees, a multi-leveled resort with swinging bridges and spectacular views of waterfalls, a little train that went swinging around the cliffs like a roller coaster, a real ape playhouse.

When we reached the base of Tenleaving Mountain, an

elevator opened its two huge doors, each sliding sideways. I spotted the electric sensors, but the thing did have a Wizard of Oz effect. We pushed our bikes up into it. The cabin was big enough for two electric carts or a half dozen pseudo horses. The lights came on, the doors pulled together, and the elevator lifted us into an octagonal glassy dome.

All the Tenleaving guests weren't precisely apes, but we all had flat faces, short torsos, long arms, and most of us had thick but flexible wrists.

I felt awkward pushing the bike up to the room reservation terminal, dressed in skin shorts, but everyone else was in species clothes, from naked fur to head to toe wraps.

"They don't show anything," Marianne said, looking at two people whose genitals were invisible under their fur.

"No," I said, picking the room cards out of the top of the terminal which obligingly printed me a map to go with them. We went out the fifth door onto a swinging bridge, pushing the bikes and holding on with our free hands. All around us was a river with falls, trees that dangled out over rocks, solid green vines with no leaves, just tendrils.

A shiny black couple waited at the opposite end of the bridge until we got safely across. "Fun?" they asked.

"Yes," Marianne said. The female touched the bike seat and said something in her own tongue to the male.

"Where can we get these?" the male asked.

"We brought them from our home planet," I said. "It hasn't been contacted yet."

They backed up a slight but noticeable bit. Marianne laughed as if being a refugee didn't bother her at all.

Our room was glass walls, a carved white ceiling, and dark green velvet drapes and rug—with the drapes back, the double bed on the platform in the center of the room was like a raft in the forest. When I closed the drapes, the only light came from tiny clerestory windows high in the ceiling.

"It doesn't bother you that we're refugees?" I asked Marianne.

"Tom, don't let those fools depress you," she said. "Trung figured out the gates, drunk as he gets. We're as smart as most of them."

"Trung figured out the gates?"

"Yes," she said, stripping off her sweaty bike clothes. I looked at her belly but she wasn't showing yet, of course. "You shocked?"

"That doesn't count for Federation admission."

"Well," she said, "It can help."

"Marianne, are you . . ." I had been about to ask her if she was smuggling information back to Carstairs, but didn't want any listening wires to hear her answer.

She looked at me, faintly trembling, then looked around and saw a door I hadn't noticed before, between drapery and folds. "Bet it's the shower."

It was. While she showered, I worried about her, hoping that she wasn't smuggling the information to Carstairs because then she would get caught. Carstairs was too sloppy.

When she came out, I did ask, "But what does Trung do with the gates?"

"Ah, Tom."

"Marianne, has he told anyone?"

"The officials don't know unless this room's bugged. What would they do to him?"

"I'm sure the Federation can detect gates. They block gate access over most of Karst."

"Tom, I shouldn't discuss this with you, but Trung and I have Federation protectors."

As I stripped and showered, I wondered if she was afraid to talk because the room might be bugged, or if she was afraid I'd turn her in to Black Amber. That was a depressing thought.

We'd brought lightweight tunics and pants in bags behind our seats, and underwear, things that we could wash and dry each night. "Where do we have dinner?" I asked after we'd both changed into the tunics.

Marianne opened the drapes. As we stared out over the landscape of trees, bridges, glass-walled rooms, a rainbow in the river mist, she said, "What about room service?"

* * *

About ten at night, we were lying under the covers with the drape remote control box under our pillow. Marianne put her hand on my stomach and touched my navel. I felt clammy, cold. *My child will grow up thinking all the time in Karst One.*

At eleven, she said, "It's all right, honey."

Now furious and wide awake, I knew why my fellow-human a generation back killed a Barcon. If a Barcon came in the room now, I'd kill it. Controlling our reproductions, hell. I wasn't ready for this.

"What," she asked, "bothers you the most about it?"

"That you didn't ask me more, that we didn't discuss it."

"I want you to help me. All this is natural, this nervousness. I asked them about frozen zygotes in case."

"In case what?"

"In case something happens to you before I have two children. I want one more of yours."

Immortal sperm, what a great idea. I felt better, but couldn't get an erection. We went to sleep.

In the morning I woke up to a fine erection. I closed the drapes and ran my thumbs around Marianne's nipples.

The next night we went to a bar. Marianne couldn't drink alcohol or take any drugs, so we sat and watched the other ex-brachiators get drunk. "Funny," Marianne said, "I feel very comfortable around them, but more like an animal."

I'd noticed the same thing. With Gwyngs, I strained so much to understand them that I wasn't aware of myself. With other humans, I was just me. But with these guys, I was an ex-tropical brachiator with odd habits, but the other guys were also funny in just the right ways. We went with cliffs, climbing trees, lianas, and swinging bridges.

The shiny blacks with the pointed noses came over with three furry sapients. The female shiny one said, "I'm Jasper Thirteen with Jasper Fourteen. Are your machines . . . was great expense involved?"

Jasper Fourteen asked directly, "Can we borrow them?"

"To ride?" Marianne asked. In English, she said, *"We ought to see if we can patent the concept."*

They raised their hands, fingers curled toward us, and brought them down—yes, yes—twice up and down. The three furry people watched.

Several thousand dollars worth of Roger Strigate bikes. Marianne adjusted the seats for them. I thought they'd head to the elevator, but no, they rode out on the walkways, across the swinging bridges. I had to look. Marianne threw a fit against a chair-size cushion in the lobby, kneeling beside it, clutching at the piping, biting into the upholstery, choking on her laughter. The Jaspers came back and he said, "Very nicely scary, like xenophobia movies."

"Will you sell them?" she asked.

Marianne said, "We could sell you the design."

"Are they patented?"

"Not here, but . . ."

He pulled a camera out of his vest and took all kinds of pictures, then handed Marianne a plastic credit chip. "Our thanks. The design could be improved for slow travel balance."

"You're supposed to use them on cart paths," Marianne said, pocketing the credit chip and wiping her face.

"We'd like to ride them down the cart path from the elevator," one of the fuzzy guys said.

I remembered the incline coming up and shook my head.

Karriaagzh came for us on the fourth day, in bare feathers frayed by the clothes he usually wore. He stepped through the meal hall like a xenophobia movie character, hocks rising high, beak slightly parted to show the flat pointed tongue tip, feathers tight against his head, yellow eyes fixed on me. I hadn't seen him in a while, I realized, and not in bare feathers in over a year. That was why he was looking so alien. Then he looked at Marianne and his feathers loosened.

He said, "Tom, Marianne, the Wrengee, and another of Isa have asked for help, so come with me. You have time to get your machines and clothes." He went to the edge of the room, stared down at the roily water and the rocks, then crouched and shuffled back. When he was well away from the edge, he sat down, palms on the floor.

"You want to go with us to our room?" I asked.

He flicked his crest at me and said, "No, thank you. Heights to me are not, as you mammals say, humorous."

I remembered Granite Grit climbing up rocks, not thrilled but not anxious, either. Did Karriaagzh's species have an aversion to heights that Granite's species didn't have, or was this personal, a phobia?

We got our bikes and clothes and went out. When we got back, a young shiny black kid was fingering Karriaagzh's scales, while the kid's parents dabbed at each other nervously. Karriaagzh had his eyes closed. The kid reached for the crest feathers just as his mother grabbed him.

"Tell him to be gentle with them," Karriaagzh said.

"We're back," Marianne said. As Karriaagzh rose, the other guests began chattering again. Marianne went up to him, reached up and stroked his shoulder feathers.

"I've been lonely," he said, "and off by myself."

Marianne said something in a language I didn't recognize. Karriaagzh wiggled feathers all over his body and said, "How did you learn *that*?"

"I called up your language from Linguistics records," Marianne said. "Does it bother you to hear it from mammal lips, not a beak?"

"You smear some sounds," Karriaagzh said. He tightened his feathers. "I should have worn my mammal clothes, to remind me of where I am."

As we left with him, the brachiators behind us talked even louder. When the elevator reached the base of the cliff, Karriaagzh sighed and rubbed the ridges about his eyes.

"Does Black Amber approve of this?"

He spat air and wiped his beak with his fingers. "If I agreed with her, she'd switch to take my old position."

I didn't think so, knowing the Gwyngs, but I didn't say anything. He'd driven up in an electric cart, too small for the three of us and the bikes.

"I'll run," he said, bouncing on his hocks. Marianne touched his arm again as she went by him to get in the passenger seat.

His seat was missing, so I piled our bike bags there, sat on them, and began heading back to Karst City at maybe twenty-five miles an hour. I said to Marianne, "I'll slow up if he starts panting."

He didn't pant at all for thirty miles, just strode along behind us, head level, neck flexing, drafting the cart. I could see him in the rearview mirrors. "Tough old bird," Marianne said.

"The age is an act," I said.

Karriaagzh saw us off at the Karst transport center. Marianne looked at the transport pod and said to me, "It's so small."

Karriaagzh sat down on his hocks and flicked his nictitating membranes back and forth. Air hissed out of his nares, then he said, "You both need experience. This may not be as pleasant as a truly good first contact, but there'll be no surprises. The Wrengee asked to talk to Tom, now."

Terrific, I thought, we don't have to worry about the aliens we're contacting, just the other aliens, those pretty little Sharwan, who don't want the Federation in their space. "Is this contact point adequately defended? I'm not sure I want Marianne to go."

"It's as well defended as Karst itself," Karriaagzh said. I remembered that Karst had been bombed to glazed rock about 500 years earlier.

We both climbed into the transport together, knees intermeshed. I tightened down the hatch bolts, then we went through the longest series of lurches I'd ever experienced.

After a claustrophobic fifteen minutes, Marianne said, "What's happening?"

"Long route," I suggested. The air seemed stale, the sides of the egg . . . no, they couldn't be collapsing.

Another twenty minutes later, we stopped lurching. The arrival diode flashed and I opened the hatch.

Travertine in his olive feathers helped me out. He looked from Marianne to me and back again, holding the door half opened. "You," he said and pulled the door the rest of the way up. "I'm replacing Granite this contact. Hope the round-about trip didn't upset your mate."

Marianne said, "Hello, Travertine."

"Capable of recognizing me, thanks."

Wool said, "Climb out." He wore regulation pants, two lumpy nipples showing above the waist band, his fuzzy chest sweat-matted.

We climbed out with our luggage and saw a big screen playing Wrengee movies. The one walking into the camera angles now had inflamed wattled earlobes and rips in his scales as if ornaments had been torn out of the drilled holes. Wool said, "Recognize Ersh?"

"No, the one in front?" I asked. "How did you get in touch with them?"

Wool sighed. "Another bunch thought they were making a deep-space first contact, but it was just these clowns changing their minds."

"Unless we're going to talk to them right now, show us to our room," I said. Wool pulled himself up and went to the computer. He wrote something on the pickup slate and the printer sprayed us a map.

"Follow the guide lights," Travertine said. Wool pushed another button and green lines began glowing in the ceiling, pulsing toward a door.

"Nothing irises open," Marianne said as we passed through it. "You know, like a camera lens?"

"Too complex to keep in good working order," I replied, "when you might have people bouncing each other off the doors."

She said in English, forgetting that Travertine could be bugging us, *"The Wrengee look creepy."*

"They're very blunt spoken," I said, wondering if we were being tested for hard-wired reactions. Travertine was a trifle hostile to both Gwyngs and humans after his conspecific, Xenon, was treated coldly by Rhyodolite and me. When our transport was stopped by the Yauntry, Xenon must have panicked because he felt caught between xenophobes. His moves frightened the Yauntry into killing him.

Marianne looked at the thick glass against three of the bulkheads. "Holograms," I said, looking in the usual Karst standard watch station place for the buttons. "They've given us New York City, Mabry's Mill, clouds, savannah with riverine jungle." The bunks were like square cells against the fourth wall.

Marianne came over to look at the buttons and said, "I've always thought lawns and shrub borders said a lot for where humans grew brains." She pushed the button for savannah and riverine jungles.

Two Ahrams were in the bunks. One of them, male judging by his crest, rolled over and blinked at us, then watched us through half-open eyes as we checked out our double bunk, under an empty one.

Finally, the male Ahram muttered, "We're getting a large Wrengee delegation, if we're doubling Karst species in a room now."

Marianne said, "I'm looking forward to it."

"Red Clay, isn't it? Red Clay, you can't react if she's threatened. Ree, from Linguistics?"

"Most of my training," she said, "was at Berkeley, on my home planet."

"Refugees."

Marianne didn't answer that. We both got into our double bunk and seethed for a while.

Cooking and food storage, for those of us who heated food or chilled it, was in one central area. We tracked in, following a map Wool printed for us. In the kitchen sat two guys of a species I'd never seen before, a couple of very roughly bear-stock creatures, about six feet tall, slender, furry with protruding eyes. They'd both crossed their legs so their ankles rested on opposite knees. The brow hair on one kept falling into her eyes. They were drinking steaming liquid from porcelain cups. Marianne said, "Hello."

They looked at us and said, in Karst Two, "Awake or sleep after your meal?"

"Awake." I began looking through the food lockers and found Homo sapiens' basic rations grain mix, some greens labeled "edible for Humans, Ahrams, Hiveo, Barcons," and six gallons of Jersey milk.

They sighed and said, "Small sleep period coming. Intermittent sleepers/us."

, I could tell by the big eyes. "Have you heard anything more about the Sharwan?"

"Sharwhang?" The two crepuscular people talked to each other. Finally, the female said, "The ones who've been disrupting contacts. We're many gate changes away from them/guarded, too."

The male went over the refrigerator and pulled out some of the greens—they were Hiveo. I'd never met Hiveo before. Already, they seemed very nice since they hadn't called us refugees.

"Not so long wait now," the female said. "So far these people seem non-xenophobic. Why didn't they join the Federation at first contact?"

"The Sharwan threatened them."

"People who threaten will exploit," Marianne said. "Tom, what do we do with this ration?"

"Grind and microwave it in milk," the male Hiveo suggested.

"Ersh asked for you. He's embarrassed, though," Wool said.

Marianne didn't say anything—she sighed and found a laser disc and earphones and began saying odd sounds under her breath. I recognized the odd sounds in a few minutes as another language of Station 467 Charge Species, Isa Planet species. Marianne's pronunciation improved phenomenally during the next seven hours.

"The Sharwan radio and comm pod traffic has been heavier," Travertine said. Marianne, still listening to the tape, reached out and tweeked his long olive belly hackles. He rubbed her awkwardly around the nose.

I suddenly wished Marianne hadn't come here—risking herself, risking my child. We waited, the gravity nets on higher than usual power, gate detection probes thrust out by the mass driver coils. A television transmission from

Wrengu said that Equirew Research Facility had been closed off.

"Maybe the Federation should contact a new species when it sends out satellites," Marianne said.

"No," Travertine said in English, *"the Voyager naked schematics aren't enough."*

"I'm not sure most humans are ready for contact, Marianne." She turned to me, her face so placid I knew she was angry.

We didn't say more, just listened to the radio bursts of coded messages. Wool turned on a computer programmed to lock onto face images in over a million possible raster and scan frequency patterns. I watched images flicker on the screen—and saw us watching as the aliens.

"Some people go eat," Wool said, "or sleep. We don't need to be craving either when Ersh and the others arrive."

Marianne said, "Tom, I am hungry." Yes, what she ate now was serious for the baby. We went off to the eating area. When we were alone, she said to me, "Why don't you want humans to be contacted?"

Self-pity? "I'd be a parole jumper loser again."

"Tom, they'd forget about that. You could help so much."

"I didn't turn you in to Black Amber, did I? Marianne, I'm just not sure about humans in space. We're such an intense species, xenoflip-flops."

"We didn't invent xenophobia movies."

"And we haven't passed the space gates test."

"Trung . . ."

"He imitated." I cooked a stew of the grains and bean grits in the pressure microwave while Marianne tossed a salad.

"Black Amber said I was working through the linguistics curriculum as fast as anyone with a provincial education, not that my Berkeley mentors would like that label."

I said, "I hate humans sometimes." She watched me while she ate as if she really had to plan her answer to that. I felt guilty. Finally, after we finished our stew, I said, "Your parents were Weather people. You were a radical."

"Tom, my kind of radicals believe people are basically good."

"That wasn't . . . I thought the radicals in Floyd were a bunch of elitist snobs. Something not for rednecks."

"Oh, the Hip Drugs Klan," Marianne said, "but I've never been religious, understand."

In English, I said, *"But you were a grad student."*

"Tom, sometimes you can be ridiculous."

"We've got a contact to work," I said. "And I do love you. Whatever you and Trung do . . ." I knew I couldn't turn them in.

Marianne rubbed her eyes with her palms, the heels of her hands, thumbs pointing outward, fingers curled. "What do you think it's going to be like?"

"Ersh didn't seem impressed with us the first time."

We put the bowls in the ultrasonic cleaner, then ran them back through the microwave to dry them before we put them up. The ultrasonic cleaner fluid didn't get recycled often—so I liked to microwave my station dishes after I used them.

Marianne asked, "Why don't we use paper plates?"

"Storage," I said. We went back into the station center and found a long cushion. I sat down on it, legs crossed tailor-fashion, and cradled Marianne's head against my thighs and belly. She twined her left hand's fingers through mine.

"Good," Wool said. "Your quarrel has abated. Please don't re-activate it."

"I've never quarreled with Tom," Marianne said, neck going stiff as she rolled her head to look up at him. Wool voided pungent anal oil. Marianne sniffed and said, "Okay, I lied."

"We're all tense," Wool said.

The Barcons shambled in as if drawn by the anal gland odor. One of them sprayed the air—the odor disappeared.

For the next hour or so, nobody said much. Wool showered and came back with a portable drier in one hand. He ran it over his body while he lifted tufts of fur with the fingers of his other hand. When a gate probe alarm rang, he yanked out the hair he had between his fingers.

"Let's make sure it's Ersh," Travertine said.

Wool wiped the hair off his fingers, and said, as he pushed a button on the console, "Re-Contact for Planet Station 467." Travertine was speaking Wrengu through another microphone. Wool put earphones on his small round ears. Marianne sat up, still holding my hands.

"Is it Ersh?" Wool asked.

Travertine said, "Yes." His head feathers rose, then settled. He blinked all of his eyelids across both eyes, one eyelid at a time. "He wants to speak to Tom." Travertine's upper bill rose, muscles between his eyes tight, bulging, then it fell in a soft click, not as loud as Karriaagzh's anger clap, just a snick sound like a ballpoint pen point being retracted.

"Well, let's bring them in," Wool said.

Travertine said, "They'd prefer that we try to speak only their languages, but I explained that some of us don't know them."

Marianne said, "Tell them I'm eager to learn from them directly." She said something choppy in the language she'd been studying.

"Better be," Wool said. "He's here."

"Now?" I asked.

Travertine sent docking procedure schematics. Finally, he said, "In about three and half minutes. They're gating a capsule into our station. Ersh and one other."

We walked back to the capsule receiving area. The air turned blue, then the alien capsule popped into our space. The capsule was white with a sealed door not unlike our own capsules. The creatures inside pushed it out and it fell on the deck, tilting and rocking.

When it stopped rocking, Ersh and the other dinosauroid stuck their heads out, arms behind them. They stared at us, their ear wattles pale, then they stepped out, knees bending like human knees. The second one forgot to leave his gun in the capsule, stared down it as if his hand was embarrassing him, if that's what a sudden earlobe wattle blush meant.

Marianne said, in soft Wrengu, *"Hello."* Ersh went up and cautiously loosened her headband, then ran scaled fingers through her hair, lifting it at right angles from her head.

"It drapes," Ersh said as Marianne laughed. He still held Marianne's hair out. "Do you breed for this?"

"Do we breed for what?" I said.

Not completely understanding Wrengu yet, Marianne asked, "Did he want to know if we bred for long hair?"

"You must," Travertine said. "It's an ecologically unreasonable amount of hair."

I signaled *yes* flippantly.

The other Wreng ran his finger up Wool's tunic sleeve and asked, "Why do filimented ones mask their bodies?"

"You need help, Ersh?" I asked, trying to get the Wreng on track. For a creature who'd been so blunt before, Ersh wasn't bringing up issues now. "You embarrassed to have allied with oppressors?"

"Yes, I'm not here to play with strange hair. Help us now, Red Clay. We made a mistake, but still don't know if you represent a worse one."

The other Wreng laid a hand across Marianne's waist and whispered in her ear. She said something in the other language. He whispered again. She, paler than usual, moved his hand a bit lower and gestured *yes*, then murmured.

"Are the Sharwan on your planet?" I asked.

"Yes," Ersh said. "We want them off."

Wool said, "Control doesn't like to fight house to house."

Marianne and I both were sent to bed after twelve duty hours, regardless of the continuing discussion—Ersh was obviously amused, wriggling his mouth flaps at us as we shuffled off to bed.

When Marianne woke up, she vomited hard as if her body had been invaded by something she could expel this way. "I don't understand. I want this baby."

A Barcon opened our toilet door and said, holding out

a package of dry crackers, "Don't drink liquids in the morning."

"I feel sick, too," I said.

"Not uncommon," the Barcon said, squatting down beside us. She touched me—my skin was clammy. "Many males acquire nausea when mates are pregnant."

"Are you going to be okay?" I asked Marianne.

"Yes. Let's go talk to the feathered lizards."

"They are warm-blooded," the Barcon said.

We went out to the meeting room. Ersh asked, "What can you do for us?"

"Do you want to have us kill them all?" Wool asked. I knew it was a testing question, but Marianne stiffened.

"No," Ersh said, "some don't steal from us. And, worst, some of us help them steal."

"What's your status on your home planet?" Marianne asked. She'd memorized questions in Wrengu or else picked up the language fast—I was a little intimidated.

"My own status now—affected by coming to you."

"We can't get rid of the Sharwan instantly now that they're in your system," Wool said. "Not without destroying all of them. We think we can persuade them."

Ersh's face flushed red, blue, yellow, then he said, "If we'd gone with the Federation, a barricade would have been simpler?"

"Much simpler," Wool said.

"They've bombed us more anyway."

"Changing their minds will be a long process—are they exploiting you that badly? We dislike direct attack. Conflict creates its own dynamics."

"I can give you contacts with those of us who are resisting." Ersh said, "Red Clay, I apologize."

"Apologize to his wife," Wool said, "because you've probably committed her womb's child to help you. It will be a long struggle. Maybe not that many of your people are resisting?"

"Or you could abandon us to them," Ersh said. "Perhaps that would be proper. We are nobody's parallel here."

"No," I said. "we don't abandon anyone." Travertine looked at me and raised his shoulder feathers.

"I am to be killed if captured by the Sharwan," Ersh said. "May we stay with you? I've brought many texts. Between us both we know all our major languages."

The Federation people stared at one another, then Wool said, "If we get back soon, we can put you in language operation group next week. Refugee cadets can be very useful."

Ersh's scales shook slightly, but he had no rings in them to jangle. His con-specific said, "The whole universe has collapsed in on us."

We gated the whole station into the Karst Oort Region and transferred to a smaller transport.

"This is fast," Marianne said, her knees between mine.

As soon as we gated into a Karst terminal, three waiting Barcons began punching bioassay holes in Ersh and his companion. Wrengee? Isaian? What would they call their species? One of the Barcons fingered Ersh's mouth tissue.

As we watched, Black Amber came in and said to Marianne, "Why didn't you stay in Karst City like most (hint of sensible) pregnant placentals?"

"I'm not most pregnant placentals," Marianne said. "And I like the work. I'm going to continue to do it. My child will be part of it."

Black Amber said, "I'll drive you home. I want to be with you both (intense undifferentiated feeling)."

"I need to translate for Ersh," I said.

Wool came up, stopped ten feet alway, one knee bent, his fingers picking through his fur. "Sub-Rector," he said as though identifying her, not greeting her.

Black Amber said to Wool, "I need/want Red Clay (and his pregnant one). You translate for those." She curled up a foot at Ersh and his companion.

We went to Black Amber's beach house, but all the children were older now and very aware that we were never going to be Gwyngs. Two days later, Marianne said that she missed our apartment and our neighbors and so we left Black Amber. When we said good-bye, she stalked out toward the ocean, not speaking.

We took a bus home—home, yes.

* * *

Marianne's birth group was a bunch of high-powered women of whatever species, all amazed that they couldn't just high-power along now.

"Pregnancy," Marianne announced when she came back from the first meeting, "is why women don't do as well as men. We lose energy in pregnancy. It adds up, especially over a thousand years or so."

I was feeling queasy myself and didn't think much of her theory right then. Was she going to make me feel guilty the whole time? "I'm not going to take advantage of whatever's going on with your hormones."

"Hormones?" For a second, I thought she'd explode— her eyebrows went up like a mad cat's back and her face around the lips looked like a shucked clam, white and all the rest of the metaphor. She shrugged and went to the terminal. "Yangchenla's not in a birth group. She's got Tibetan midwives. Agate's in my group. It's weird, Tom. Really weird. They seem even more alien now, like some human maternal defense program has kicked in, but we're all having babies the hard way."

Black Amber came over a week after Marianne's first pregnancy meeting, almost slinking around Marianne. Black Amber finally sat down on one of our sofas, legs curled under her, arms hooked together at the thumbs, a nervous Gwyng for some reason. I looked at Marianne— we twitched our eyebrows at each other. Black Amber's brow hair rose slightly, then she said, "Linguist, why risk yourself/the nymph?"

"I'm back now." Marianne wrapped her own arms around her waist, low as if protecting her womb from Black Amber's eyes or ultrasonic voice.

Black Amber muttered to herself in Gwyng and walked around Marianne, then said, "Linguist, couldn't you have had a primitive human bear it for you. The Barcons can do gamete implants."

"I don't ask other women to carry Tom's and my child." But Marianne looked distressed, as if she'd never known she had an option.

I said, "I didn't know we could do that."

"Not now/too late," Black Amber said. "*Shershee mink in cooler?*"

Jersey milk? "Yes," I said. Black Amber went back to the kitchen.

"She acts like she owns us," Marianne said.

"I thought you liked her."

"Tom, did you know that I could have hired one of the Tibetan women to bear my child?"

"No. Would you want to do that next time?"

"No, of course not. No. But I wanted to know, I didn't want you making decisions about this for me, okay."

"Marianne . . ."

"You wouldn't cooperate with Yangchenla."

"She was manipulative."

"Black Amber approves of me, and didn't approve of her." She smiled bleakly for all that Black Amber didn't know about Trung's gates.

"She accused me of having sex with Black Amber."

As I said that, Black Amber ambled toward us with milk in a glass. She rolled her tongue into a tube and began sucking as it noisily. When she paused, she said, "Red Clay too stinky for sex. Loyal in body to you/mind to me. We-who-share should be friends."

"Honest, I didn't know about gamete transplants."

Marianne said in English, *"It's all right, Tom. I'm going to go through with it."*

"Not to exclude with language," Black Amber said.

But Marianne didn't translate.

About two months into Marianne's pregnancy, I tried to get assigned out. "Rector's Man," I said to Chalk in his clammy tile-walled office, "I'm going through what Marianne's going through—vomiting in the mornings."

"Not everything as much as she, though," Chalk said. I noticed him scratching his lower belly. His breasts were swelling. "Wouldn't it be inappropriate for you to go on watch now? Doesn't she need you?"

"She'd be jealous, but . . ."

"Better stay with her. The Barcons aren't sure whether you're competing with her or sympathizing with her."

I said, "I've never heard of a human male getting morning sickness."

"The Barcons say your condition is described in the human anthropological literature." Chalk whistled slightly and raised his nose. "So, you may both study. And you both can help me with cadets."

At least I didn't develop breasts, I thought as I stared at his, the way Barcon and Jerek men did.

One day during Marianne's pregnancy, I brought home a third-year cadet, a pug-faced male with a barrel round body and pied head hair. We'd been talking about the impact species had on each other, beyond the technological changes, and I invited him to come home with me.

The elevator door rose and I saw Marianne slouched on a sofa by the window and around her in the dimly lit room, two other shapes—Agate's shiny face skin caught the elevator light. The other one groaned. They were all huge-bellied—Marianne, the non-human women. I asked, "Is it all right for us to come in? I'd asked a cadet . . ."

The cadet said, "I think we can talk another time." His face was moist around the eyes, as though he had sweat glands only there.

Marianne looked at me—face pale, her baby visibly moving her belly. "We were saying about men . . ."

The one in the chair interrupted, "But you don't need them after impregnation." She turned into the light—another pug face. The cadet closed the elevator and went down.

"Marianne, don't you need me?"

"I said I did. I just wondered about Domiecan males, why you don't talk about him."

Agate said, "We all have different ecologies. Human and Jerek babies are helpless."

"I'm gland Domiecan babies aren't," the pregnant pug-face said. She crooned, "Baby baby," and stuck her huge belly up off the chair and lay her hands over her navel.

Was she going into labor now? I felt like I was the alien

and they were all of a species—pregnant females, a single word, not two, in Karst One. I stood there in my officer's uniform wondering if Jereks and Domiecans had morning sickness. "Are you all having males?" I asked, sounding dumb in my own ears. Marianne knew about the fifth month that she was carrying a boy.

"No," Agate said. She stood up, belly breasts squashed down against support cups in her hip leathers, mashed by her pregnant belly.

I wondered how much pregnancy alone hurt, much less labor. "I think I'll go back to my bedroom, or would you rather have me go out for something, Marianne?"

"It's all right, Tom," Marianne said. "We're still the same people we were. You could talk to us before, sit down and chat now."

"We delivered her baby," Marianne said after she'd helped with the Domiecan's labor. "And it got up and walked around. Tom, it was weird—a baby walking two hours after delivery, walking up to Bir and finding her breast, then sniffing at us. She had to call it off."

"Pig babies are like that," I said.

Marianne shuddered so hard I thought she was going into labor. She said, "You forget they're not human."

"Yeah."

"They aren't human. They aren't really our kind of mammals."

"It's all right, Marianne."

"Her hip bones came apart, but they snapped right back together again. I thought she . . ." Marianne laughed, shuddered again, and sat down beside me, not reaching for me but rather huddled against me. "Tom, be there for me."

"When you have our baby?"

"Yes. Yangchenla's off with the Tibetans."

Oh, not that I'd sired the baby, but that I was the same species, a second human in the birth room. But then, that's why I got involved with Yangchenla when I was the only modern human around. I hugged her and said, "Sure," somewhat uneasy.

"Do you ever want to go back?" she asked, her body relaxing, curving up against mine. Her shoulders were thin and bony, very odd over her pregnant belly.

"Sometimes I wish I could change a lot of things."

"I want to go back. Karriaagzh said we could, for a visit, just a visit," Marianne said, "after the baby's born."

"When did you talk to Karriaagzh?"

"Last week, when you were out. I wanted to go back for the delivery, but Karriaagzh insisted that I work with the pregnancy group. Tom, we are a bit xenophobic. You haven't been to see Ersh."

"Xenophobic? You and Me? With Karriaagzh and Black Amber in and out of the apartment? You might be uneasy—that's natural for pregnant creatures." Wrong thing to say—I felt her stiffen.

"Karriaagzh is so concerned," she said, "his throat glands are developing. I visualize him regurgitating into my child, Tom." She said in English, *"Not into my human baby."*

I said, "We'll go to Earth then, as soon as Karriaagzh and Black Amber let us. For a few months, maybe." I became uneasy as soon as I promised that.

"You withdrew from the other sapients, too, Tom, when contact with Isa and Wrengee went wrong. Humor me." She sighed as she got up, pushing off from the sofa with her hands, awkward, and went into her room. I heard her crying and felt helpless, Warren's head being rebuilt by the Barcons, Marianne going to be delivered by non-human females. And I hadn't been to see Ersh. More than *little* twinges of xenophobia.

I went with Marianne to the Institute of Medicine where the Barcons organized and monitored the pregnancy groups. The Institute building for midwifery was cream-colored, with faint blue and green marbling to it. Inside, the floors were synthetic mats, soft underfoot, running down wide white halls. Marianne said, "Here," and we opened a door to the room where her group met. Bir, the pug-faced Domiecan, stood with her child, cunning as a dog, on a leash. An olive-colored bird like Travertine held a bundle of fabric, her utterly helpless baby that couldn't even keep its own body warm. She pushed her beak down into the bundle and hummed. Then her throat surged. The still pregnant others, Agate and a Barcon female among them, sat in chairs or reclined on floor mats.

"You want to help?" the Barcon female asked me.

"I'd prefer just to help with Marianne. It's a custom among our culture groups." Not mine, but Marianne said California radical fathers helped with deliveries.

They looked at each other, almost the way contact and diplomatic teams tended to do after leaving the new species they'd worked with—eyes checking out eyes to see how we'd all taken the deal. The Barcon female rumbled, "Marianne is upset with us, our involvement in her pregnancy. She needs us to help her get over this fear."

"Yangchenla had hers with just human help," Marianne said.

"Dangerous," the Barcon said. "We often have to repair primitive wombs. The babies die, or are murdered if the family wants a different sex baby."

"Her little girl is fine," Marianne said.

Agate said, "Since Chalk will be at my delivery for the first milk, let's allow Tom to be with Marianne."

Black Amber watched Marianne as though my human wife was a most strange creature, swollen up in the belly, still the same person, but tired all the time now—almost as tired as she'd been during the first three months when the fetus was locking his connections to her womb.

"You/Linguist have been invaded," Black Amber said, her hand stretched toward Marianne's belly, the fur on the long fingers sweaty. "Wombs protect from the placental construction your nymphs build. Placentas run wild in unwombed bodies/space."

"If I'm so disgusting now, why do you keep coming over? Surely you've seen pregnant placentals before."

"You need host wombs." Black Amber licked her fingers with a dry tongue. I looked down at my sponsor's own belly—pregnant yourself, heh, Black Amber, and no one's gong to take the nymph this time.

"Want to look at it?" Marianne said to Black Amber. She reached for her tunic hem, lifted it up. Her navel was protruding now on top of her blue-veined belly, a small mound on top of a great one. Black Amber touched her own belly, shuddered and ran her hand down inside her tunic pants, stroking her Gwyng birth hairs below the pouch hole. Amber's eyes opened so wide I thought she'd pulled back the bone plates around the sockets. Marianne dropped her tunic top as the baby squirmed inside her.

Black Amber said, "I've seen those bellies before, but not so hairless/colorless. Hostile to show . . . (question)." She wrapped her arms around her body, webs making ridges against her uniform top. "But I am not hostile to you." Her eyes grew glossier with the oil Gwyngs lubricate their eyes with, cry with.

"You want to see me in labor?" Marianne said.

"No/yes/no/confusion."

"I don't want you to see me in labor."

"Early stages will be done at home/monitoring my protégés as sponsor," Black Amber said. "Linguist, I, you, pouch kin-through-my hurt/wounding (on your planet). Many years ago, yes/true, but . . . ah, my little placental, you reject/hurts."

"I'm sorry," Marianne said, "but I'd like you to leave now."

First from one hand, then the other, Black Amber smeared thumb gland secretions on Marianne's forehead, finally just furious with my human wife. I grabbed Black Amber by the left elbow as she pulled away. Marianne began sneezing as she stumbled into a chair, sat down heavily in it, then went to the stranger's bathroom. We heard water running.

"Frustrating," Black Amber said, her elbow still in my hand.

"Why did you mark her face?"

"To put my hands on her where she thinks." She pulled herself away and called for the elevator, stood facing the door as if she'd left already. I watched her a second, then programmed our door to lock after she left and went to Marianne.

"Monitoring me," Marianne said. She reached down for the soap again, lathered her hands, and scrubbed her forehead again.

"If you keep the thumb gland secretion on, Gwyngs will avoid you." I heard the elevator doors opening for Black Amber out in the main room.

"She's going to show up when I'm going into labor—she's monitoring me—Tom, do something."

"She wanted to touch you where you thought."

"That was hostile. I've studied Gwyng physiology." She sneezed. "Tom, she doesn't even try to keep her babies alive."

"She doesn't want healthy pouched nymphs to die."

"Why doesn't she brood it herself in her own *fucking* pouch then? Or are Gwyngs too parasitical to mother their own children?" She stared around at all the strange fixtures for other species in this guest bathroom and said, "Cloacal bitch, pisses through the birth canal." Then she laughed and said, "What would one more *uhyalla* pregnant or postpartum female matter? Let her see me. I'll freak her out. She's xenophobic about placentas—let her eat mine."

"Marianne!"

"That's what alternative birth centers in Berkeley do, serve up fried placentas to the mothers and birth guest."

She began laughing so hard I thought I ought to hit her to calm her down, but she was pregnant. I grabbed her shoulders and then went side to side against her still muscular flank, hoping she didn't know this was a Gwyng embrace. Strands of her long hair were plastered to her face. When I pulled them away, she said, "Oh, Tom, I'm so tired of being pregnant. I wish it were over."

Yeah? After the baby was born, we'd be parents forever.

Our apartment was great for pacing with the atrium hall, the kitchen in back, the big room in front. Marianne could pace in circles or back and forth or pretend she was going to the kitchen for tea or milk, or even actually go fix tea and come pacing back with the teacup warming her hands. The Barcons forbade her group the use of caffeine or alcohol, so Marianne drank peppermint tea, lots of it, then paced until she had to use the toilet, often, since the baby cramped her bladder.

I didn't know whether to stay with her or leave her alone those last weeks, but I figured I'd get in less trouble if I kept her company. Agate and Chalk, both sets of breasts swollen over their loin straps, stayed with her a few nights. Marianne was teaching Agate English.

"Whof nesht?" Agate asked in what she tried to make English.

"Next? Maybe we'll go into labor together? What happens then?" Marianne said, continuing to talk English.

"Bosh . . . both . . . group big enoush, shplit . . ." Agate said.

"But I want you to be with me," Marianne said. I wondered if she meant it, then realized she'd learned Karst One from these people when she was first a stranger here.

Neither Jerek sat up straight now, but lounged in their chairs, spines curling their bellies and breasts forward. Agate was not so hugely pregnant as Marianne—Jereks, I thought, must be born tiny if she's as far along as Marianne.

"It's odd," I said. "All over the universe, do all sapients give birth as do other creatures?"

"Except Gwyngs," Chalk said.

"Nobody's made artificial wombs?"

"Yes, but they're so expensive, prone to mechanical problems, very expensive. Only very decadent Jereks use them," Agate said.

"We also have some cut-from-male babies," Chalk added, "when the female dies and ova are saved."

"It can be done with humans, too," Agate said as though I ought to volunteer now. "The baby makes the placenta on the abdomenal wall. The male belly must be supported by sling clothes, then the baby is cut out and the placenta scraped away."

"Not customary for human males," Chalk said to Agate. Marianne was smiling at me as if to say, now you know how weird it can be in a birth group.

When the Jereks left, Marianne began pacing again. I asked, "Do you want to take a walk outside?"

"No, Tom. Do they really know anything about human childbirth?"

"The Barcons work on everyone."

"They destroyed the pigment cells in Karriaagzh's skin."

I said, "Ask the Tibetans if the Barcons have ever delivered one of their women, or patched up a human womb."

"I want to go to a human hospital. I never believed in home deliveries." She tried to giggle. "I feel like I'm constipated. I've got a blood tester here. Tom!" Her voice—she was in labor, now.

"Where is it?"

"In the top drawer of my dresser."

I went and found a steel grey box with a hinged cover and brought it to Marianne. She opened the cover. Inside were panels of diodes and a plastic-capped needle. She pried off the plastic and stuck herself with the needle, held her fingers on it for a few seconds. The machine clicked, then was as silent as a battery watch. The second diode from the top lit up.

"I've got oxytocin in my bloodstream. This is it." She pulled her finger off the needle. "Tom, start timing my contractions."

"Tell me."

"Well, well, I guess that's the first one."

I looked at my watch, then said, "Why don't we call your birth group coordinator now."

"Not yet. Tom."

"Was that another contraction?"

"No, I'm going to try to go to the bathroom."

"Do you want me to go with you?"

"Tom, I'll leave the door open, okay?" She sounded annoyed. I noticed when she stood up again that the pregnant bulge had dropped. She saw where I was looking and put one hand under her breasts, then the other hand under it. "Definitely dropped."

While Marianne was in the bathroom, I typed messages to Chalk and Agate both at the Rector's Offices and at their residences. She came out and looked at me funny, her face sweaty, her hair in tangled black strings. "My water broke."

"Oh?"

She went to the computer and flicked it to voice mode, called her birth group. Then she said, "Tom, contraction."

"Is that fast, fifteen minutes?"

"Shit. I'm calling the birth center for transport." She started pacing again, in circles on the big room's rug. I knew not to suggest that she sit down—pregnant creatures were restless. Even on the farm, I'd learned that.

The elevator stopped on our floor—two women from Marianne's birth group, Bir and the Barcon, came out with a gurney. I was relieved not to see Bir's precocial son. Marianne wailed, "Where's Agate?"

"She's coming," Bir said. "She's going to be there."

"Get on the stretcher or walk down with us," the Barcon said.

"You're experimenting with me."

"We've worked with human women enough on repairs to know what should be," the Barcon said. "and one of my species had done some human obstetrics while on your planet."

"No real experience," Marianne said. "I'll walk into that elevator."

"Fine," the Barcon said as if she had tranquilizers ready in case it wasn't. Bir made what Domiecans must consider to be soothing noises, like a purring bulldog, the noise fluttering out of her bent-up face.

Marianne braced herself against the elevator's back wall, hands on her knees. She went pale. Still fifteen minutes apart. "We better hurry," she said.

"First birth human females generally labor for up to sixteen hours," the Barcon said.

"Well, I'm not going to," Marianne said. She straightened unsteadily. I got in and held her shoulder.

The elevator door slid up. Marianne's eyes wobbled in their sockets as if she were looking at the door most closely.

We got into the electric ambulance—Marianne refused to lie down so the other women loaded the gurney on the roof and raised the back seats.

At the birth building, I saw Chalk and Agate waiting with a vase full of flowers. Marianne smiled and walked up to Agate, said, "Thanks. What kind of room did you get me?"

"One with human comforts, come on now," Agate said, taking Marianne's hand. Marianne looked behind at me to make sure I was following.

The birth place was a suite, opening up on one side to a medically outfitted surgical room that it shared with two other birth suites. The birth suite proper had two small rooms—one for labor, one for delivery. The labor room was a miniature Earth living room, with a fake fireplace, newly installed ceiling beams like Marianne had had in her Berkeley house bedrooms, two leather couches like Warren bought with drug money. The Barcon opened a refrigerator and put a pitcher of cracked ice on a walnut table half the size of a card table. One corner was blocked off with a toilet cubical. There was no door between this room and the labor room—I could see several obstetrical devices—a table with stirrups and an obstetrical stool, the gleaming metal speculum, an incubator. Still, even the delivery room had homey touches, wooden walls, an over-stuffed chair in one corner, drapes. Marianne had told me earlier all of it was sterilized.

Bir left. The olive bird female wheeled in an incubator with her own baby in it, lifted him up, wrapped him in a blanket, fed him, his tiny arms flailing around her beak, then took him into the toilet box.

"She licks him clean," Marianne said. The bird came back out, tucked her baby back in the incubator, on his belly. He looked very much like a newly hatched chick, except for the size and the arms.

"Tom," the bird said, "I am Mercury. I will help." She looked over at the incubator. Her baby twitched his eyes and looked back at her.

I wondered where the father was, if the males of this

bird species helped with the young, but I didn't say anything, just looked at Chalk.

Agate took Marianne into the labor room to check her cervical dilation. When they came out, Marianne was wearing a tunic down to her calves, snapped up the front, her nipples puckered up under it—fear, not arousal.

"Is it too cold for you, dear?" Agate asked, touching the cloth over Marianne's breasts.

"No," Marianne muttered. "It's embarrassing."

"We have music—classic *Rolling Shones, Bach, bluegrash*," Chalk said. Mercury crouched beside her child's incubator and the Barcon left.

Marianne stood staring at the hallway door for a long time, then another contraction hit her. She bent at the knees and hips, holding her stomach, her lips pursed as she blew breaths in and out.

Agate pressed a button on a handheld chronometer—metal case as matte black as her nails. She slipped it in her tunic pocket.

"Music . . . music would be nice," Marianne said. "Or study. I don't want to just wait for the next one."

I wondered if Black Amber would come to see Marianne in labor. And why was Marianne's labor so fascinating to her?

"Work with me on English," Agate said. "*Laid, lay, lie*, those words of imparting."

"Not all of them are imparting. Some of them are self-actions. *I am going to lie down.*"

"Now?"

"Yes, I can still talk to you. I'd rather rest between contractions."

"But *she lay out the speculum.*"

"Don't remind me." Marianne tried to laugh. She sat up and removed her headband, then lay back down. "The problem is remembering that the past tense for one is the same as the present tense for the other."

"Same sounds, but not the same words, and not even in the same linguistic class. A word of self-movement compared to a word of imparting."

"We call them both *verbs*," Marianne said.

"Common bound morphemes?"

"Except for the irregular ones. *Shit*." Marianne sat up groaning and gripped her knees while Agate punched her chronometer again.

"Count the breaths."

"Not . . . *damn* . . . meditation." Marianne floundered to her feet. I rushed up to help her. "Hurts," she said. "Really hurts."

"Should we check again?" Chalk asked.

Marianne stared at him, then at Agate. "I want to go home."

"Marianne, try to relax in the early stages," Agate said. "Our womb musculature is alike. I've delivered . . ."

"You don't know that much about humans," Marianne said. "I want to . . . oh." She gripped my arm, shifted her hand to my shoulder and pulled. "Leave me with Tom."

The Barcon said, "You need to trust us more."

"Let's not make an issue of it now," Agate said. "We'll be in the delivery room. We have to monitor you."

"Agate, I'm sorry."

Agate lowered her nose very slightly, then said, "I need your trust. You're going to deliver my child."

"Stay with me then." Marianne found Bach's Goldberg Variations, and put the disc on. We listened between her contractions. Agate rubbed away Marianne's face sweat with the furry backs of her hands.

Then Black Amber did show up. She stood with a hand on each side of the door, webs spread and throbbing as she watched Marianne. She was dressed as a Gwyng, just the neck straps and the long front piece to cover the pouch holes and genitals, ribbons to hold that against her body. "I am/was concerned," she said.

Chalk came out of the delivery room fast when he heard Black Amber's voice. "We're not having visitors yet."

"I'm her sponsor."

"Sub-Rector, I don't think you really want to see this," Chalk said.

Marianne said, "Feed her the *fucking* placenta."

Black Amber's webs pulsed in waves not too unlike the muscles rippling on Marianne's belly. "Don't understand hostility/hurt. Difficult for me/I overcome distaste for/I'm trying to support (un-Gwyng to associate with pain)."

"Un-Gwyng?" Marianne said. She looked like she wanted to say more, but couldn't. Groans tore through her throat as she squatted. When the contraction passed, she said, "Agate, the pain. Painkillers?"

"I don't think you've been in labor that long," Agate said.

"*Damn you*, it hurts."

"Come in here, we'll check. Black Amber, we'll let you visit later, okay." Marianne went in with Chalk.

"You go look, too," Black Amber said.

"I don't want to see her organs when she's going through this."

"Hurt sex drive, Red Clay?" Black Amber asked. She oo'ed slightly.

"I don't want to discuss it with you, Black Amber."

Chalk came out and said, "She's halfway dilated."

"What does that mean?" I asked.

"Your son's going to arrive soon."

I could hear Marianne scream, then say, "It hurts, it hurts, it hurts," chanting that over and over.

Black Amber collapsed to the floor. For a second, I thought, God, Amber's a real bitch attention distractor, then I saw that she was oozing from every orifice—eyes, thumb glands, pouch, cloaca.

The pregnant Barcon came out, pulled a phone out from the cabinet by the fireplace, and called other Barcons, then knelt over Black Amber to feel her neck.

"What happened?" Marianne asked.

"Black Amber fainted," the pregnant Barcon said. Other Barcons came with a gurney, muttering to each other in Barq as they strapped Black Amber into it. I was relieved to see that she wasn't bleeding—all the secretions were clear, oily. But she seemed unconscious.

One of the Barcons pulled a strap down over Black Amber's ankles and said to me, "*Uhyalla* still can surprise us with freshly observed behaviors."

In the delivery room, I heard Agate murmuring to Marianne, who answered her back in a slurred voice. Then Marianne cried out, "Tom."

"I'm coming." What had happened to Black Amber? I'd have to find out later—my wife wanted me. I went in and saw her standing between the two smaller Jereks, her arms around their necks, leaning into Agate, who herself was paler in the face skin, that T of naked flesh was dark grey, not black. I quickly went to take Agate's place.

"Um, standing between two men," Marianne said, her eyelids down, eyes dull. "And finally they gave me pain-killer, Tom. They're not sure what's going on."

"Rapid deliveries are unusual for the first child," Chalk said. I knew his loyalties were to Agate.

The contractions came rapidly, more rapidly. Marianne seemed lost in her body, sweating, muscles standing up in ridges in her legs, along her back. Her nipples oozed fluid. Finally, Agate said, "Get her to the chair, if she can still stand."

I felt her heart racing, the muscles spasming beside me, and wondered if we shouldn't use the table, call in the surgical Barcons, take her quickly to a hospital on Earth. Marianne said, "Would hurt to lie down." She squatted suddenly, not falling, pulling against us. Quickly, Chalk, I, and the female Barcon maneuvered her to the birthing stool, spread her knees on its supports.

Marianne began screaming full out with each contraction. I was horrified, couldn't look down there, held her hand between my hands and rubbed her face with my thumbs, stroking over and over. Agate tore away the lower part of the tunic—a shocking rip, *she's torn Marianne*, I thought for a second.

Then we were just dealing with it. The baby's head, all slick and bent, came sliding out into someone's hands while I continued to hold Marianne's head, watching her eyes suddenly widen. She shuddered, went, "aagh," and I heard the baby cry for the first time.

Everyone cheered.

Marianne had to look at him, cuddle him. "He's beautiful," she said.

Actually, he looked like a tiny old man who'd just wiggled out of a hot wet cave where he'd been trapped for nine months. He was wrinkled, blotchy, but so alert, staring at Marianne as though he'd been hearing her for months and finally got to see what she looked like.

Agate and Chalk and our Barcon didn't look so alien now, visibly exhausted, rumpled fur. Chalk had a scratch across his nose—Marianne must have done it flailing around, but he'd never said anything. I said, "Thank you so much."

"I hope Marianne's well enough soon to help with me," Agate said. "It is beautiful, even if difficult."

After Marianne and the baby were sleeping, I went out to see what happened to Black Amber. The Barcon woman told me the other Barcons had taken her to another Institute building across from the birth building.

When I came in, I remembered when I'd first seen her re-built as a Gwyng after being surgically shaped to look human. She wasn't cut and stitched up this time, no surgical tubes sluiced liquids under the clear plastic bandages, and she was sitting up in the bed, but she looked wounded. I said, "We'd be happy to have you come visit now. Marianne's son was born—eight pounds six ounces." I said the weight in Karst One figures.

She closed her eyes as though shutting me out.

"I'm sorry if Marianne was rude to you, but she was hurting."

Without opening her eyes, Black Amber said, "Horrible to volunteer for such pain."

"What happened to you?"

"Conceptual overload. Embarrassing in a Sub-Rector."

"You could have chilled out."

"Time couldn't turn away her screaming voice, the parasite child distorting her body."

"In the end, it was beautiful."

"Hormones washing the brain. Hormones I (and other Gwyngs) don't have."

I wondered how many pregnancies a Gwyng had in her lifetime, if they could even be called pregnancies compared to what other species went through. "Are you going to be okay?"

"I suppose," she said. Her eyes opened, focused on me, closed again. I left.

= 10 =

Time, Bound With Ceremony

As Marianne held our son, Karl David, against her in the elevator going up to our apartment, I thought, everything about families is forever. We'd be parents even after he was grown. Reeann smiled down at Karl, two damp places over her breasts, and he rubbed his eyelids with tiny fists, then cried a thin cry—*why am I here,* maybe.

Marianne grimaced, almost a smile, milk coming out of her breasts again, and said, "Sam and Yangchenla found a place near us. I asked her if she wanted to put her girl in the play group. At least there'd be one other human baby for Karl."

Yeah, and the real life of the universe is built from sticky soft stuff, sperm, women's gooey insides, milk, and baby shit. All this was making me feel uneasy—the milk dripping from Marianne's breasts, the feeling that behind Karl's eyes was a soft baby brain taking up impressions that would affect him in ways that I couldn't fathom. He'd never grow up completely human here. I didn't tell Reeann what I was thinking, just said, "That's nice."

The elevator door slid down and we got out. Karl's eyes looked around. "See," Marianne said, "it's your home."

He stared back at her and groped for her breasts, nuzzled them through her blouse. I felt jealous, then fierce—my woman, my child. "Kids are a bit embarrassing," I said, instantly regretting I'd said that.

Marianne just laughed, looked at me, then laughed

again. Karl looked up at her face and blinked. She said, "He's going to think Daddy's embarrassing soon."

I felt myself blush, remembering my parent's locked door and Warren laughing as he led me away. Child witnesses came with being a father.

"Oh, Karl," Marianne murmured. "Oh, Karllet."

I checked my mail through the computer as Marianne carried Karl to her bedroom to change his diaper:

> I WANT TO TALK TO YOU ABOUT THE BARCONS— WARREN
>
> BARCON CHARGE OF YOUR BROTHER NEEDS YOUR HELP—INSTITUTE OF MEDICINE.
>
> CONGRATULATIONS ON YOUR SON—CADMIUM.
>
> I NEED TO SEE YOU *NOW*—WARREN.
>
> YOUR BROTHER THINKS HE IS HIDING FROM US— INSTITUTE OF MEDICINE.

Warren and the Barcons weren't doing well, obviously. I put a WE'RE HOME message in the computer and went back to check on Marianne and Karl.

He was lying on her bed, one hand grasping her finger. She was sitting beside him, looking. When she noticed I was there, she said, "He's going to be different from us, learning Karst One as a first language."

"I thought about that." We were both speaking in Karst ourselves.

In English, Marianne said, almost to herself, *"It's a bit scary."*

"Warren's upset with what the Barcons are doing to him," I said in the same language. Karst One demanded an attitude modifier and I didn't know quite how I felt, but didn't want to admit that so definitively, with the implication of being confused in the root of the no-attitude modifier.

"Warren," Marianne said, then switched back to Karst. "Is he doing drugs again?"

"I didn't know he could find drugs here," I said.

"Some people can find drugs anywhere."

"Fortunately, they can't reduce his rank if the Barcons test him out positive."

Marianne, not commenting, bent down and nibbled Karl's belly.

A Jerek sterile, fur patchy as if she'd been in combat recently, came up to me when I went down to the Gwyng store. "Red Clay," she said, looking around, the T of face skin wrinkled, flaking around the nose, "Warren wants to see you." She didn't wear leather loin straps, but instead, canvas, some sort of synthetic fiber.

"You want to take me to him."

"Yes."

I'd thought that Warren didn't find the Jerek steriles sexually attractive, but now he was hanging out with one. "Let me call Marianne."

"Don't."

"I have to."

"The medical beasts."

Come on, I thought, he only thinks he's hiding from them. "How long will this take?"

"Eighth rotation at the longest."

The Jerek waited just outside while I went in the store and called up to Marianne. "Hi, you be okay if I went out to check on something that came up in my messages?"

"I guess. How long?"

"Eighth rotation, maybe."

I gave the phone back to the Gwyng who ran the store. She said, nodding at the Jerek, "Those (drug users) steal/ make physical danger."

We took a bus to the northside slums, the little Jerek hugging herself and shivering. I felt terribly conspicuous in my officer's tunic and pants around all the others dressed in shabby species clothes, some in visitor's brown tunics or pre-cadet white. When I saw other blue tunics, I felt almost relieved until I remembered that officers who visited down here were generally after interspecific sex. That's what I looked like I was after, following this Jerek sterile.

"What's your name?" I asked her.

"Moolan," she said, not giving an Academy mineral name contact designator.

"That's a Jerek name, right?"

"Right." She turned her nose down and stared at me, full frontal challenge face. I remembered that most Jereks gave their tunnel as part of their names. She said, "In here."

We went into a hall that stunk of alien pisses, lit by bulbs covered in wire-reinforced plastic. Was this a ruse? Moolan opened a door and went in, bare feet patting on a concrete floor. The room was dimly lit, as dark as Chalk and Agate's tunnel, but the air was stuffy, the same medicinal stink as Warren's drug operation.

He was inside. I heard her say, "I need some," and his laugh.

"So, Warren," I said, walking into the room.

"Little brother the officer." He was lying on a cushion, wrapped in imitation furs.

"Warren, this isn't good for you."

"Shit, getting ripped up inside the brain is?" He said to Moolan, "I evaporated it out just right for you."

She seemed to know what he was talking about, where it was—a small vial full of bluish powder that she poured onto her thumb nail, below the center ridge, just a tiny trace of the powder. She snuffed the powder off her nail and stared at us gravely, almost frozen.

"Keeps her from coming after my cock," Warren said.

"I wondered."

"I love her, but not for that," Warren said.

Moolan said, very slowly, "This would kill me, this wonderful drug, if I weren't dying already. Wonderful lethal conditions."

"Is it too late for you to have your ovaries out?" I asked.

"O-o-oh yes-s-s." She began nibbling her tongue, none too gently, then she stiffened and cried out.

"Fake sex," Warren said. He got up and stroked her, then picked her up in his arms and carried her into a colder room. Not knowing if I should or not, I followed him. He laid her down on a mattress covered with something like Velcro. She twisted against it, shedding fur into it.

"Warren."

"Barcons were killing me."

"They said you thought you were hiding from them."

"Why don't you both just let me go to hell in my own way? I found where I fit. We take care of each other, Moolan, me, the rest of us flop-outs."

"Warren."

He said in English, *"Can't you say nothing but my name?"*

"They said you'd still be you."

"My body, with different memories. Things didn't connect. They were killing the real me inside the brain."

I didn't say anything, remembered the false memories in another brainwipe victim, then realized that I'd thought *victim*. Finally, I managed to say, "I'm sorry I brought you here."

"No problem. Most drugs here do less damage than speed. More advanced biochemistry, right. Some do worse, but the damage is so much more fun."

"Warren, you weren't using drugs in Richmond."

"What the fuck you think Prolixin is?"

"Why did you want to see me?"

"Call off the Barcons. It's my life, and it's no worse in this slum than any other."

Warren bared his teeth in a grin that didn't quite work and said, "We need drugs to smooth out the xenophobia in my slum here. Good drugs turn us all into *Technicolor* fascinations." He used the movie word in English.

His bare feet had raw sores on the tops of his toes, and one heel oozed a clear liquid. He was freezing with his Jerek; shouldn't I turn him in for his own good? "Warren, you could do better than this. We can't be that much different."

"Scares you, doesn't it?"

"I won't ever become like you."

"Call off the Barcons, little brother, or you'll be sorry."

"Warren, I can't abandon you."

"Shit, don't. Come visit. Try some drugs." His grin

was crooked, as though his brain couldn't quite communicate through his facial nerves, signals scrambled.

I didn't say anything more, just walked out alone, looking to the street like a whore's customer. When I got out of the slum, I cried, the tears burning as though they'd clotted inside like bad blood and came out half scab.

Everyone on the bus with me went silent, then murmured until I got off. I took the elevator up. Marianne said, "He's using again."

"Yes." I slumped onto a couch. "What do I do?"

"I asked what the drug laws were here. They're relatively liberal—the Barcons pull in dealers when the drug use in a population goes over a certain percent. It's a hundredth percent total living hours for where we're living. I found out through the computer."

I went to the terminal and called up the percent for where Warren was living. Two percent total hours. A twentieth of the population could stay stoned all the time. All the population could get stoned one hour a day. "What do they do to dealers?"

"Don't ask," Marianne said.

"He had sores on his feet," I said to her as I typed a message to the Barcons in charge of Warren: WE MUST TALK. Then I stood up, almost tripping, slightly dizzy. "Is Karl sleeping?" Marianne nodded, then hugged me sideways like a Gwyng. We went in hip to hip to watch our sleeping son.

Appalled again at how tiny he was, I said, "I don't want anything ever to hurt him, or you."

Marianne squeezed me and said, "All I hope for is that nothing damages us permanently. Any of us."

That sent my thoughts back to Warren.

"We don't understand why you insist on continuity of personality. If we remove his addictive nature without changing his memories, he'll know he was changed, and if he considers it tampering . . ." The Barcon trailed off without concluding the statement. We were sitting in my little Academy office, a report from the Institute of Control

about the Sharwan and the Wrengee on my terminal
screen.

I was getting very depressed today, no good news. "He
wants you to stop treating him. He said I'll be sorry if
you don't leave him alone."

"He's a known drug technician. He's marked to be
brought in if the rate becomes excessive. Then we treat
him as is prescribed."

"What's that?"

"Drug aversion."

"He wouldn't use drugs again?"

"Officer Red Clay, he could never even go near them."

"What can be done?"

The Barcon sighed. "A personality re-structuring with
some false memories."

"How many years do you think you'd have to cut out to
give him a drug-free past?"

"We haven't examined that issue completely."

"He's been using since he was fourteen, not excessively, but . . ." I felt as though I'd been drugged myself,
some amphetamine that burned the myelin off my nerves
and left me jangling. What, I asked myself, was I defend-
ing? "Can you give him memories of tapering off, of stopping? Cancel these last few weeks?"

"Will you authorize?"

"He'll hate me forever."

"We . . ." He sighed.

I looked up sharply, having not heard a Barcon sigh like
that. "What is the problem?"

"We will try to keep him as human as possible, but
stopping the drug involvement is most critical, right?"

I remembered where he was living, in a cold room with
a Jerek sterile. "Can you do anything for the Jerek he's
living with?"

"Her cell signature isn't on the drugs sold there. Since
she's also not Academy or Institute, she can do what she
wishes, which includes dying of pernicious anemia. Or of
drug toxicity. Do you want that for your brother?"

A little slip of skin, sweat—Warren tagged each cap he
handled as his product. And dying of drugs, several of

Warren's old Earthside connections managed that without precisely overdosing—couple of murders, couple of suicides, a car crash. I said, "He never used badly, he'd always detox on his own every couple months, before Mica came. Before v'r . . . this."

"You don't think this Karst, this Federation, isn't stressful to me. Barcons go to the Northeast Quadrant, too."

"And what do you do to them?"

"Re-build them and send them home."

"Oh, could you please do that. Back home." Getting Warren back to Earth now would be as difficult as extracting the Sharwan from the Wrengee planet, but I was going to force myself to be a little optimistic here.

"We must see how the reconstruction works," the Barcon said. "Have you given us your permission?"

I felt like I was too exhausted to do otherwise. "Yes."

The Barcon stood up. "We will tend to your regrets if that proves necessary."

"Only if I allow you to," I said, almost ready to retract my decision, wondering if I could.

The next day, Bir from Marianne's birth group came to watch Karl while Marianne and I went to a First Contact Party. One of my cadets, a Yauntry from Frosted Granite Corporation, had been aboard an observation station when their charge species gated out.

We went through the strange tunnel entrance at the Rector's Lodge—"like a womb, we all get re-born here," Marianne said—and came in late to the large lodge room filled with all the seating instruments. A Barcon was already filling drug orders for some of the cadets. I spotted my cadet, Simla Doth, who had small northern Yauntry teeth and snow-white hair, but brown eyes, not green or grey.

"Sorry I'm late."

He fingered his sash. Beside him was a representative of the people he'd contacted; vaguely Gwyng-like, but with smooth bare-skinned faces. They both seemed to smile at each other, then Simla took me aside.

"I wondered why you made us cadets first, not people

of the Institutes. Now, quickly, we've been on both sides—
first contact and first contacting.''

"It is like an initiation."

His face crinkled up in a Yauntry smile, almost like
mine. "Great fun, though."

"If it goes smoothly," I said.

"Topaz is most experienced."

I remembered her from my own First Contact Party, the
tri-colored almost human-looking woman, so serious.
"Yes. Hers are good teams to be on." I looked around
and saw Marianne talking to Karriaagzh. His throat organ
throbbed once; I felt vaguely like he'd made a pass at her
and went over.

Marianne smiled and said, "Tom's worried about his
brother."

Karriaagzh's inner third eyelids flicked—why did this
upset him—and he said, "Drugs are terrible."

"Even supervised like this?" Marianne asked, waving
her hand at the Barcon on the drug dispenser.

"I have many pleasures," Karriaagzh said. "Perhaps
you mammals will snoop later?" He stalked off, hocks
flexing high, feathers quivering.

Marianne asked, "What was that about?"

"He, I guess, he masturbated, or something, by throwing up, no, regurgitating in a toilet that's decorated like a
baby bird."

"And you watched him?" Marianne sounded more
shocked that I'd watched than he'd done it.

"Rhyodolite made me."

"Karriaagzh needs friends," she said.

I went up to the drug box, thinking about smoking dope
one last time, with Warren. With Warren, not here in front
of my cadets. Not in front of my wife, either.

The Barcon on the box said, "Red Clay, we don't think
you should take drugs now."

"I'd like to smoke one of my home planet drugs with
my brother." I wrote *tetrahydrocannabinol* on the drug
box scribe pad. "This, but in the plant."

"One last time?"

"The Institute of Medicine is going to fix him, right. Make it where he can't stand drugs, purge his memories."

The Barcon talked into a communicator, then said, "One last time," as he keyed the dispenser to disgorge a small metal box. I slipped it into a pocket in my tunic, under my dress sash.

When I turned around, Ersh was standing there watching me. Someone had ripped three jewelry rings out of his scales. He looked exhausted. "I'm a refugee." He used the Karst One term for that word, with all its connotations, and sighed as if he knew them all now.

"I'm having a rough time with some of my conspecifics," I said, "and my wife had a baby three weeks ago, so I'm sorry if I'm less than completely polite by your standards."

"Not at all," Ersh said. "I was rude myself, but then you were afraid of me."

For the rest of the party, I stayed around the fringes of the party, with the Barcons against the wall, while Marianne talked to everyone, fascinated. I was glad she liked it.

When we got home, Bir's son had his forefeet up against Karl's crib, sniffing through the bars, while Bir explained, "They're born utterly helpless, not strong boys like you."

I almost expected him to bark; he looked so much like a puppy with his face beginning to pug up.

"So you're back," Warren said. Moolan stood holding the door as though she was thinking about pushing me back out. Warren was stretched out on his mattress, back and one elbow against the rear wall, operating a pump that loaded needle cubes. Odd how quickly he'd adapted to some of the new technology.

"I brought you something. I guess you'll think it's an unsophisticated drug now, marijuana." I opened the box for the first time since I'd gotten it from the Barcon at the party, tilted it, all dark green sticky buds with visible resin beads, toward Warren. Moolan sniffed the air and shut the door.

"They even packed paper," Warren said, getting up off the couch and taking the box out of my hands.

Moolan sighed, and picked up a bone she was using as a biting stick. She said, "I want to detox for a while, but there's a waiting list. Everyone in Karst City wants to detox . . . for a while."

I remembered dopers talking like that, as if everyone in Southwestern Virginia was using, just the good folks being secretive about it. "Can you use tetrahydrocannabinol?" I asked.

She raised her hand and rocked her fist, neither yes or no, almost the fingers out, palm down rocking that was the human sign "ifsy-shitsy," then went and curled up by Warren, her furred skin not touching him, he being too hot-blooded for her comfort. They'd compromised on the room temperature, too cold for him, really, with his bare feet.

"You want to smoke some with me or is this a pure gift?"

"One last time," I said. We locked eyes and I looked away first. He laughed as he rolled a small tight joint, popped it in his mouth and drew it through his lips. I suddenly didn't want to smoke with him. Warren, I didn't know Warren really, I realized. Nor had I realized before this moment how much I'd changed—so straight, so hardworking, so middle class, but not a human middle class. But then Warren paused in the ritual and stared off at the door, not his 1,000-yard war stare, but something else, softer.

He looked back at me and said, "You know, here there are just a hundred more ways to get into trouble."

Moolan bit her stick. Warren lit the joint with an electric heat point and sucked in deeply, then handed me the joint, his fingers clammy against mine.

The Barcons grow extremely good shit. Instantly stoned into tunnel vision, I was sorry I'd done this. Warren said, "My," and took another hit, then breathed the smoke into Moolan's mouth in a drug kiss. She shivered and left for her room. "Stare at the wall for days," Warren said after she'd closed two doors, the noises of them battering against me. I didn't know if he was referring to her or us.

He was still bigger than I was, but I suspected I was in better shape if I had to beat him up. The Barcons, of course . . .

"The Barcons?" Warren asked, coiled against the wall.

I stared at him, seeing his wrinkles as places where he'd begun to die under the skin.

He got up and put on some Jerek stone chime music— I braced myself, but it was in tune. "Relax," he said. "Maybe I do need saving?"

Who was Warren? I didn't know if he was taunting me or agreeing to whatever the Barcons would do. "Only if you want help," I replied, wondering where I'd drawn that cunning from. I sounded sincere, even to myself. He kept looking more and more like a stranger, like a fifty-year-old druggie with amphetamine-dried muscles. Alkaloids and acids etched his skin. An old degenerate ape, my brother. I managed to say, *"I remember you from when I was eight, ten."*

"You didn't even know what was going on."

"I suspect not, but you're still my brother." We were talking to each other in English, but not in country dialect, formally from my days here and from his social workers.

He took another hit from the joint—how could he do that much of that cannabis—and said, *"Shit, we're not having any fun, are we? Can you get out okay?"*

"I can call . . ." I was about to say one of the Barcons who knew I was making this visit, but managed to mangle that into *". . . a cab."*

"Shit, not a cab?" Warren began to laugh.

I had to walk to the street and find a call box, feeling most hideous. The Barcons came for me quickly and even more quickly detoxed me. I know they were waiting close. As soon as I was straight, I thought I remembered that Warren seemed resigned to whatever procedures the Barcons would use to help him.

A few days later Marianne was telling me about the nursery her child-bearing group planned to start. "We need enough of each species of child to make sure the sexual socialization will be generally species normal. Yangchenla finally agreed to put her daughter in the group; we've got two other Tibetan women interested.''

The phone buzzed. She, thinking it might be a call she was expecting from her birth group, answered, stiffened, and looked at me, then said, ''No, we must tell him. Yes, it's our custom. We aren't at all like Gwyngs. *Shit.*''

I got up and took the phone, adjusted the earpieces for me. A Barcon voice said, ''Your brother died of a drug overdose. We are still with his body. His Jerek found him.''

''Deliberate?''

''We aren't sure.''

''Let me come down there.''

''We can bring you in fast. Go to the roof of your building.''

''Warren's dead,'' I told Marianne, but I realized they'd told her that.

''I'm sorry,'' she said. ''You're going down there?''

''Yeah. His Jerek, why didn't someone . . .'' I felt so responsible and so helpless.

''Karl and I will come with you.''

''They're picking me up off the roof.'' I remembered seeing a few helicopter-type craft around, not many, not big ones. It isn't safe for a woman and baby, I wanted to tell her, but then that neighborhood wasn't safe for anyone—Warren died in it.

''Maybe you should wait until they bring the body in?''

''No, I want to talk to his Jerek.''

Marianne sat down and curled up in a little ball, then said slowly, ''Don't blame her. Or yourself.''

''I brought him here.''

''Don't do that to yourself,'' she said. ''You have me, you have Karl.''

I kissed her on the forehead, then went upstairs. The small helicopter was waiting, too small for Marianne and Karl to have joined us. We rose, bouncing in the updrafts between buildings and parks, all the different architectures rolling away under us, alien trees whizzing past.

"We will come back with you," the Barcon pilot said. "There are some options for the body."

"If he wanted to be dead, let him stay dead," I said, suddenly feeling almost angry with him, then guilty again.

"We will observe you, sedate if necessary."

"It's customary in my species to grieve," I said. "And I better *goddamn well* be allowed to do it."

"I understand the implications of the expletive," the Barcon said. We dropped down on top of Warren's building and went spiraling down grim clanking iron stairs. Rust like blood was rotting them.

Warren lay on a Barcon gurney, eyes open and glazed, stains around his ears and neck where I could see the skin, fresh ashes in the wrinkles on his forehead—smeared there? His feet were so white—the sores were barely visible.

I turned and saw the little Jerek, Moolan. She bent her body and rocked slightly, then pulled at her pelt. Huge tufts of fur came out, even where she wasn't pulling.

Then I saw the words Warren had scrawled on the wall, in English, FUCKERS, I'VE OBLITERATED YOU ALL.

When I gaped, one Barcon grabbed me while another cut around the words and peeled the layer they were on away. The walls were paper, laminated paper and plastic, I thought, numb in the Barcon's hands, staring at the clean void in the dirty wall.

"Mourning in moderation, we permit," the Barcon holding me said.

"Why didn't you bring him in?" I said to Moolan.

"He was beginning . . . happy. We were going to get well."

"We were fooled," the Barcon said. "One of us who specializes in humans warned us that sudden cheer without good reason could be lethal."

"We were lethal to him," I said.

"No, he was lethal to himself," the Barcon holding me said. He pushed his knuckles against my throat pulse point, then let me go.

"Should I die now?" Moolan said.

"What tunnel?" one of the Barcons asked. She looked away, not answering them.

"Is it too late to spay her?" I asked, desperate to save someone now.

"What motivation for continued medical stablization?" the Barcon who'd asked her about her tunnel said.

Moolan shivered and wouldn't look at any of us. One of the Barcons handed her her bone-biting stick. She put it in her mouth and nibbled gently. I, not knowing what would become of her, went back to Warren on the gurney, pulled his eyelids down. They felt like chicken skin.

Then I heard Karst Two—Cadmium. He seemed to move into the room as if his body were a puppet controlled by his will. He came up and embraced me, rocking side to side, murmuring sounds my computer simply transformed into other murmurs. I heard the Barcons talking, recognized their word for Gwyng.

"Why do you come to a death, Gwyng?" the pilot who'd brought me asked.

"He's friend/pouch kin equivalent," Cadmium said as I found I could finally cry.

"We will sedate fiercely if you Gwyng-freak on us," the pilot replied.

"He's all right," I said. Cadmium rubbed the tears away from my eyes with his long thumbs.

Moolan moaned from her corner and cried out, "Am I worthless?"

Cadmium turned to stare at her, eye assault between two species that knew precisely how to do it. I said, "Maybe she could try detox?" She was shedding so much fur I expected she'd be bald within a day.

Cadmium asked me, "What ceremony do you wind around a death?"

I looked at the Barcons by the gurney and realized they were waiting. "We have a memorial service, *a funeral*, and do remembrances at the burying."

"We'll take you to your house. Agate and Chalk ask that we bring the Jerek, too."

"No," Moolan said, "not to Jereks."

A Barcon grabbed her by her loose neck skin and lifted

her by that and the skin at her hip. She twisted inside her skin, almost scratched him, then dangled limp in his hands. He took her out to the street. Cadmium and I followed, he touching me, from time to time, on the face with his knuckles.

The Barcon pilot took off in his helicopter above us while the other Barcons loaded Warren's corpse. Cadmium said to them, "Let us follow alone/Red Clay with me (in my care)." I saw Amber's electric car then and nodded.

The Barcon in charge grabbed his groin tits, rubbed them, and said, "Be sure to follow. Be sure to arrive. No Gwyng tricks."

"No," Cadmium said, flexing one thumb slightly. He sucked at the gland hole and got in the driver's seat. I got in beside him, staring at the Barcon ambulance, not crying now.

As he pulled out behind the Barcons, Cadmium said, "Ersh feels like he betrayed you, advising against the Federation at first contact."

"I feel like I betrayed Warren."

"We need you for us, not to follow unliving meat."

"That's harsh, Cadmium. I messed him up."

"Made him take drugs?"

"Let the Barcons work on his brain. He was afraid he wasn't going to end up being human. I wanted him to still be Warren."

"Who was Warren?"

"Who was Mica?" I said, regretting ever having saved him even for a little while, then hating myself for that.

Cadmium said, "I don't know with any more certainty than you know who Warren was."

"Are you trying to say we didn't know our brothers?"

"All of us deliberately don't know things about our own species that are transparent to others. And even the Barcons can only map a brain at part of its time."

Had I really known Warren? Maybe I'd tried to have the Barcons rebuild the forty-eight-year-old ex-con into what I thought he'd been at nineteen, before he joined the Army. He'd thought it was the Barcons making him alien to himself when it had been me. "Cadmium, I feel so guilty."

"Do you need to feel guilty for a while? I can stay with you if the Linguist would permit."

How oddly put, I thought.

"You are so good at joining together," he said. "You helped me re-evaluate my being stimulated by birds—not so xenophobic now."

"Warren killed Mica."

"Accident. The universe commits them daily."

I watched all the creatures we were passing—accidents once made now trying to sustain themselves? Accidents who every day denied they were accidents, trying to justify their existence, their rightness, forgetting the nightmare of centuries of fish dying in evaporating tide pools before some accidental lungs made life on dry land possible. Life was horrified of seeing itself clearly.

Then I saw a Domiecan like Bir cuddling her small child so much like a bipedal dog and thought of Marianne nursing our son, so helpless he needed two parents. I said, "It can't be just an accident."

Cadmium said, "With my mind I can see this as both." He waved one hand, then put it back on the wheel when he turned a corner.

Life was both—accident and design. I could see that, too, even with my brain. In front of us, Warren was dead, by design and accident. A small muscle in my eyelid twitched, bunched, and twitched again. "He wrote on the wall that he was obliterating us."

"Us/himself/those not himself."

We were passing by open girder houses of the olive bird people now. I remembered seeing country houses at night with the shades open—the sense of house as hollow container. That sense made people seem fragile out on the surface of a world. These people seemed even more fragile, in their spaces that didn't contain them, open to the weather, just layers and layers of surfaces. And Warren was beyond all of it now—obliterated or whatever, I didn't know what to believe—his corpse traveling back to my apartment in an alien hearse. I said, "We need a lacquered wooden box to bury him in. And formal clothes for his body."

Cadmium picked up a phone and Gwyng-talked into it, then asked, "What shape box?"

"Slightly wider than he was, slightly longer."

Cadmium talked again and then we were home, driving into the basement.

"Don't bring his body up," I said to a Barcon standing by the hearse, not wanting Marianne to suddenly face that, not while nursing, not unless she wanted to.

"It's cooler down here," the Barcon in charge said. He stayed with the body while another Barcon came out of the hearse with Moolan in front of him, her arms pinned behind her in his right hand while his left hand was holding the scruff of her neck. I thought that was a bit rough, then noticed his cheek was torn, red scratches through the black skin.

"I refuse to see other Jereks," Moolan said.

I said, "Why don't you get them together away from us? We humans have our own grief."

"I thought your brother would stay through my death. He cheated me," she said.

I tensed, ready to tear her into little shreds, when Cadmium touched me lightly and said, "You'd regret it."

The Barcons held her downstairs while Cadmium and I rode up on the elevator. When the doors opened at my apartment, I saw Dorge Karmapa and three other Tibetan men. "May we support you in ceremony," Dorge said. Behind him, Marianne, holding Karl, nodded slightly to urge me to agree.

"Yes," I said. "Can you perform a burial service?"

"Burning has been our custom, but he was your brother."

Cremation, good. We could take his ashes back to Earth someday. Cadmium gave my elbow a quick squeeze and went into the visitor's bathroom. Then I saw Agate, Chalk, and Lisanmarl. "Moolan is downstairs. I can only take so much."

Lisanmarl said, "We're both deformed, but her way shames all steriles."

"She wanted Warren to be with her when she died."

The Jereks all gasped, then took the elevator down. I

said to the Tibetans, "Warren's corpse is also down-stairs."

"Bears are building a box for the corpse as is your custom," Dorge said. "My brothers will wash and dress it. We regret that your people and mine have not been close."

"Tom, have the Barcons bring the body up," Marianne said. "We can lay him out in his bedroom. Didn't your people hold wakes at the house?"

"*Funeral* home in my day," I said, slightly insulted, but there was no funeral home here. "Bedroom will do." Marianne told the Barcons over the intercom to bring Warren's corpse up.

"You've seen him," Dorge said, "you don't need to see more." He led me back to my own room. Marianne followed, then Agate and Chalk came in without Lisanmarl.

"What will happen to Moolan?" I asked.

"Lisanmarl fought her to agree to accept help. She will not die without tunnel," Chalk said. Agate handed him their tiny baby, so much smaller than Karl had been as a newborn. Chalk pulled up his tunic and put his son to his breast, both hands covering the tiny body, keeping him warm.

I imagined the two small Jerek steriles rolling on the ground, fur dropping off in clots, Moolan so weak, Lisanmarl so tough, sure of herself.

Agate and Chalk sat with me, then Cadmium came in, ducking his head slightly to them. I smelled alcohol. His armpit webs were damp. When Gwyngs died suddenly while young, it was a great tragedy; when they lost their sanity, other Gwyngs felt they were socially dead and so the body might as well follow. I said, "Our grief must confuse you."

"I try to care for my living human friends, not become human myself," he said.

One of the Barcons who'd worked on Warren's brain came in, clutching her lower belly. She stared at me with those almost human eyes, jaw flexing at the inhuman joints, then said, "We at least made him less paranoid.

We should have attacked the drug cravings first, but he was better before he began the drugs."

I almost said, you messed him up, you left him a stranger in his own mind, but then realized a Barcon who had come to me for comfort must be very agitated. "Yes, he wasn't xenophobic."

The Barcon sighed and loosened her grasp on her lower belly. "We try not to invest so much, but saving others is our pride."

And, I realized, he wasn't just obliterating me, my attempts to save him, but the Barcons and their pride in what they did, Moolan and her wish to have company when she died, everyone who'd hassled him, wanted something from him. I said to the Barcon woman, "Suicide's selfish."

Cadmium said, "Ersh wants to know if he can share your death-release ceremony."

"Yes," I said, almost saying no.

Cadmium went to my terminal and entered a cadet code, then the message, awkwardly picking out the Karst One characters as he mumbled to himself. "When should he come?" Cadmium asked when he'd gotten Ersh on-line.

"Whenever," I said.

Cadmium typed a time two hours from now, then said, "We will have the former-alive in the wooden box by then."

While we waited for the coffin, I told them stories about Warren that I realized were my personal myths, creating with words the Warren I wanted to remember.

At the crematorium, Rimpoche Dorge Karmapa stood on a dais the Tibetans had brought with them, an embroidered cloth image behind him that seemed to be of a sapient in general, not human, Gwyng, or bird, although there was a suggestion of feathers stitched in with fresh thread. Warren's coffin was open. I went up to see him and he wasn't the wax-works Warren that an American mortician would have presented to us, but the muscles of the face had been massaged loose and he was in a European suit. I listened while Dorge talked to Warren as though he were alive and very sick, "All components of being are transitory, therefore being is transitory.'' He rang a bell over Warren, then began chanting a Tibetan I could only grasp vague words from: white light, demons.

For an instant, I was outraged that Dorge was cremating Warren with a pagan ritual, but Warren wouldn't have been more pleased to be buried Baptist. Dorge handed me a flower and said, ''Tell him that life regrets his absence.''

I threaded the flower between his fingers and said, ''Life missed you, Warren.''

Other Tibetans began softly to beat drums. Grouped together in the back of the service room, Cadmium, Ersh, and the other non-humans watched us.

Dorge said, ''Warren Easley has moved from a physical state to a mental state. He lives now within the minds of those who knew him while his corpse goes to the fire. No one can claim a complete knowledge of him. He was, as we all are, attached to Eternity.''

I looked behind me as a conveyor belt took Warren's corpse to the fires. Karriaagzh was standing in the doorway. When the coffin disappeared behind two bronze fire doors, Dorge bowed to me and I to him, then he came down off the dais and cautiously embraced me as if fearing a rebuff. I gripped his back as if we were saving each other from drowning.

THE BEST IN SCIENCE FICTION

THE TOR DOUBLES

Two complete short science fiction novels in one volume!

BEN BOVA

Buy them at your local bookstore or use this handy coupon:
Clip and mail this page with your order.

Publishers Book and Audio Mailing Service
P.O. Box 120159, Staten Island, NY 10312-0004

Please send me the book(s) I have checked above. I am enclosing $_____
(please add $1.25 for the first book, and $.25 for each additional book to
cover postage and handling. Send check or money order only — no CODs.)

Name _____

Address _____

City _____ State/Zip _____

Please allow six weeks for delivery. Prices subject to change without notice.

BESTSELLING BOOKS FROM TOR